The Vineyard of the Nietzschean Priest

☨

"Good people, hark!

What speaks the deepest, furthest dark?

"I was asleep -

Deep from dreaming I awoke: -

The world is deep

Deeper than the day can hope

And deep its pain –

Lust - deeper even than heartache

Pain says: go away

But lust wills eternity -

Wills deep, deep eternity!"

- Zarathustra's Roundelay, Friedrich Nietzsche

To Brian Cleeve

The months had become years, and times and places had flowed into each other without ever a trace of her, except in some memory of a dream ...

The Vineyard of the Nietzschean Priest

A Novel
by

Eamon Kiernan

Acknowledgement

Many people helped me with this book, often with great kindness and at some cost to themselves. I am especially grateful to:

Jim Bruce
Michael Duffy
Annemarie Skjold Jensen
Yvonne Vetjens
Sean O`Dwyer
Steven O'Neill

- Eamon Kiernan

Paperback ISBN 978-8792632-11-1
Second edition

Published by
Whyte Tracks, Copenhagen

Contents

Glossary

*The following is a list of persons who are mentioned more or less prominently in the story. Fictional characters are marked with **

Persons

Antonelli, Ferdinando OFM (1896-1993)	Italian Franciscan friar, liturgical scholar, Curial official and Cardinal. An important figure in the reforms of the Roman Catholic liturgies before, during and after the Second Vatican Council
Bea, Augustine SJ (1881–1968)	German Jesuit priest, biblical scholar and Cardinal. President of the Secretariat for the Promotion of Christian Unity. A leading progressive voice at the Second Vatican Council
Beauduin, Lambert OSB (1873–1960)	Belgian Benedictine monk. Reformer of monastic life. One of the initiators of the movement for a vernacular liturgy in the Roman Catholic Church in the early twentieth century
Blessed Virgin Mary	Title given to the mother of Jesus of Nazareth
Breen, Benignus (Billy) OFM*	Irish Franciscan priest, informer and paedophile
Bugnini, Annibale CM (1912-1982)	Italian Vincentian priest, liturgical scholar, advisor to the Second Vatican Council, Secretary of the *Consilium*, Secretary of the Congregation for Divine Worship, Papal diplomat in Iran. The central figure in the reform of the Catholic liturgies before, during and after the Second Vatican Council
Chomsky, Noam (born 1928)	American linguist and radical journalist. Author of *Syntactic Structures*
Clavis, Didimus Thomas*	Dissident Catholic priest and mystic

Congar, Yves OP (1904-1995)	French Dominican friar, theologian of ecumenism and Cardinal. One of the leading progressive voices at the Second Vatican Council
Costelloe, Marie-Louise ODC*	Irish Carmelite nun. Follower of the spirituality of Saint Thérèse of Lisieux
Courtney, Isaiah*	Irish seminarian. Protégé of Michael Cremin
Cremin, Michael*	Irish priest, official of the Roman Curia, Bishop of Limerick, and Cardinal. Having shaped his life according to the post-conciliar freedoms, he finds himself with nowhere to go
Davidek, Felix Maria (1921-1988)	Moravian priest. Clandestine bishop of the persecuted Church in Czechoslovakia
Deeler, Launcelot OSB*	American Benedictine monk, educator, and paedophile
Fielding, Corinna*	Irish woman. Girlfriend of Michael Cremin
Forgione, Francesco OFMCap (1887–1968)	Italian Capuchin friar, stigmatist and guide of souls. Canonised in 2002 as St. Pio of Pietrelcina. Known as Padre Pio
Freeman, Pontus*	American journalist accredited to the Second Vatican Council
Frings, Josef (1887-1978)	German priest, Archbishop of Cologne and Cardinal. A leading progressive voice at the Second Vatican Council
Ghislieri, Antonio (1504–1572)	Italian Dominican friar. Pope Pius V. Implemented the reforms of the Council of Trent. Promulgated the first binding norm of the Mass of the Roman Rite. Canonised in 1712
Gregory, John*	English taxi driver based in Rome. Assistant to Thomas Clavis
Guardini, Romano (1885–1968)	Italian-German priest, educator and liturgical reformer. Advisor to the *Consilium*
Guéranger, Prosper OSB (1805- 1875)	French Benedictine monk. Abbot of Solesmes. Liturgical reformer
Hegarty, Gerry*	Irish priest. Friend and associate of Michael Cremin
Heidegger, Martin (1889-1976)	German anti-metaphysical philosopher

Hippasus of Metapontum (ca 500 B.C.)	Greek philosopher. Believed to be the discoverer of incommensurability
Hogan, Augustine (Gus) *	Papal notary, Professor of Canon Law and Curial official. Teacher and Superior of Michael Cremin
Hovda, Robert (1920-1992)	American Catholic convert, priest of the Diocese of Fargo, liturgical reformer and social activist
Jesus Christ	see Jesus of Nazareth
Jesus of Nazareth (ca 4 BC–33 AD)	Jewish spiritual teacher and reformer who was crucified by the Roman authorities. Believed by Christians to be the Christ and the Son of God, through whom salvation from Sin is made possible
Judas Iscariot (ca 6BC– 30AD)	Follower and friend of Jesus of Nazareth. Noted for his betrayal of Jesus with a kiss
Jungmann, Josef Andreas SJ (1889-1975)	Austrian Jesuit priest and liturgical scholar, advisor to the Second Vatican Council and the *Consilium*. Originator of Kerygmatic Theology. Author of *Missarum Sollemnia*
Kaiser, Robert B. (born 1930)	American journalist accredited to the Second Vatican Council
Kapleau, Philip (1912-2004)	American Zen master (Roshi)
Kostuva, Felix SJ*	Croatian Jesuit priest, Curial official and Archbishop
Küng, Hans (born 1928)	Swiss priest and theologian. Advisor to the Second Vatican Council. A leading progressive, he is noted for his conflicts with the Vatican and for the ecumenical project World Ethos. Author of *Infallible? An Inquiry (Unfehlbar? Eine Anfrage)*
Lefebvre, Marcel (1905–1991)	French missionary priest. Archbishop of Dakar, Superior General of the Congregation of the Holy Spirit, founder of the Society of Saint Pius X. Excommunicated in 1988
Liam the Librarian	See Liam O'Casey
Little Flower	See Thérèse Martin
Luther, Martin (1483-1546)	German Augustinian friar and reformer. One of the originators of Protestantism
Martin, Malachi (1921-1999)	Irish priest, former Jesuit and biblical scholar. Noted as an exorcist and a novelist

Martin, Thérèse ODC (1873-1897)	French Carmelite nun. Originator of a new spirituality she termed the Little Way. Canonised in 1925. Promoted to Doctor of the Church in 1997 under the title Doctor of Love. Author of *The Story of a Soul (L'Histoire d'une Âme)*. Sometimes referred to as the Little Flower
Marx, Karl (1818-1883)	German materialist philosopher. One of the originators of Communism
McManus, Frederick R. (1923-2005)	American priest, canon lawyer, liturgical scholar, advisor to the Second Vatican Council, member of the *Consilium*, Chairman of the ICEL. A central figure in the introduction of the vernacular Mass in the English-speaking world
McQuaid, John Charles CSSp (1895-1973)	Irish missionary priest. Member of the Congregation of the Holy Spirit, Archbishop of Dublin and Primate of Ireland. Superior of Michael Cremin. Upholder of conservative theological positions before, during and after the Second Vatican Council
Michel, Virgil OSB (1890-1938)	American Benedictine monk and liturgical reformer
Montini, Giovanni Battista (1879-1978)	Official of the Curia, Archbishop of Milan and Cardinal, Pope Paul VI. A leading progressive voice in preparing for the Second Vatican Council, he came to regret much of what he implemented as Pope
Moro, Laura*	Roman woman. Girlfriend of Michael Cremin
Murphy, Leo*	Irish businessman. Financial advisor to Michael Cremin
Nietzsche, Friedrich (1844-1900)	German sceptical philosopher. Author of *Thus spoke Zarathustra (Also Sprach Zarathustra)* and *On the Genealogy of Morals (Zur Genealogie der Moral)*
Nightbird, Isadora*	American student. Participant in a course taught by Michael Cremin at St. John's Abbey, Collegeville, Minnesota
Nordheider, Jean*	Lecturer in Philosophy at the Catholic University of Louvain (Leuven). Mentor to Michael Cremin
O'Casey, Liam*	Irish priest and librarian at the Vatican. Assistant to Augustine Hogan. Known as Liam the Librarian

Ottaviani, Alfredo (1890 –1979)	Official of the Curia and Cardinal, Pro-Prefect of the Holy Office. A leader of the conservative faction at the Second Vatican Council
Pacelli, Eugenio (1876-1958)	Papal diplomat in Germany, Secretary of State and Cardinal, Pope Pius XII
Padre Pio	see Francesco Forgione
Plato (428 BC–348 BC)	Greek philosopher. Author of *The Republic*
Poggi, Angelo CM*	Milanese student of Liturgy at Louvain (Leuven).
Pope John Paul II	see Karol Wojtyla
Pope John XXIII	see Angelo Roncalli
Pope Paul VI	see Giovanni Battista Montini
Pope Pius XII	see Eugenio Pacelli
Pope Saint Pius V	see Antonio Ghislieri
Pythagoras (ca 580-490BC)	Greek philosopher, mathematician and mystic
Rahner, Karl SJ (1904-1984)	German theologian, originator of an influential anthropo-centric turn in theology
Ratzinger, Joseph (born 1927)	German priest, theological advisor to Cardinal Frings at the Second Vatican Council, Archbishop of Munich and Freising and Cardinal, Prefect of the Congregation for the Doctrine of the Faith
Roberts, Thomas d'Esterre SJ (1893-1976)	English Jesuit priest. Archbishop of Bombay. A noted progressive voice during and after the Second Vatican Council
Roncalli, Angelo (1881-1963)	Papal diplomat in Bulgaria, Turkey, France, Patriarch of Venice and Cardinal, Pope John XXIII. Convoked the Second Vatican Council in 1961 to initiate a dialogue between the Catholic Church and the modern world
Ryan, Dermot (1924 - 1985)	Irish priest and scholar of Semitic languages. Member of the *Consilium*. Archbishop of Dublin
Saint John (?-ca 90AD)	Follower of Jesus of Nazareth. Called "the Beloved" on account of his close relationship to Jesus. His Fourth Gospel is believed to be a first-hand account of certain teachings of Jesus and events in His life. Author of the Book of the Apocalypse

Saint Peter (? –ca. 64AD)	Galilean fisherman, friend and follower of Jesus of Nazareth. One of the leaders of the early Christian Church. Believed to have received special authority from Jesus and to have been the first pope
Saint Thérèse of Lisieux	see Thérèse Martin
Saint Thérèse of the Child Jesus and the Holy Face	see Thérèse Martin
Saint Thomas Aquinas (1224-1274)	Italian Dominican friar, philosopher and theologian. Canonised in 1323. Doctor of the Church. His synthesis of Church teaching with Aristotelian philosophy has dominated much of Western thought. Author of the *Summa Theologiae*
Sister Marie of the Holy Trinity	see Marie-Louise Costelloe
Sodano, Angelo (born 1927)	Curial official and Cardinal. Secretary of State to Pope John Paul II
Suenens, Leo-Jozef (Léon-Joseph) (1904-1996)	Member of the Governing Body of the Catholic University of Louvain (Leuven), Archbishop of Mechelen-Brussels (Malines), Primate of Belgium and Cardinal. A leading progressive at the Second Vatican Council
Villot, Jean-Marie (1905-1979)	Archbishop of Lyon and Cardinal. Secretary of State to Pope Paul VI, Pope John-Paul I, Pope John-Paul II
Wagner, Johannes (1908-1999)	German priest and liturgical scholar. Advisor to the Second Vatican Council, head of Coetus X of the *Consilium*, advisor to the Congregation of Rites
Wojtyla, Karol (1920-2005)	Polish priest. Archbishop of Cracau and Cardinal. Pope John Paul II. A progressive at the Second Vatican Council, he later adopted pragmatic conservative positions

†

Prologue

Rome. Limerick
2004

Michael Cardinal Cremin. His Eminence, the Cardinal. Your Eminence, Eminence. The new cardinal was looking at himself in the mirror. No matter how he turned the title in his mouth, the words had resonance. And no matter how he pulled at his face and twisted it, what looked back out at him was most distinguished.

He closed one eye and looked at the side of his face which was lit by the eye that was still open. Then he did the same with the other eye. It was intriguing. He was two persons in the one face. Like Oscar Wilde's Dorian Gray. A great story. There was a thrill of decadence to it which had given him no end of titillation when he was younger. And it was quite perceptive of human nature. Wilde, of course, had simplified things. A clear distinction between good and evil. Hiding the true self away in a portrait in an attic. In reality, of course, good and evil were a matter of perspective, and the true self was plain to see in the face of everyone; plain, that is, to those with eyes to see.

When he closed his left eye and looked upon himself, he saw what everybody saw, the Bishop of Limerick, in Ireland's Mid-West, who held more sway in the Roman Catholic Church than that minor post would suggest. A strong, decisive man. A man not unattractive to women, as he was constantly being reminded. A man at the vanguard of his time. He had been through most, if not all, of what made the Church what it was. The experiments in freedom of the 1960s. The great flowering of the Second Vatican Council. The reaffirmation of Catholic discipline in the reign of Pope John Paul II. In the light that shone on him through the many short-lived dramas on the stage of history, people could see something of what they themselves might yet become. He was one of those perfect beings you find in the media. A face of the times.

When he closed his right eye a different man emerged. The force, the ambition, remained; but they belonged to a man of shadow, a man who was no stranger to the extremities of human passion, but who dwelt beyond them in a mysterious quiet, in depths well hidden from prying eyes. A man known to no-one, unless he chose to be known, and well satisfied with that. This was a rare human face. In his experience, few had possessed it. Fewer still had retained it to the end. The faceless face. The face under the mask.

He glanced round the little bathroom with its gold fittings. There was a self-warming seat on the toilet. There were current affairs magazines in a little recess in the wall. And that generous mirror. Flying had never been so comfortable. It was a private plane, of course. Lent to him by his friend, Leo Murphy.

He took up one of the towels which had been warmed for him on an array of heating pipes. It was fine cloth, and they had even embroidered it with his crest. A very nice touch. He dried his hands and stepped out into the oval cabin with its designer furniture and soft wood veneers. He was the way he wanted to be: alone.

Hardly anyone anywhere had been like him. Only Jean Nordheider, really. What would Jean think of his elevation to Cardinal, he wondered. Now was the time to make plans. To look for allies. The pope himself was not worth bothering about. An old, spent man propped up by medication. Cardinal Ratzinger was the obvious choice, but the smooth German seemed to have been sidelined recently. Perhaps he should try all the cardinals, one after the other. Only those eligible for the conclave, of course. Not that it was a pleasant prospect. He thought very little of his fellow princes of the Church. But first Nordheider.

"Do you need anything, Your Eminence?"

It was the stewardess. He looked up at her, surprised, his attention captured by her perfume.

"Need anything? No, no," he said, and wondered was he telling the truth. It was her eyes. They reminded him of something.

In the end, it was Nordheider who contacted him. A letter with the coat of arms of the Catholic University of Louvain, brought by courier and waiting for him on his return.

> *My dear Michael,*
>
> *Forty years, and you have been on the increase, I on the decrease. Now, as you approach your zenith, I approach my nadir, but gladly. I am retiring from the University on May 15th, next. It is time philosophy was released from my unworthy clutches. There will be a small get together at the Department to see me off, and I would be pleased to welcome as my guest of honour my most eminent student, perhaps my only student. Will you come?*
>
> *May your Eminence be more than a mere title.*
>
> *Yours ever,*
>
> *Jean Nordheider.*

His most eminent student. Perhaps his only student.

Jean meant it, too.

Would he come?

Yes, he would come.

†

The Vineyard of the Nietzschean Priest

1

A Student at Louvain

1

The academic year of 1959-1960 found Michael Cremin in Belgium. He was studying to be a priest in Dublin, but his Archbishop, John Charles McQuaid, had sent him to the Catholic University of Louvain to learn languages and study philosophy and theology. The KU Leuven, as the university was officially known, was a very famous place, and it was full of renowned philosophers and theologians. But the only philosophy course he had got to attend was the one taught by Dr. Jean Nordheider.

A Catholic philosopher, supposedly, Nordheider's doctoral research had dealt with Saint Thomas Aquinas, which was a highly appropriate subject, Michael knew. His thesis, however, was so replete with irony that the faculty had taken diametrically opposed positions on its value, some regarding it as a work of genius, others seeing it as nonsense at best, and at worst, blasphemy. It smelt vaguely of heresy, but in all the attempts to label it with the usual labels, from Gnosticism onwards, not one could be made to stick. Nordheider's public defence of his thesis had attracted a motley audience from the obscurest nooks and crannies of the university, and beyond. Among them was Archibald Freiling, the analytical philosopher, who had spent his time since the 1920s trying to prove that he had been plagiarised by the overrated Wittgenstein. Also present was Raoul-Christophe Bachmann, a historian with the distinction of being the first to claim that the Holocaust was a lie spread by World Jewry. Professor Karl Schmidt, the expert on Hittite, whom many had believed dead, as he had not been seen in public for many years, hobbled in on a stick, wheezing, and demanded that all present be supplied with port from the university cellar to add conviviality to the discussions. The Professor had the foresight to bring the university port with him, on five kitchen trolleys, pushed by his assistants. The Dean of the Faculty of Arts, who was chairing the proceedings, thought it wise to acquiesce, as Professor Schmidt, on his previous appearance, a banquet in 1951, had taken offence at a remark of the guest of honour, General de Gaulle, and had gone for him with his stick. The news of free drink spread rapidly, and the student taverns quickly emptied themselves, with a rowdy crowd making their way to the lecture hall and filling the back seats, greeting the Dean's attempts to maintain order with derision. The Belgian Communist Party, who believed Nordheider to be a disciple of Marx, had sent a delegation, as had other, more obscure radical organizations, and were surprised to find themselves standing in line with their bitterest enemies to claim Nordheider as one of their own.

In a pontificate less tolerant of ambiguity than that of John XXIII, the publication which emerged from Nordheider's thesis would no doubt have been placed on the Index of Forbidden Books. As it was, it was brought out to a flurry of rather dubious acclaim by an obscure Antwerp publisher, Sacramentum Mundi. Every intellectual persuasion, apart from traditionalist Catholics, had something good to say about it, and it remained in print for many years, with the modest, though steady sales turnover which is typical of the recommended reading of academia. The book had come to the attention of a Catholic bishop, Leon-Joseph Suenens, a long-standing member of the governing body of the university, who enjoyed a close friendship with Pope John. Bishop Suenens was impressed enough to go over the heads of the faculty authorities and procure a lectureship for the young Doctor of Philosophy.

By the late summer of 1959, when Michael Cremin arrived at Louvain, the scandal of Nordheider's doctorate had started to die down, to be replaced by the even greater scandal of his style of teaching. The Department of Philosophy had not taken kindly to his being imposed on them by Bishop Suenens, and had taken revenge by assigning him the worst duty they could come up with, that of conducting introductory courses in philosophy for students of theology. As Louvain was full of theology students for whom these courses were obligatory, they were sure that their unwanted colleague would be so swamped by student numbers, and by the resulting examining work, that there would be no danger of him rocking any of the various boats in which the Department believed itself well on course.

Nordheider responded with considerable ingenuity. He had been assigned a thoroughly unsuitable office in a draughty and unheated wing of Arenberg Castle, which was some miles from the philosophy department in Cardinal Mercier Square. Now, he retaliated by insisting that his courses be held in Arenberg Castle itself, which normally saw only students of technical subjects, and by scheduling his courses for impossible times in impossible places, which were also subject to change at short notice. Latin was the language of scholarship at Louvain, but Nordheider chose to lecture in English. In this, he had the approval of Bishop Suenens. Like many, the Bishop was concerned about the vendettas between the French and the Flemish speaking staff, which at times threatened to incapacitate the university, and the failure of Latin to provide the common ground was plain to see. The Bishop himself was active in the Liturgical Movement, which for many decades had been preparing the way for a greater use of local languages in the Catholic rites. Suenens, who was soon to become Archbishop and Primate, believed that the time had come to put an end to Latin as the sole liturgical language of the Church.

Providence had determined that none of the chess moves of Louvain university politics would adversely affect Michael Cremin. The House of Studies where he was staying, a small Jesuit residence in the neighbouring town of Heverlee, happened to be within walking distance of Arenberg Castle, and lectures in Nordheider's rather quaint English were a relief to him after his struggles with the French and Flemish accented Latin of the Louvain theologians. Jean Nordheider, though odd, was unforgettable: a tall, thin and very pale individual, lost in an academic gown which was many sizes too large for him and hopelessly blotched by chalk dust. When Michael first saw him on the podium, he thought he looked like the outline sketch of a new species of bird, a bird whose maker was still undecided about providing the capacity to fly. His voice was nasal and penetrating, a combination of rasp and whine, creating a strange effect of rarefaction and coarseness.

Nordheider's students would lose their way pedalling their bicycles through the narrow streets of Louvain in uncertain weather, usually at awkward times which forced them to miss their breakfast or their dinner. Those who made it to the latest change of room in the ramshackle castle found themselves lost a second time, as they were dragged at breakneck speed through the history of philosophy from the Milesian School to the present-day; or to what was deemed the present day, as the course seemed to end with the First World War.

When they returned after the Christmas break, with little more than scattered fragments of names and concepts in their lecture notes, the course turned more and more to the philosophical questioning of theology. Perhaps this provocative slant had always been there without them noticing it, but the students were now brought up against the harsh reality: they were the prey of a master ironist, who never advanced a position of his own, but took pleasure in undermining their most cherished beliefs with exquisite forms of dialectic. Nordheider's lecturing had become a precision instrument of destruction. Few of them were able for it. By the end of January, most of them had left. The lecturer did not seem to care.

2

January 30 was the day that changed everything. It was a Saturday, but as a student on Dr. Nordheider's course, Michael Cremin had to go to the university. But he had been on the move quite early anyway, because it was the feast of Saint Ildephonsus, and Michael, whose turn it was on the roster, had been required to serve the Mass of an elderly Spanish Jesuit who was named after this saint. After breakfast with the community, he had found some time for Burridge's *Shorter History of Philosophy* from 1942. It was the only elementary guide which contained anything on Franz Brentano, the Catholic priest who had helped to initiate Phenomenology, and whom Nordheider had praised, rather faintly, the week before. By 8:00 a.m he was in the lecture hall in Arenberg Castle.

Since the Christmas break, the class of sixty or seventy students had dwindled to ten or twelve. It had been odd, but fascinating to see them all leave. Michael was obliged by Archbishop McQuaid to post home a monthly report of his doings, but he had decided that he would no longer mention this particular series of lectures. He would probably be ordered home immediately if he told them what was happening. For the afternoon, he had decided to visit the Irish College in Louvain, which was run by the Irish Franciscans. The night before, he had been idly turning the pages of the Directory of Priests in Louvain, trying to pronounce the strange names he came across. Ildefonso Garcia SJ.

Harke Lubbers SJ. Korbinian Gusius SJ. Placidus-Maria Globowski SJ. Then he found the Irish Franciscans: Benignus Breen OFM. Canice Whelan OFM. Columbanus Deegan OFM. The familiarity of these names had warmed his heart, and he wanted to go over to their friary and introduce himself.

At the lecture that morning, a French nun, obviously irritated by something, decided to speak up. "What you are saying is completely wrong, Dr. Nordheider. There are truths about which it is possible to be absolutely certain. In the domains of Faith and Morals, truths are made certain by the infallibility of the pope."

Nordheider thanked the nun for her unsolicited contribution, then he seemed to fall into himself, getting caught up in his academic gown. Having worked out what he wanted to say, he rose to his full height, licking his lips.

"Infallibility, Sister. What is that? Is it a little dove whispering in the brain of the pope? No, it is not. It is, of course, a dogma, one promulgated at the First Vatican Council. This Council was held from 1869 to 1870. What about the hundreds of popes who lived before this Council? Are all Their Holinesses now deemed infallible?"

"It is when a pope invokes infallibility that he is infallible."

"Latin is the sacred language of the Church. Is a pope then infallible only when he uses Latin?"

"It is not Latin that makes a pope infallible. It is the Holy Spirit."

"Does the Holy Spirit speak only Latin? If the Holy Spirit speaks only Latin, then how can He be omniscient or omnipotent? If He also speaks other languages, is He then infallible? Hardly. Because the differences between the languages make differences in the interpretation of doctrine inevitable. Minor differences, perhaps, but differences all the same. And differences mean disagreements. Can we expect the Holy Spirit to disagree with Himself? Surely that would be most uncatholic?"

An embarrassed silence descended on the lecture theatre. A group of Franciscans pointedly walked out, swishing the ropes of their habits.

"Your assumptions are wrong, Doctor," the brave nun called from her seat.

"But, Sister, we are assuming nothing! In these lectures, there is no God, and the Holy Spirit is as inspirational as a pipe of opium, no more and no less. There is one rather far-fetched assumption of modern times which will serve to make my meaning clear. I refer to the Assumption into Heaven of the Blessed Virgin Mary, which was proclaimed infallibiliter by Pope Pius XII in the Apostolic Constitution *Munificentissimus Deus* of 1950. This is a quite remarkable assumption, you will agree. Imagine now that a blind and deaf person is to be instructed in this new dogma. There is a language created for such persons by a professor in Seville, a language composed of taps on the palm of the hand. We find, however, that we cannot use it to communicate with the subtlety that the language of Virgil and Horace made available to Pope Pius. All we can say regarding the Assumption is, that the woman went up somewhere, as in going upstairs, for example. We cannot separate going upstairs, perhaps to darn the socks of Saint Joseph, from being assumed into Heaven! And indeed, why should we? Surely darning a man's socks is a worthwhile pastime for the Blessed Virgin?"

"That is completely wrong, Doctor Nordheider."

The French nun again. Nordheider grinned at her.

"Pope Pius is with his Maker, and as we speak, he is doubtless developing further his competence in theology. Happily, there is now another we can take guidance from, one who regards the great diversity of mankind as a blessing rather than a curse, and who is therefore prepared to acknowledge the provisional nature of the language in which we attempt to formulate our truths. I refer to Pope John XXIII. You have heard of this man, Sister?"

The nun did not answer, but there was an angry murmur among what remained of the audience. Nordheider gripped his gown at the lapels and beamed down at them.

"Potzthuidenschiit! You Catholics are intellectually dishonest. You have no business attending a university. I tell you, when you come to sit the exam I will set, you will either abandon your beliefs or you will lie through your teeth, if you want to pass. And I believe I prefer the latter, Potzstraal!"

At this point the courageous sister, grim with anger left the lecture theatre, followed in a show of solidarity by the three or four students that remained. Michael Cremin was now alone with the dangerous Doctor of Philosophy.

"So. Boy. Do you also leave?"

The young man plucked up his courage. "You said we would be assuming nothing in this course. I think we were assuming a number of things."

"What was assumed?"

"A shared position on the nature of language and truth. But you and the Sister have different conceptions of language and truth. The students assumed proper communication was taking place, but it wasn't. And you assumed the ignorance of everybody who was here, bar you yourself."

Nordheider stared fixedly at Michael for what seemed a long time. "This lecture is now over," he said. "I will be expecting you in my office at three. Please be on time."

3

Michael Cremin changed his plans. Instead of visiting the Irish College to exchange pleasantries with Benignus Breen and Canice Whelan, he spent the rest of the time walking distractedly through the shops in the centre of Louvain, or sitting nervously in the cafes of the Old Market, while pondering over what exactly he had got himself into. Nordheider did not make a solid impression, morally. It occurred to him that the lecturer might be a serious sinner in dire need of conversion. For a moment, Michael dreamed that he might be an emissary of God, sent from holy Ireland, the land of saints and scholars, to save the soul of Jean Nordheider. But it was more likely to be a simple question of authority. You just couldn't talk to a lecturer in the insolent way he had done. Not even a lecturer like Dr. Nordheider. The waiter came with another cup of the strong black coffee, one more than he could afford. He would apologise to Dr. Nordheider. And then? Well, then, Michael would let the lecturer see the wonderful certainty of the Roman Catholic Faith. The ancient beauty of the Rock of Peter on which his house was built. Fortified by prayer, he would invite Jean Nordheider to consider the state of his soul.

It turned out differently. As Michael walked through the gate into Heverlee Park, things looked new to him. There was an old gate lodge he could not remember having noticed before. It had a name sign hanging from a black iron post, where it was creaking slowly in the wind. It was a decrepit edifice, with its rotting wooden walls and its haphazard roof slates peeling with sickly green lichen. The gate lodge was called Jerusalem, he saw with astonishment. Then, past a ruined chapel, Arenberg Castle itself, which reassured the eye with four or more stories of reddish-brown brickwork and tall glass windows. But Michael was not reassured. The Christian omens were not good, and this played in his soul like a nervous wind.

The lecturer's office was situated at the top of some uneven flights of stairs in a little-used wing of the castle which looked out on an overgrown courtyard. The door was open. Jean Nordheider was perched in an armchair, where he was inhaling smoke from a water-pipe and blowing it in slow aromatic clouds towards the ceiling. The wide bowl of the pipe rested on the bare floorboards. It was of brass or copper, shaped like the mouth of a gargoyle, and a dark red tube sewn with gold thread emerged from it and curved like a snake towards the lecturer's mouth.

"Enter."

Anxious now, Michael closed the door behind him and sat down on a hard stool which had been placed to one side. For a long time there was silence.

"Your name, boy?"

Michael told him who he was and why he was in Louvain.

"So. They are starting to send their talented ones abroad now. They want to open minds, for a change, instead of nailing them shut. Only a preparation, no doubt. There will then be indestructible nails when the time comes for the nailing. What do you think of the new pope, John XXIII, Mr. Cremin? Michael?"

Nordheider had put down the pipe. His thin red tongue licked over his lips. With the smoke taste, he seemed to be testing the flavour of the young man's name.

"I admire him so much, Doctor. He welcomes everyone as a brother. I read how he likes to enjoy life, to laugh, even at himself. They say he is bringing a new spirit into the Church."

"This pope, my dear Michael, is not a Catholic as we know them. He is perhaps a Humanist. Or a Deist. Perhaps an adherent of one of the ancient heresies. Ah, but fear not my jests, dear Michael. This pope is a man of love. A true humanitarian. Strange how such an exotic being could survive in the arctic waste of the Vatican!"

Michael had been taken aback by the seeming slander against Pope John, but now he relaxed a little. The lecturer was able to appreciate Pope John as a man of love. Like the atheists and the communists. Perhaps his lecturer was one of these unfortunates, whom the example of the pope was now drawing towards the Faith. A happy thought.

"The other contenders at the conclave of 1958 were hopeless fossils, Michael. Cardinal Siri, for example. For him, the history of thought ended in 1274. Everything since then, just a commentary on the *Summa Theologiae*."

"May I ask, are you a Catholic, Doctor Nordheider?"

"No."

"Are you an atheist?"

"No."

"What are you, then?"

"I am nothing."

"How can you say that? And how could you read Saint Thomas Aquinas and not believe?"

"It is precisely because I have read Thomas that I do not believe. I do not want to believe. I hate Thomas Aquinas. Do you know that there are ten thousand and seven different intellectual positions considered in the *Summa*? I have counted them. Thomas is a fat, ugly warthog who goes to the pool and drinks all the water. Then he piddles and fills the pool again. There is nothing in the pool for anybody who thirsts for knowledge but the piddle of Thomas. Thomas was an ignoramus. He never knew what it meant to lie with a woman, let alone that special jingle in the muscles that comes with the illicit forms of sensuality. He never tasted any real pleasures, not even the intellectual ones. He never expanded his consciousness. He never doubted. And he never wanted anything except what he was told to want. Thomas Aquinas knew absolutely nothing."

Michael was stunned by what he had just heard. If he were to follow the pricking of his conscience, he would have to get out of there immediately and have nothing to do with this man ever again.

"How lucky we are with Good Pope John," Nordheider continued, seemingly unaware of his visitor's discomfort. "The present pope is a very different kind of man. A good man."

The discomfort subsided. A man who praised the pope, particularly a pope of such obvious sanctity as this one, could not be an enemy of the Faith, whatever his words might at first seem to mean.

"Pope John, Michael, is possibly a true individual, a rare species in the Roman Catholic Church."

"They are returning to God because of him, Doctor. There are thousands of conversions. The atheists and the communists. He has opened a door for them. Maybe you will convert, too, Doctor Nordheider."

"I must confess that I am beginning to feel that I could indeed be at home in the Roman Catholic Church. I would never have thought it possible."

Nordheider rummaged through papers scattered over different tables. With a cry of delight, he found what he was looking for, a photograph, which he handed to Michael. It was a black and white print of a young nun in the habit of her Order, gazing serenely into the camera.

"That, Michael, is what has kept me as far from the Church as it is possible to be. That, Michael, is the so-called Thérèse of the Child Jesus and the Holy Face, known to us as Saint Thérèse of Lisieux. Now that Good Pope John is in, this little Thérèse is out. The Church is to become a place for healthy individuals, at last!"

Michael disliked hearing his lecturer talk this way about a saint, even if it was a saint he did not know much about. He felt again that he should leave. The lecturer seemed to notice, and he put more warmth into his voice.

"Thérèse of Lisieux is quite a challenge, I'll admit. I had intended to deal with her grotesque Little Way in one of my lectures, but I found myself unable to do so."

"No doubt it was the authorities that held you back from so unwise a step, sir."

"What? Of course not. It was her writings. The spirit behind her writings. I could not grasp hold of it."

Despite himself, Michael was intrigued. Nordheider was clearly affected by the writings of a saint. It was perhaps a sign of incipient conversion.

"This cult of spiritual childhood. It is pernicious. Obnoxious. It is the very antithesis of what I stand for. You cannot use a child to hone your arguments and perfect your rhetoric. All you can do with a child is be displeased with it, and spank its bottom for a while, but then you have to put it out of the room, and you can be certain that it will come back in again at the most inopportune moment. I would make a laughing stock of myself if I attacked the appalling Thérèse with the weapons of reason. The way to deal with the nonsense of a child is to ignore it. But I believe her time is over. Pope John is opening up that little secluded garden where she was whiling the time away pretending to be a princess. The Church will now face up to the realities! The Church will value the courage to be!"

"I do not follow you, Doctor."

"It is the parable of the servants and the talents, is it not? Jesus Christ praised the servant who made profitable use of what he was given, and he also praised that servant who made unprofitable use and lost his talent. It is the servant who kept the talent by making no use of it who was condemned. Surely this applies to Thérèse of Lisieux as much as to anyone? She had a life and she refused to use it. She refused to be herself. How can that be pleasing to God?"

To the inexperienced seminarian, this was new and daring language. Despite himself, he was fascinated.

"Good, Michael. I am pointing the way. You can learn nothing from a little girl who entered a convent because she did not want to grow up. Plato! Nietzsche! From these substantial beings you can learn. Do you know why I am so glad to meet you, Michael?"

The lecturer looked deep into his eyes, and Michael Cremin began to feel somehow exalted. He was used to being no more than a lowly seminarian of the Archdiocese of Dublin, where the ordained priests did not even use his name when they were ordering him to bring their books back to the library, or to pick the muck off their football boots.

"You used the word "communication" to me yesterday, Michael. It is not a word that one hears often. There are very few people in the world who are aware that this concept is of importance. The pope is one. Obviously, you are another. The kingdom that is to come is a hermeneutic kingdom, where we will endlessly approach and re-approach ourselves through communication with strangers on the presupposition of equality. I think, Michael, that you might be a man of the future. It was my intention yesterday to end the course on account of the low attendance. Now, I will not end this course. I will continue it. For you alone. It will be your course, Michael."

4

It will be your course, Michael, Jean Nordheider had said, and so it was. He gave Michael a selection of texts from the history of philosophy, some of them in the original languages, and he did not seem to care when Michael understood very little. One evening, they took a short walk together along the small river which traversed the grounds of Arenberg castle.

"Well, Michael. We have tried to grasp the importance of Kant and German Idealism. We cannot know the thing-in-itself. History is Spirit becoming itself. What liberating positions these are! When you contemplate them, do you feel liberated, Michael?"

Michael would not have thought that his feelings had anything to do with understanding. But the Gospels did say that the truth would be liberating.

"Doctor, Kant and Hegel do not take proper account of the Fall of Man. Of the fact that error of thought, and the fragility of physical existence are part of what man is. Of the fact that Revelation has been given to help us. And redemption."

"Do you find Kant palatable? I mean, do you like him?"

"I can't say."

"I can say, Michael. I detest Kant."

"You mean his books?"

"I mean the books together with the man who wrote them. You mentioned the fragility of physical existence, just now. Immanuel Kant, Michael, was a man who eschewed the body, with particular reference to his own body. In order to ensure that no excitement of a sexual kind could disturb the smooth pace of his thought, he refused to allow himself to take pleasure in the form of the body, male, or female, and he took measures against himself that were most peculiar. He doused his sex with cold water and he slept in clothing which resembled the strait-jackets in which lunatics are placed in order to restrain them. It is said that when he died the embalmers were surprised to find that his pudenda were almost non-existent. Do you think, Michael, that such a man can be a man of knowledge? Undoubtedly he had what passes for knowledge, but is it not so that if there is knowledge that can be said to be of the body, then this underdeveloped man would have no choice but to claim that such knowledge is not knowledge at all?"

"It is so."

"So, Michael, the reason for this abject failure on the part of a so-called great thinker is because he did not believe. Immanuel Kant had no faith! And you will find, Michael that the vast majority of professing Christians do not have faith, either."

Michael stared at the lecturer in confusion. Why was he bringing up faith now, when he claimed not to have any faith?

"You will look hard in your Church, Michael, for any true evidence of belief that God and His creation are good. Take celibacy. A teaching on sexuality that ignores completely the insights of Sigmund Freud. A teaching, in fact, that takes the truth and says that it is not true. Do you wish to spend your life saying that the truth is not true, Michael?"

"Of course, not, Doctor. I want to be a priest! I want to spend all of my life worshipping truth and serving truth."

"Then do so, my dear Michael, do so. There are so few who have the courage to do so. You believe that you have what is termed a Vocation. You believe that you have been singled out by the Almighty God. Your Church has confirmed this for you. But what have you ever done? What effort have you made?"

"I'm a seminarian, attending classes, preparing for ordination!"

"But what is inside you? Do you know this at all? Or do you pretend you do not have a body like most of the Catholics I have met? Thank Heaven for Good Pope John and his healthy respect for the pleasures of his stomach. A pope who can give us a happy belch after his dinner will certainly change Catholicism as we know it. So, Michael. Will you look at the bodily impulses which your retrograde Archbishop wished you did not have? Ask them what they may have to say to you?"

"In the interests of truth?"

"Of course. Or would you prefer to evaporate completely into the mind, to leave behind upon your demise the emasculated stump of a penis and a sad pair of wizened testicles to sum up for the world who you had been? Think it over, Michael. When you are certain, if you are certain, we will proceed."

5

Think it over, Michael. He did think it over. He thought it over every minute of every day for almost a week. It drove him across half Louvain, from one hopefully wise Father Confessor to another, as he tried to break the moral conundrum of listening to his body while avoiding sin. He was at an age when his appetites did not find a balance by themselves, and Jean Nordheider's invitation gave him sleepless nights in which the devil had complete command over his imagination. More than once, he found his hand reaching for his penis, longing to ease the pain of his manhood, in that detestable sin which he had been combating with brisk exercise and cold showers in the seminary. He would then lie in bed until the grey light of morning came, hating himself for his failure.

The confessors were of little help. "Think of Our Lord on the Cross," they sniffed from behind the metal grille, and closed the wooden shutter on him as quickly as they could.

In Michael's fevered imagination, thinking of the Lord on the Cross only made things worse. The crucified Jesus was somehow desirable, and now, in addition to the horrible sin of self-pollution, he had that most dreadful Sin against Nature, and not only that, but also the truly appalling blasphemy of connecting this with the Holy Lord. He was a sure candidate for the Sin against the Holy Spirit, that Sin which the Gospels say can never be forgiven. There was no doubt in Michael's mind that he was already damned and destined for Hellfire for all eternity. This thought, frightful though it was, still had an odd glamour to it. Being a Great Sinner was every bit as exceptional as being a Great Poet, or a Great Warrior. Not everyone could go so far.

There was a youngish Italian priest staying at the Jesuit residence, a Vincentian whose name was Angelo Poggi. He hailed from a dependency of his Order in the Archdiocese of Milan, and was in Louvain to study the Belgian Liturgical Movement. Angelo Poggi was connected in some vague way with the influential Roman liturgist, Annibale Bugnini CM, and he believed in the abolition of Latin in favour of a Vernacular liturgy, as he liked to tell anyone who would listen. He believed himself ahead of his time on many issues, and was regarded as something of a nuisance around Louvain.

One morning, after a night of erotic fantasies, which he was beginning to take pleasure in, despite himself, Michael decided that he would mark the seriousness of the matter by confessing his sins immediately, to the first priest he could find. This happened to be Angelo Poggi, who, like Michael, was late that morning, and had missed the community breakfast. Michael got down on his knees before the Milanese Vincentian, who glanced up and down the corridor, as if to ascertain that they were alone. Calmly, he listened to Michael stutter out his sins and spoke the Latin words of Absolution. Then, in a show of compassion, he suggested that they breakfast together in the nearby refectory, which was now empty.

"I used to be like that, too." Angelo Poggi checked over his shoulder and poured the coffee. "You know, Jesus forgives. Always. So there's nothing to worry about."

"But I just can't stop it, Father."

"Angelo. Call me Angelo. You can't stop it? So why do you try? I stopped trying years ago."

Michael was aghast. "Father, you don't try to be chaste?"

"There is no point. And I do not know what it is to be chaste. I do not know what is a sin when something cannot be stopped with the best will in the world. They are not treating you well in your seminary, Mr. Cremin. Michael. We are not angels. We are human beings."

Afterwards, when he tried to work out why he had agreed to follow the doubtful Vincentian, Michael remembered that odd glitter in Angelo Poggi's eyes, and the waft of freedom it seemed to represent. At that time, Michael was very insecure: a young fellow from a small and backward country who had to struggle hard not to go red whenever he was addressed by someone in authority. Angelo Poggi had the allure of the accomplished cosmopolitan, and he seemed the epitome of self-confidence. To cap it all, whatever liberties he was taking, Angelo was a priest in good standing, and that evoked respect and trust.

"There is a special club here," Angelo said to him one evening. "I am a member of this club. It meets in an establishment where one is safe from interference. The members of this club understand certain things."

"What things?"

"For one, that moral codes are for children and for cowards. The real man does whatever he wants."

"Even mortal sins?"

"There is no such a thing as a sin, mortal or not. Come to the club with me, I can get you onto the guest list. Very exclusive!"

Angelo brought Michael to the streets behind the railway station, and then beyond them, to a secluded villa, set on its own tract of land and hidden behind high iron railings of black and gold. In the approaches, they walked past half-lit places where men had their clothing down round their ankles, and were jerking, grimacing and groaning, being serviced sexually by girls who were making a good show of enjoying their work.

They are priests, Michael heard Angelo say, his heart sinking. No serious transgression, the Italian went on. There was that assurance. The Church was coming round to a more balanced view of human sexuality. His own bishop, for example, the well-known Cardinal Montini, was a practicing homosexual. Secretly, for the moment. There was no harm in a priest, even a cardinal, being before his time, was there? It was Montini who had recommended that he take a look at Freud and Psychoanalysis. Michael could join in here, if he liked, here in the shadows. He did not have to go any further if he didn't want to. There were male prostitutes, too, if that was what he preferred. Wasn't Good Pope John about to renew the Church, dare he say it, from the bottom up?

Michael was too frightened to speak, but his mind was clear. What Angelo Poggi had said was ridiculous. Cardinal Montini was known to have been in the running to succeed Pius XII, despite being only an Archbishop at the time. The thought that this holy man could be a sodomite was preposterous. And anyway, Michael did not have the faintest idea of what to do to join in. The antics before his eyes simply disgusted him.

Now they had reached the gate which led up to the villa. Angelo whispered something, a wad of banknotes changed hands, and the gate creaked open to admit them. A short expanse of bleached gravel and they came to a door, which was ajar. They found themselves in a hallway, and then in a large ballroom which was dimly-lit, but full of people. Michael recognised some of the faces from the newspapers and from official events he had witnessed. There were churchmen among them. And businessmen and politicians.

A small glass was pressed into his hand by a white-gloved waiter. It was heavy for its size, and the sweet liquid was a cloudy brown colour. A gong sounded, and the guests disappeared into the curtained shadows.

"Where are they going?" Michael whispered.

"To do their thing. Some of them will study the stars in the heavens or the realities of other worlds. A few will be taking the vinegar. I will show you. Come."

With some reluctance, Michael followed Angelo through one of the doors and down a narrow flight of stairs. This led to a quieter room, sparsely furnished, in the centre of which was a single wooden stool, above which a bare light bulb dangled from black, pleated wires. He watched in wonder as a woman emerged from a shadowed area on the other side of the room, naked but for an array of leather belts studded with metal. Brandishing a whip, she commanded the priest to strip naked and to sit on the stool. She then chained his arms, using manacles attached to long chains which she pulled down from the shadowed roof beams, pulling the chains so tight that even from a distance he could see the red welts beginning to form on Angelo Poggi's skin.

Before Michael's young eyes there unfolded a long ritual of pain and humiliation, which ought to have sickened him completely. But to his surprise, when the reek of Angelo's sweat wafted over to him, with its tang of fear and decay, he felt himself becoming aroused.

This was no ordinary sexual excitement. A sudden power was rising from his rampant loins, filling him with a brazen lust he had never before experienced. He began laughing at the hapless wretch before him, abused by a woman paid for the task, his pitiful little erection peeking out from behind loud cries of misery. The woman loosed one of the manacles and ordered Angelo to masturbate. She then looked over at Michael, fixing his eyes with hers. Michael felt the air go strange around him, stranger even than before, colder, harder, louder, and the light bulb began to throw a strange oily sheen around the room. The woman now appeared to be sexless or androgynous, and to be completely bald, but for a thin black stripe in the centre of the skull. Half her face seemed to be composed of thousands upon thousands of maggots writhing in and out of each other in a sickening way. The eye sockets were empty of eyes, and Michael found himself drawn into them by an urge to know what was inside them, an insatiable urge; and all the time his loins were throbbing painfully and boiling with heat, overpowering him. Aroused like never before, Michael rubbed frantically at his trousers as if at a mad itch. His insides seemed to break wide open, his semen erupted from him with quick agonizing spasms, and he fell to the ground, washed with a vile-tasting mixture of surprise, satisfaction and sheer disgust. What he remembered next was the sight of the naked Angelo Poggi lolling in his chains, fast asleep, and snoring contentedly. Then he was walking through the windy night towards Heverlee, alone.

In the days that followed, Michael tried to avoid Angelo Poggi at the university and in the Jesuit Residence. Whenever their paths happened to cross, he would turn on his heel and walk away. It was, of course impossible to avoid him completely, and at mealtimes he would sometimes glance across the refectory towards him, always to find that Angelo was staring at him. He knew from the facial expression that Angelo was deeply troubled by this standoffish behaviour. With a thrill of excitement, one reminiscent of that night of sin, he observed Angelo's attitude towards him change from one of bewildered hurt to one of crushed betrayal, and finally to one bordering on terror. The eyes that looked furtively across at him seemed to sink deeper into their sockets every day, and the somewhat thickened face seemed to be collapsing into different components that had nothing to do with each other. Michael Cremin realised that all this brokenness was due to his silence, to what the troubled Italian was making of his silence. It was a thrill of power, like a dark wind, but he thrust it resolutely from him and turned back to his food.

6

When Michael Cremin met Jean Nordheider again it was to say No. What had been proposed at their last meeting, he told him, was a laudable philosophical endeavour, which ordinarily he would be delighted to pursue. But he would now be discontinuing their relationship. He remained deeply grateful to Dr. Nordheider for the honour shown him, and he would take many useful insights back home with him. The lecturer listened to him without a word, then bid him a polite goodbye.

In fact, Michael was suffering tortures he felt obliged to keep secret. His sleep was ruined by the unstoppable memories of what he had seen in the villa. His body ached for a repeat of that orgasm, and no cold showers and no desperate runs around the sports field could kill that ache. Indeed, not even the usual grim picturings of buxom farm girls rolling in hay-ricks could help him, as he pumped himself to exhaustion in the oft-soiled bedclothes. He was in extremities of conscience, and under the circumstances, he saw no possibility of going to Confession. No confessor could offer any advice other than to abandon his vocation to the priesthood, and this Michael would not countenance. Thus excluded from Sacramental Confession, and consequently from Holy Communion, he languished in Mortal Sin, in permanent fear for his soul. In his few calm moments he noted wryly that he was excluded from the Sacraments by the very desire to partake of them worthily, a moral no man's land which the manuals of theology seemed to have no description for, and no remedy.

One night, when he could take it no longer, he got up from the stale, sultry stench of his bed, wiped himself dry with the sheet, got dressed and went downstairs to the chapel, where he knelt in front of the Tabernacle. For a number of hours he entreated God to remove the dangerous desire from him, but to no avail. When dawn broke, and the tired fingers of grey light crept slowly over him like old spiders, he still burned as much as before with this clamouring lust, which demanded to be fed with nothing other than the sight, sound and smell of pain. It was obviously drug-induced, because he remembered the little glass of brown spirit they had pressed on him. It wasn't his fault. And God was not there for him. In this horror, God just was not there. It occurred to him that the Bible had many stories of serious sinners in dire situations, and that if he looked hard enough, he could probably find a comparable story with the happy end of salvation. But at that moment he had no interest in the Bible; he had no interest in stories about other people. He wanted his own story, and this was it. It was said of God that He liked to enter such stories in person in order to put them right, but there was no sign of Him knocking on the door for Michael Cremin. It was a crying injustice. A fly came from nowhere and began buzzing around him. He caught it in his hands. Then, allowing himself for an instant to be someone else, only for an instant, he crushed the fly between his hands, savouring the feel of something dying against his flesh, savouring the dull fire, horribly familiar, that flared in his loins.

If it had not been for the absence of God to him in his angry desperation, Michael might have sustained his vigil. Then, it might not have been he who found Angelo Poggi. As it was, he made his way back to his room with almost an hour still to go before breakfast. His room was on the third floor, and when he pushed open the door from the landing, he saw him. Angelo Poggi was dangling by the neck from the cross beam below the skylight, his tongue driven out of his mouth by the violence of the rope. The chair he had kicked himself from lay overturned below him. Angelo Poggi's room was on the first floor. He had chosen this place, just in front of Michael Cremin's door, to hang himself.

The young man ran to the room of the nearest priest, Fr. Lubbers, who staggered bleary-eyed up the corridor in a stole and administered the Last Rites while Angelo Poggi was still hanging there. He was not cut down until shortly before noon, when the doctors, the police and the Jesuit superiors had finished conferring with each other. There were three other Italian priests staying in the Jesuit Residence, none of them close to the deceased, but these now took it upon themselves to deal with the formalities. Nobody was allowed near Angelo Poggi's room while they were cleaning it out. Their insistence on personally bringing the rubbish to the city dump led to all kinds of rumours as to what that room had contained.

Through all this, Michael Cremin kept his silence. He attended the Mass and the Holy Hour that were held for the repose of the dead priest's soul, sharing the general feeling that the three Italians were reading the prayers at a most unseemly speed. When they hurried from the altar, omitting to extol the virtues of the deceased in the usual way, their embarrassment was plain to see. The whispered excuses of language problems, or of the bad cold of one of them, could not hide the fact that they had been unable to discover any virtues to extol. After the body was driven away for transport to Italy, nobody ever spoke of the matter again. It was as if Angelo Poggi had never existed.

All that day and night, Michael was swathed in a strange inner calm that was like a foretaste of death. It was not the calm of the resolution of conflict, but another kind, the calm that comes when conflict dies unresolved because it has run out of fuel. A dirty kind of calm. He knew that it reflected the state of his soul, but he believed he could do nothing about it. In no way was he responsible for the death and the certain damnation of Angelo Poggi. But his hand was in it, nevertheless. He had known the life this priest was leading, and he had done nothing to dissuade him. It was too complex for the usual catalogue of sins, but anyway, he could not mention it in Confession. There was no chance at all that his Vocation would survive, if he did. Nobody had told him this, because he had not asked anyone, but he was certain of it. He was beyond the moral pale, where there were no maps, no compasses, and no guides. He did not want to be there, but he was there. He would have to make the best of it, come what may.

7

One morning, shortly after Angelo Poggi's death, the porter at the residence shuffled across the wood-floored hallway to where Michael Cremin was studying a notice board before setting out for the university. "Oh, you're the rich little one, aren't you?" the porter whispered, pressing a folded note into Michael's hand. The porter was a bit soft in the head, and Michael thought no more of him as he read the message. It was from Dr. Nordheider, and Michael's heart began to beat faster. He was invited to call to the lecturer's office later that morning. The note did not say why.

Michael took a leisurely walk over the short distance to Arenberg Castle, but it was still with some nervousness that he took the uneven stairs and strode down the now familiar corridor, which smelt of Jean's tobacco smoke. Nordheider was standing by the open door of his office, waiting, his books under his arm, glancing at his watch, for once attempting to be on time for a scheduled lecture.

"Well, Michael?" he asked, his voice playful.

"Yes," the young man answered, and that was enough.

When they plunged together into Plato's *Republic*, it was almost as if they had never been parted. This was a great and commanding work, a seminal work of the Western Tradition, replete with intellectual jewels of every cut and hue. Allowances had to be made for the many barbarisms, but Plato was largely acceptable to a Catholic Christian of their day. Perhaps the most brilliant of the jewels was the Parable of the Cave, that deceptively simple story of people dwelling in ignorance inside a cave, chained together facing a wall, unable to move their heads, seeing nothing except shadows cast on the wall in front of them by the light of a fire burning somewhere behind them. Despite their chains, these prisoners do not realize that they have been imprisoned. They know nothing inside the cave as it truly is. They perceive nothing at all of a land outside the cave or of the bright light of the sun. If someone told them that they were seeing only deceptive shadows and then tried to get them to see more of their true reality, they would regard him as the worst kind of criminal. With its many layers of meaning, and its call to the reader to wake up out of sleep, the Parable of the Cave had a similar feel to the Parables of Jesus in the Gospels.

"Michael, Plato tells us that the sunlit land outside the cave is the home of the Knowledge of the Form of the Good. Unfortunately, he was unable to state clearly what the Form of the Good was, or what it might mean to have the knowledge of it. Is it not strange that this heavenly place remained so ill-defined?"

"But we must enter heaven to know heaven, Doctor. And if we return here to speak about it, we are forced to use a language that has no proper words for it. That is one good reason why Plato couldn't write more clearly."

"And why are we so sure that this sunlit land is indeed a heavenly place?"

"I do not follow you."

They were strolling easily by the small river that flowed past Arenberg Castle. The wind had picked up a little, and the long grass was waving before them as if to point out the way.

"Ah, Michael, you cannot come to know anything that you do not know already, that you have not always known since the beginning. And you can only know it now according to the measure of how you are prepared to accept it."

Jean seemed perplexed by something. Then, as if an insight had dawned, or a decision had been taken, his brow cleared and he began to smile.

"The joys of inversion were not known to Plato. But they are known to us. Practising against the grain. Exploiting the sources against themselves. Using corrosives to create. Have you tasted this delight, Michael? They gave it to Christ on the Cross, did they not? The dish of vinegar."

Vinegar. That had been one of Angelo Poggi's words. Dr. Nordheider had no doubt meant well by mentioning the great sacrifice of Jesus, but it brought Michael back to something he was hoping to forget: the dreadful sight of the celebration of cruelty and of the ruin of personalities, and the dreadful knowledge of his complicity. He swallowed hard. Red with embarrassment, he held the lecturer's gaze. Then he walked away.

Again, Michael Cremin was plunged into his secret agony of soul. He had thought that hard work on the philosophical texts would purge him, but the agony was proving stronger. After a time, he found that he could indeed bear it.

Some days later, a package arrived for Michael by post. Jean Nordheider had sent it. It was a typescript copy of a philosophical work in German. Written by someone who was still alive, for a change: Martin Heidegger of Freiburg, Germany. Michael had heard many vague things about this philosopher, none of them good. The work bore the title: *Vom Wesen der Wahrheit (Platon)*. Of the Essence of Truth (Plato). Jean Nordheider had included a note specifying the most significant chapters and pages. With the help of a dictionary, Michael slowly made his way through the ponderous sentences. The German philosopher interpreted the Parable of the Cave as revealing a truth that is man-created, rather than the eternal unchanging truth that Plato himself must have meant. With a shudder, Michael saw how Heidegger passed rather quickly, almost contemptuously, it seemed, over the passages which described the emergence of the prisoner into the sunlit land, but expended no small eloquence on his return to the cave, which now seemed to be the place of history, of the struggle to understand, of political activity, of all those sources of meaning that make human life identifiably human. The sunlit land itself, the experience of the sun, all this had no purpose but that of the backdrop of a stage, as it were. It was simply the horizon of nothingness, against which all that existed existed as itself.

The implications were profound, he wrote to Nordheider, who was away from

Louvain for some time. There was no eternal, unchanging truth, there was no separate existence in a sunlit land, there was only the twilight existence of the cave, and the special openings for truth that were made possible by the flickering of the shadows, which put one in the way of dreaming of the perpetual shining of the sun. If the prisoners in Plato's cave were to be set free, they would be free to work out their existence inside that cave, and nowhere else. The inverted story was coherent, and it had as much a claim to validity as the face-value version.

Never had the fragile beauty of Belief in God shone out so clearly for Michael as now, as he sat at his desk in his sparse little room in Louvain, sealing the envelope for Jean Nordheider. Belief in God was the tiniest candle-flame flickering in an immense darkness, and the great whole, the belief together with the darkness, had a stark symmetry to it that was overwhelming in its necessity. Neither could survive without the other, and only both together were complete. Now he could see the cosmic relations behind his moral predicament. He had not turned away from God by accepting the mark of experience, he had turned towards God in a new and deeper way. It was not the straight way, but the straight way had been blocked. It was a roundabout way with many detours, but it was a way that was open. The more he thought about it, the better he felt. It was the magnificent achievement of the Church to have at hand a symbolic remedy for every spiritual incapacity. It was the meaning of Sacrament that the presence of God be possible even in dimensions of reality which had fallen away from Him. The Grace of God was possible, always and everywhere. Even for him.

When Michael Cremin confessed again, at the university church in Louvain the next day, using the established formulae, and avoiding unhelpful detail, he felt at peace again at last. And he allowed that sense of peace to wash away the nagging feeling that he had lost something very precious indeed.

8

"So, Michael," Nordheider said, as they walked by the little river, which was twinkling happily in the morning sun. The weeks and months had passed very quickly, and it was already time for the young man to prepare to go home. "There is one further author we should look at. Friedrich Nietzsche. The poet of the death of God. What do you think of the phrase, 'God is dead?'"

"It is an abominable blasphemy."

"Is it really? There is a related idea in Feuerbach. Feuerbach was referring to the God commonly believed in, which he regarded as a creation of the minds of the believers, an idol, so to speak. In view of this, would clear thinking not require you to regard the common concept of God as something dispensable?"

"It would, Doctor, if Feuerbach was right."

"When you consider your own belief in God, have there been any changes over the years in what you have understood of Him?"

"There have been many changes, Doctor."

"If you were now to go back some years and take the understanding of God of that year and state that this was the only correct way to conceive of God, surely that would be a serious error?"

"A most serious error."

"And would this not apply with equal force to the understanding of God you now have, and to any future perception of God?"

"Yes, it would."

"Is there not then a justification to Feuerbach's view that the God that is spoken about is a creation of human minds?"

"There would appear to be one, but that is not the same as saying that God is dead. God cannot die."

"You are saying then, that the experience of death is not one that is open to God?"

"No. Yes. No."

"Did not Jesus die? And was not Jesus God?"

"He rose again."

"Did His Resurrection not logically depend on His death?"

"Doctor, this is not logic, or reason, this is Faith."

"Are logic and reason then repugnant to your faith? Is your faith repugnant to reason?"

"No."

"Then, let us give fair consideration to the death of God and Friedrich Nietzsche. I am a philosopher, Michael. I will leave theology to the theologians. In a short time, I will return you to your diocese with a mind made deeper and broader than most there will have. What becomes of you, Michael, depends not on me, but on you and your religious superiors. The way is almost at an end. Let us walk this last little stretch together. With courage and goodwill."

'German nihilist in the line of Schopenhauer. An influence on French existentialist thought. Also noted as a poet and a composer of music'. Thus Burridge in the entry on Nietzsche. That did not say very much, but luckily Burridge listed the main works by this man. *The Birth of Tragedy. Thus Spoke Zarathustra. On the Genealogy of Morals. The Antichrist.* Books with titles like that would have been forbidden to him in Dublin. There was also an incomplete magnum opus called *The Will to Power.* Not an edifying title, either.

It was *Also Sprach Zarathustra* that Jean asked Michael to read. This proved to be a black-bound tome of 400 odd pages which sat heavy in the hand. The frontispiece offered a brooding picture of Friedrich Nietzsche, taken from a contemporary etching. He looked rather like Josef Stalin, Michael thought: bushy black eyebrows and an outsize moustache, which made the lower part of his face look like a garden of weeds.

This was not a book that a Christian could read with assent. Not only does the protagonist announce that God is dead, and that something called the Superman is His successor, but he specifically attacks central Christian themes such as Compassion and Prayer, and he presents new teachings of his own in language clearly stolen from the New Testament. And turning up regularly, something called the 'Eternal Recurrence of the Same'; obviously a worldly substitute for the Christian idea of Heaven. The Superman is the man who is capable of believing in the Eternal Recurrence. This makes him a self-energising entity who affirms the totality of existence. The existence he affirms is a self-creating and self-destroying vitality, a monster of life force, which devours everything in its blind striving to surpass itself.

Michael was not surprised to learn that poor Nietzsche had ended his life insane. His perspectivist outpourings were the height of bad logic. Affirming all of existence must also mean affirming Jesus Christ and the Christian ideals, and this Nietzsche was clearly unable to do. The man was a failure by his own standards. A philosopher destroyed by his own thought. The best that could be said about him was that he had had the mind of a priest gone wrong: he could not live without worshipping God, but he refused to worship God. So he had to spend his time reworking reality inside his head so that he could have the experience of worship without acknowledging God, at all. A sad case. A salutary example of the dire effect on the mind of false teaching.

Michael did not realise how angry Nordheider could be. The philosopher's face was drawn tight, his eyes were poisonous slits, and a vein throbbed dangerously in his forehead.

"You have understood nothing," he hissed. "Nothing!"

Contemptuously, Jean Nordheider opened the book in the middle of Part Two, at a short section called On Overcoming Yourself. Tapping the pages with his fingers, he ordered Michael to summarize the main point. It proved impossible to do so satisfactorily, and Michael soon gave up.

"If you cannot make anything of these few short pages, Mr. Cremin," said the lecturer, wearily, "you will utterly fail to understand the direction mankind has taken in this century. Modern art and modern music will be nonsense to you. Politics will shock you. Philosophy, poetry and literature will confuse you. You will live a ghetto existence inside your Church like the rest of your kind, and you will never understand why the truths you profess to live by are so irrelevant to so many. Now. These pages are about the Will to Power. The Will to Power is an interpretation of life and living creatures. Life is that which must overcome itself again and again. Only I am life. I am struggle and aim and conflict of aims. I am will. Will to power. I am creator of Good. And of Evil. The greatest Good and the greatest Evil belong together in my exertion of my power. Now, I ask you to dispute this, to prove that it is wrong."

Over the next hour or so, Michael grappled with Nietzsche's teaching, as Nordheider had presented it. He tried to refute it with what he thought were Christian teachings on the nature of life and living creatures, but he was forced to admit that every Christian truth he advanced could be understood perfectly well in terms of the Will to Power. No Christian value could not be revalued in the light of the Will to Power. No truth of Revelation could not also be seen as an exertion of the Will to Power. Even Belief in God could be considered an expression of the Will to Power. This mad German sceptic had smashed every valid truth to nothing, and yet had found a viable way to walk on, or so it seemed. It was a way of radical self-affirmation, not a Catholic or a Christian way, but a way nevertheless. It seemed to lead somewhere, even if one could not say exactly where.

"I do not ask you to call yourself a Nietzschean, Michael. I ask only that you assent to what has a valid claim to your assent, and that in other cases you refuse your assent. The men of your Church often prefer cowardice and dishonesty. They do not engage with Nietzsche. They know they would lose, and they are afraid to lose. Do not be afraid, Michael. Be a loyal priest of your Church. Be loyal to your God. I have tried to enable you to do this without subterfuge and without shame."

"I will be loyal to God, sir."

"Be loyal with honesty, Michael."

9

It was unthinkable for Michael Cremin to leave Louvain without expressing his gratitude to Jean Nordheider in some tangible way. He had agonized over what he could do to both please his teacher and mark the quality of their time together, and eventually, he came across some translations from the Old Irish in a second-hand bookshop. He pawned his watch to be able to buy this rare book. But when Michael met up with his teacher, Jean Nordheider refused to accept it. He refused with great kindness, but he gave no reason. It seemed to Michael that his debt to Jean Nordheider was just too great for him to even acknowledge, let alone repay.

While the aircraft took him on the slow journey from Brussels to Dublin via London, Michael Cremin passed the time by reading in different books he had brought with him and noting down his thoughts in a jotter. Man was an artist. Man was a poet of truth. Man was not the prisoner of an eternally fixed reality. Truth was something to be endured, in the nobility of tragedy; the painful and the repulsive were to be affirmed just as much as the beautiful and the holy. Even by a priest. Especially by a priest.

Jean Nordheider was not asking him to be a Nietzschean. He could never be a

Nietzschean. He believed in God and in Jesus Christ and in the Holy Roman Catholic and Apostolic Church. But there could be a Nietzschean edge to his belief. Faith in God was perhaps the greatest sublimation of the Will to Power. Adherence to the teachings of the Church was perhaps God's chosen means of this sublimation. It was the way of education of life-force, the turning of it towards the Good.

These were unusual thoughts. But they seemed to be very much of the time that was coming. Michael was sure that the Holy Father, Pope John XXIII, would approve.

Michael leafed through one of the books, then closed it and leaned back in his seat. He had not wanted to go on Jean Nordheider's word alone. That would have been dishonest. But Jean's dismissal of Saint Thérèse of Lisieux was indeed justified. The autobiography of Saint Thérèse had very little to recommend it. Not that it was a bad book. Far from it. It might even have touches of genius, in places. But it was not for their time. Not for the times that were coming.

Outside, on the wings of the plane, the propellers turned almost invisibly, and the dull beating of the engines kept its own regular time. Little Thérèse Martin had never flown in an airplane. She had never learned foreign languages, nor read much at all, it seemed, not even in the literature of the Church. And the one time she had spread her wings a little, on a pilgrimage to Rome, she seemed to have been deeply shocked by the coarseness of the pilgrims. That was the reality of her spirituality of childhood, her Little Way. Shrinking into herself like a sensitive little princess, who was too good for the raw living all around her. Take the famous conversion experience of Christmas 1886. All Thérèse did was walk down the stairs of her home to take part in the family celebrations. To be sure, she had had to overcome herself to do so, and in what seemed a personally significant way. But still, all she did was walk down the stairs to a warm room in a warm house and into the arms of her loved ones. At that same moment, there were probably hundreds of urchins lying destitute in the streets of Paris, dying of the cold and the hunger, abandoned by those who were supposed to be caring for them, and seeing nothing at all of Christmas.

Later, as a nun, all Thérèse Martin did was let the other nuns treat her like dirt. And when she contracted TB, all she hoped for was to die quickly. As an informed Catholic, Michael Cremin was well aware of the supposed value in such behaviour. Especially the value of serious illnesses borne well, and of a holy death. It was the eschatological life. It was that personal asceticism the Church taught to all its members, and asked in greater measure of those in religious vows. But there was just too much of it in *The Story of a Soul.* Thérèse's behaviour had made her illness worse than it would otherwise have been. That was not right or good. To teach absolute confidence in God in one's weakness, as Thérèse had done, was laudable. No doubt about that. But to actually aspire to be weak? That was going too far. To be so focused on weakness just increased that weakness. That was not right, at all.

As they headed out over the Irish Sea and into the darkening evening, they hit some turbulence, and the plane rolled and dipped erratically. Some of the passengers were visibly afraid, clinging to anything within reach that looked fixed and safe. Fear, Michael mused. It was the great constant of the Catholic life. Fear of God. Fear of sin. Fear of being damned to Hell for all eternity. It had done him good to read Nietzsche. Nietzsche had been a fearless thinker. It occurred to him that that was also true of Saint Thérèse of Lisieux. It was unusual, but the fear of God did not play a role for her at all. Hers was a fearless spirituality. But she had read nothing, studied nothing, accomplished nothing. It was Nietzsche modern man could learn from.

The plane steadied itself, and Michael recalled his last few days in Louvain. Once his bags were packed, he had walked one more time down the raucous streets behind the railway station, where he had been with Angelo Poggi. He was not consciously seeking anything, yet somehow he knew where to go. It was as if some instinct had been active over the preceding weeks, taking secret note of the small ads in the newspapers. Again, the villa without a name had emerged before him on its own tract of land, darker than the surrounding twilight. This time, the approaches were empty and silent. The man at the gate admitted him without a word, as if he was expected, and pocketed the wad of banknotes which Michael proffered. He had got the money only the day before, from the resale of the Old Irish translations. It seemed just enough. Michael had assumed that he would only get as far as the gate, and would then be turned away, but now he was inside again. The bleached gravel crunched under his feet like a carpet of eggshells, and the door to the villa swung open. A sombre-faced man was standing there, dressed in black coat and tails, a high starched collar buttoned tightly at his neck without the adornment of a tie.

"My condolences," the man whispered. They walked together through the empty ballroom, down a flight of stairs and into a long windowless cavern, which was full of the paraphernalia one would associate with a torture chamber. There were naked bodies locked onto various ugly instruments. Men and women in masks were operating different apparatus to punish their victims, performing sex acts as they did so. Occult symbols decorated the walls.

"You're just looking, I take it?" whispered the man who had admitted him. Michael nodded. He spent about an hour moving from one sadistic scene to another, breathing in the smells of pain and bodily secretions. Relatively quickly his excitement had subsided. He was completely in control, and that was what he needed to know. He felt nothing, nothing at all. Not for himself, not for the victims, not for the sick men and women who were torturing them. It was just one grim scene among many that made up the tapestry of life.

"I'd like to go now," he said to the doorkeeper who had admitted him.

"Yes, Father," breathed the doorkeeper, and gravely led the young man outside.

On the morning of Michael's departure, a letter from Jean Nordheider had reached him from Canada. As the plane began its descent into Dublin, Michael read it one more time.

My dear Michael,

I greet you from the wilds of Manitoba. I congratulate you on your graduation from my secret school. I did not know that I had a school, secret or otherwise, or even any pupils, until you came along. You are likely to be the only graduate. Communication was the key that let you in. It is the concept of the future, a far more useful one than Truth. It will not be long before we see a pope praying in public with Protestants, Hindus and Buddhists. It will not be long before all the religions of the world, and indeed all the nations and cultures of the world will join together in the struggle to become One World of Brothers, as the glorious Ninth Symphony of Beethoven tells us.

Yesterday, I met the bishop of this place, a congenial fellow, who is just back from Rome. He tells me there is soon to be an Ecumenical Council of the Vatican, to decide the future direction of the Catholic Church in our times. It will be history in the making. My advice to you is to try to be part of it. Perhaps your bishop will have need of someone with your skills in foreign languages, and may be persuaded to send you to Rome.

Yours ever,

Jean.

It was a signpost pointing out a way he might not have found himself. But what chance was there of following it? He would be a seminarian again, nothing more.

†

2

The Seminarian in Dublin

1

The Dublin Diocesan Seminary was located in Clonliffe College in Drumcondra, a few miles from the centre of Dublin. When Michael Cremin walked again through the grey gates, his suitcase in his hand, he realised for the first time how ugly the place was. The building was a grey-brown block of limestone with only an array of drainpipes and a squat, blunt cross on the roof for decoration. That stony symbol was supposed to mark Clonliffe as a place of holiness, but it looked like two banishing fingers on a scowling facade, telling the city and the country that there was something wrong with them.

Over there by the trees was the bicycle shed, where he had once smoked a cigarette with Frank Begley, one of the older seminarians. His first cigarette and his last. In a day or two, he would be wheeling out his bicycle again and heading off down the Drumcondra Road on his way to the university. He and Gerry Hegarty would be cycling together, trying to keep their clerical hats from being blown away by the wind. Out of earshot of the superiors, Gerry liked to shout things like "Janey Mary" in his North Dublin accent, hoping for a bit of a swear without actually committing a sin. Seeing Gerry again was one of the more pleasant prospects ahead of him.

Michael and Gerry Hegarty were a "pair," as the typical organisational unit was termed in Clonliffe. On their first day as seminarians, Michael had happened to arrive at the college at about the same time as Gerry, which meant that they were bundled together for almost everything. They sat together in class, in choir and at meals. They studied together, did chores together, and walked around the perimeter of the college together when ordered to take some exercise. Because C came before H in the alphabet, Michael was always the senior of the pair, and Gerry always the junior. Michael and Gerry had little enough in common, but doing everything together as a pair, as the rules required, meant that they had become friends, insofar as friendships were possible in the regimented, ascetic and self-observational world of their training.

What they shared, of course, was what was called a Vocation, a sense of being called by God to the priesthood. Gerry's vocation had been largely a matter of course. In Ireland at that time, it went without saying that one of the purposes of marrying and starting a family was to supply the Church with new priests. Gerry's parents and Gerry himself were content to walk this established path. Gerry saw his faith very much as he saw Dublin and Ireland. It was something he was naturally part of, where he was happy enough to do his bit, without worrying too much about the reasons why.

Michael Cremin's vocation, indeed his belief in God as a whole, was more complex. It had been the unlikely figure of Martin Luther, the German reformer, who had awakened in him the possibility of the priesthood. In his history classes at school, Michael had been intrigued by the picture of the young Luther lost in a thunderstorm, being forced to his knees in abject terror, and vowing to become a monk. There was a commanding logic in promising God that you would dedicate your life to Him in return for being saved, and Michael was drawn to Luther, as a result. The history teacher always portrayed Luther as a wrecker of the Church who was now burning in Hell, but Michael's sympathy for him kept growing. The Church of the 16th Century had been appallingly corrupt. For example, selling Indulgences so that the pope in Rome would have enough money to build Saint Peter's Basilica. It was fraud on the grand scale, and there was no denying that Luther had been right to oppose it. Even the Reformation catch-phrase, "justification by faith alone" had a lot to recommend it. The Catholic believer was caught in a mesh of obedience to external authorities. The Protestant had broken loose, and could stand alone before God; a man free to do whatever he believed God willed for him, justified by his own conscience, without anyone to forbid him. That, at least, was the Protestant theory, even if they fell way short of it in practice. Oddly enough, the Catholic Church affirmed the truth of Free Will far more clearly than the Protestants. But the Church was a highly-regulated community. Free Will did not seem all that free if the hierarchy of superiors forbade something in a particular case, as often happened.

Then, in October 1958, shortly after Michael's second year in the seminary had begun, a cardinal few had ever heard of, the obscure Angelo Roncalli, became pope under the name of John XXIII, and asked the Church to change. It was like the coming of spring after an unusually long and gloomy winter. There was a new lift to the air, and shyly, in many different places at once, hives of activity sprung up which grew richer and more colourful by the day.

There had already been a Pope John XXIII in the Church: the shady Neapolitan, Baldassare Cossa, who reigned at the time of the Great Western Schism. Tired of harassment by the rival claimants to the papacy, he convened the Council of Constance in 1414 in the hope of getting rid of them, only to be got rid of himself a few months later. In 1958, the new Pope John would have had his own scenarios in mind. But it was intriguing that he should choose the number XXIII, which was the same number as the antipope, Cossa. The new pope was creating a space for his pontificate that was both inside and outside the papal tradition. The more Michael thought about it, the more fascinated he was.

In fact, anything that any pope would have done would have fascinated Michael Cremin. The Church was the emotional centre of his life. When he was very young he had lost his mother, and the void caused by that loss had been filled by the Church. Priests and nuns were almost always kind to him, kinder than other people. And very often they were better educated and more charismatic than others. Sacred music thrilled him when he heard it. The public liturgies of the Church were always solemn, beautiful and comforting to him. Those sacred threads which held him together were themselves held together by that great and holy man, the Supreme Pontiff in Rome, the Vicar of Christ. When the Church taught Michael how to pray, he prayed regularly to his dead mother, who, he was told, was now an angel in Heaven and watching over him. In his child's imagination, his angelic mother was connected with another powerful being, whom he called the Lady of the Eyes, and who had much in common with the Holy Mother of God, the Blessed Virgin Mary. He tried to live as the Church taught him, and he found that it gave him what he longed for most: a well-lit and well-protected path through life and a mother who would never abandon him. He felt special to Mother Church, and becoming a priest would make him more special still.

Even so, without Pope John XXIII, Michael might never have persevered with his vocation. He was knowledgeable for his age, and there were too many discrepancies between what the authorities told him and what he knew to be true. He was moved as much by doubts and by moral outrage as he was by faith and trust. But Good Pope John had come over Michael like a light, laughing breeze, turning his suffering in the Church into joy. Here was a pope saying that things could change. For the better. Mistakes had been made in the past, serious mistakes, but there was no shame in admitting them and correcting them. The Church was to be brought up to date. Above all, Pope John XXIII smiled out at you from the photographs, as if he enjoyed being alive, a happy contrast to the aloof, stylised poses of his predecessor, Pope Pius. The boat of Peter the Fisherman was to be opened wide to the peaceful lapping of the waves on the many fertile seas, and to the inexhaustible warmth of God's shining sun.

As their studies progressed, it was clear that Michael Cremin and Gerry Hegarty would make very different kinds of priest. Everyone vaguely knew that Gerry would be useful for something some day, but he was a little too plain-minded for comfort. The details of the Berlin Air Lift of 1948, which was news again as Berlin became the flash point of the Cold War, were of greater interest to him than theology, in which he was out of his depth. Gerry had become famous in the seminary for using an adding machine to try to explain one of the miracles of Jesus: the one where He feeds a large crowd with just a few loaves and fish. The course teacher, Professor Oakeshotte, felt that Gerry's catering-size loaves and whale-size fish were disrespectful of the Gospel, and he demanded that Gerry retract, which he did immediately, and with good cheer. But Gerry had added an explanation. Feeding the Five Thousand, Gerry had argued, was actually a far better miracle than was commonly supposed. Instead of simply filling bellies, the Lord had taught people that the simple things in life were holy, and that there was enough of them to go round, if people were happy to take a bit less, and the distribution was planned in the right way. Sarcastically, Professor Oakeshotte offered Gerry the opportunity to prove his point: a weekend of research into baking and fishing practices in Galilee at the time of Christ to be followed by an extended essay on the matter. Gerry apologised, but it was not enough, and Professor Oakeshotte wrote a long letter of complaint to the authorities. By this time, however, Archbishop McQuaid had taken the unusual step of entrusting Gerry with duties in the central administration of the Archdiocese, under the watchful eye of the responsible Monsignor. So, instead of being expelled for insolence, Gerry gave another, even more abject, apology, which Professor Oakeshotte was prevailed upon to accept. From then on, Gerry avoided the academic side of the priesthood as much as he could.

For all their differences, Michael and Gerry liked and trusted each other, and they were glad to be a "pair" again after the year's separation. One afternoon, it was a dreary day in late October, Gerry saw Michael take a note from the pigeon hole assigned to him for his post. It was a note on blue paper, the kind of note one got from the Dean. One only received notes from the Dean when there were unpleasant matters to be discussed. Michael crumpled the note angrily and put it in his pocket. Gerry decided to go over and see what was happening.

"It's a practical problem, Gerry."

There was indeed a lot on Michael Cremin's mind. Returning to Clonliffe and re-entering the routines of his training had put his Louvain experiences in a new light. He saw no reason to deny his experiences; which would be dishonest, and therefore immoral. But those rich experiences had come to him while he was in a different country and in a different world. Now, when little flashes of them came back to him, he was puzzled and disturbed. While he still regarded his experiences as good ones, he could not expect the superiors to take this view. If they knew the full content of them, they would be more likely to regard him as incapacitated for the priesthood. Now that note from the Dean, Father Hogan. They must have found out about him in Louvain. They were planning to get rid of him. One night very soon, the seminarians would go to bed as usual, and when the new day dawned, Michael Cremin would not be there. He would have vanished without a trace, like a speck of dirt someone had discovered on one of the Archbishop's kitchen knives. Much as he disliked Clonliffe College, it was still a horrible thought.

"Some trouble follow you home from Louvain?" Gerry asked.

"Depends on how you see it. All I know is, I have to go to the Dean's office. Heaven knows what he's been told about me. You still working in the Administration? You must be able to get at the records. Any chance you could have a look at my file? Just to see if anyone has been spreading lies or malicious rumours?"

"Lies and rumours, eh? We'll have to put a stop to that."

Shortly before Michael had to meet the Dean, Gerry came back to him.

"You never told me your real name is Mick!"

Michael flushed red. "At school, some people used to call me that. I never answered them."

Laughing at Michael's embarrassment, Gerry told him what he had discovered. One of the Irish Franciscans in Louvain, Benignus "Billy" Breen OFM, whom Michael had never got to meet, had been keeping a quiet eye on him and had sent regular reports about him to the Clonliffe authorities. The reports termed him "the Candidate" or "the Candidate, M.C." or "the Rev. Mick Cremin." According to Father Breen's final report, "the Rev. Mick Cremin" was guilty of "intellectual singularity" and of a "dubious friendship" with the named Angelo Poggi. Luckily, that report also stated that "an intemperate and licentious tendency is not conspicuous in the Candidate." Michael's contacts with Angelo's netherworld seemed to have gone unobserved. It was not so bad, after all. There would be some explaining to do, but Michael could face the Dean without fearing the worst.

2

Augustine Hogan, the Dean of Clonliffe College, was somewhat out of place in the Dublin seminary. He had once been a Professor of Canon Law in Rome, and no-one knew what calamity had brought him down from those dizzy heights to land at Clonliffe, where there was little opportunity for scholarship. Gerry Hegarty, who had good sources of information, used to say that it was simply a matter of religious obedience: Archbishop McQuaid had made it known that he wanted him, and Gus Hogan had come. Unlike the Archbishop, Gus Hogan was a little uncertain when it came to wielding power, which meant that people did not take him too seriously. But there was a goodness about him which evoked affection and a certain respect.

The room which Father Hogan used as his Dean's office was small, cold and sparsely furnished. Pictures of Archbishop McQuaid and the new pope looked down from the wall on a small desk, some hard, wooden chairs and a dark linoleum floor. The first question he put to Michael Cremin was about Angelo Poggi.

"I knew this priest a little," Michael began hesitantly, unwilling to divulge anything, but more unwilling still to lie. "An unhappy man. He took his own life. I might have been able to help him. I just wasn't equipped for it. Is suicide the Sin against the Holy Spirit? The sin that can never be forgiven?"

Gus Hogan answered distantly. "We cannot know for certain. God is the judge, and God is surely merciful."

He glanced at the young man sitting on the edge of his chair, clasping and unclasping his hands. When he spoke, it was with a new firmness.

"May Father Poggi rest in peace. Let us draw the curtain of charity over his passing. As for the Sin against the Holy Spirit, Mister Cremin, isn't it more likely to originate in a place such as this?"

He handed Michael a sheet of paper which bore the crest of the Irish College at Louvain. The signature was Father Breen's. The date was recent. It described the villa beyond the Louvain railway station which he had visited with Angelo Poggi, and some of what went on there. The game was up.

"His Grace may wish to take a lenient view," said Gus Hogan. "We are advised that such places of ill repute – which will never darken the shores of Ireland, thank God – can easily be mistaken by the unwary for more innocent places, because they are licensed by the government. Nor is the true nature of such places immediately apparent to the unwary, because the sinful acts are confined to secret areas of the place. Had you been at the Irish College under our jurisdiction, rather than some Jesuit house, where anybody can walk in off the street, you would have had no connection at all with this place. His Grace may want to weigh these facts in the balance. But that is entirely a matter for His Grace. You won't be surprised to hear that we are deeply concerned about your Vocation. Now, as for yourself, you'd better make a clean breast of it. You'll write a letter explaining yourself to His Grace. You can sit at the desk here. There's pens and paper in plenty. You'll be doing without your dinner and your tea. And when I'm back at about nine this evening, I want you to be finished."

Michael Cremin stared after Father Hogan as the door slowly closed behind him. It was shocking. And for the first time ever, they were not going to tell him what to say. The light of hope darkened over and froze inside him. He was lost now in a grim world of finality, beyond all consolation.

Something helped him, something he had not earned and could never have expected, like a measure of water appearing miraculously on his tongue after days, if not years, in a desert. It was a memory. Shortly after his mother had died, when he was very sick, he had dreamt of a beautiful woman, a queenly personage, one who no longer wore a crown, and who was gracious and loving and who cared for him, but who was unreachable. She had the most extraordinary eyes, a bit like his mother's, but brighter than he remembered, and those eyes told him that She was not completely unreachable. If he tried hard enough, She would let Herself be reached. The doctors said that that was the moment when his will to live returned. To Michael, She was the Lady of the Eyes, and he was very sad when his father and stepmother did not take the dream seriously. Michael had as good as forgotten Her. Now, for no reason perceptible to him, as the words slowly formed under his pen, he thought of Her again:

Dear Holy Spirit.

He stopped, shaking his head over what he had written. He wasn't writing to the Holy Spirit, but he wished he was. Michael took a new sheet of paper, and began again with the proper formalities. He wrote and wrote, not caring about the formulations, plunging deeper and deeper with growing resolution into his memories of Louvain. And as the hours passed and the pages filled, he realised that almost without meaning to, he was writing to the Lady of the Eyes. That is to say, his heart, or part of his heart, was yearning towards this beautiful, loving and compassionate being and was compelling the rest of him to follow. A timid gratitude emerged, and he looked anew at those events in Louvain. He began to feel the poison that had been left in him, and as that poison began to fill his perception, but without clouding it completely, he saw himself steeped in those events as in a barrel of tar, thick, cloying and corrosive. It was clear to him how horribly unclean it was to take pleasure in the inflicting of pain, even if only as a bystander, or in the imagination. The last lines he wrote were a plea for Forgiveness. Forgiveness that such thoughts and desires could find nourishment in him, that he had become so ruined a person. Never would he inflict or receive harm, never would he be present at or encourage the celebration of pain again, ever.

When he had finished, it was almost night, and there were tears in his eyes. Although he wiped them away, they kept coming, and his eyes were still moist when Father Hogan returned. The Dean glanced at the pages Michael had written, and gave the young man a searching look.

"I won't be reading these," he said. "I can see there's no need to. Nor will anybody else be reading them. You can keep them."

"I don't want them," Michael croaked. "Can we burn them?"

Father Hogan handed Michael a box of matches and watched him set the papers alight. As they blackened to nothing in the unlit fire of the fireplace, Michael asked for the Sacrament of Penance.

Afterwards, Michael was at peace. He lay on his bed, his hands under his head looking up at the flaking plaster above him on the ceiling. Peace was a warmth that lapped at the walls of his self like a private sea. Peace was also a sense of fullness, such as he might have after a good meal. He had confessed. But he had not told Father Hogan that he had gone back to that villa a second time. He had not wanted to tell him. After all, he had gone back there to free himself. By facing down the horrors. This second visit was not part of the sin. But as he lay there, a thought arose, only to vanish almost as soon as he had perceived it; the thought that his remorse was insincere. He did indeed regret his complicity in what had been done in that villa, but he had confessed because he had been found out. So why this satisfaction? He was reconciled with the Church, but he had retained the prize of sin: he was more himself than before. And that was how it was meant to be, he thought.

3

Michael's studies began to move with greater ease. Friedrich Nietzsche and the Will to Power were banished to a far portion of his mind, like upstart clouds from a spotless horizon. He thought no more of Louvain, and the memories of Angelo Poggi and Jean Nordheider were so far away as to belong to some shadow person that he might once have been, but no longer was. He immersed himself with grateful zeal in the texts and tasks set by his teachers and he realised that he believed. He understood the principles of the Catholic Faith, and he assented to them and loved them.

In the summer, after their exams, the seminarians usually went to help out in a parish or in another of the many areas of pastoral work for which the Archdiocese would later need them as priests. Shortly before the term ended, Michael was the only one of his year still without a placement. Then, one afternoon, Augustine Hogan took Michael by the arm and led him outside to talk to him. It was a beautiful sunny day, and they strolled round the driveway by the main steps of the College.

"Young Michael." The Dean was in good humour. "We might not have your brains, but we're not all fools. And we're compassionate and lenient where we can be. His Grace, in particular, is very kind-hearted. We've been keeping a close eye on you, and we're starting to like what we see. Now. You know Dan Smith, who is training with us for the Diocese of Kerry? Well, poor Dan was all set to help out with an Irish Summer College down in Ballybunion. But he's ill with pneumonia or something. So we're sending you down to Kerry instead. You'll not be there for a rest, mind, so make sure you make yourself useful. The studying can go a bit too far. Makes a lad one-sided. A bit nervous. So you get stuck in down there washing the dishes and so on, and show us you're all right. And when you get back here after the three weeks in Kerry, we'll put you in one of the parishes."

With a parting nod, the Dean went back inside, and Michael went to pray in the college chapel. There was gratitude in his heart, and it glowed all the more strongly as he began to see the extent of the generosity that was being shown him. All this time, the superiors had been ready to expel him, but their hand had been stayed. The Lady of the Eyes had interceded for him with God.

4

Coláiste Íosa was a four winged, pebble-dashed building on the outskirts of the sleepy seaside town of Ballybunion. The college grounds were surrounded by farmland, and two of the adjoining fields doubled as football pitches and as grazing for some local cattle. The students of Irish boarded there, in rows of bunk-beds in underventilated dormitories. Every morning there were classes in the Irish language, and every afternoon there were sports events or visits to the beach. In the evenings there was a Céilí in the big assembly hall, where an accordionist would sound out the lively jigs and reels, and the students would happily give themselves over to the complex Gaelic set dances, which they picked up with ease.

Michael Cremin spent most of his mornings in the kitchens, which were run by a formidable woman known to everyone as Bean an Tí. Bean an Tí was something of a healer, and rather than call in the local doctor, she used to prepare her own poultices for bruised limbs and herbal drinks for fevers and digestive upsets. These were rare, as she supplied the sixty or so residents with three simple but wholesome meals every day, which managed to combine freshness and variety with an ingenious use of leftovers. Bean an Tí was unimpressed by Michael's clerical status and used to work him hard, watching over his performance without mercy. The toilets in the assembly hall were in particularly bad condition after the Céilís, and if his onslaught with mop and cloth was not good enough, he would be obliged to clean them a second time before retiring for the night. He'd be no use in the confessional, Bean an Tí remarked, if he wasn't able to clean out a toilet.

Michael attended the formal classes in Irish whenever he could. He often joined the students on the beach in the sunny afternoons, and although most of them were younger than him, he was drawn into the camaraderie that characterised their time together, and soon felt an integral part of it. This sense of belonging was new to him, but it had an innocence about it that put it beyond question. In the Jesuit House of Studies in Louvain, the residents had been in unspoken competition with each other, and there had been factional divisions along national and ecclesiastical lines. At Clonliffe, there was no feuding of this kind, but there was no escaping the feeling of being watched, as one of Archbishop McQuaid's paternalist traits was to encourage spying and reporting, so that trouble could be rooted out before it actually happened. Here in Ballybunion the young people simply accepted each other. Learning Irish was fun, and they were glad to be there.

Michael found joy in this temporary community. He was able to participate in the Céilís in the evenings, and it was no small thing for a seminarian to see the light in the eyes of a pretty girl and take her briefly in his arms, as the steps of the dance brought them together for a moment. What some might have condemned as an occasion of sin, was, in fact, remarkably innocent. The sexes did indeed come into close proximity with each other, but they did so while concentrated on a complex dance sequence, for which their joint contribution as part of the whole dancing community was essential. In this way, a boy felt himself a man and a girl felt herself a woman as part of something greater. There was no tearing of the fabric into the lonesome dyads or self-trumpeting monads typical of the more fashionable dance forms, and one felt in harmony with present, past and future.

5

It was within this horizon of innocence that Michael Cremin fell in love. He had never been in love before, and it took some time for it to dawn on him that what was happening to him had a name, and that the name was love. She was called Corinna Fielding. He had first noticed her at breakfast one morning, having been captivated by the particular way she had of holding her head to one side, as if she was listening to voices on the air that were speaking only to her. But he did not dare to approach her. Then, for some reason, at a Céilí shortly afterwards, she had crossed the length of the assembly hall to ask him to be her dance partner. He had responded in kind at the next dance, when it was the turn of the boys to choose. This continued at the Céilí the following evening, and after a few days, it was clear that this was how it would always be. He would be her choice, and she his. Corinna had curling, blonde hair that swept almost to her waist, laughing blue eyes and a way of speaking that somehow reached deep inside him. It was as if there was a hidden string behind his navel which only her voice could touch, and once touched, it would resonate forever.

Many of the men of Clonliffe, schooled in the prevailing techniques of pastoral ministry, would have tried to use this growing friendship for what their manuals deemed her good, keeping a look out on their walks for crucifixes and statues of the Virgin to steer her towards, ensuring a supply of rosary beads and prayer books, and seeking to turn the conversation towards the beauty of the vocation to motherhood or to the religious life.

But Michael did not think of behaving like a priest at all. Although it was by definition summer in July, he suddenly knew in his heart that it was summer when he walked with Corinna in the more secluded places around the college grounds, where they would never be alone, as such, but could nevertheless enjoy a certain privacy. Although he knew that God had created a world of beauty that was intrinsically good, and that its goodness remained, independent of the plunder of fallen Man, he had not known till that moment, when Corinna plucked some apple blossom for him, that goodness was also a gift, and signified in the aroma of apple blossom, could reach right to the centre of the heart.

Instead of occasions for prayer, Michael now looked for occasions of returning this sense of gift to Corinna. It might be the surprise of a hazel branch which he had hidden from her until the right moment. It might be simply waiting to walk the short way together with her from the classrooms to the dining hall. It wasn't so much the outward action that counted, although there were some things she liked, and some she did not like, and these he respected. What counted was his attention, which in a sense lifted her into herself, and the way she would light up from within when this happened, gave him more joy than anything he had ever seen. He dreamt of her almost every night in quiet and noble dreams, and they made the day a happy one before he even got up. Her presence was always with him, not insistent, but gentle, like the scent of summer flowers borne through an open window.

Corinna returned his feelings. She liked to be with him and she told him all kinds of things about herself. He knew nothing about women, and the strange feminine charm that overlay her stories made her life an enchanted book to him, only that the wonder of it was in very ordinary things. Corinna came from a place near Bray, County Wicklow, where her father was a doctor. She liked bright green and blue colours, which she usually combined in some way, a blue head band with a green blouse, or a green ribbon with a blue pullover. She liked to collect seashells, and used to pull Michael over to out-of-the-way parts of the beach in the search for new specimens. She also liked to talk about the tragic fate of Queen Marie Antoinette, whom she had learned about at school, and was exploring further through historical novels. They touched each other only at the Céilís, within the formal framework of the dance steps, and felt no compulsion towards those places out of sight of the teachers, where people were known to drink alcohol and to fumble with each other in daring ways.

The time of parting came upon them quickly. Corinna was eager to discuss how they could stay together, but Michael ignored her awkward attempts to broach the subject. There was simply nothing to be said on the matter. He was returning to the seminary; and whether he liked it or not, it was impossible for him to have a woman friend. It did not occur to him that Corinna might have needed to hear him say this to her, in words that showed her he cared for her. It did not occur to Michael that his silence might be a cruelty.

The courses were over, the bags were packed, and students and teachers were dispersing in all directions. Corinna must have expected that Michael would walk the half mile or so from the college to the railway station with her, as her special friend, but he did not. He kept far to the rear, leaving her with her girl-friends. He could see her as she walked ahead of him, glancing around from time to time, perhaps seeking him, as so often at breakfast during the weeks they had shared. On the train, he chose a carriage far from hers. He felt a need for the fact of parting to be crystal clear.

About half-way through the journey, Michael was approached by one of Corinna's friends. She told him that Corinna was ill from crying, and was calling for him. She needed him, could he come? Worried now, he followed the girl down the train. Sure enough, there Corinna was, sitting, or rather lying, with her head between her knees, her face wet, her golden hair hanging lifelessly, stuck together in thick, ugly strands. She had been using her hair to wipe away the tears. She looked up, and as so often before, their eyes met. Each held the eyes of the other for only an instant, but it was an instant that might have contained all of time. Michael saw everything: how she had trusted him only to be cast aside without even a farewell; how she had been humiliated by him, publicly crushed by his disdain. Michael realised that he felt nothing for her, nothing at all. Corinna's renewed crying followed him, as he turned away, but with a new tone to it, a tone that rang out for all to hear: the bell-tone of the triumph of Hell.

Something must have dawned on Michael Cremin, because later, he took another walk through the train to Corinna's compartment. He did not know what he would say or do, but anyway, Corinna was not there. Even her things were gone. There was no-one there at all. He'd probably catch up with her at the station in Dublin. He returned to his seat, and sat there awkwardly for the rest of the journey. But in Dublin, too, he could not find Corinna. She must have got off the train at one of the Kildare stations. Corinna was gone. It occurred to him then that all kinds of things were gone. Things he had no name for.

With tears of regret pricking at his eyelids, Michael headed for the bus that would bring him across the city to the seminary. When he arrived, it was beginning to rain, but he could not bring himself to go in through the gates. He retraced his steps a little and walked up and down the Drumcondra Road for a time, his feet kicking against the cracks in the asphalt footpath, almost as if he did not have the strength anymore to hold himself erect. A policeman who was passing by wheeling his bicycle offered to help. Feigning cheerfulness, Michael declined, and strode down Clonliffe Road and through the College gates. On the driveway, he came across some of his fellow seminarians who were gathered there for a surreptitious smoke, but he did not greet them.

"So that's what Kerry's done for Cremin," said one of them, loudly enough for him to hear. "Not only a snob, but bog ignorant now, as well."

There was no point in going back to them to take away the impression of brusqueness, because then they would see that he was crying.

6

At breakfast the following morning, Michael was unable to eat. He had slept badly, and he was overcome by a nervous horror of the large refectory. Even in the summer, when the place was almost empty, they were obliged to eat in silence. But this silence only created a loud and disgusting echo for the rude sounds of chomping and swallowing and of greedy mouths slurping at tea-cups. His throat was so dry he felt it was cracking, and whenever he swallowed anything, he immediately felt sick. Luckily there was a message for him, and he was able to make a quick escape from the unpleasant food and the leering companions. The note was from the Dean, Father Hogan. He wanted to see him at once.

They walked together in the grounds for some minutes and Gus Hogan asked some polite questions about Michael's time at the Summer College. Then he changed the subject.

"I'll be heading off to Rome, soon. Back to the University of the Lateran. I wouldn't mind staying here, really. But they want me over there. It's an exciting time to go to Rome, of course. I suppose you've heard about the Ecumenical Council the Holy Father is setting up?"

"I have, Father. A great thing for the Church."

"A great thing, to be sure. His Grace, poor man, is run off his feet getting ready for it. He has great ideas, of course, as you'd expect from His Grace. The Council will be the perfect opportunity to consecrate all the world to the Immaculate Heart of Mary, as Our Lady asked for at Fatima. His Grace wants Our Lady to be declared the Co-Redemptrix. I hope it all works out for us."

"And why wouldn't it work out?" Michael asked, surprised.

Gus Hogan thought for a while before answering. "Best to let sleeping dogs lie, in my view. There are far too many people at a Council. Hard to keep a rein on them. And they're very tainted with Protestantism on the Continent. They don't uphold the priestly discipline like we do. Worker priests wearing overalls and saying Mass in factories. Priests shouting for the freedom to do what they like. The signs are not good, if you ask me."

Michael decided that it was time to bring matters to a head. "Father Hogan, I am in love."

"Ah. I see. You're in love. And would this be accompanied by any matters pertaining to the sixth commandment?"

"I want to leave the College and marry the woman I love."

"And has she said she'll have you?"

"No."

"There you are, now. A good girl, obviously. The Will of God is clear. And holy purity?"

"The thoughts are clean, Father."

"Sound. Now to your placement." With a smile, the Dean told Michael that he had been assigned to the Pro-Cathedral, one of the better placements available.

"Unless, of course, you'd rather go and get married, instead."

"No, no," said Michael, his head spinning. He had always wanted to go to the Pro-Cathedral for a pastoral placement. And Gerry Hegarty would be there, as well.

7

Dublin's Pro-Cathedral was an unprepossessing building hidden away behind O'Connell Street, the main thoroughfare of the city. It was the Archbishop's Episcopal seat and it also served a small parish which included some of the poorest of Dublin's poor. But in all that Michael did, from rostering the altar boys, to listening to the stream of the needy who came looking for help, to the evening Rosary and Benediction, he was surrounded by the memory of Corinna Fielding, and it often felt as if there was a touch of apple blossom to the mix of old, wet clothes, floor varnish and incense that was the cathedral's natural odour.

One afternoon, over a cup of tea with Gerry Hegarty in a local tea-shop, Michael reached into his shirt pocket, pulled out a crumpled envelope, and handed it to Gerry. It was addressed to the Most Reverend John Charles McQuaid MA, H.Dip, DD, Archbishop of Dublin, Primate of Ireland, at Archbishop's House, Drumcondra.

"What's all this?"

"It's my resignation. I'm getting married. To her."

"To her? After knowing her only three weeks?"

"Yes."

"So this is it."

"Yes."

"And your vocation?"

"It's a load of rubbish."

"And is that what you said in here?"

"More or less."

"I hope it's in Latin."

"Will you give it to him?"

"To His Grace?"

"Yes."

"I suppose I could put it in the post for him."

"I mean give it to him personally."

"Personally. And will you be wanting a reply?"

"No."

"Give it to him yourself."

"I'm not going back."

Gerry looked Michael in the eye. Then he puckered his lips into a grimace, and pocketed the envelope.

"Right so. I'll do this last favour for you. I'll see that His Grace gets it when he's back from wherever he is."

"Thanks. I'll be off so. There's a train to Bray in about half an hour."

Gerry looked at his friend through half-closed eyes. The feverish colour of the face. The fingers clutched tightly around the coffee-cup. Michael had been like this on more than one occasion since returning from Louvain.

"I'll let you know, so," said Gerry.

8

When things were slack at the Pro-Cathedral, Michael had studied telephone books, train and bus timetables and local maps. From the railway station at Bray, a bus would take him a short way out towards Greystones. Across the road from the bus stop there would be a small mountain with a radio mast on the summit. Two hills lay to the right, and the road between them would lead into the small valley which sheltered the village of Carraig Bán, where Corinna lived.

Michael arrived at Doctor Fielding's Surgery in the early evening. This was a small flat-roofed annexe which adjoined a modest two-storied house. Surgery hours were coming to an end, and a tired-looking nurse sized him up with little, glinting eyes before admitting him to the waiting-room. There was a reek of stale cigarette smoke in her wake. Michael had changed out of his clerical garb in the train, and was trying to look smart in blazer and tie. Hard, wooden chairs lined the walls, which were hung with posters proclaiming slogans to do with healthy living. There was a small table in the centre of the room, piled with old issues of *Reader's Digest* and *National Geographic.* At the back, there was an antique chest of drawers, with a small mirror built into the dark wood upright. He stood there nervously for a moment, readjusting the clumsy knot in his tie and straightening his hair.

Doctor Fielding was not what he had expected a country doctor to be. He was tall, thin and quiet of manner, and his clear, blue eyes, so much like Corinna's, were shy and retiring, but with a forced extroversion. Michael had prepared what he wanted to say, but he was tongue-tied without his notes. After fumbling for them in his pocket, he dropped the page. Doctor Fielding picked it up and glanced at it, raising his eyebrows as he caught its message. Michael turned red with embarrassment.

"Young man," the doctor said, "my daughter will speak to you herself."

Michael never forgot the sight of Corinna framed in that doorway. There was a sudden rise in the evening sun, which surged through the window and singled her out. And the sun lifting her towards him with light seemed to bring God's seal of approval to his beating heart and his longing.

"Corinna, love," he croaked, "Will you marry me?"

She did not look him in the eye.

"After the way you treated me?"

"I'm so very sorry."

She nodded solemnly. All expression had left her face.

"Michael, I'm engaged to someone else."

Slowly, Michael became aware of a presence of pure anguish inside his body, an anguish her words had created and which he was powerless against. She had infused him with ice. She was swinging a hammer at his frozen belly, and his belly was breaking open. There was a slow trickle of his innards towards oblivion.

Years later, after intermittent periods of brooding detective work, Michael was able to piece together what had happened. Corinna, although barely past the age of consent, had betrothed herself to a very wealthy man. She had sacrificed herself partly for her father, whose debts her suitor had contracted to pay, but also for a place at medical school, which he had also promised to finance. In a few short weeks, Corinna had changed. The gentle innocent, the romantic admirer of Marie Antoinette he had come to love in Ballybunion had ceased to exist. In later years, she had a career in medical research. Michael would read of her achievements in the newspapers, and shake his head over her seeming disregard for ethics. She was not what he believed she could or should have been, and he sometimes wondered what part he might have played in making her that way.

9

Michael Cremin did not return to the Cathedral Parish, but travelled from Bray directly to his family home in Foxrock in the South of Dublin. His father was appalled to see him in civilian attire, and to find him so depressed. His stepmother's main worry was that he had somehow disgraced the family. Michael's father guessed that a girl might be at the root of it all. An adroit telephone call to the diocesan authorities procured a leave-of-absence for Michael, and he prevailed upon his son to rest at home for a while. However, perhaps because his nerves were still raw after Corinna, Michael could not spend any length of time in the same place as his stepmother. Her unwillingness to listen to him, her direct way with words, and her constant finding fault with everything were too much for him. After a week or so, Michael forced himself to be strong enough to return to his pastoral placement, which still had a few days left to run.

The first person he met was Gerry Hegarty, who was sitting on the steps of the Pro-Cathedral, enjoying the midday sun.

"So it's yourself," Gerry began.

Michael swallowed to ease his dry throat. "Did you give His Grace the letter?"

Gerry looked at him with an amused half-smile. "Actually, it got lost. I'd say His Grace was very disappointed."

"It got lost? Thank heaven for that."

Gerry stood up and walked with Michael into the shadowed cathedral. "So are you getting married then?" he whispered, after genuflecting.

"No."

Wisely, Gerry did not inquire any further. However, when things became difficult in the months that followed, Michael knew from many small gestures of kindness that Gerry understood how wounded he was. He could not speak of it. How could this multiple betrayal ever be explained? Corinna had offered him her love, and he had accepted it. Then when the time came to return to his studies for the priesthood, he betrayed Corinna. Then, he abandoned the priesthood to try to win Corinna back. And when she refused him, he went back to the priesthood, as if nothing had happened.

But there was worse. It was indeed largely out of guilt that he had wanted to go back and marry Corinna, guilt because he had wounded her, and was terrified of the meaning of that wounding. How could that wounding have come so naturally to him? How could he wreak such havoc on the life of another person without even thinking? He was a Judas, always prepared to abandon what God had given him for whatever seemed better. And he remembered clearly the sado-masochistic events in Louvain. He knew of the dark and cruel power residing in them. He had gone there a second time, to demonstrate that he was able for that power, that it had no hold over him. And he had broken with that power, forever. Or had he not? Was there no release? No, he thought, not ever. There was only endurance. And the Will to assent to that endurance. There was surely a radiance that would break through the horror and light everything up. But that radiance was nowhere to be seen.

10

Late in September, shortly after the new term at Clonliffe College began, one of the senior diocesan secretaries stopped Michael Cremin while he was on his way to class. It was a summons to the presence of Archbishop McQuaid. Michael was conducted across the College grounds to the red-bricked mansion that housed the Archbishop's offices. There he was placed on a lone chair in a draughty corridor outside the private office and was told to say the Rosary while he waited to be called. Michael knew it could be a long wait, and he was in full view of people through the open windows. At least they were not making fun of him, he thought, as he fingered his beads.

He mumbled his well-practiced way through the Joyful, the Sorrowful and the Glorious Mysteries, but Corinna was far more urgent to him than the prayers. She had written to him care of his parents a few days before, saying terrible things: "You don't love me, you just love the idea of yourself loving me, because you feel guilty for hurting me." And: "You don't love God. You just love yourself. There's nobody greater than God, so if you spend your life serving God, you'll be greater than anybody else. That's why you want to be a priest." Her words had hurt him so much that he wanted to leave the seminary, just in case they might be true. He was so unworthy. It would be a relief to be expelled.

The Archbishop's study was a shrouded place. Dr. McQuaid, to Michael's dismay, was standing to receive him. His was a concentrated and formidable presence, charging the air around him with force. It was an Episcopal presence, as the Catholic Church then conceived it, both priest and judge, redolent of hard work in abstract worlds and of great renunciation. Nervously, Michael dropped to his knee and kissed the large, dull amethyst which glowed from the Archbishop's left hand. Apart from this so-called Borgia ring and the pectoral cross around his neck, the Archbishop was dressed in a simple black cassock like any of his priests. The purple skull cap he usually wore over his tonsure lay on top of a pile of papers on the desk behind him. As Michael took the chair he was offered, a hard, creaking one that dug into his back, the ambience suggested a courtroom to him, one where the usual human bustle was reduced to two simple qualities, absolute right and absolute wrong. Michael looked up at the Archbishop to try to see a little more of him. The eyes he saw were lively, though tired; and not unkind.

"Tell me," began Dr. McQuaid. They were separated by a small table of carved ebony. "In your lectures at Louvain, did you meet with the name of Chomsky?"

There was a book by this person on the desk behind him. The spine was towards them, and Michael could read the title. *Syntactic Structures*, it was called.

"I am sorry, Your Grace. I have never heard of him."

"In time you will. In your view, Mister, is it possible to conceive of the nature of language without reference to God?"

"It is surely undesirable to try, Your Grace."

The Archbishop looked above him and beyond him.

"If what men call meaning is not founded on the loving adoration of Jesus Christ, the Second Person of the Blessed Trinity, it is founded on the worship of the Fallen Archangel. Is it not so?"

"Yes, Your Grace."

"Is this the girl?"

Wondering, Michael took the photograph which the Archbishop had picked up from a small file in front of him. It was a good likeness of Corinna Fielding. He did not even have a photograph of her himself.

"A good Catholic girl from a good family."

"Yes, Your Grace."

"It is implicit in this man Chomsky's work on language acquisition that a mother could spend her time reading blasphemous literature to her children and they would learn their native language just as well. Tell me, what did you speak of to Miss Fielding, and she to you?"

"We spoke about things that interested us, Your Grace. French history. The sea."

"I, too, take pleasure in good conversation. And I cannot imagine good Catholic parents doing anything other than speaking to their children in a way that is appropriate to them and which communicates their love to them."

"Yes, Your Grace."

"You have excellent results in Latin. Considerable prowess."

"Your Grace is more than kind."

"Have you tackled Seneca?"

"A little, Your Grace."

"Seneca, as you know, was a disciple of Wisdom. Then he became the teacher of young Nero, as close a version of Antichrist as has yet darkened the earth. Do you know the outcome?"

"Nero was responsible for the persecution of the Church, Your Grace. There was terrible bloodshed."

"Indeed. Seneca, for all his fine ethics, was powerless against this enemy of Wisdom lying at his bosom. And the lesson, Mister? Is it that God's Will charges Wisdom to be the teacher of Antichrist, come what may?"

"I expect so, Your Grace."

"No, Mister, that is not the lesson. We are in this world, but we are not of it. Our Lord Jesus Christ charged us with the preaching of the Gospel in this world, which has been usurped by Antichrist. But we do not accomplish this task by adjusting the tenor of our speech to the babble of Evil. As we offer to evil men the means to repent, we do not become like them. We preach the denial of self. And the help and sustenance of the Sacraments."

Michael began to relax. The Archbishop seemed to want to enjoy some pious conversation, nothing more.

"The establishment you visited in Louvain," he paused in mid-sentence and watched Michael quail before him. Then he continued sombrely, enunciating every syllable with the effort of clarity, "in that unspeakable place, your soul was in mortal danger. There can be no purpose or intention good enough to protect a priest from being destroyed, if he willingly enter such a place, unless it be the administering of the Sacraments under Apostolic authority. All the more so for a mere seminarian, who under normal circumstances would not even be allowed outside the precincts of the College. The fact that you were there to help a brother priest in his difficulties is no excuse whatever. Under normal circumstances, you would now be expelled from here in complete ignominy, with your character tainted for the rest of your life. I have written to the Jesuit General, and to Archbishop Suenens of Mechelen-Brussels. I have expressed my complete incredulity at the lax governance of the House you had the misfortune to stay in, which is a disgrace to the religious life. I have conveyed to the Father-General and to the Belgian Primate Our most grave concern at what was allowed to occur under their very eyes. The response has been appropriate."

"Your Grace, I am deeply sorry."

"It is likely, Mister, that in the decades to come, structuralist ideas like Mr. Chomsky's will be in vogue, even in theology. It is likely that we will begin to lose sight of the Fall of Man, and what it means for us. Then it will become increasingly difficult to conceive of the difference between Good and Evil. It may even seem acceptable for a priest of Our Lord to go where you went. May it never come to pass."

"Never, Your Grace."

"As I say, Mister, my hand was stayed. The Father Visitor whom Father-General Janssens dispatched to Louvain to thoroughly investigate that sorry affair assures us that no blame attaches to you. The Father Visitor has gone even further on your behalf. The responsible Congregation in Rome, independently of any request of mine, has urged strongly that you continue to receive priestly formation. I may say that I had first intended not to admit you to Ordination. But I have since weighed many things in the balance, including my own failing in the matter. Had my paternal vigilance been what it should always be, Mr. Cremin, you would have been as safe as a lamb at pasture."

"I'm sorry, Your Grace."

"Let it be a lesson to you. His Lordship of Kerry has informed me that there was not the slightest shade of impropriety in your dealings with Miss Fielding. I am satisfied that you still have the potential to respond to your vocation. The matter is now ended."

Michael licked his dry lips. "Thank you, Your Grace," he stammered

The Archbishop rose to his feet and extended his hand. Michael kissed the Episcopal ring and withdrew. When he tried to open the door, his palm and fingers were clammy with sweat and the doorknob kept slipping in his hand. When he finally got out, he went to his room, and spent the rest of the day there, unable for anything. The Archbishop's words had impaled him like knives, but he had been spared the worst.

11

Sacerdos in aeternum. A priest for ever. That is what Michael Cremin would be, in this life and the next. An indelible mark would be placed on his soul by the Holy Spirit, and his whole being would be radically changed. No matter what sin he might stain himself with, no matter what act of betrayal he might commit, he would retain that indelible mark for ever. It was a comforting and uplifting thought.

The most awesome of the privileges of a priest was the power to effect the transubstantiation of Bread and Wine into the Body and Blood of Jesus Christ. This great Eucharistic event of God's self-giving was embedded in the Rite of the Mass, and it was efficacious *ex opere operato*. It was a great comfort to Michael to learn the meaning of this. The Rite of the Mass was valid independently of the quality of the local setting and of the moral character of the celebrant and congregation. No matter how dismally Michael might fail to live up to the ideal of the priesthood, no matter how deeply he might fall, God's Grace would still be made available to the faithful through his celebration of the Rite. The Mass was an inexhaustible fountain of love and mercy, and he, as a priest, was called to work that fountain for evermore. Sin would never prevail against him, just as the gates of Hell would never prevail against the Roman Catholic Church.

Much of the work of the Ordination Year was dedicated to understanding the Rite of the Mass and learning how to perform it perfectly. It had to be performed perfectly, as anything less than that put the celebrant at the risk of Mortal Sin. The Missal in general use was that promulgated by Pope Pius X in 1910, in the edition made typical by Pope Benedict XV in 1920. There had been some adjustments under Pius XII, and a new edition was now due, which Pope John XXIII was busy with in Rome. Although the priest had everything he needed in one book, the Mass was anything but easy to celebrate. The Rite consisted of two interwoven structures, the Common, which was invariable, and the Proper, which varied according to the day. To work out the Mass of the Day meant applying a complicated set of rules. There was a Mass provided for every day in the year, according to the seasons of the Church. But the year as a whole was overlaid with variations for the feast-days of saints or of special ecclesiastical events. Almost every day in the year was a special feast of some kind; often there was a coincidence of feasts on one day. The rules then diverged for places like monasteries, where there were a number of priests available to say the different Masses, and for lone priests. In the latter case, only one of the coinciding Masses could be said, and prayers from the other Masses were to be added at appropriate points. The Mass to be chosen depended on the degree of dignity which prevailed among the feasts. There were eight degrees of dignity. The feast of the greatest dignity was the one to be kept, and the others were transferred to the next free day. Certain days of significance were privileged, and could not be displaced by a higher feast, for example, the days leading up to Easter. There was also some scope for local customs and for special requirements.

The list of rubrics at the beginning of the Missal told the priest quite clearly what Mass to say, but there was always a lot of detail to manage. Even if the priest had the Proper in place, all it meant was that he had the different coloured bookmarks at the right places in the Missal. He was only beginning to get ready for the Mass itself. He still had to attire himself correctly in the cumbersome vestments with their unwieldy buttons, ribbons, sashes and tassels. If it was a High Mass, he still had to see to it that Deacon, Subdeacon, Master of Ceremonies, Thurifer and the acolytes all turned up and got themselves attired in time. Once the solemn procession began, and they at last entered the Church, he had to remember which side of the Altar was North and which South, because the Gospel had to be read from the North and the Lessons from the South.

Three tones of voice were stipulated for the celebrant at different points: audible, secret, and audible only to those at the altar. The Bread and Wine had to be held in a specified way in specified fingers of the hand, and there was no small risk of letting them fall. There were twelve different Signs of the Cross required of the priest during the Canon of the Mass alone; each of them had to be made perfectly. He dared not neglect even one of them. There was so much that could go wrong so easily.

If the externals were so fraught with significance, what about the prayers themselves and the momentous events they were intended to commemorate and re-enact? There were no words to describe them. The priest approached the Canon by silently venerating an image of the Crucifixion, then lifting up his hands, joining them, lifting up his eyes, and then bowing deeply before the altar, he rested his joined hands on it, and began. The stipulated inaudibility of the Canon was believed to reflect the inaudibility of the Lord's lonely prayer in the Garden of Gethsemane and His silence during His Passion. It was an image of Holiness and Sacrifice, inaudible to worldly ears. The first words of the Canon were the mysterious *Te igitur, "Therefore to You, most merciful Father."* That wherefore the priest was on his knees at the altar in solemn rite, moving towards the Consecration, was not stated; it belonged to a different dimension of reality, one beyond the reach of human language. Most esoteric of all was the phrase *:mysterium fidei:* the mystery of faith. Flouting the rules of punctuation, it hung suspended on two colons in the middle of the consecration of the Wine without an explicit connection to what went before or after. The black dots of the colons might have been hinges, and the phrase itself might have been a window which the right touch could push open. If so, it was a window to another world. Thus it was with the Roman Canon in its textual entirety. It was a logician's nightmare, unless the logician was also a believer, and could find holiness in the strange grammatical relations which pertained. Perhaps the greatest ritual treasure of the Church, the Canon had been handed down without change since the time of Pope Gregory the Great in the Seventh Century. For this reason, the priests Michael was working with could have changed places quite easily with a priest of a thousand years earlier. They could also have changed places geographically, even with priests from the most faraway places, because the liturgy was in Latin, and independent of language variations. The Mass was thus a permanent, ongoing miracle, linking the faithful across the barriers of time and space with the Sacrifice of Jesus, in the permanent centre of the Real Presence.

12

For the Christmas festivities of 1961, Michael and Gerry Hegarty had been sent to an outlying parish, Saint Bartholomew's in Cabra, to help out with the different ceremonies. Together with a few others, they were able to stay overnight in the big parochial house, where they had free access to newspapers and the radio. Pope John's Council, which was now officially known as the Second Ecumenical Council of the Vatican, or the Second Vatican Council, for short, was to be convoked that Christmas Day of 1961, to begin in the autumn of 1962. The formal convocation was widely reported, and Michael and the others were following the discussions on the radio.

"Isn't it a funny one," Gerry Hegarty remarked to the little group, which was gathered round a cheerful fire and a huge pot of tea. A large valve-powered radio set dominated the room from a place of honour on the dark wooden sideboard, where it was crackling with uncertain life. "The pope's announcing a new Pentecost at Christmas instead of Easter, like a big, fat turkey, or something from Santa Claus."

"One more incisive statement from the Hegarty brain, I hear," remarked Frank Begley, a late vocation who knew how to drive a car, and felt slightly superior as a result. "You'd have to record anything Gerry says and play it backwards to get any sense out of him."

"I'm serious, now. It is a very odd thing."

"Look Gerry," called another. "If he announced it at Easter there wouldn't be time enough to get ready."

"It's not starting till October," Gerry answered. "There'd be plenty of time."

"Gerry, listen. The pope likes Christmas. It's a happy time. And it's going to be a happy Council. That's the symbolism of it."

"Why isn't Easter a happy time? The time of the Resurrection?"

"No-one gives you presents at Easter. All you get is a bit of chocolate, if you're lucky. Easter is too complicated for the average atheist. This is the pope's Christmas present to the world."

Gerry stood up to make himself heard. "But there would have been no Pentecost without the Death of Our Lord and the Descent into Hell and the Resurrection. There's no Pentecost from stuffing your face at Christmas. Where's the Cross, now, in all this guff about a new start?"

"What about ICBMs and the Arms Race, Gerry? Is thermonuclear war not a big enough cross for you?"

Gerry folded his arms resolutely. "The Lord came to save us not from wars but from sin!"

Frank Begley got up from his chair and rested his arms on his ample belly. Because of the festive season, he was sporting a red check waistcoat over his clerical black. "When Gerry's ordained, lads, we'll give him an extra Roman collar for his mouth. Listen. There's one of them strange animals known as Modernists here among us. The species is distinguished, lads, by never letting you see what it really is. There it is, the Great Irish Modernist, Michaelus Creminus, the scourge of Louvain. Let's hear what it thinks. Gentlemen, I give you the right answer!"

Frank pulled his ample self to attention and waggled his fingers over his puckered lips, miming a herald's trumpet. Michael laughed and shook his head.

"Hey, lads Cremin's laughing," someone mocked. "Maybe Modernism's given him a sense of humour!"

Michael ignored them. "This Council is a good thing. You heard what Pope John said. The world is changing. It needs the Faith now more than ever. The Council will work out how to present the Faith to the world. In terms the world can accept. It's going to be a pastoral council. The Church is going to pull down the walls and learn how to communicate to everyone in the world. Learn to understand. People agreeing to be together and work together for the good of all without hard and fast positions that they stick to like enemies at war."

"That's Ecumenism."

"Ecumenism is part of the Council. You heard the pope's words. We're moving towards the Church Universal. The brotherhood of man. The Catholic Church!"

"You are all wrong," Gerry Hegarty insisted. "The Church is a fat, lovely turkey, who'd better watch out, because now it's Christmas."

13

Finally, the great feast of ordination drew near. The academic part of their training had been completed at University College Dublin or at the Pontifical University at Maynooth. The practical part had been completed at Clonliffe, comprising lectures, tutorials, and practice sessions at makeshift altars. Initial soundings had been taken regarding their first postings as priests. One or two wanted to go on the Missions. Many listed their home parishes as the destination of choice. A few wanted to continue their studies in Rome, Michael Cremin among them. The spiritual preparation came last. It was a formal retreat, designed to remove the seminarians from their everyday lives and place them in a structured round of penitence, fasting, prayer, and meditation. Each candidate was to seek the consolation of the Holy Spirit and to test his own readiness to serve as a priest.

When the great moment came, Michael was well-prepared. On the altar of the Pro-Cathedral in Dublin, to the ageless sound of the *Salve Regina,* he lay prostrate before the High Priest, Jesus Christ, and in His Name, Archbishop McQuaid laid hands on him, invoking the Holy Spirit, and made that change to his substance by which he became a priest for ever. Michael's heart swung high with the music and the marble columns not far from him were the gateposts of a fertile plain of holy sound which was closed to disorder forever.

The first Mass of Father Michael Cremin was scheduled for three days later, in his home parish of Foxrock. Family and friends from far afield gathered at the Church together with a large contingent of the curious, who remembered the shy, young man from the neighbourhood, and were wondering if he would manage to get the Mass right rather than making a show of himself. But nothing had been left to chance. He had three days to go through everything again and again, and the Deacon with him was an old hand at helping out with first Masses.

For the first time, Michael elevated the Host, murmuring the sacred formula of consecration: *hoc est enim corpus meum quod pro vobis tradetur: this is My Body which is given for you.* God Himself now lay fragile between his thumbs and forefingers, and they began to shake. With tremendous concentration he forced himself to continue. Only after Communion had been given out and he was standing to read the Last Gospel did he relax a little. Then the strain hit him again. His hands shook and his fingers sweated so badly that they slid off the pages of the Missal. But it did not matter. The hosts were safe. And the Gospel passage was the beautiful Prologue to the Gospel of Saint John, which he knew off by heart.

Afterwards, at the small celebration his parents had organised, everyone congratulated him on how well the Mass had gone. But the memory of that flimsy wafer of bread, changing substance in his hands, remained with him. God had made Himself vulnerable, defenceless, and those poor fingers of his, weak and slippery, were not good protection.

14

Foxrock was a busy parish, and the newly-ordained Father Cremin was a welcome arrival. He was full of enthusiasm for the priesthood, and though officially on holiday, he was easily prevailed on to say Mass and to hear confessions, setting one or other of the regular priests free for other duties.

Michael would not have believed that his old neighbours would seek him out for Confession, but they did, and in dispensing this Sacrament to them, Michael experienced the impersonal beauty of the priesthood. He was a consecrated vehicle for Grace. His personality could meld with the presence of God as the human failings of those he knew were spread out before him, but did not concern him, except as a priest. It happened one Saturday that his father came to his confessional. Patrick Cremin came anonymously, of course, but Michael recognised him immediately. He was a good man, Michael believed, but there were things burdening his soul, things beyond Michael's ken for the most part, dating back to his son's childhood, and even before. But all his father could do was hint vaguely at these things, only to return immediately to the classic laundry list of sins which he had learned to be content with, like many of his generation. Giving Absolution seemed a little poignant to Michael, but he suppressed his unwanted feelings, and with a special prayer, he commended his poor father to God.

Perhaps the greatest joy Michael now had was his freedom from the rules of the seminary. He went on long walks and on bus trips with no object but to test the feeling of having freedom of movement. He was under-informed about what was happening in the world, and he devoured the books, newspapers and radio broadcasts that had been denied him in Clonliffe. One of the major issues of the time was, of course, the coming Second Vatican Council. The journalists had recognized it to be an epoch-making event, a great watershed in the history of mankind. At least, they seemed determined to present it as such, in their own way, and were vigorously asserting their independent voices against the censorship of the Vatican.

To his surprise, Michael learned that when Pope John had first broached the idea of an Ecumenical Council with his senior cardinals in January 1959, they had turned their backs and walked away to show their disapproval. Even now, with the Council almost ready to begin, the Curia, the executive which governed the Church in the pope's name, was obstructing everything. As a priest himself, bound to obedience to ecclesiastical superiors, Michael could not understand how the pope could meet with so much opposition. Particularly on a matter of such great solemnity as a Council.

Michael's former Dean, Augustine Hogan, was back in Dublin for a short visit, and with a few of the other new priests, Michael travelled to Clonliffe to see him. Gus, who was enjoying his new life as a Professor at the University of the Lateran, was happy to talk about the preparations for the Council, which he was witnessing at first hand.

"That's the Obedience problem for you, Michael. The pope has suspended the usual rules, but he hasn't made any new ones. So no one can figure out what to do."

The pope's key concept was *Aggiornamento*, but nobody quite understood what he meant by it. It seemed to refer vaguely to making the Church more receptive to advances in secular knowledge and to the realities of modern life. Opening the windows to let in the fresh air, as he once told an admiring crowd.

"It's a concept with no foundation at all," Gerry Hegarty called out. "The pope's just making it up as he goes along. All he wants to do is play the Good Shepherd on the newsreels."

There was loud laughter around the table. Ordination was not inspiring anyone to take Father Gerry Hegarty more seriously than before.

Gus Hogan then told them what the Council would be all about. Contrary to tradition, the pope had refrained from determining the subject matter himself. Instead, a questionnaire had been sent to all the bishops in charge of a diocese and to selected ecclesiastical institutes and faculties of theology with the aim of eliciting those themes which the Church as a whole felt to be particularly significant. Despite this inductive, almost democratic process, most un-Roman in style, the majority of the Vota, as the replies were termed, were very conservative. The issues which were pressing on the Church in their day were the issues that had always pressed on the Church: the clarification and condemnation of the errors of the World, a tidying-up of liturgical rites and canonical procedure, and a further exaltation of the Blessed Virgin Mary. Gus was certain that the Council would not bring anything new.

Gus Hogan had brought a priest with him from Rome, a Father O'Casey, who worked as an assistant librarian at the Vatican. Liam the Librarian, as he was generally known, dropped dark hints of a different story.

"You can't go by those Vota," he whispered over a quick cigarette out in the grounds. "Those Vota are only there to keep people quiet while the real work gets done."

Liam told them of the Vota that were conspicuous by their absence. For example, that of Eugène Cardinal Tisserant, the Dean of the College of Cardinals, no less.

"There's a story for you," Liam whispered, glancing around him to make sure that Gus was out of earshot. "But you'll never hear it told. It was Tisserant who ran the conclave which elected Roncalli. And Tisserant was rushing around the Sistine Chapel excommunicating people for breaking the oath of secrecy!"

Michael was intrigued. "Who did he excommunicate?"

"Tardini, for one. But it got lifted afterwards."

Tardini was now dead. Pope John had elevated him to cardinal and made him his Secretary of State. At the time of the conclave, he had been running the Secretariat of State as an Archbishop.

One rising star they often read about was Augustine Cardinal Bea, a biblical scholar, who had been a confessor to Pope Pius XII. Pope John had decided that the time was ripe for Ecumenism and he had set up a top-level Secretariat for the Promotion of Christian Unity under Cardinal Bea. Bea was a German Jesuit, a fact which seemed to invite no end of snide comment.

Germany had, in fact, despatched some particularly influential theologians to Rome, and these were being turned into household names by a Press eager for charisma. Karl Rahner and Hans Küng, together with their French compatriots, Yves Congar and Jean Daniélou, rolled with others through the newsprint like a pantheon of heroes. They were gifted and determined men, and they stood for a paradigm shift in theology. In Ireland, nobody seemed to take these New Theologians very seriously. They were not careful scholars, Michael heard during a complacent lecture Gus Hogan gave at Maynooth University. They had turned away from the sound method of Saint Thomas Aquinas in favour of dubious hermeneutic and critical approaches without foundation in Scripture or Tradition. Moreover, they were animated by a reprehensible sense of historical grievance. For them, Catholic theology had been denied a fruitful dialogue with the American Revolution of 1776 and the French Revolution of 1789 as well as the Enlightenment philosophy which had nurtured them. In their day, they believed, theology was being denied a dialogue with Communism, Sociology, Psychoanalysis, and so on, as if any sane mind would ever engage with such nonsense. A good Catholic needed only to glance at the list of errors these theologians advanced as examples of the historical progress of mankind to see how dangerous the ground was on which they were treading.

Michael wondered, not for the first time, if Gus Hogan had not begun to lose touch, if he was so sceptical of these radicals and their prospects of success. Whatever their motivation, the New Theologians were obviously writing better books than anyone else. And they were fearless enough to sound the bells in favour of free inquiry at the Council. Yves Congar and the others had enjoyed the support of Angelo Roncalli while he was Nuncio to France after the Second World War. Now Roncalli was pope. Something had come of age. Something you could not quite put your finger on.

15

One morning, while disrobing in the Foxrock sacristy after Mass, Michael was surprised to find an oldish priest leaning in the doorway, studying him. The visitor had an ill-kept look about him, and there were little spots of dried blood on his chin from shaving.

"The name's Christopher Beatty. Thought I'd drop in and have a look at you."

Michael walked over and shook his hand, a little nervously. He knew the name. Father Beatty was a Parish Priest up in the Wicklow Mountains. Something of a rogue.

"You're a bit young for my taste. But I suppose we'll have to get along."

The visitor turned and left, leaving a whiff of cheap brandy on the air behind him. Michael sat down and put his head in his hands. They couldn't have done this to him. But they had. Later, a phone call from Drumcondra confirmed it. He was to be the new curate at Saint Enda's, out in the wilds between Blessington and Arklow, working under none other than Christopher Beatty. It was left to Michael himself to deduce that his application to go to Rome had been turned down.

By the end of the week, Michael had officially taken up his first posting as a priest. He introduced himself to the parishioners at Sunday Mass and was shown to his room in the parochial house by the senior curate, Tom Deegan. Father Deegan, like the third curate, Paudge Faherty, had been at Saint Enda's for over a year, and they had been curates at other parishes before that. They knew their way around fairly well, and luckily, they were disposed to be kind to the newcomer. An added poignancy for Michael was the fact that Saint Enda's was not far from where Corinna Fielding lived. But the hard work in the parish made it easier to keep the memories of her from troubling his mind. After a few weeks, he had settled in as well as could be expected. Ordination had not given him an easy manner with people, and pastoral work did not come naturally to him, but he was willing to do his best.

The most serious difficulty at Saint Enda's was its nominal head, Father Beatty. He was the worst parish priest in the Archdiocese, if not in the entire country. He liked to go on wild drinking sprees, leaving the work to his long-suffering curates. No matter what they did, they would be roundly berated for their incompetence on Father Beatty's return. Father Beatty had many tiresome eccentricities. One was an obsession with cuckoo clocks, of which the parochial house had far too many. Another was his refusal to tolerate any mirrors anywhere.

"I won't have you young fellows admiring yourselves in the mirror all the time," he liked to say to his curates.

One always knew the priests of Saint Enda's, thus the diocesan lore, by the odd fit of the Roman collar, by the wild shock of hair they never combed properly, and by the chins torn open from shaving without a mirror.

Shortly after Michael's arrival, Father Beatty disappeared, only to reappear at breakfast some weeks later, reeking of stale drink. There was a strained silence as he took his rightful place at the head of the table.

"Which of you boiled these eggs? Whoever boiled this egg isn't pulling his weight in the Parish. Was it yourself, Father Paudge? I'd say it was. They should never have let a Galway man into the Archdiocese. Or was it you, Father Tom? Sure, you can't even wipe your arse by yourself. Tell you what, Michael, go in and put a hot drop in the teapot, will you? There's a good lad."

"Yes, Father Beatty. Sorry the tea's cold, Father Beatty."

This was Michael's life now. Running errands for the parish priest. Helping Father Paudge and Father Tom deal with his rages and rebuild the parish after his disasters. Strangely, the parishioners liked Father Beatty, and were prepared to put up with him. Not that they had much choice. A priest did not come to this parish in the mountains voluntarily. Either he was a priest like Father Beatty whom they were transferring in disgrace from somewhere else, or he was a young priest, like the three curates, and had little say in where he went. All three of them knew they had been sent to Saint Enda's because they were thought to be the most able for the pressure there. It was simply part of the priesthood, and anyway, their sojourn in the Wicklow mountains was not likely to last too long, two to three years being the average. Not a few of those put through their paces by Christopher Beatty had risen high in the Church after their release.

"Have you heard, Fathers? His Grace is off to Rome for the Council."

"Yes, Father," came the diplomatic reply. Father Beatty could still surprise them. They would not have thought that he had heard of the Council at all.

"Isn't it a great thing His Grace will be there in Rome to sort them all out?"

"A great thing, Father Beatty."

"Ah, that's a grand sup of tea, Michael. Sure, the Church would be gone to the dogs without us Irish. The rest of them can't read the Gospel straight, that's how it is with them. Did you get the slates fixed on the roof like I told you to, Father Paudge?"

"I did, Father Beatty."

"Well, I'll head out later on to have a look at them. I'll probably have to do them again myself. Catholicism, Irish style. That's what the Church needs. And His Grace is the man."

"Yes, Father," chorused the curates.

There was indeed reason to believe that Archbishop McQuaid would have considerable influence at the Council. Unusually for an Irish bishop, Dr. McQuaid was a member of a French religious order, the Congregation of the Holy Spirit. Only the other day, the newspapers had carried reports of the cordial invitation extended to him by Archbishop Lefebvre, the Superior General of the Congregation. Dr. McQuaid would be joining Lefebvre in a network of influence which was centred on the French-speaking missionary orders and their territories. If one added the potential of the Irish diaspora, there was a large number of Council Fathers who could be expected to respond positively to a cause promoted by McQuaid.

"His Grace'll be coming home a cardinal, mark my words."

It was a rare moment of agreement between Father Beatty and his assistant priests. As if to underline it, he carried his dirty dishes to the sink himself instead of pushing them across the table towards one of the curates as he usually did. Then he went to bed. The curates heaved a sigh of relief. They could get on with the business of the parish, after all.

16

On October 11, 1962, the Feast of the Divine Maternity of the Blessed Virgin Mary, Pope John XXIII opened the Second Vatican Ecumenical Council in Saint Peter's. The length of the Basilica from the doors to the papal altar under the cupola had been transformed into a huge Council Chamber, or Aula, as it was to be known. High tiers of seats with collapsible tables had been erected on each side of the nave by teams of workmen. These were now filled according to rank by the 2500-odd bishops of the Catholic Church, who now constituted the Fathers of the Council. Closer to the papal altar, large tribunes had been constructed for the various invited guests who would observe the Council at close hand.

"Gaudet Mater Ecclesia – Mother Church rejoices," Pope John began. His speech did not offer the usual blanket condemnation of the modern world as a cesspit of error and moral confusion. Instead, John spoke positively of the "research methods and the literary forms of modern thought" in the light of which the doctrine of the Church was to be studied and presented anew. John spoke eloquently of the "medicine of mercy" that the Church would now offer to the World through patient dialogue. His condemnation he reserved for those "prophets of doom" who had made the Church so fearful of change for so long. It was clear to his listeners where those "prophets of doom" were to be

found: among his own Catholic bishops, and in his own Curia. Pope John had done no less than call for a revolution.

When the official translations of the pope's speech, and even the official Latin text, proved to have been heavily altered, it seemed that the old guard at the Vatican had managed to strike back. The pope remained serene in the face of this disobedience. He simply quoted his own original words on all occasions. It was these, needless to say, not the obfuscations of the Curia, that were sent around the world by the admiring press.

Father Paudge and Father Tom were in full agreement with Michael Cremin that it was high time for changes in the Church. But, unlike Michael, they were not keen theologians. What interested them most was the practical advantage that would accrue if the Laity had a greater role to play in parish life. They understood this to mean a lightening of their heavy workload so that they might have a few hours off every now and again for a rest. Paudge and Tom were a lot less enthusiastic about the Liturgical Movement in Europe and America, which was pushing for an end to Latin. They had heard of the so-called Dialogue Masses in Germany, in which a kind of choirmaster led the congregation in reciting translations from the Latin while the Mass continued on the altar as usual. Even if they had liked the concept, which they didn't, and even if the Archbishop had permitted it, which he would never have done, Fathers Paudge and Tom would not have burdened themselves with yet another organisational problem by trying out a Dialogue Mass in Saint Enda's.

The Liturgical Movement had dreamed up all kinds of theatrical elements to teach things to the congregation and to generally freshen things up: Masses in old castles with the priest and the congregation forming a circle around the altar, Masses in the open air with copious lightings of fires, and so on. They had even persuaded Pope Pius XII to tinker around with the ceremonies of Holy Week. But it was all very far away for Paudge and Tom. Such liturgical innovations might suit decadent, industrialised places like Germany, where the people might not go to Mass at all unless they were bribed by the promise of interesting experiences. But they did not think this necessary for an Irish parish like Saint Enda's. Irish parishes were simple places and poor places. Irish Catholics were strong and simple in their faith. The Mass itself was enough for them. Michael was unsure on the matter. He had a liking for experiments, and the simple Irish parish badly needed some education and some self-respect. But he too was worked to the limit by his duties.

As the winter months passed, Michael Cremin never ceased to be amazed by the terrible fragility of his parishioners and their lives. There was hardly anyone who remotely corresponded to the most basic expectations of normality. There were old bachelor brothers who slept in the one bed and who were so hard to understand that they seemed to be speaking their own language. There were large families with no income who were permanently on the brink of starvation. Hardly anyone went to school beyond the age of twelve or thirteen. The community was devastated by illnesses that no civilized country should ever suffer. Into this deprivation, Michael tried his best to bring the Good News of Jesus Christ. He spent hours cycling to far-flung homesteads to bless the sick and encourage families to say the Rosary. He spent nights holding the hands of the dying whose only hope was that they would not have to die alone. He rounded up the children for First Communion and Confirmation instruction to be repeatedly astonished at their lack of knowledge of themselves or the wider world. And no matter how often he told them that Jesus had been poor like they were, he knew it never changed the simple fact that they should not have been so poor in the first place, and should not have to stay so poor.

These pastoral experiences sharpened Michael's mind in a way theology alone would never have done. Cardinal Frings, the Archbishop of Cologne, had emerged as a major force at the Council, and in the reports from Rome, Michael recognised in Frings a new kind of pastoral thinking, one which emerged from the direct encounter with human suffering, just as he was beginning to experience it at Saint Enda's. After the collapse of Nazi Germany in 1945, Frings had been faced with severe hardship among his flock, while supplies of coal and food were shipped out of Germany every day to feed the victors. Frings had preached that the cold and the hungry should go and steal whatever they needed in order to survive. He had done fantastic work in rebuilding the shattered morale of the people. Archbishop McQuaid, in his own way, was also very concerned about social deprivation, and his particular model of pastoral social services was very influential in the Church. But where McQuaid was feudal and paternalist, Frings seemed more focused on people's rights as human beings. McQuaid filled the begging bowl generously enough, if he thought you were a deserving case, but Frings wanted to get rid of begging bowls altogether. Though old and sick, Cardinal Frings was a most formidable personage. Because of him, the first working day of the Council had ended in shambles after barely twenty minutes. The first task of the Council, Frings had argued, the election of the members of the Expert Commissions, was simply impossible. All the Council Fathers had to go on were lists of names drawn up by the Curia. But they could not be expected to elect people they did not know. Consultation was required on who exactly was best qualified for which task. An emergency vote set aside the Order of Business and the great nave of Saint Peter's erupted with cheering and stamping of feet. Frings and his allies, Michael noted with admiration, had prevented the bureaucrats from planting their own people in the key positions. The Council was forced to take a more honest course.

17

After Easter, 1963, Pope John's Encyclical Letter, *Pacem in Terris*, appeared. Again, this unlikely world figure had taken the measure of the age to perfection. For the first time ever, a pope took literally his title of Universal Pastor and addressed his words not to Catholics alone, but to "all men of good will." Instead of focusing on the Fall of Man, and Original Sin, as popes were expected to do, he spoke in praise of the "fundamental human rights" first proclaimed at the French revolution of 1789 and formally declared by the United Nations in 1948. In another break with the dominant view of Catholic Tradition, he presented these rights as absolute, and seemed to many to imply that the human social order rather than the individual soul was the focal point of Redemption through Jesus Christ. He called for freedom of conscience, not only for Catholics, but for men and women of all persuasions and of none, and he called for an end to discrimination against women and minorities. Where previous popes had admonished men and women to seek the peace of Christ through individual repentance of their sins, Pope John called on them to seek peace through the settling of social conflict and through an end to all wars. He called for nothing less than a new world order of the brotherhood of man, and this in a world still terrified by the East-West confrontation and by the looming threat of nuclear annihilation.

These were inspiring words. When Cardinal Suenens travelled to New York as Pope John's emissary and presented a personally autographed copy of *Pacem in Terris* to the Secretary General of the UN, it seemed somehow right and fitting. In the person of Leon-Joseph Suenens, radical theologian and Primate of Belgium, it seemed that the Old World and the Old Belief had travelled to the New World, bearing a sacred scroll from the ancient source to the tabernacle of a new generation.

Pacem in Terris was Pope John's last message to the Church and the World. On June 3, 1963, in the company of his closest friends and collaborators, he died, fortified, it is said, by the Sacraments, and with a Monstrance by his bed, offering his death agony for the success of the Second Vatican Council and for world peace. Everywhere, men and women wept unashamedly. For many whose hearts he had touched, it was as if they had lost a beloved member of the family.

Even Father Beatty at Saint Enda's seemed to feel the loss of Good Pope John. He sobered up enough to lead the parishioners in memorial services. Votive candles appeared around the pictures of the dead pope in the parochial house. When the conclave began, Father Beatty went down to a bookmaker in Arklow to place a bet on the result. His tip for the next pope was Cardinal Montini, but the odds were so short that there was hardly any money to be made.

18

It was an August day, but the weather was unkind to anyone outside in the open air. A gale was blowing down the mountains, and it was raining, so that the rain lashed into your face whichever way you moved. Each of the curates had calls to make in remote areas, and only bicycles to get them there. It was early evening when they were home again, hungry, and sodden to the skin. Father Tom had brought a quart of oxtail soup back with him in a small milk can – a present for the priests from two elderly sisters. He left it on the gas ring to heat up and joined Paudge and Michael in setting the table. Another parishioner had given them a loaf of home-baked soda bread, and yet another a couple of jars of home-made jam. They were tucking into a cheerful meal, when they heard an ominous creak from the staircase. Father Beatty was on the move.

"There you are," he growled through the open doorway. "Anyone'd think you'd skipped the country. Have you no concern for the Parish?"

"Sorry, Father," mumbled the curates.

"There's a phone call came today from Drumcondra." Father Beatty savoured the grave silence which suddenly filled the kitchen. "About Father Michael. He's to go to Rome."

Michael dropped his spoon in surprise. It clattered against the porcelain soup bowl and fell on the floor, where one of the cats began to lick at it.

"Young Father Michael was never cut out for parish work," Father Beatty grunted to the curates. "Still, he won't be long in Rome before he'll be wishing he was back with us here in the mountains. Mark my words. But we'll have a small sup of whiskey to see him on his way."

A phone call to Drumcondra confirmed what Father Beatty had said. Michael's request had finally been approved. He was to take advanced courses in theology at the Gregorian University.

It took a few weeks to arrange for Michael's departure. When the day finally came, Father Paudge generously offered to drive him to the station in Arklow. As they rattled off in the old Austin, Michael did not look back at the grey parochial house, lost half way up the bare hillside, miles from anywhere. He had done his best during his year at Saint Enda's. And he had tried to like it. Now he was off to Rome. It had seemed impossible. But even the impossible could happen.

†

3

A Priest in Rome

1

Rome was a place of constant surprises. The flat-roofed villas of the city were herded tightly together on flat hills snarling with traffic, but inside they had tiled courtyards that were spacious and quiet. There were orange trees and lemon trees growing in gardens, and sometimes huge palms with ancient stone benches offering shade and rest. The historic quarters were mazes of little dark alleys with peculiar shops, and the darkest of them could converge without warning on a carved white fountain blazing with light.

The Pontifical Irish College, which was close to the Basilica of Saint John Lateran, was Michael's new home. On account of the Ecumenical Council, the College was bursting at the seams with people. Most of the Irish bishops wanted to live there during the Council sessions, as did their staff. There were also a few individuals from Africa and Asia who could not afford a place to stay in Rome and were relying on the fabled Irish hospitality. Space was tight, but the College was full of good humour, and the gossip and banter were a perfect introduction to ecclesiastical affairs for an eager young man from home.

The Council, of course, was the major topic of conversation, and Michael was an avid listener. He already knew some of the more senior residents from clerical get-togethers at home. Liam O'Casey, for example, one of the Vatican librarians, whom Gus Hogan had once brought to Dublin. Liam was a rather dubious character, but all the more interesting because of it. Gus Hogan, who was now a Professor of Canon Law, was also living at the College, and was doing a lot to help Michael to feel welcome. The new rector of the College, Monsignor

Denis O'Hare, was also a congenial fellow. But Gus and Denis were timid and vacillating, and a bit out of step with the times. Before he became Pope, Cardinal Montini, together with Cardinal Suenens, had established a distinction between the theology of the Church *ad intra*, as she is in herself, and *ad extra*, as she presents herself to the world. This created a whole new way of thinking about the Church that was becoming fundamental for the Council. And Gus and Denis payed it no more attention than the orange trees and lemon trees outside, or the blazing light that caught the terracotta paving in so many wonderful ways. They had grown tired in the priesthood, like so many others. As far as they were concerned, *aggiornamento* had passsed away with Pope John. It was business as usual from now on.

Business as usual? Michael shook his head when he heard it. Business as usual was what most of them were hoping for. The perpetuation of what they had learned as seminarians. Of what they had been taught to believe was God's Will.

Gus Hogan and Denis O'Hare were fine fellows, of course. Like all the rest of them, really. And they had a sense of humour, too, in their own way. But they were trickles of water twisted out of an old towel, while Pope John had been a glorious fountain of water turning the place into a great splashing river, rushing God alone knew where.

2

A year previously, an opportune evaluation by the Nijmegen theologian, Edward Schillebeeckx OP, had enabled Pope John to order the rejection of the discussion papers, known as Schemata, which had been drafted for the Council by the Preparatory Commission. An exception was *De Sacra Liturgia*, the Schema on the Liturgy, which had been deemed of a sufficiently high standard. In view of its subject matter, *De Sacra Liturgia* touched on the most fundamental, and potentially divisive, questions concerning the Catholic Faith, but in what seemed a secondary, practical way. Through this Schema, a most disturbing question was revealed, the question of whether changes to the Mass Itself were at all conceivable.

Changes to the Mass were dangerous. The Mass of the Roman Rite was generally believed to have been placed beyond all possible change by the Bull of Pope

Saint Pius V, *Quo Primum Tempore*, in 1570. The Liturgical Movement had long argued that using the different languages of the peoples in the Mass Rite instead of Latin would enrich the experience of the congregation. The defenders of Latin also had good arguments. The Latin words of the Canon had been established and venerated for many centuries. No translation could render the sense of these words with the required precision. To try this would put the purity of the doctrine expressed by the Canon at risk. Also, the syntax and semantics of the world's languages diverged in important ways. If all languages were admitted to the Mass, how could the Rite retain its sacred unity? Surely, it would collapse like the Tower of Babel?

As a priest, Michael Cremin had great respect for the Latin words of the Mass. But at the Irish College, when the younger priests were among themselves, he often took the part of the reformers. They should follow Jesus Christ rather than Pope Pius V, Michael argued. Jesus Himself had looked to see how the Rites of His day had fitted the needs of the people; he had not wanted to fit the people into the Rites. Not for the first time, Michael noticed that he was bolder in his views than the others.

One evening, after a day spent running errands between the College and different offices of the Curia, Michael received an intriguing note from the Rector. Archbishop McQuaid had arrived in Rome for the Council. Michael was to hold himself ready at all times, because the Archbishop wished to see him. The Rector was unable to say when or for what reason.

The summons came late on a sunny afternoon. Michael was led towards the spacious, corner office which up to then had been the Rector's, and was told to wait by the door, which was slightly ajar. The Archbishop was telephoning, and in the effort to make himself understood through the Roman telephone system, he had raised his voice, and Michael could hear almost everything.

"Intrepid Lutherans and adventurous Calvinists. And the ill-mannered young doctors of theology from our own universities. There's no end to it, Vincent. There are paid American journalists pronouncing on the meaning of the Council, day in, day out. No, Ottaviani was boycotting the Aula at that time. Who would blame him, after the treatment he received? He called them a gang of revolutionaries to their faces. It was well spoken. Yes, his speech was too long, but he was prevented by bad eyesight from giving it as written. There is a bishop, Vincent – I shall not speak his name – who has circulated a prayer about Cardinal Ottaviani. This prayer is, that God may open the eyes of His Eminence, and if that prove impossible, that He close those eyes for ever. Can you imagine it? A prayer for the death of the Cardinal. Circulated in Saint Peter's, itself. We are showing as much venom as at the court of the Borgias. There is a new spirit abroad, Vincent. The Spirit of the Council, they're calling it. Oh, and we saw it that day in all its finery. They were rapping their tables and stamping their feet and clapping and cheering as poor Ottaviani tried to get back to his seat. Like a Communist mob, Vincent!"

The humiliation of the Pro-Prefect of the Holy Office was still an event of great interest, a year after its occurrence. Cardinal Ottaviani had been berating the Council for allowing consideration to changes to the Mass. When he exceeded the time limit, the microphone was switched off, leaving him stranded in mid-sentence, as if he were some insignificant junior man, rather than the giant of the Curia that he was. And rightly so, in Michael's view. Why should the time limit be more generous for Cardinal Ottaviani? And that lame excuse of bad eyesight. Cardinal Frings' eyes were just as bad. But Frings went to the trouble of learning his speeches by heart so that he would not go over time by having to improvise at the microphone. It was Frings, not Ottaviani, who was giving real leadership.

"You have been listening, Father."

Michael looked up in dismay. The Archbishop was standing over him.

"Inadvertently, Your Grace. I was told to wait here. The door was open."

"What did you hear?"

"I have already forgotten, Your Grace."

The Archbishop stared into Michael's eyes for a long time. "You are steeped in reticence. As I knew you would be. It will be of use to you, Father, to be steeped in reticence. I have asked a number of men I can trust to provide me with assistance. To be, in effect, my eyes here in Rome, and perhaps on occasion my hands. You shall be one of them."

"I am at Your Grace's service."

"You will deliver messages for me. In the course of delivering messages, it will be quite natural for you to see things and hear things. You will use your judgement. If something has a bearing on matters of interest, you will report it. And you will forget what you have done as soon as you have done it. There will be no reward, of course, save for that reward attendant upon humble obedience."

"Yes, Your Grace. Thank you, Your Grace."

3

The Pontifical University Gregoriana was situated across the river from the Vatican in the Piazza della Pilotta, which was no great distance from the Irish College. On his way to lectures, at least during his first few weeks there, Michael liked to walk past the Forum and the Coliseum and the other remains of Imperial Rome. There was no grandeur like this back in Ireland, and there was no reason not to admire it. In general, there was more freedom for a priest in Rome than in Dublin, and there was no reason either not to take notice of the pretty girls who were dressed so revealingly, to his eyes at least, that it was impossible not to look at them. If he had not been a priest, he would have tried to get chatting to one of these girls, but it was right and proper for him to drop his eyes and pass them by. After a while Michael chose a different walking route because the tourists slowed him down too much, but the pretty girls seemed to be everywhere.

The weeks leading up to Christmas were spent on exam preparation. These exams took the form of public oral demonstrations of Thomist syllogisms, in Latin, of course, and were quite excruciating. But Michael passed. By the end of the academic year, barring accidents, the degree of STL, Licentiate in Sacred Theology, would be his, and then he could move on at his own pace towards the Doctorate.

After the last of the exams, when the Rector had mumbled the last *placet* over his nervous responses, Michael had dawdled a little on the way home. It had done him so much good to pass his exams that he felt like walking over to the young beauties who hung about the Piazza Navona and asking one of them for a kiss. There was a dark-haired and bright-eyed one sitting all by herself, a little lonely, perhaps. He might have risked it, but he was a priest. With a sigh, he offered it up to God, and went on his way.

A lot of Michael's time was spent in the university library, which was watched over by priest-librarians with suspicious minds. The collections were justly famous, but access was restricted. One had to state a good reason on requesting a book, and the most interesting works, though neatly catalogued, were unavailable, at least to him. On reflection, however, the restrictions were not that surprising. The desire to explore outside one's field was redolent of intellectual pride. Prayerful study, and not indiscriminate reading, was the life of a scholar-priest.

The Gregorian was a place of cultivated frugality. Everything was of good quality, but nothing ever suggested comfort or rest. Even the professors' rooms on the upper floors were without adornment and differed little from the monastic cells many of them returned to after their day's work. Founded by Saint Ignatius Loyola to educate his elite new Society, the Jesuits, it had remained one of the leading centres of institutionalised Thomism. Only a short walk away, the Ecumenical Council was airing questions that few would have imagined could ever be aired. But huddled in its conservativism, the Gregorian seemed to take little notice. There was hardly a whisper of daring concepts from German and French sources to ruffle the tranquillity.

But Michael knew better. There was a hidden undertow churning behind the appearances, and it threatened to become a dangerous whirlpool. As a messenger, he was moving easily between Archbishops McQuaid and Lefebvre and their friends. He had seen that the bland, clerical smiles worn by many bishops concealed a Church that was increasingly at odds with itself.

Again, Michael dawdled at the Piazza Navona. The dark-haired and bright-eyed girl was there again, sitting by herself in her winter coat, and he would rather have had a message for her than for Archbishop McQuaid.

Like the progressives, the conservatives were organising right-thinking study groups and were approaching bishops to get them to attend. Calling in favours. Proposing, praising, inviting. Cajoling and warning. Petitions to get the Council to pronounce a solemn condemnation of Communism. Petitions for new Marian dogmas. Petitions about the rules of procedure at the Council. They were on a battlefield, and the weapons were nods, smiles, hands raised in blessing, signatures and official seals.

Soon enough it became known to the observant that Michael Cremin was acting as a messenger. He was regularly waylaid on the streets of Rome by shady characters who used the pretence of conversation to size him up and make him divulge what he knew. One of the most persistent was Pontus Freeman, a Rome-based journalist, who followed Michael all the way up the Via dei S.S. Quattro one day, and then ran him down in the coffee bar where he was trying to hide. Resolving to say as little as possible, Michael resigned himself to the unwanted company.

"You're Irish, aren't you? What do the Irish think about the Armageddon in the Aula? I am referring to the showdown between the Grand Inquisitor Ottaviani with his gang of bad guys and the free world. It's like high noon in Tombstone, Texas, except this time the Marshal's the bad guy."

"They're more on the conservative side, Mr. Freeman."

"Yeah, that's what I was thinking. I don't like that guy, McQuaid. Doesn't look good at the microphone. And outside the Aula, he's like a crazed animal, snarling at people he doesn't like. It's getting out of hand. They should tie him up in a cage so that reasonable people can make themselves understood."

"For your information, Mr. Freeman, Archbishop McQuaid is a very learned and very prayerful man."

Pontus Freeman looked at him slyly. "You know, I like you. Call me Pontus, all my friends do."

Michael did not answer. He had the measure of this man now. He liked to use people. Otherwise he had no time for them. He was reminded vaguely of Angelo Poggi in Louvain.

"Ottaviani and McQuaid haven't a chance," Freeman was saying. "Bea and Suenens. They're the stars. They've got the image, you see. We're using them as the good guys to sell our newspapers. The day the free press arrived in the Vatican, Michael, is the day the outcome of this Council was decided. Aggiornamento means public opinion. And public opinion means us."

"The Council sessions are secret, eh, Pontus. No-one's allowed in. And the Fathers of the Council obey the rules of the pope."

Pontus Freeman chortled loudly. "Like hell they do. And they aren't the pope's rules, anyway. He's on our side. Let me tell you about the rules. Do you know who's sitting right up there near the altar in the best seats? Hearing and seeing everything? The official observers from the other Churches. And I can tell you, they're not worried about being excommunicated by Ottaviani for not keeping some secret that helps the bad guys. They're not Catholics, so they're excommunicated anyway. They like to talk. So do the German bishops. Some of those guys don't believe in God at all. And they're out there on the steps of St. Peter's every lunchtime looking for a journalist to take down what they want to say. Those guys learned their press management from Josef Goebbels. I couldn't plant a story better myself. You shocked, Michael?"

The fish eyes were narrowed over the young man, who was shaking his head in disbelief.

"Well let me tell you something else, son. Those Germans have been organizing refresher courses on theology for all the bishops at the Council. You can imagine, if you're the bishop of some diocese in the African jungle you're not likely to be up to date in your theological reading. And all of a sudden you have to get over to Rome for a Council. You'd be ashamed of your lack of knowledge, wouldn't you? And you'd be very grateful to all those learned Germans who are helping you out like real friends and brothers in Christ. They probably even paid for his air ticket. Do you reckon he's able to spot the German slant on things? No way. It's a bit like programming their minds, and they don't even need drugs to do it."

"Sir, the bishops serve the truth."

"Yeah? Whose truth? You know Bob Kaiser, who writes for *Time*? Do you know how he's so well informed? So penetrating. So far-seeing? Well, I'll tell you. He has his own pet Archbishop. That's how. A guy called Thomas d'Esterre Roberts SJ, who just happens to be Archbishop Emeritus of Bombay. Last year, this guy actually lived with the Kaisers. Said Mass in there every day, squatting on the living room floor like a kaffir doing voodoo. Kaiser drove this guy to the Council every morning and then picked him up again and drove him home, where he told Kaiser everything. There's no document Kaiser didn't get a copy of within the day."

Michael rapped the table in exasperation. "Archbishops do not live with journalists from *Time* magazine!"

"Kaiser's ex-Jesuit. They're like the CIA. Once you're in, you're in to stay." The American was suddenly hard, focused. Then he smiled and relaxed. "Anyway, this guy Roberts is a real maverick. An upper-class English twit who went native down there in the monsoons and the vindaloo curries. Do you know what he did when India became independent in 1948? He hitch-hiked round the world. Yup. Just skipped off from his diocese and hitch-hiked round the world, like some beatnik on drugs. Turned up at the Vatican two or three years later to offer his resignation. It's one of the great mysteries of all time why he wasn't carted off to a lunatic asylum. Now he's here. And he's dynamite. He's a walking Council all by himself. There's nothing they'll ever think of in that Aula that Roberts hasn't already tried out in the Bombay slums. He's seen it all. He's done it all."

"You are speaking about a man who is a consecrated Archbishop of the Roman Catholic Church. Are you not ashamed of yourself?"

Pontus Freeman reached lazily into his shirt and scratched at his neck. "Look, son, the Roman Catholic Church is a thing of the past. You don't have to believe me, but the events will bear me out as they unfold. You keep your eye on Annibale Bugnini, the guy who was in charge of the Commission on the Liturgy till he got fired. That Schema on the Liturgy is like a nuclear warhead. It's all there in miniature, son, all that's coming. And no-one can see it. I had a profile on that Bugnini guy that would make your hair stand on end. But I had to tear it up and throw it in the Tiber. The guy's too well connected."

As Secretary of one of the Preparatory Commissions, Father Annibale Bugnini had been in operational charge of drafting the Schema on the Liturgy under the supposedly watchful eye of Cardinal Cicognani, the Prefect of the Congregation of Rites, who had passed away in the run-up to the Council. The new Prefect, Cardinal Larraona, had summarily dismissed Father Bugnini, and had secretly begun redrafting the Schema along conservative lines. He was aided in this by two senior officials, Joseph Löw CSSr and Ferdinando Antonelli OFM, who up to then had been friends and colleagues of Bugnini. Nicknamed "homo ambiguous" around Rome, Antonelli had been promoted to Bugnini's former post of Commission Secretary. The sudden death of Father Löw in September 1962 brought the dirty tricks to light, and Cardinal Larraona was forced into an embarrassing about-turn when the Council began. In the meantime, Pope John himself had intervened. In a quiet but effective move, he had appointed Bugnini a *peritus*, an expert advisor to the Council, which effectively rehabilitated him and his original Schema.

An assistant to Father Bugnini had begun to teach at the Gregorian, and Michael went up to ask him if what he heard was true. The assistant was in a mood for conversation.

"Liturgically, we need to go back to our roots, Father, as well you know. How sad it is that so few are prepared to accept this as they ought to. Even at the Council. And this despite the clear line given by Good Pope John, may he rest in peace. My dear Father, the ancient language of Saint Feargal and Saint Columcille, surely it is as adequate a language for prayer as Latin?"

"No doubt it is, Father."

"And your great Saint Patrick, Father, did he not learn the language of the Irish in order to bring them the Gospel in the way they could understand and accept?"

"Yes, he did, Father, thank God."

"Thank God, indeed, Father. The Vernacular, Father. That is the example of the early Christians. The example of the Church Fathers. It will lift Holy Church to new heights of glory. *Laudetur Jesus Christus!*"

"*In aeternum, amen,*" Michael murmured.

Father Bugnini's assistant had told him almost nothing, but Michael did not give up. He visited different libraries and read up as much as he could on the contentious issues of the liturgy. Certainly, a lot was at stake. The so-called Liturgical Movement, predominantly a German, French and American phenomenon, was in the ascendancy. A Bull of Pope Pius X, *Tra le Sollecitudini*, had given the Liturgical Movement one of its catchphrases, 'Active Participation'. But things had taken a more radical turn with the Belgian liturgist, Lambert Beauduin OSB. At the Mechelen Congress of 1909, Beauduin had called for a democratisation of the liturgy, by which he meant the active participation of the congregation as a community and the use of texts in the Vernacular. This clearly entailed a downplaying of the interiority of personal prayer in favour of public expressions of prayer life in social space. Almost overnight, powerful allies emerged from nowhere to join with Dom Beauduin, chief among them the German Benedictines of Maria Laach, and some close advisors of the pope. It was miraculous, almost; one of those spiritual impulses that come unexpectedly to correct imbalances and fashion things anew. Eventually, Beauduin had gone too far and had been silenced by the Vatican. Perhaps for this reason, books by or about Lambert Beauduin were almost impossible to procure, even though some of his followers were now periti at the Council. Among Dom Beauduin's early friends, Michael was surprised to learn, was Angelo Roncalli, the late Pope John XXIII.

4

Sacrosanctum Concilium. The Sacred Council. This was to be the title of the final version of the Schema on the Liturgy. Michael Cremin broke the rules and procured himself an advance copy. By the time he had finished reading it, shortly before its promulgation, he had turned a corner, his mind anything but clear.

The sacred Council has set out to impart an ever increasing vigour to the Christian life of the faithful; to adapt more closely to the needs of our age those institutions which are subject to change; [...] Accordingly it sees particularly cogent reasons for undertaking the reform and promotion of the liturgy.

That was to be the first article, if the pope approved it. *Accordingly*. It was certainly no example of stringent reasoning. But if the conclusion was valid, it set a whole new tone. A tone amazingly critical of the mainstream liturgical tradition.

"New to the Greg?" came a voice in English.

The man who had interrupted Michael was no Roman. He had eyes which shone a brilliant blue colour and were set back in the face like in two deep caves. Untidy red hair, greying in places. A thin reddish beard. Dressed in a suit of dark green tweed which had seen better days. The man was pleasantly familiar, like someone in an old story book.

"Not that new, really. I'm just thinking a bit."

"Gregory. John Gregory." The man handed Michael a visiting card, which bore his name and the legend 'English-Speaking Taxis'."

Michael told him who he was.

"Studying Theology?"

"What else."

John Gregory had a magazine with him, an old issue of the American weekly, *Time*. The cover story was devoted to the Second Vatican Council. John tapped the cover with his finger.

"Bit too simple for you, Father Michael," came the answer. "But I like things kept simple."

Michael took the magazine and turned the pages. The international journalists were extremely well-informed. Many bishops had a poor knowledge of Latin and relied on press reports in other languages to keep abreast of things. The journalists were thus proving to be more effective opinion-makers at the Council than the Fathers themselves. John Gregory knew this well. A lot of his income was generated by providing bishops with the international newspapers of their choice. Some of the leading journalists had a strong sense of mission. Robert B. Kaiser, of *Time*, for example. During the First Session in 1962, liberal bishops and theologians had got to know each other at Kaiser's buffet suppers and had forged alliances in the warmth of his hospitality. And on returning home, not a few bishops had found themselves under pressure in their dioceses, as a generation of lay Catholics became theologically literate by reading Kaiser's articles.

John Gregory heard all about it in his taxi, as his illustrious passengers, their minds heated up by daring talk, their tongues loosened by alcohol, boasted of the great things that were coming. They were going to scrap Latin. They were going to scrap the Mass completely. They were going to scrap the Papacy. They were going to recognize the Jews. They were going to recognize other religions and freedom of religion and freedom of conscience. They were going to open up the closed orders. They were going to re-write the Rules of all the religious orders.

"I hope we can talk again!" Michael said, eagerly. This taxi driver knew more than he did about how they were getting the Council to work. But when John

Gregory agreed to meet him regularly, Michael saw something else in his eyes, something more than a shared interest in the Council. John was concerned about him and wanted to help.

As often as he could, Michael drank coffee with John Gregory, and frequently the taxi-driver asked him to explain something he had picked up from one of his passengers. He listened carefully while Michael did so, occasionally helping him with intelligent questions. In explaining things to his new friend, Michael's own thinking grew clearer. The Church was believed to be founded on unity. But the only unity they seemed able to cope with was uniformity. And uniformity was stale and dead in comparison with the fullness of passionately-held differences. The Innsbruck theologian, Josef Andreas Jungmann SJ, to whom most people deferred, had defined liturgy as the prayer of the Church. Not the prayer provided for by Vatican legislation, but that prayer actively engaged in by the faithful. What seemed a dry, uninspiring distinction was explosive in its import. All at once, what people actually did was more important than what they were supposed to do. And what they did together was more important than what they did alone. It levelled the field, in a way. Local Mass customs were potentially as worthwhile as the Mass of the Popes. Popes and bishops were not more privileged liturgically than priests. And the clergy were not in principle more privileged than the laity. But the key element was Jungmann's sources. He had not thought this up by himself. He had come upon it through the most painstaking study of liturgical history the Church had yet seen. This was, in fact, the liturgical concept of the early Church, that golden age of Christian inspiration. Jungmann was actively opposed by another learned man, Canon Martimort of Paris and Toulouse, who favoured the Mass of the Popes as the primordial model. Concepts of liturgy were clashing against each other irreconcilably. It could not be otherwise. And why should one of them be deemed less Catholic than another? It was time for a bigger picture. A unity in diversity.

One day, John Gregory was late. John had never been late before, and Michael ordered a second glass of water, wondering what had happened. When John arrived, all flustered, he explained that he couldn't stay. A woman in his neighbourhood had been taken ill and he had just taken her to hospital. A mental breakdown. Not the first time. Now he was taking her daughter home, as he had promised. Michael glanced through the window at the girl standing by the taxi. It was the dark-haired and bright-eyed girl he had once seen sitting all by herself at the Piazza Navona. She looked so forlorn, standing there by John's taxi. Michael was reminded of some of his former parishioners in the Wicklow mountains. Affliction made no difference between old and young, strong and weak. With a sigh, he offered a silent prayer for her, and wished John Gregory well.

5

One afternoon, while Archbishop McQuaid was walking in the garden of the Irish College praying the Divine Office, Michael plucked up his courage and approached him. A week previously, after he had delivered one of the Archbishop's messages, someone had stopped Michael on the street and thrust a little package into his hands, whispering that he was to make sure that the Archbishop was informed of its contents. The person disappeared before Michael could make out who it was. The package proved to contain a private record of certain meetings of the Preparatory Commission on the Liturgy from two years previously. Michael had done his best to check the authenticity of these notes. A picture had taken shape, a picture of some urgency.

"Young Father Cremin, no less. What a pleasure. I trust Father will confine himself to essentials?"

"It's about changes to the Mass, Your Grace."

"Changes to Holy Mass? Indeed. Tell me. Do you regard Holy Church as a safe haven in every storm?"

Michael felt uncomfortable. Dr. McQuaid was testing him again.

"I do, Your Grace."

"You are right to do so. Nevertheless, Holy Church is permanently under attack. The enemies of God do not rest. We must maintain the purity of the Holy Sacrifice of the Mass. At all costs. This purity is intolerable to Protestants and Jews and the like. They are conspiring against the Mass! They have always done so. And now they are perched in the Aula of Saint Peter's, privy to the most sensitive discussions. It is a most serious mistake to allow in these strangers. We shall prevail upon Pope Paul to have them removed!"

"Your Grace, the question of the Mass may not be the work of outsiders."

"Be specific, will you?"

"As Your Grace's messenger, certain facts have been made known to me with regard to the drafting of the Schema on the Liturgy. To be conveyed to Your Grace. Evidently, the initial mandate of the Preparatory Commission was for seven areas of thematic focus. The Secretariat under Father Bugnini — apparently on his initiative alone — extended this to twelve themes. These new themes include the areas of the greatest controversy. Concelebration of Masses. The participation of the faithful in the Holy Sacrifice. The educational meaning of Liturgy. At the first plenary meeting of the Preparatory Commission on the Liturgy, a thirteenth theme was added: the drafting of a dogmatic prologium. This prologium states a certain theology of liturgy as it relates to the life of the Church. A theology that is controversial. Your Grace, after hardly any discussion, the prologium was approved by a quick show of hands, and became part of the Schema. There was no way to check how those votes were counted. Now this prologium provides the legitimation for calls for substantial change."

"You say this is the doing of Father Bugnini?"

"Yes, Your Grace. Very few plenary sessions were held by the Preparatory Commission on the Liturgy. The work was done mainly in sections and subcommissions, with communication by letter. Only one man knew the overall picture at any one time, the man who co-ordinated things. Father Bugnini. No one else, unless Father Bugnini took him into his confidence. And Father Bugnini was in the habit of telling different versions of things to different people."

"Communication in Rome has always been circuitous."

"Indeed, Your Grace. But the point I am making is this: it is impossible to say where Father Bugnini received the instructions to widen the scope for the Schema. He seems to have acted independently of all valid authority. Your Grace, at the last plenary session of the Preparatory Commission on the Liturgy, Father Bugnini was explicitly accused by some of the members of dishonesty and manipulation. Your Grace may not be aware that many Commission members were taken completely by surprise by the total content of the Schema they were supposed to have drafted together."

Michael handed over the little moleskine notebook the anonymous package had contained. Dr. McQuaid perused the pages with their tiny handwriting.

"Father, the gist of this is not new to me. But it is not common knowledge. Now it is known to you. A mere student. Barely ordained. Chance events would seem to be singling you out for a strange prominence. But you will resist this temptation, Father. You will refuse to know something when it is not your station to know it. Privileged knowledge you will pass on to me, leaving it to my judgement. And you will expunge it from your memory. It must be as if you had never known it."

"Your Grace can trust me completely."

"Father, it is the liturgy of the Mass that will be the major issue of this Council. It is the only issue which will affect all the faithful, clerical and lay, all Catholics of all ages in all countries, and for all the times that are coming. The only issue which will have immediate and lasting impact. I have long detected a wind of change, Father Cremin. And it is an ill-wind, to be sure."

"Your Grace, there can be no changes to the Mass. Surely it is impossible."

"Last year, Father, Pope John ordered that the name of Saint Joseph be inserted into the Canon of the Mass alongside the Blessed Virgin. We would never oppose the honour due to the stepfather of Our Lord. But there was a great clamour on behalf of this insertion during the First Session of the Council. And the loudest voices, I tell you, were those of people who on an ordinary day wouldn't give tuppence-halfpenny for Saint Joseph. They wanted to be able to say that the Canon had been changed. That there is papal approval for changing the Canon. And for changing the Mass Itself. But let us be clear. Pope John did not change anything by inserting these felicitous words. Popes have made such useful alterations in the past, without them constituting a change. But there is a vociferous and unmanageable element lurking in the shadows of this Council. An element that is not loyal to the Council, or to the Holy Father. They are trying to twist things. Confuse the ill-informed. Create an engine of impiety. Some of them do not even belong to our faith."

"And Father Bugnini is one of these?"

"There has been a lack of clear and firm leadership. An excitable individual such as Father Bugnini might easily lose the run of himself in such circumstances. And play into the hands of our enemies."

"So Father Bugnini is being used to attack the Mass?"

"Father, the Mass may be attacked, but it cannot be destroyed. We may have lost a few skirmishes on the wording of the Schema on the Liturgy, but we will win the war, as always. We know this. Even so, I do not like to be surprised by events. I have asked you to be my eyes. Be especially alert, Father Cremin. Report anything of interest."

"Yes, Your Grace. Thank You, Your Grace."

Michael had spoken as he believed he should. But he had been careful to keep something hidden. He had a sneaking admiration for Bugnini and those brazen liturgical reformers, and he did not want his superior to see it.

At the Irish College, the talk over meals often concerned the leading progressive theologians at the Council, among them Karl Rahner SJ, who was a *peritus* to the liberal Cardinal Koenig of Vienna. Father Rahner was not known as a liturgist, but some in the College felt that the Schema on the Liturgy had drawn from his theology, much as the water in the taps might be drawn from a hidden reservoir they could not see.

"It is Rahner's Anthropocentric Turn. If you read carefully, it's there."

"And a good thing, too. The Anthropocentric Turn is long overdue in theology."

"Nonsense!"

"Look. Rahner shows us what it means to ask questions. The question is fundamental, not the answer. God is in question. Man is in question. The question of God and the question of Man are in reality the same question, and the same engaging in questioning. And Jesus Christ is the answer."

"Can you understand that?"

"No!"

As he poured out cups of tea for the arguing priests, Michael was happy to keep quiet and listen.

"Rahner's a Heideggerian," someone said. "And he never defines his terms properly."

"So you've read him then," sneered another. Michael took note of the shame-faced way a number of them dropped their eyes. They'd been reading Rahner for years and were afraid to say so.

Finally, Augustine Hogan spoke up. "Fathers. This Anthropocentric Turn is utterly pernicious. We can't allow any derogation from the fundamental distinction between Grace and Nature. Anything else will lead us straight into the denial of Original Sin."

"You're saying it smacks of heresy, Gus?"

"I might be, I suppose. In the abstract."

"You can't prove Rahner a heretic. It's been tried before."

"The man is a weasel, obviously. He would have us do theology in the subjunctive mood. Surely, when Our Lord charged us with the task of preaching the Gospel, he intended us to do it with conviction and with clarity?"

There was no answer to that.

Not long before, a mass intervention by German-speaking cardinals had caused the draconian censorship restrictions imposed on Karl Rahner to be lifted. Even so, Father Rahner was still one of the most suspect theologians in the Church. To get hold of his books, Michael had to beg his way into the library in the Jesuit Generalate in the Borgo Santo Spirito. There, he found a long river of speculative dialectic, which was a world all its own, but not totally unfamiliar to him. It was reminiscent of the potentiated facticity he had discovered in Heidegger when he was in Louvain, and it was not at all uncongenial. It was a mental landscape that reeked of the brokenness of human striving, and was quite fascinating. In Rahner's world, it seemed to be a far better thing, a far more human thing, to struggle to believe than to actually believe. Rahner's ideal Christian, as far as Michael could see, was like a character in a novel by Graham Greene, the self-styled Catholic agnostic. A man incapable of faith, a born double-agent tortured by his shifting loyalties, wreaking a kind of constructive havoc as he contemplates his agony of soul. If Sin and Salvation were dialectically related, it was hard not to conclude that somehow Sin was good.

6

At the Irish College one day, shortly after this first brush with the existentialist theology of Karl Rahner, Michael came upon Liam the Librarian, who waved in his face a copy of *De Ecclesia* which he had picked up somewhere. *De Ecclesia* was the controversial Schema on the Church which was on the agenda of the Council. The Schemata were secret, but that did not prevent clandestine copies from being circulated.

"Give us a look." Michael made a grab for it, but missed.

"It'll cost you," Liam taunted.

"I'll say a prayer for you."

"A prayer? From you? I'll give it to you for a packet of fags. Twenty Sweet Afton."

"It's a deal."

Michael saw that *De Ecclesia* was very short, only 25 pages or so, but over 50 pages of explanatory notes had been added. "This looks like a bit of a mess. Are you sure it's all there?"

"Here's a question for you." Liam licked his lips, slyly. "Is the Church a perfect society with an unchanging juridical structure or is the Church a Sacrament, or is the Church something else? What do you think?"

"Knowing you, Liam, I'd say the answer is, the Church is something else."

"Too poxy right. They said there in the Aula the Church is the People of God. There you are now."

"The People of God. What's that? A rock-and-roll band?"

"You're not far wrong. And there was a bishop in there a while ago saying the Church is a sinning community on a pilgrimage through time."

"It would want to be a nice short pilgrimage for the People of God, wouldn't it?"

"Right you are. And no talk of Sin, either, if you don't mind. There's another bishop who wants the Church to apologise to the modern world."

"Apologise for what, Liam?"

"For being the Church."

"Maybe it's just tactical. To move the debate to a better position."

"Listen. If that was the Church when I was a boy, my mother would never have let me go on for the priesthood. I'd be saving my soul loading barrels for the Guinness brewery."

Michael took *De Ecclesia* away with him for a closer look. To go by the news reports, the discussions of the Schema in the Aula had been dominated by Cardinal Suenens. Suenens had urged that the Church be a charismatic Church enjoying the full freedom of the Holy Spirit. Not just the Clergy, but the Laity also had a spiritual mission. Women too had their unique spiritual mission given to them by the Holy Spirit. The Church should, in fact, be feminist. To underline the urgency of the matter, he had a whole new Schema on the Church in his briefcase, drafted by his own personal staff in Mechelen, which he would put to the Council all by himself, if need be. Such bold vision had proved unwelcome in the Aula, but outside it, fame was assured.

When Michael came to return the copy of the Schema, he found Liam the Librarian on the roof of the Irish College. Liam was sitting on a low parapet with his cassock pulled up to his waist and his legs dangling into space. He was enjoying a cigarette and taking in the fine view over the city of Rome. When he saw Michael, he gave a ribald chuckle and gestured towards the dome of Saint Peter's in the near distance.

"Have a look over there at the Feminist Church. The thing always looked like a Brussels Sprout, anyway."

"Suenens is more popular then the pope, I hear," Michael replied.

The librarian launched a globule of spit into the Roman air. "You mean that big speech in the Aula? Look, it wasn't Suenens at all who wrote that speech. It was Hans Küng."

Michael wondered if this was one of Liam's little jokes.

"This is how it was. Suenens is wondering what he can say to shake up the Council but he has no ideas left of his own. So over he goes to Hans Küng and asks for a quick speech. And the rest is history."

What Liam said could well be true. The Council had brought a number of star theologians to Rome, for whom some ambitious bishops were quite willing to act as mouthpieces. Father Küng was one of the best of them, and the suave Belgian was well able to spot a winner.

Liam the Librarian stubbed out his cigarette. "So what do you think then, eh? Is it more a woman's tit than a Brussels Sprout?"

Michael looked across at Saint Peter's. It still looked like a Basilica to him.

7

At the end of the Second Session, the Council approved the Schema on the Liturgy. It was then solemnly promulgated as an Apostolic Constitution by Pope Paul VI and became an official, though not infallible, teaching of the Church. Progressive forces were highly pleased by Article 50, which permitted the use of the Vernacular in appropriate places in the Mass Rite. Hardly a month later, however, in January 1964, Pope Paul issued the decree *Sacram Liturgiam* which prohibited the use of the Vernacular pending the approval of translations by the Holy See. With this legislative act he satisfied almost no-one. Progressives who were eager to avail of the possibility of using the Vernacular in their liturgies found themselves forbidden to do so. Many of them went ahead regardless. Conservatives who abhorred the thought of the Vernacular, and who insisted on the tight constraints which could be read from the new Apostolic Constitution, were appalled that the introduction of the Vernacular had simply been postponed to a date in the near future. As Archbishop and Cardinal, Montini had been an imperturbable and effective power-wielder. Now, only a few months into his reign as pope, he seemed beset by a strange insecurity. He was becoming a scarecrow in a gale-force wind, blown this way and that, unable to maintain a firm line.

Michael Cremin, like many young theologians, welcomed *Sacrosanctum Concilium* wholeheartedly. The pope's apparent lack of resolve seemed to them a strength for the Church rather than a weakness. People with forward-looking convictions were not blocked before their time had come, people like the impressive Father Bugnini. But reading with understanding, as he was able to do, Michael saw that *Sacrosanctum Concilium* was remarkable for what it did not specifically say. So much was left hanging in the air for others to clarify, and to oppose each other while doing so. This too seemed a strength rather than a weakness. When he later came to hear of Annibale Bugnini's secret group of experts which had been preparing for the Vernacular long before there was any sign of official approval, it was revealed as no less than the planned outcome.

Active Participation in the Mass. Now it specifically meant including the Vernacular. It seemed obvious. But it wasn't. There had always been papal approval for the Vernacular in the Mass, but only as an exception in special cases. It had not been normative. *Sacrosanctum Concilium* did not make the Vernacular normative, either. Not exactly. Nevertheless, it had obviously been made inherent in the norm of the Rite in some way. It was strange how unreliable the meanings of words were. When Pope Pius X introduced the concept of Active Participation, earlier in the century, he had not been concerned with the Vernacular, at all. He had been writing specifically about church music. It was people like Lambert Beauduin who had connected Active Participation with the Vernacular, recognising the Pope's innovation as grist to their own particular mill. As for church musicians, the ones Michael knew disliked the idea of the Vernacular more than anyone. For them, Active Participation meant the pure sound of trained voices filling silent places with the austere beauty of Gregorian chant. The congregation were welcome to participate actively, of course, but let them get lessons first, and join the choir, if they wanted to sing. That was quite obvious, really.

Michael Cremin was resting in the gardens of the Villa Borghese as he turned these things over in his mind. It was more parkland than cultivated gardens, but it provided a good example, all the same. The general way to participate actively in a garden was to passively enjoy it. Only a few people needed to be gardeners. But there was a deeper issue: the life of prayer. There was the unchallenged assumption that prayer had to be passive. Your body and mind had to be solitary and fixed in one place like you were nailed to a cross. But there wasn't just the cross, was there? What about the Resurrection?

"You're John's friend, aren't you?" someone said.

Michael glanced up from his reverie. It was the girl he had seen at the Piazza Navona. The girl his heart had gone out to when John told him that her mother was ill. She was sitting beside him on the bench. He hadn't noticed anyone sitting down.

"How's your mother?" he asked.

"I haven't got a mother."

Michael wondered what this might mean.

"She's just too sick to be a mother," the girl said. "She can't do anything."

"The Church is our mother, too." The words sounded trite, but Michael hoped that they might help her in some way.

"The Church can't put its arms around you, can it?"

Michael had to admit that this was true. Intrigued, he looked at the girl more closely. Then, carelessly, he caught himself in her eyes. Those eyes were bright, tangled pools you could dive into and never come back up from. Michael blinked a little. Then he got up and went away. He had nothing to say to her. Nothing at all. Those eyes. And that young girl's musk that had quickened his senses with sexual promise. He had not been ready for it. But he was not able to forget. He knew only too well what it meant when there was nobody there to put their arms around you when you needed it. Did this girl need someone's arms around her? His, perhaps? But he was a priest. There was no telling what it might mean for him to put his arms around a girl. He found that the whole thing bothered him. She had stirred him in a way dangerous for him. It bothered him and would not let him go.

By this time, Michael had transferred to a doctoral programme at the Gregorian, which made him largely self-managing. After meeting the girl, he drifted about the city for some weeks, not much able for his usual routines, and with no-one to enforce discipline. He was thinking a lot of the dark-haired and bright-eyed beauty. He wanted so much to be close to her. One day, when he found her at the Piazza Navona, he took a risk and asked her for her name.

"Why should I tell you?" The bright eyes were mocking him.

"It's friendly," he ventured. Even to his own ears, it sounded silly.

"It's not friendly to just get up and walk away, like you did in the Gardens."

"No, I suppose not. Don't tell me your name then. But I'll tell you mine. Michael. Michael Cremin."

Michael began to go red. He had left out his title of Father. Why had he done that?

"I'm Laura Moro," she said, taking his hand, and the look she gave him went straight to his heart. She was a woman. She was mystery. A mystery that could touch him.

Laura Moro agreed to meet with him, and on walks around Rome that grew longer each time, Michael tried to get to know her. She was eighteen years of age and was a dressmaker by trade, but she did not want to work. Laura did not believe in God, but she believed in the Devil. There was no sign of God anywhere, she asserted, but you could see the Devil's power all around you.

"But God is Love." Michael summoned all his conviction. "Do you not believe in Love?" She shook her head, and Michael was overwhelmed with concern.

Each time they met, in a completely natural way, she touched him. A hand on his hand. A hand on his shoulder to brush away some dust. Taking his hand in hers, sometimes, very briefly, not long enough, not often enough. It was completely different from the infrequent handclasps or backslaps which men gave each other. It was feminine, a perfumed wind blowing from a place far distant, a wonderful place. It lifted him like wind in the flagging sail of a slowing ship, and urged him towards where he knew he ought to be. It was the gift that only a woman could give. He returned to his university work with new strength and began to plough through it at an astonishing pace.

One day, some weeks into their friendship, he met Laura as planned and found her quite distraught. Her mother, who had been refusing to let her visit her, had been released from hospital. On arriving home, she had proceeded to have a new breakdown, and had been re-admitted to hospital that very day. The night had been terrifying. Michael took Laura home, and tried to get her to eat something.

It was not the right time, of course, but there could never be a right time. "I think I love you," Michael told her, his heart beating fast.

Laura looked into his eyes. "If you get me pregnant, I'll kill myself."

She undressed and stood shyly in front of him. Michael stared in wonder at the beauty of womanhood that was given to her, and at the secret places, which he looked away from almost immediately. He took her hand and pressed it to his lips. She reached for his mouth with hers. The kiss was awkward, and Michael stepped back from her overcome by nervousness. Then, he went to the door, intending to go. Laura, now half-dressed, met him there. She stared long into his eyes and kissed him on the lips. "I love you, too," she whispered.

Nobody had ever told Michael Cremin that they loved him. Not his mother, not his father, not even Corinna Fielding, and certainly none of his fellow clerics. Not even in his dreams were those words ever spoken to him. It was the love of God he was aspiring to, and how abstract and unreal a love it now seemed.

Love, he had been taught, was Sacrifice and Service. It had nothing to do with sensual enjoyment. It had nothing to do with him, the individual, Michael Cremin, in his earthly reality. There could be no better proof of the emptiness of this teaching than Laura. The intimacy of her lips on his for a few paltry seconds was enough to dispel years of priestly formation like a puff ball in the wind.

Michael chose to believe that Laura was essentially a good person, just as he chose to believe that the love he felt for her was essentially good. But again and again he was forced to reconsider. Laura had a taste for dangerous excesses and she cared for hardly anything that was objectively good, true, or beautiful. Try as he might, she remained more interested in Satan than in God. She refused to go into churches with him, but she would pull him over to the display windows of occult bookshops and gaze in fascination at the strange symbols on the dust jackets of the books. In one of these bookshops, whose owner she knew, she was allowed to bring back the books she bought after reading them, and exchange them for new ones. So, despite her lack of money, she had a constant supply of unhealthy reading. Also, there was no denying that her sexual allure made up a large part of the attraction, and this was troubling for Michael.

Laura's father was from Turin, but she had never known him. He had abandoned the family shortly after she was born. Laura's mother was from Silesia, a part of Germany which had fallen to Poland in the carve-up of Hitler's Reich after 1945. The family, with hundreds of thousands of others, had walked westwards for weeks, with the old and the sick dropping dead beside them, until they arrived at the sparse plains of the River Weser, where they were allowed to settle. Laura's grandfather had escaped to Bavaria, where he shot himself on hearing of the death of Hitler. There was a photograph of him in the flat. He seemed young for the rank of a General of the SS, and he exuded a cold resolve, no doubt fashionable at the time, which Laura thought highly attractive. He had been a believing Nazi up to the bitter end, she told him proudly. Laura herself was Italian, born in Abruzzo.

Michael and Laura began to lie naked together on the sofa or on the bed, and to share tenderness with their mouths and hands. Michael was disconcerted by the pleasure that seemed to come over her with such regularity. Such abandonment to sensuality was fascinating, and he felt admiration for it, even if he could not follow. The hardening of her nipples. The rushes of moistness inside her. Above all, her eyes. They would cloud over, as if they had been smoked from the inside, and would stay fixed on his as her body curved up and down beside him, moaning softly, taken by the slow power all around them.

Then, one evening, he forgot to go home, and they spent the night together in her mother's bed. Tired of resistance, and only half-awake, he put himself inside her, crying out at the sudden snick of entry. She hooked her arms around his neck, urging him deeper and deeper. His climax, when it came, was as close an approximation to Heaven as he had ever imagined.

"Our love is God," Laura remarked, when he had anxiously reminded her of the spiritual realities. And in the crescendos of orgasm, it was hard to think otherwise.

But there was so much that Michael was unable to say to Laura. Their love-making continued to give great pleasure, but that first explosion of joy had not been repeated. He chased it in every orgasm, but it was always just out of reach. Also, the stirrings of his conscience were growing more and more insistent, and he was often miserable. Michael was no longer convinced that celibacy was necessary for the priesthood. The books he was reading suggested that celibacy was only a secondary, external discipline. But he was not sure. He had promised the Church a life of celibacy, and implicitly, he had promised it to God. A promise to God could never be merely external. For a time, this kind of questioning occluded the more concrete matter of Sins against the Sixth Commandment. But the day came when he had to admit the truth. No amount of rationalisation could persuade his shivering conscience that this love-making between him and Laura was right and good. The sexual pleasure began to be a poor compensation.

Shortly after this realisation, Michael discovered that Laura had left him. She did not show up for a rendezvous, and the letters he wrote went unanswered. At a loss, he sought out the occult bookshop she frequented, and asked after her there.

"I know where that one is," came the heavy whisper. The owner had drunk acid once, Laura had told him, and so always spoke in a whisper. He glanced with distaste at Michael's clerical dress. "Ran off about a week ago. With her boyfriend."

Michael forced down a violent reaction. "Thank you," he muttered and turned very carefully towards the door.

"By the way," the voice whispered after him, "she's pregnant."

It was night when Michael returned home to the Irish College. He had spent a while on his knees in his favourite churches, but when that didn't help, he bought a bottle of wine and drank it at the Piazza Navona. It tasted so bad that he poured half of it away. He didn't want to talk to anyone. He went to bed and did not get up for a long time.

The best scenario, no doubt, was that Laura would marry this boyfriend Michael had never heard of before, and bring up the child as a loving mother. She might have the child and give it up for adoption, again not too bad a scenario. Was Michael the father? God alone knew. If she turned up at the Irish College, her infant in her arms, he would work out a financial deal for her with the superiors. This was done from time to time, as it had to be. In return for silence. The ugliest scenarios were the more likely ones, an abortion, suicide, or both. And he couldn't even be certain that the bookshop owner had told him the truth. No matter what, he who loved her was powerless.

It was a truth so painful that it was beyond expression. Michael screamed silently like a heart cut out from a body and impaled upon a battlement, awaiting its dry death in a mocking wind. And roaming in his blood like a poison was the certainty that Laura had betrayed him. Betrayal was a thousand rodents gnawing at his innards, making him break out at times with unspoken and unspeakable rage. Nothing was of any help. Nothing at all.

In his extremity, Michael turned to the Sacrament of Penance. He chose a small Jesuit church on the edge of Rome where no-one could possibly know him. There he opened his soul with complete candour to the old priest in the confessional.

"I can't give you absolution, you know," coughed the priest. "It's such a grave matter, you'll need to go to your bishop. But the crux of it is this: you're not a sincere penitent."

Michael burned with resentment, but he held himself in check.

"You asked for forgiveness like you were a parrot, repeating words you don't understand. That poor girl you seduced, and perhaps put in the family way. What can you ever do to make amends? And all that fleshly pleasure you stole for yourself, can you honestly say to Our Lord that you want things to be as if you never had those pleasures?"

"I can't say I see anything wrong in the pleasure," was Michael's grim response.

"Go to your bishop, Father."

Michael stared at the little wooden slate behind the wire mesh which had just been rapped shut on him. He had been refused Absolution. It was unthinkable. He genuflected deeply, then stormed out of the Church, pushing his way through the summer crowds on the street outside. Trust him to be landed with some conservative old fogy. There were surely better priests.

"There's a priest not far from here" said John Gregory. "He's been known to help people no-one else could help." He and Michael were sitting in John's taxi beside a street-side coffee bar near the Gregorian.

"Anyway it shouldn't be a surprise to anyone, should it? Our Lady told us this 120 years ago at La Salette. And again at Fatima. Wholesale changing of sides to the Devil."

Michael knew that John Gregory had come to disapprove of him. John knew Laura, after all, not well enough to know what had become of her, but well enough not to be neutral in the matter.

"John. I fell in love with this girl, and you think I've changed sides to the Devil?"

John solemnly lifted his paper cup and took a sip of coffee. "Not a great recommendation, is it, Michael? For a priest, I mean."

John was right, of course. But was Michael to lose this friendship now, too?

"What's this priest's name?"

"Clavis."

"How do I find him?"

"It just happens."

8

John Gregory had been careful to park his taxi some distance away and to take Michael Cremin through a maze of narrow alleys before approaching his destination. The young nun who opened the door was courteous and composed, but no more than that. She left them standing in the cold hallway, and they tried not to breathe too deeply of the strong, wax polish that had been scrubbed into the wood of the walls and floor.

"Il Padre will see you." The nuns who looked after the old man called him simply Il Padre. John knew him as Clavis. They had propped him up with cushions on a hard chair in a common room. Both his hands were knotted around his stick. He had a high forehead, with wavy white hair, and a pronounced nose which seemed squashed to one side. He was very thin. His head was sunk deep into the hood of a black cape. It made him look like a Benedictine monk. His voice was warm and musical, rich in overtones, a trifle high-pitched, perhaps, and a little husky.

"Draw the curtains, John, will you, please? I am not as sturdy as good Sister Clara, and the draught is unnecessary."

The taxi-driver did as bidden, and pulled over two chairs. The old man's eyes were deep in their sockets, the skin hung in folds around them, but the eyes themselves were clear, almost young in their freshness.

"Father, I've brought someone to see you. Father Michael Cremin. An Irish student at the Gregorian."

"Leave us, John, if you please."

Michael drew closer to the old man. "I have been unable to receive Absolution, Father. That is what troubles me."

"And are you determined to repent, Father?" The old priest spoke warmly and gently, but his steady gaze was discomfiting.

Michael plucked up the courage to speak frankly. "Father, I broke my vows as a priest. With a girl. But I don't know what you mean by repentance. I have difficulties with the concept. And with the concept of sin, which fails to illuminate this matter."

"To repent means to admit that you are wrong by your own fault, and to implore forgiveness, cleansing yourself with sorrow for what you have done. And Sin, Father is not a concept. It is a refusal. A real one. It is the refusal of God's love for the sake of the worship of self."

Michael felt the shame rise and spread throughout his body, his face turning a deep red. The old man was looking into another world, now. His eyes were bright with pain.

"Father Clavis, sir. I wanted my girlfriend to know the gift of love. I thought I could show her through love how to believe in God."

"It is simple common sense to first stop and see whether such a gift would be welcome. And you, Father, do you want to remain a priest?"

"Of course, Father."

"What is your reason?"

Michael was disturbed by the question. And more disturbing still was his inability to find an answer.

"It is my life," he stammered, finally.

The old priest seemed bowed as if his thoughts were a weight he was carrying. "A priest must struggle to know and serve God. And you cannot attempt this struggle and at the same time be yourself. You have been told this often."

"Father," Michael began, hesitantly, "is the Church not beginning to teach differently through the Council?"

"If so, the Church is wrong."

"May I ask if you are in good standing, Father?"

"I returned my Canonical Mission to the Roman authorities."

Michael tried to fit this irregularity together with what he knew of Canon Law, but he couldn't.

"If you'll permit the remark, Father, you are not a priest in good standing with the Church!"

"If so, it is God's Will." Clavis was inscrutable.

There was really nothing more to say, Michael thought. The old man had a strong presence, but he was a renegade. He did not speak from the heart of the Catholic Church. It would not do to listen to him. Michael turned towards John Gregory. John seemed to have read his thoughts. John's face was clouded, disappointed. Michael felt a sadness growing inside him, but John Gregory had already turned back to the old priest.

"John. The good sisters won't be able to keep me here for very long. Help me to find a place."

"I will, Father."

"A place by the sea."

9

"Clavis?" Pontus Freeman scratched at his neck. "Never heard of him. Sounds like one more priest whose brain has exploded here with the religious heat."

Michael was sitting in a coffee bar with the American journalist. It had probably been a mistake to consult him.

"Can't be his real name, anyway. You know, Michael, appearances are magic mirrors. You look into them, and the last thing you're going to see is any kind of reality."

Michael looked pointedly at his watch, but the American did not take the hint. "Take this Council, Michael. You know what my editor wants back home? He wants a story on the Germans here at the Council. Being one of the world's great geniuses, my editor already knows what's going to be in that story. These German bishops are all former Nazis, see, and this story is going to blow the lid on them. Now, how can my editor know the picture before he's got the facts checked?"

"He can't, Pontus."

It was a fine autumn afternoon, and they were sitting out in the street, shielded from the thoroughfare by the wooden trellis of the cafe.

"I'm tired of it, Father Michael. Tired of making up the truth. Ever wondered what became of Bob Kaiser, the guy writing for *Time*?"

"He went home to write a book, I heard."

"He sure did. And do you know where he finished up? In a psychiatric institution, that's where." Pontus Freeman's voice had grown weaker. "I just can't get it out of my head. Kaiser looked down on me like a piece of trash. Never invited me to his Sunday nights. But I just can't get it out of my head. Do you reckon that Kaiser was ripe for the Largactyl and the electric shocks?"

"It would not seem so from his articles."

"No way. He was saner than all the Vatican put together. Now, do you know who locked Kaiser up in the nuthouse? A guy who was carrying on with Kaiser's wife behind Kaiser's back. That's who. This guy wanted the husband out of the way so he could screw the wife all he liked while the kids were playing with their toys out there in the hallway. So he persuades Kaiser's circle that Kaiser is having a breakdown, and Kaiser's circle persuades Kaiser to check himself into the clinic for observation. Then this seducer gets Kaiser's wife to write to the clinic with the kind of behaviour details that excite the professional interest. So Kaiser gets detained for quite some time. Now Kaiser's wife knows why she's suddenly committing adultery, even though she still loves Kaiser. It's all because of Kaiser's breakdown. So Kaiser's wife and Kaiser's friends think they're doing the right thing by Kaiser, the poor guy having a breakdown and all that. And Mrs. Kaiser turns more and more to the seducer for comfort in her distress. Neat, eh? It's like the early days of the CIA. Good, clean dirt that does the job."

"Poor Mrs. Kaiser, if that's what they are saying about her."

"It was a priest. She fell for a priest. An Irish priest, at that. A Jesuit bag of slime called Malachi Martin."

Michael shook his head in dismay. He knew Dr. Malachi Martin. A biblical scholar, and some kind of factotum for Cardinal Bea at the Institute for the Promotion of Christian Unity.

"What would God's judgement be on that, Father Michael? A seducer priest. And Mrs. Kaiser was pregnant at the time! It sickens me so much that my head's all messed up. I want to get that guy Martin and wring his neck like a squawking chicken. They sicken me, all that gang of liberals and progressives. They sicken me just as much as Ottaviani and his goddam conservatives. You know, it was Bob Kaiser got this Council to work the way it did. They were all in and out of Kaiser's household, enjoying Kaiser's hospitality, talking theology all the time. All the big progressive names. They all knew about Father Martin, all of them. And they all stood back and just watched it happen. All those priests of God. They watched a fellow priest abuse friendship and hospitality. They watched this priest commit adultery with the name of God on his lips. And they watched him destroy the personality of that husband and father."

"No-one tried to help Mr. Kaiser?"

"Not one single voice was raised. And these are the guys who are shaping the Catholic Church of the future. I tell you, if I was God, I wouldn't be turning up in their churches on a Sunday."

Michael shook his head. The American was making him uneasy.

"If you ask me, Michael, it was sort of deliberate. These bishops and theologians got a secret thrill out of watching Martin destroy Kaiser. They're bad men. Those guys won't be satisfied with a bit of Vernacular here and there in the liturgy. Deep down they've got a hunger for the Black Mass."

Michael shivered. But there was something tugging at his memory: a time in Louvain with dark perversions opening out before him. There were such black seeds. Even in priests.

"You mean Satanism?"

"Most of those guys would be totally shocked to hear that word used. They regard themselves as pure as the driven snow. But who needs Satanists? Our guys will just tilt things towards whatever gravitational pull they feel inside them. They're not overly concerned with knowing where that pull comes from, being kind of busy with Justice and Peace, and so on. Michael, I'm not a guy who likes churches, and I've never done much praying, but sometimes when I arrive home I get down on my knees and I beg God to do something, because it's just not right."

"Maybe you're misreading things, Pontus."

"It's a professional assessment. That's why I don't want to go back twenty years in the lives of those Germans and start digging. I'm kind of expecting to be sprayed in the face by a geyser of hot shit. Seek and ye shall find, and all that. I'm not neutral any more. So what do you think, then? About the Germans and their connections?"

Some quality in Pontus Freeman persuaded Michael. A moral force that had not been there before. "I don't know, Pontus. But I'll check it out."

"They want me to come home, son," the journalist continued, sadly. "Now that the Catholic Church is committing hara-kiri at our invitation, I am needed elsewhere. Arizona. There's a whole new religion they're going to start out there. The Jesus People. LSD, sex, and a few simple rules. But I'm just sick of the whole thing. Want to know where I was for a few days last week? Normandy."

"France?"

"A place called Lisieux. You see, one night when I couldn't sleep, something popped into my head. It was a picture postcard of Saint Thérèse. I know, because I saw the same postcard at the station the next day. So totally spontaneously I gave myself a little holiday in her home town. And I got talking to someone about her Little Way. You know what, Michael, it's a clean thing. Her heart is clean and her mind is clean. I never thought I'd ever get away from this filth, but maybe I can."

Michael wished Pontus Freeman well. He did not want to disappoint him about Saint Thérèse of Lisieux.

10

"You may speak, Father Cremin" Archbishop McQuaid was suffering from a slight cold and his voice was hoarse. Michael looked at the disorderly sheaf of notes in his hands. His researches on the Church in Germany had surprised him and confused him, and had then inspired him to take a completely new perspective on things. A decidedly progressive perspective. But he had no idea how to say this to Archbishop McQuaid.

"Father Cremin. Obviously, you cannot read your own handwriting. Not unusual a malady. I gather you have information on certain members of the German Episcopate which you received from a journalist in advance of print. We are pleased to be kept up to date. But please confine yourself to the essentials."

Michael tried. "Your Grace, Holy Church has held herself to be indefectible by the Grace of God. Now, at the Council, many Fathers are asserting that this is not the case, that the Church is, in fact, susceptible to defects, and has at this time many serious defects which are crying out to be remedied. There is a preponderance of the German Church here, Your Grace, and this can be explained historically by the relations between the German bishops and Hitler's Third Reich. In particular, by the shameful inaction of the German Church regarding the evils of Nazism. Complicity is not too strong a word for this, Your Grace."

Dr. McQuaid sat opposite him, distant, but attentive. "Continue, Father."

"In 1933, Cardinal Pacelli had negotiated a Concordat between the Holy See and the Reich. We cannot deny that this Concordat bestowed a form of papal recognition on Hitler's Reich, and this may explain the helplessness of the German bishops in the face of the ugly reality. At Advent, in 1933, Cardinal Faulhaber of Munich felt conscience-bound to condemn National Socialism as completely inimical to Christianity. Yet, this same cardinal could write to his fellow bishops after a meeting with Hitler in 1934 that he was certain the Führer believed in God and belonged to the Christian tradition. Later, it was Faulhaber who provided the first draft of the Encyclical *Mit brennender Sorge*, which Pope Pius XI issued from Rome in 1937. This Encyclical was a very clear condemnation of the false religion of the Nazis. All German Catholics were warned concretely and explicitly of where they stood: they were to choose their personal sanctification against the dictates of the State, quote: "at the cost of every worldly sacrifice." Yet, this same Faulhaber welcomed the Fall of France with as much patriotic fervour as any Nazi. He even ordered a *Te Deum* to be sung in his cathedral when Hitler's life seemed miraculously spared after an assassination attempt. And despite all this, Faulhaber himself was on Nazi assassination lists, not to mention the constant betrayal of interna by informers in his inner circle. After the so-called Reichskristallnacht of 1936, he braved the Nazis by providing a car for the Chief Rabbi of Munich when he had to flee the city. For this Faulhaber was stoned by hired mobs and ridiculed in the press...."

"I had the pleasure of meeting Cardinal von Faulhaber," Archbishop McQuaid broke in. "A man of deep piety, of course."

Michael had noticed the emphasis his superior placed on the "von". He had wanted to avoid that title of nobility, so unbecoming for a priest and a bishop.

"No doubt, he was, Your Grace. But how does all this vacillation seem to us today? He recognized the evil around him. Why did he not take a more consistent stand? He could have officially left Munich that day together with the Chief Rabbi, never to return."

Archbishop McQuaid laughed loudly. "Was he to abandon his diocese and leave his flock to the wolves? You have said yourself that his Chancery was riddled with spies. Who do you think would have taken over in his absence?"

Michael caught his breath. "A German Catholic bishop in those times, Your Grace, was ill-served by the mainstream theology. It rendered him incapable of any effective protest against rightful authority, and this Hitler had been vested with, no matter how evil his use of it. The German bishops had been expressly charged by Pope Pius XI to put a stop to every blasphemy, but any attempt they made was pathetically easy to ignore. Alfred Rosenberg, the Nazi ideologue, was even able to use Church newspapers to distribute his educational pamphlets. Large numbers of the faithful joined the Nazi Party and remained party members until the collapse of the regime, despite the *brennende Sorge* of Pope Pius for their souls. Even some priests were party members."

"Father Cremin." The Archbishop's tone was peremptory. "We Ourselves know only too well how difficult it is to deal effectively with a blasphemous government."

We Ourselves. An Apostolic plural. Something usually reserved for the most solemn occasions and for the pope alone. The tone was decidedly frosty. Michael sighed, and continued.

"Your Grace, the Catholic Church in Germany was able to document cases of martyrdom, where individual Catholics defied the Nazi regime in obedience to their consciences. Bernhard Lichtenberg, for example. When the Nazi euthanasia programme started, Monsignor Lichtenberg wrote personally to the Chief Medical Officer of the Reich, in order to remind him of the sacredness of human life and of his personal responsibility before God as a doctor. In 1935 he appeared personally at the Ministry of Hermann Goering to demand an end to torture in the concentration camp at Esterwegen. He made a point of including prayers for Jews and for other persecuted and despairing persons at his services at the Cathedral in Berlin. He was tortured by the Gestapo, and died on his way to the concentration camp at Dachau. That is how it was, Your Grace. To preach in the name of Jesus Christ meant that you broke the laws in force, with all the consequences."

"Praise God for Father Lichtenberg and his fine example." Archbishop McQuaid brought his hands together in prayer. "But you will have noted that he was not a bishop charged with the care of a diocese? He was free to speak and act as a bishop could never have been. He endangered only himself. And you will have noted the complete and total support he enjoyed from his bishop, Count Preysing?"

"Total support, or token support, Your Grace? But the question is this: if Bernhard Lichtenberg could do it, why were there so few others who even tried? There is one very simple answer: a massive failure of conscience on the part of millions of German Roman Catholics. They were exhorted in their own language by the pope to be ready for every sacrifice, but they were not ready. And their excuse? They were too busy following the orders of rightful authority, just as the Church had always told them to do. Monsignor Lichtenberg and a few others had responded perfectly to the Evil of Nazism, as exhorted to by *Mit brennender Sorge*. But they alone had been able to. They were geniuses, exceptions. So they were not the correct measure. How fruitful it would have been, Your Grace, if the German Church had been able to conceive of Evil in structural terms. Faulhaber and others might then have distinguished more clearly between Authority as God-given and that form of authority shaped by evil men for the purposes of systematic abuse. Your Grace, our Church has forbidden people to read Marxist and Freudian works. But thinkers with sociological and psychoanalytical approaches were able to see through Nazism far better than German Catholics. An 'authoritarian character' has been diagnosed as that psychological weakness which made the Germans so susceptible to dictatorship. But, Your Grace, this 'authoritarian character' is precisely what Catholic education too has always cultivated."

At a sign from his superior, Michael was forced to stop. "I'm almost finished, Your Grace," he said.

John Charles McQuaid looked down at the young priest in front of him. A clever fellow, of course. And he had been making progress. The Archbishop decided that his youth still excused him.

"Father, permit me to correct you. There is no such a thing as Evil that is structural in nature. There is only the personal Evil of individual men and women, who through their ill-motivated actions create structures of injustice and oppression. If you are of the contrary opinion, I advise you to reconsider that opinion at your earliest convenience. Tell me, do you believe that the German bishops collectively chose to ignore the Encyclical of Pope Pius XI?"

"I believe they failed in Holiness, Your Grace, at a time when Holiness was essential."

"You have read *Mit brennender Sorge*, I take it? Then you will be aware that it states very clearly that the only true witness a Christian can bear for Christ in the midst of collective unbelief is by the method of personal sanctification?"

"Yes, Your Grace, but instead of working on their sanctification they were implicating themselves in genocide!"

"Be silent, Father. Tell me, is there ever a time and place in this vale of tears when Holiness is not essential?"

"No, Your Grace."

"No doubt, Father, there will be a time when you will also sit in judgement over me. Poor John McQuaid, you will say. He tried hard to be Archbishop of Dublin, but he was lacking in Holiness when it was sorely needed. No doubt you will be right as regards my unworthy person. But tell me, in whose name will you be judging? In the name of Our Lord Jesus Christ, who told us never to judge?"

Michael felt the strength draining from him. He realised that he was stranded in the middle of a serious mistake, one whose meaning he was not yet able to comprehend.

“You will now continue your historical exposition, Father.”

“I’d rather not, Your Grace.”

“I said, continue.”

Michael swallowed hard, and faced into the inevitable. He clutched his notes as if they could protect him, but his handwriting seemed to blur before his eyes.

“To a man such as Josef Frings, Archbishop of Cologne since 1941, now a central figure at the Council, it must have bordered on a new Revelation as he struggled to help the widows and orphans to keep themselves alive in the rubble of their homes during the bitter winter of 1945 and 1946. The forced labourers from Poland and Russia were moving homewards, leaving a trail of revenge rapes of German women behind them. There were 15 million Germans who had been deported westwards by Poland and Czechoslovakia in a savage act of ethnic cleansing, and who needed a place where they could begin again. Most of the habitable buildings had been requisitioned by British officers, whose main task was to organise the mass shipment of any remaining German resources to Britain. Any German still in any form of a job at the end of the war was deemed a Nazi and was forced into the official Denazification Programme. There he languished, unable to work, while Allied functionaries wore him down with an endless series of questionnaires and interviews. Wherever the Russians held sway, able-bodied males upwards of the age of 11 were transported as forced labour to the Soviet Union. Very few of them returned. All over Germany, the precious harvest of cabbages, turnips and potatoes, which might yet preserve the land from outright starvation, was endangered through a shortage of labour. The massive German industrial conglomerates were being demolished and their assets shipped abroad as reparation payments, leaving behind the curse of unemployment and economic dependency. What had Catholic Teaching to say about all this? With homelessness and hunger, immorality was widespread. Was Frings to make its condemnation a greater priority than the homes and the food? Many millions of marriageable young men had not survived the war. Was he now to discourage mixed marriages as the Church wanted him to, or was he to thank God that there was someone willing and able to start a family, whatever his religion? There was the problem of former Nazi party members and the war crimes tribunals. With a few spectacular exceptions, only the lower and middle ranks were brought to justice. Were these to be scapegoated, while the leaders got off scot free? There was the emergence of the full truth of the Holocaust. Where was anybody to find enough will power to start his life again, if that awesome burden of guilt was imposed on him? By 1946 Josef Frings was a cardinal and the leader of the German bishops. In the case of all ordinary Germans, he declared that any guilt had been well and truly expunged by their sufferings. He re-admitted all those to the Sacraments who were willing to receive them, no matter who they were or what they had done. It is not surprising that a horizontal theology, a theology of the social, would come up alongside the traditional theology of the contact between the individual soul and God. Where simple, everyday human life was so difficult to achieve, its beauty and fragility were all too apparent. An inherent sacramental quality was revealed. The different practices that make up ordinary human life were clearly in and of themselves meaningful, an insight which threw doubt on the traditional interpretations of Original Sin. In his Interventions at the Council, Cardinal Frings has been arguing for a concept of Church as Sacrament. Not the direct, special contact of the individual believer with God as primary in the life of faith, but the permanent, unbroken contact of the believers with each other and with God in the given everyday, by virtue of their being Christians together. Does it not reflect more truly the Teaching of Jesus in the Gospels? The Old Theology was not able to prevent the Holocaust. That theology is equally powerless now in the face of the Arms Race and the threat of nuclear annihilation. Perhaps the German lesson is valid for us all, Your Grace. We are a Church of few saints and very many sinners. Perhaps we are indeed an *ecclesia semper reformanda,* as these Fathers claim."

John Charles McQuaid gave a thin smile.

"Have you decided to become a Protestant?"

"Of course not, Your Grace!"

"The Rahner crowd. The Bugnini people. Are they are your friends?"

"I keep to myself, Your Grace."

"I would hope so. The *ecclesia semper reformanda* is an illusion sown in resentful minds by the devil. It is not the Church that requires reforming, it is the people in it. The Church herself is immaculate, and always has been. This 'horizontal theology' as you call it, this, too, is illusion. As for the doctrine of Original Sin, there has never been, and never will be, the need for a revision. Now, tell me. By what authority have you set yourself up in judgement over the German Episcopate?"

"Your Grace requested that I keep my eyes and ears open, and report useful information from time to time."

"So I did. Open eyes and open ears. Reports. Nothing more."

"I beg You Grace's pardon?"

"You are not aware of any failing? You believe you are simply using the mind that God gave you? Well, then. You shall have time to reflect. We hereby impose upon you an immediate Penance of silence and confinement for twenty-four hours. At this time tomorrow, you will tell Us if the opinions you have aired here today are still your opinions."

Michael retired to his room and lay on his bed for a while, staring at nothing. There was a terrible crushing weight to the Archbishop's displeasure. He felt ill, like he was coming down with the flu.

Confined for twenty-four hours. Penance. Reflection. Archbishop McQuaid had no formal authority in the Irish College, but no one questioned the matter. It was an ironic situation. If Michael chose to leave, he could not be stopped. He could thumb his nose at the priesthood, and walk away, and no one could prevent him.

As the little clock on the rough wooden table ticked away the minutes and the hours, the thought of escape grew more and more attractive. He had every reason to tell John Charles McQuaid exactly where he could stick his idiotic skull-cap and his disgusting amethyst ring. This Penance was simply ridiculous. It revealed McQuaid for what he was: a tyrant; a small man terrorizing his environment, measuring everything by his own mediocrity.

Never did Michael Cremin see more clearly what animated the radicals at the Second Vatican Council. The stomach-turning lip-service to senseless customs and empty formulae. The shameful reliance on Law and on the letter of the law.

The clinging to a pyramidal structure of formal obedience, because anything else would force them to change their lives. The clinging to frozen concepts of other-world perfection, because anything else would force them to go out and actually live. The refusal of experience, because experience meant uncertainty. The refusal of real, bodied, earthy love because the risks of love were too challenging.

One hundredth part of what he saw was reason enough to get out. The Catholic Church was a criminal, unreformable institution, squatting on the Gospels like a thuggish elephant, blocking the way to God.

But Michael's heart sank. He could not leave. He had nowhere to go.

In the morning, somebody left a breakfast for Michael outside his door. Later, the same kind person came again with tea, bread and jam, disappearing before Michael could see who it was. He had just enough time to eat before his summons to Archbishop McQuaid.

While he waited in the ante-room, the sounds of heated argument could be clearly heard from the Archbishop's study. Then, the door was flung open and a huge bull-like man swept past him in a flurry of black and red. It was Cardinal Conway, the new Archbishop of Armagh and Primate of All Ireland, and he was in foul humour. He and Dr. McQuaid were not getting on. McQuaid had once rated William Conway highly, but he was known to disapprove of his indiscriminate networking in Rome. Dr. Conway's circle liked to blame McQuaid for the rift, suggesting that the older man was jealous of Conway's elevation to Cardinal.

Michael entered the room in the hectic wake of the Belfast man, and found Dr. McQuaid seated in an armchair, gazing out the window, the picture of repose. Michael knelt and kissed the Episcopal ring. When he tried to get to his feet, a lordly wave of the hand stopped him. He remained there on one knee, angry, humiliated, but also deeply afraid, like a prisoner about to be beheaded.

"I require only one word from you, Father. Yes or No. Do you wish to maintain the position of yesterday, to wit, that you are in a position to judge the German Episcopate to have been lacking in Holiness?"

Michael swallowed hard. According to what he knew, the standpoint of yesterday was correct. But there could be equally little doubt that it was not for him,

Michael Cremin, to say so.

"No, Your Grace."

"You will hear of my further decisions through Monsignor O'Hare."

"Yes, Your Grace."

"That will be all."

"Yes, Your Grace. Thank you, Your Grace."

11

Meanwhile, in Saint Peter's, it was proving very difficult for the bishops of the Roman Catholic Church to find agreement on what their Church was intended to be. In the debates on *De Ecclesia*, one finely-worked ecclesiological point was blocked by another in chapter after chapter, and the text seemed destined for an unedifying stalemate. Pope Paul VI, believing himself betrayed by theologians he had previously encouraged, imposed a last-minute Preliminary Explanatory Note to clarify the line of interpretation: the Papal Office was to be read as retaining its primacy. If the Council rejected this Note, he threatened, that would be the end of *De Ecclesia*. It was an unusually clear statement for Pope Paul. However, in an inversion of textual logic, this Preliminary Note was appended at the end of the Schema, and never found its way to the beginning, even upon promulgation. The oddly-shaped Dogmatic Apostolic Constitution which emerged carried a familiar title: *Lumen Gentium*. A coinage of the indefatigable Cardinal Suenens, this was the name the Germans had chosen for their own alternative Schema in 1963. *Lumen Gentium*. The Light of Humanity. Inevitably, given its genesis, *Lumen Gentium* was full of contradictions which would have to be reconciled afterwards. But as names do, these title words resolved everything into coherence already. The Church was a light, a safe thing, and a warm and pleasant thing, a thing set there for all human eyes, and whatever else it might shine on, the rough path ahead, for example, or the hard-won strength of the saints, it shone primarily on all humanity on its light-worthy collective journeying through time.

By this time, Michael Cremin was taking much less notice of the work of the Council. On the orders of Archbishop McQuaid, he was serving a time of penance in Saint Damien's, a Ukrainian house of religion in Trastevere. It was a time of austerity and semi-confinement. Every morning, he rose at 5 AM, doused himself with freezing water from a stone jug, which was all he was provided with in that spartan place, and prayed the Divine Office in the oratory with the community. After the frugal breakfast, invariably black bread thinly spread with margarine and a cup of lukewarm herbal tea, he went to the Gregorian. Once out of sight of any possible spies, he headed for a coffee bar, reached for the cache of money he had secreted in his cassock, wolfed down a sandwich and a cup of coffee, and then went about his university work. He was under orders to return quickly to Saint Damien's for the rest of the long penitential day.

At the Gregorian University, the signs of change were increasingly obvious. The tonsures and military-style haircuts sometimes sported an elegant quiff which had been protected from the barber. The students still wore the prescribed garb of their dioceses and congregations, but there was an undone top button here and there that would have brought censure not long before. Young clerics had always told jokes about the Church when they believed themselves unobserved. But the groups of smokers gathered in stairwells and porches had a new scatological tone to their conversation which might once have been deemed sinful. The New Theology was definitely in. Theologians and would-be theologians were abandoning the traditional stringent syllogisms in favour of declared perspectivist approaches which began often enough with themselves, their feelings and their dreams. Little by little, they were discovering Catholic echoes in Marx and Freud, and Freudian and Marxist echoes in the Bible and the Patristic literature. A priestly ideal was being detected in the figures of psychotherapists and Maoist revolutionaries. One or two young men were wondering why they were spending their time on their knees in clammy Roman churches instead of on their feet in a South American jungle, ministering to the true poor.

The Ukrainian monks of Saint Damien's had never heard of such a thing as New Theology. Even Old Theology was a far distant object to them, as was scholarship of any kind. In his first weeks there, Michael used to go looking for people to talk to about theology, but, no-one would talk to him on any matter whatever. Then he went on foraging trips for something to read. But there were no books of any kind, there were not even bookshelves. The Ukrainians were evidently bound to ignorance by some provision of their Rule. Michael could not but admire the cold elegance of this Penance. He had played the role of an expert intellectual. Now, he was kept away from the satisfactions of the intellect, but was not isolated enough to ruin his studies.

The only one who spoke to Michael was the Father Superior. Every day, after returning from the University, this monk took him for a conference of spiritual direction. This consisted of one tedious question again and again, in different guises: "Where is the peace of Christ in your life, Father?" Or, "Why are you not quiet, Father?" Or again, "You have a stormy conscience. Why is that?"

Michael's answer was always the same. "I'm studying hard, Father. I'm studying hard."

At this, the old Ukrainian would simply shake his head, and send him away, to accost him the next day with more of the same. It was unbearable. Particularly because it was true. Michael's life was indeed dry, anxious, and impatient, and it was made all the worse by his resentment of the superior's intrusions. After some weeks, these consultations came to an end. Michael thought at first that the old monk had simply given up on him, but he had, in fact, been taken ill. The priest who took his place had a poor command of both Latin and Italian, and no other common language. The language barrier put these afternoon meetings on a more congenial footing, and Michael was able to relax.

12

The days and weeks at Saint Damien's ran into each other like long silverlines of water into an old puddle. Then, when Michael Cremin crossed the Tiber, one day, having mingled a little among the tourists at the Bridge of the Angels, he found Jean Nordheider waiting for him.

The Suenens-Montini distinction between the Church *ad intra* and the Church *ad extra* had given rise to the controversial Schema XIII, which dealt with the Church and the Modern World. Schema XIII had also received impulses from the Lay Observers. These Observers had been one of the brainwaves of Pope John, and a colourful mix of them, both Catholics and Non-Catholics, had been accommodated in the Aula, close to the speaker's podium and the High Altar. The Non-Catholics among them were the honoured guests of Cardinal Bea's Secretariat for the Promotion of Christian Unity. No expense was spared, and the itinerary included workshops and get-togethers with selected Council Fathers. Many of the Lay Observers were formidable theologians within their own Churches and had an astonishing knowledge of Catholic sacred texts. Cardinal Bea, like Pope John before him, understood the educational value of these get-togethers and of the friendships which emerged.

Michael had suspected that Jean Nordheider was in Rome, and was perhaps involved with the Lay Observers in some way. At times, he had detected what he thought were signs of his presence: a whiff of a certain kind of after-shave in unexpected places, or the aroma of a particular kind of tobacco smoke, again in the oddest places: a railway carriage perhaps, or in the foyer of an art gallery, once even in the foyer of the university.

"You are restless with questions, Michael." Nordheider's face was narrower than Michael remembered. It seemed like a long triangle pointed down at the chin, the eyes darting about inside it with firm purpose. "And what greater blessing can there be for a man who seeks the truth than the inability to rest? Dissatisfaction is a powerful motivator, is it not? Peace is the enemy of progress."

Michael had to smile. It was the rhetorical exaggeration he remembered of old. "How may I help you, Doctor Nordheider?"

"I can help you, Michael."

"I am glad to see you again, sir. But I am a priest now. What help can you give me?"

"Let us grind the coffee bean together, let us push boiling water through the grinds at high pressure, perhaps with a dash of fine spirit to add some bite. Over there, I see!"

They walked towards a nearby coffee bar. It was busy, but they squeezed together at a table, speaking in French for greater confidentiality.

"I cannot think of how you can help me, Dr. Nordheider."

"Communication, Michael. I still remember the day when you delighted my ears with that concept. A song of innocence. Perhaps it is now a song of experience? Let us simply be in communication. You have heard of Schema XIII, of course? A great event. The Catholic Church is at last reading the signs of the times. And this reading of the signs is changing the Church beyond recognition!"

"Why are you so concerned, Doctor?"

"A pattern is being completed. I take an aesthetic pleasure in such things. It is like raising Karl Marx from the dead and making him a cardinal. There is daring to it. And style. We are in dialogue, are we not?" He squinted over his espresso as he slurped. "As equals, of course," he added, clattering the little cup in the saucer. "Can there be dialogue without the equality of opposites?"

"No doubt you have the answer up your sleeve."

"Of course! Shall I show it to you?"

Jean did. He had taken up a residency of some kind at a private library on the Palatine Hill. There, in a room made long by the high shelves of ancient volumes and a vaulted roof, he took Michael under his wing once more.

"Pythagoras, Michael, as you know, held the belief that all was number." The sunlight was slanting through the narrow windows, drenching the long mahogany table in an impossible light. "To see the essence of entities as given by number! What delectation of the mind that must have been! To have before one the order and the beauty of all that is, seeing it as a harmonious whole, recognizing the principle of that harmony, to have the means of exploring that principle without let or hindrance. It is a form of Paradise, is it not?"

Nordheider waited for Michael's assent. "And then, Michael, along came Incommensurability. Legend has it that Hippasus of Metapontum was on a sea voyage with some fellow Pythagoreans. Hippasus had plotted a dodecahedron sphere, which, as you know, consists of 12 regular pentagons. At the centre, a new pentagon is formed, and he showed his brethren that one can begin there again, ad infinitum. He was using the old craftsman's method of mutual subtraction. Hippasus showed his brethren that there was no numerical way of expressing the ratio of diameter and side of pentagons in this sphere, because in the numerical system known to them, such a number was simply impossible. And Michael, what do you get when you draw out the lines of a pentagon so that they intersect? You get the pentagram, which was a sacred symbol of the Pythagorean Brotherhood. Just imagine it: there in the geometrical negation of all they believed in was their own holy symbol, again and again and again. How the skies must have fallen! It is impossible to see a Great Theory disintegrating, Michael. There are no explosions, no bloodied corpses, no widows, no orphans.

So Michael, they put the scoundrel to death. Like a sign from God, a fierce storm came upon them and his fellow Pythagoreans threw Hippasus overboard."

"The situation must have been comparable to High Treason."

"But this treason consisted in a discovery of the truth. Surely if one is committed to the truth, then even a truth that makes a ruin of a lifetime of supposed knowledge must be welcomed with open arms?"

"Of course."

"And the refutation of every new truth, too, ad infinitum?"

"Of course."

"So you are saying that truth lies in permanent revolution. That the strongest moral character is one who assents to permanent revolution?"

"Am I saying that?"

The soft wood of the long library seemed to come alive with sounds. The rapping of old wood straining against the shifts of weight and humidity. From outside came the loud crack of a tile as a little plant forced its way through in the struggle to grow, the staggered whistle-chatter of a family of cicadas. Jean Nordheider raised his voice to retain Michael's attention.

"It would seem that you are. And if we seek that out of which truths and their refutation; objects and their negation, emerge, surely it is not a new discovery we come to; but a formative power, the power behind all discovery of objects, behind their making and placing. This power is surely the power of assent; working in us and through us."

It was odd, Michael thought, that Jean would lead him so easily to the answer he wanted to hear. It must be to reach him in some way. The sudden music of the library forgotten, Michael answered, giving the lecturer his full attention.

"The Will to Power, Jean."

Nordheider leaned forward, speaking intensely. "Precisely, Michael. The Will to Power. It is as inevitable as a sunrise. Reality is not a seamless garment. There is no stitch that cannot be unstitched and re-stitched. There is nothing combined that cannot be recombined in a different way. And the seams in the garment are flaws. What binds separates. Eternally. A Man of Power is a Man of Flaw. Flaw is power. Does God exist, Michael? He does and He does not. He is the Architect of Flaw, He is Flaw Itself. And He needs us to bind Him through His becoming. Force on Force."

"I disagree."

"How glad I am that you disagree, Michael. We are the sum of our disagreements. All that is, is the disagreement of what was before. Is that not God, that moves invisibly through our disagreements, and like a lion trapped in a cage, awaits the fullness of His Antithesis?"

"And where is Love?"

" You still believe in Love? After all that you have seen?" Nordheider smiled and let his gaze wander around the bookshelves. His eyes were almost kind as they came to rest on Michael, taking in his calm, alert, posture, his agile mind, still ingrained with the longing for Love. "And have you put Love to the test?"

"I believe so."

"And has Love satisfied you?"

To his dismay, Michael was not able to answer.

Among other things, Jean Nordheider introduced the young priest to the vexed question of the real teachings of Jesus, which had been opened up anew by the archaeological discoveries at Nag Hammadi in Egypt and at Khirbet Qumran near the Dead Sea.

"To me, Michael, the Christian teaching has always been a desiccated and enervating teaching. A teaching unworthy of anyone with healthy self-respect. But perhaps I must look again. There may well be a Jesuan Gnosis, an impressive theurgy of self, which has been lost to us. And the Essenes? Clearly, they were far more important at the time of Jesus than anyone realised. Is it not strange that the New Testament does not mention them at all? Especially when there are such obvious parallels between the New Testament books and the Qumran writings. Perhaps all references to Essene teaching were expunged by the right-thinking copyists so beloved of Catholic education!"

"If they were ever there, Jean!"

"If they were not there, perhaps they should have been there."

"You are saying ...?"

"Yes, Michael. To protect the Church. That is to say, to protect that concept of the Church which the power holders had determined should be true. We see it again today at the Council, do we not?"

Michael conceded that this was true. The Conservatives at the Council promoted a pyramidal, juridical concept of the Church. The Progressives promoted the alternative concept of a pilgrim, penitent and pentecostal Church. Both factions appealed to Jesus of Nazareth for legitimation. But the Jesus each of them appealed to was barely recognizable after 1800 years of contested hermeneutics.

"The Church, Michael," thus Jean had summarized the matter, "is an institution of formation like any other powerful organisation. Like the State. The Military. The Enterprise. And its aim? It is to create a form of self. The Military is not there primarily to fight wars, but to make possible the emergence of a Great Warrior. The Church exists to prepare the way for a Great Servant of God, to make a Great Servant possible, so to speak, by forming his mind, body and character, by giving form to his earthly existence, effective form."

"So you do believe?"

"I believe as an enlightened man believes. In life and in the power of life. Hoping to turn its natural blindness towards what is good."

"And God's Grace?"

"There is no such a thing, Michael. But there is the belief in such a thing. And we can make use of belief. That is the meaning of this Vatican Council. Belief in God and in the Church has created a reservoir of goodness. It is time to open the gates and let the waters flow, to fertilize the land and to help feed the populace. And the means? The means is communication, Michael. Bringing together the incommensurables in the act of speech. The creation of a common framework which is permanently evolving. New seams in the garment. Again and again."

"Amazing, Jean."

But Michael was not telling Jean Nordheider everything. It had occurred to him while they were speaking that incommensurable statements were not brought together in the way Nordheider wanted him to accept. That was no more than juxtaposition. The true remained true and the false remained false. The only true common element was Love, if it was present. The greatest incommensurability of all was that of God and His Fallen Creation. This unimaginable gulf had been bridged by the Love of God for that Creation, and the possibility given to created beings to answer in kind. And this great truth, far more valuable than any insights into number handed down from the Pythagoreans, had been preserved by the Church despite the hermeneutic uncertainties that beset her.

Michael Cremin returned to Saint Damien's with his mind changed. He no longer despised the Roman Catholic Church. He no longer hated himself for being one of its priests. He had seen the potential once again. For all its corruption, the Church still had something essential to offer: a wise compromise between Man as he was and Man as he should be. It was a far cry from the goodness of Jesus of Nazareth. But that was a mythic goodness; vision, inspiration rather than reality. Yes, it would indeed be possible for him to flourish within this venerable institution. The progressive victory at the Council was a certainty. A new Church was coming. A Church that would honour the full sin-sodden reality of human life. A Church of genuine solidarity with human striving in all its brokenness. In the new Church, it would be easier for him to find his own way.

For the remainder of his time of Penance, Michael worked on his doctoral dissertation. Its theme was the possibility of a theology of communication. In the submitted version, he confined himself to a critical reconstruction of Kerygmatic Theology, which had been developed at Innsbruck in the 1930s by Josef Jungmann SJ, now an aging Council peritus. With its recourse to Augustine and Aquinas, Michael's thesis was deemed a competent piece of work, respectful of established authorities while remaining open to new advances, commendably modest in its conclusions, and above all, uncontroversial. So it seemed. He had had to prune his text to comply with faculty demands, crossing out one inspired passage after another, feeling as if he was cutting out hunks of his own flesh to throw to the rubbish. He had then felt a strong need to rewrite certain sections with an eye to variant readings in the future. He would leave a few seeds in place, he thought. Healthy seeds of the new, and like all new life, potentially subversive. It was the appropriate answer to the puling anxieties and the narrow horizons of his professors. If a dialogical theology was essential to the Church, it meant a permanent revolution of Dogma and Catechetics, whatever qualificatory clauses were demanded of him to pretend otherwise. It was Michael's hope that this would prove a permanent revolution of Love.

That autumn, after an uneventful defence of his thesis, Michael was awarded the degree of STD, Doctor of Sacred Theology. The Irish College marked the occasion with a glass of sparkling wine after dinner and a formal speech of congratulation by a proud Monsignor O'Hare. Michael's dissertation, 350 pages of dense Latin prose bound in imitation leather with gold lettering, lay on a side table for people to admire. It subsequently disappeared into the limbo of university libraries, destined to be read by few.

13

On December 8 1965, the Feast of the Immaculate Conception of the Blessed Virgin Mary, Pope Paul VI solemnly declared the Second Ecumenical Council of the Vatican to be concluded. A Fourth Session had brought the weary Council Fathers to Rome one more time. They had approved two new Apostolic Constitutions, one dogmatic, *Dei Verbum*, dealing with the nature of Divine Revelation, and one pastoral, *Gaudium et Spes*. This Pastoral Constitution dealt specifically and exhaustively with the Church as a permanently evolving Church in dialogue with the world in which she found herself. This made a total of 16 Acts of the Apostolic See which stated anew the nature of Roman Catholicism in their time. Soon there would be no other light in which the Catholic Church might be able to see herself but that well-crafted light which was shone backwards and forwards, inwards and outwards, by the Spirit of Vatican II.

However, it was not these complex Latin texts, but the images and symbols of the Council era, shot around the world at lightning speed by the media, that bore the effective message. Hundreds of bishops, archbishops and cardinals standing around aimlessly in Saint Peter's Square in October 1962, waiting impatiently for their drivers, wondering how the first general congregation of their Ecumenical Council could end in disarray after only 20 minutes. Pope John XXIII imparting a blessing to the atheist daughter of the Soviet leader, Khrushchev, as if to include her and the Communist regime she represented in the love of Holy Church. Pope Paul VI in Syria together with the Orthodox leader, Patriarch Athenagoras I of Constantinople, and their joint lifting of the mutual excommunications dating from 1054. Paul VI in Saint Peter's in September 1964, taking off his Tiara, the jewel-studded triple crown of the popes, and announcing to the congregation that he was donating it to the Poor. Paul VI in New York in October 1964, announcing to the United Nations its "solemn moral ratification." And there at the U.N., Paul's strange decision to remove his Pectoral Cross, the symbol of his apostolic office of bishop, and to allow it to be auctioned to the highest bidder. And again, Pope Paul's gift of a Golden Rose to the shrine of Fatima as a token of the Church's esteem for the Blessed Virgin Mary.

"As if Our Lady cares a whit about gold!" Augustine Hogan, for one, felt strongly about this matter. His teacup clattered angrily in its saucer, and there was an unhealthy reddish hue on his cheek.

Timothy McGovern finished his slice of toast before giving a nod of assent. "The pope isn't getting it right any more. Maybe he never did. All that recognition for the United Nations. It looks like pandering to fashion to me."

"Remember that business about the Pectoral Cross last year? When he wanted it sold to the highest bidder at the U.N.? Like some decrepit old alcoholic selling his wedding ring so he can buy a few drinks!"

"That was sold for the poor, Tim!" someone insisted.

"You'll look hard at the U.N. for any poor. The only poor around there are the ones they won't let inside the door. Listen, if the pope was so weighed down by his Pectoral Cross, why didn't he take it off in a Church like a man of God instead of at the bloody U.N.?"

"Exactly." Gus Hogan smiled at his unexpected ally. "He could have brought that Cross to Our Lady of Fatima instead of a ridiculous golden rose!"

"He did it for the world, Gus. For Justice and Peace!"

Gaudium et Spes had some fine things to say about solidarity with the struggles in the world for Justice and Peace. Yet, when the translations appeared in the different languages, theologically literate readers found many surprises. Where the Gospel of Saint Matthew (22: 35-40) records Jesus as saying that the "greatest and the first commandment" is that "you must love the Lord Your God with all your heart, with all your soul and with all your mind," *Gaudium et Spes* asserts that "love for God and neighbour is the first and greatest commandment." Was *Gaudium et Spes* disallowing a difference between love of God and love of neighbour? A bold and daring interpretation, no doubt, and perhaps a better view of things than the old view. But Michael Cremin was not alone when he wondered how they had managed to loosen themselves from the approved words of the Gospel. Not a few priests were startled by phrases which obscured the hitherto unquestioned distinction between the natural order and the supernatural. When *Gaudium et Spes* spoke of the "obligations of conscience," it spoke of them as the obligations of individual men towards themselves and their social setting, avoiding reference to God, Who up to then had been thought to speak in all the obligations of Conscience. When *Gaudium et Spes* stated that all human activity "takes its significance from its relationship to man [...] and is ordered towards man" it again saw no need to refer to God, towards Whom Catholic Teaching had always regarded human activity as ordered. The defenders of the text were quick to point out that of course God was presupposed, and always to be understood as included in such a formulation. But to include God in such an offhand way was to orient the text away from Him. Gus Hogan, for one, was heard to say that *Gaudium et Spes* gave a blatant two fingers to the Almighty.

Michael Cremin was not unduly worried by the text. He believed the fears of the creep of heresy to be both justified and unjustified. Justified, because the text manifestly contradicted many time-honoured teachings, even if its supporters did not like to say so. Unjustified, because the text did not seek to supplant the old teachings, as such. These were left standing in their accustomed validity. They were simply no longer standing alone.

It was no surprise to Michael when he heard that Jean Nordheider had indeed played a role behind the scenes in the drafting of *Gaudium et Spes.* The text was a good example of what Nordheider had termed Flaw. The logical connectors in *Gaudium et Spes,* for example, gave the impression of a coherent document, but it was not a coherent document. The ideas cohered by virtue of nothing other than the will to make them cohere, and by the grammatical expression of that will. But by virtue of the promulgation, by virtue of the speech acts of papal law-making, they did indeed cohere in the world of post-conciliar Catholic

Theology. Catholic reality had been changed. It was no longer uniform. It was now pluralist and contradictory. And perhaps the better for it. Now there would be an end to the shaping of reality by autocratic moves from on high. There would have to be dialogue between the different possible positions. It all pointed to some richer unity in a distant future.

By this time, Michael Cremin was a welcome guest in the circles of progressive young theologians in Rome. Many of these believed *Gaudiam et Spes* to be a great document of liberation and the crowning achievement of the Council. The old dualism of the Church and the World was a thing of the past. A creative tension had entered mainstream Catholic theology. The healthy clash of perspectives was now welcome.

Six years before, Michael had followed Jean Nordheider's advice and had struggled to understand something of Friedrich Nietzsche. Now, this philosopher's perspectivist and vitalist kind of thinking, right or wrong, was everywhere. The human potential movement, which the American theologians were so enthusiastic about, seemed full of Nietzschean echoes, even if they were unacknowledged. Michael's French friends pointed out that De Lubac, Daniélou and other proponents of Nouvelle Theologie openly admitted their debt to Nietzsche. And the influential Karl Rahner looked straight back to Nietzsche, if not directly, then certainly through his teacher, Martin Heidegger. What foresight Jean Nordheider had had.

14

In the period following the solemn conclusion of the Council, Dr. Michael Cremin received a letter from Cardinal Conway of Armagh, who had been a member of the executive body for implementing the Constitution on the Liturgy, the Consilium, since the previous June. He had recommended Michael for a position with the Consilium. Michael was not the only young theologian to whom Conway had offered preferment. The year before, he had won another up-and-coming Dublin priest, Dr. Dermot Ryan, for the same Curial body.

It was a wonderful opportunity. It would mean the end of Michael's time of servitude in Dublin. He would be placed at the guiding centre of the changes that were sweeping through the Church. There was no limit to where he might go. Invigorated by the news, he went out for a brisk walk through the streets around Saint John Lateran. Caught by a shower of rain on turning back, he was hurrying up the stairs to his room hoping to change his wet clothes in time for Vespers when a messenger found him. Archbishop McQuaid wanted to see him.

Michael towelled his hair, donned fresh clothing, secured a fresh Roman collar, and dashed down the stairs. The Archbishop's quarters were in turmoil. Underlings were hurrying about in confusion. Dr. McQuaid was sitting weakly in a chair, his face haggard. A glass trembled in his hand. Beside him, a doctor was quietly putting order on his equipment.

"Thank God Your Grace is well," Michael said, appalled at the sight.

"I am of no account, Father Cremin. Tell me. You are the last of my priests I'll be leaving in Rome. What am I to say about this Ecumenical Council? Has anything changed for us?"

"It's hard to say, Your Grace."

"Is it?"

"Your Grace, the Council has most certainly changed things for all of us. But it would be hard to say that the substance of the Faith has been changed. As Pope John said, it's the same teaching in new forms."

"New forms, Father Cremin? I have been reading *Gaudium et Spes*. Can I say before God that I believe it to be good Catholic teaching? Everything essential is in there somewhere. But it is mixed up with things that no Catholic should ever be asked to accept. Do these admixtures change anything?"

"It would be hard to say, Your Grace."

"Father Cremin, I now have difficulty in speaking clearly. It is the inability to be clear which is robbing me of my strength. I have a duty to speak clearly to the people of Ireland. And I cannot. I have always spoken clearly. There has never been the possibility of a doubt as to what my words have meant. Now I cannot speak clearly. I simply do not know what to say. I have always known what to say. But now I do not. The people of Ireland require it to be stated to them in the clearest possible terms what this Council has meant and will mean. What am I to say?"

At this moment of destiny, John Charles McQuaid was little more than a trembling old man. His voice was cracked and his once bright eyes were clouded with fear and worry.

"Father, not long ago, I said to the people of Ireland that because of this Council nothing had changed or would change, because the Church does not change. Was I wrong?"

"I'm afraid, you were, Your Grace."

"Leave me, Father."

The next morning, Michael received a letter signed by Benno Cardinal Gut, the new Prefect of the Congregation of Rites. It was a letter of appointment to a staff function at the Congregation with duties at the Consilium. He would be working for the most famous liturgical reformer of all, Annibale Bugnini CM, whom Pope Paul had chosen to head the Consilium. But there was a catch to it: Gus Hogan had been appointed to the same section in the Congregation, and Michael would be working directly under him. It was not in Gus's nature to welcome radical changes. But Michael put aside his misgivings. A new Mass was to be created. A whole new Church was in the making. And no amount of Gus Hogans could prevent it. He, Dr. Michael Cremin, would be there at the centre, making it happen. It was a wonderful opportunity, more than he could ever have hoped for.

The next day, Michael was summoned again to the Archbishop's presence. This time, the skull cap was balanced perfectly on his head, and his bishop's attire was secured around him like battle armour. When the Episcopal ring was thrust out to be kissed, there was a peremptory impatience in the gesture that Michael knew of old. Dr. McQuaid was himself again.

"Father Cremin! You may be wondering why I have released you from my service for a position here in Rome with the Curia. I have taken this step for two reasons. The first is that Professor Augustine Hogan will be your immediate superior. You will therefore be prevented from making any serious mistakes. And secondly, you will always remember where your loyalties lie. I will have use for you in this Consilium. The Constitution on the Sacred Liturgy is in danger of being implemented in defiance of our great Catholic Tradition. You will help to nip this in the bud."

"I will always do my best, Your Grace."

"Father, yesterday you claimed that I was wrong to say that because of the Council, our Faith has not changed. Father Cremin, it is you who are wrong."

This was not quite what Michael had said. He wanted to point this out, but the fiery, regal glint in the Archbishop's eye quelled him before he could speak.

"We require you to take dictation. You will write down what We say and you will arrange for a typed script of Our words for Our correction before Our departure for Ireland."

"Does Your Grace not wish to ......"

A wave of the Archbishop's hand brought silence. "There will be dictation. There are writing utensils on the table, as you can see. I trust Father has mastery of pen and ink? And has come with his ears open?"

Michael Cremin looked into the sardonic eye of Dr. McQuaid. He wanted to protest, but thought better of it.

"Begin as follows. No. Start again, will you? A new sheet? Good. Let us begin:

You may have been troubled by much talk of changes to come. Allow me to reassure you. No change will worry the tranquillity of your Christian lives......"

The words that Michael Cremin took down for John Charles McQuaid were to become a famous sermon, and later, a celebrated Pastoral Letter which was widely read all over the world. Troubled traditionalist Catholics were persuaded for a time that their disquiet over the Council was groundless. Progressive Catholics took heart from the apparent affirmation of the new Council teachings. But, in reality, John Charles McQuaid had no intention of affirming any new teachings of the Council. Neither had he any intention of not affirming them. He would simply act as if there were no new teachings to affirm. Many conservative bishops were taking the line that the Second Vatican Council had been a purely pastoral Council. Pope John and Pope Paul had said precisely this. Therefore, whenever a teaching of Vatican II gave the impression of being a new teaching, it was not, in fact, a new teaching, but merely an unfortunate choice of words, which was to be passed over and forgotten. Skilled interpretive work was required, of course, but the Ecumenical Council would be ignored as much as possible. Above all, Archbishop McQuaid would not have to take a clear position of dissent, nor call into question his concept of blind obedience to ecclesiastical authority. And he would never have to admit that he had been wrong.

In that spacious and well-ordered room, the tall windows open to the chilly Roman air, an image flashed into Michael's mind: the image of a funeral pyre. Consigned to the flames was the Roman Catholic Church as he and his Archbishop had known her. For a brief moment, the image flared in him commanding his attention. The Church was a dying star floating on a sea of sadness. But being afraid of his superior, and being too compromised already by his own assent to what was coming, he ignored the warning. And that cold, heartless night in Rome was the last time that Michael Cremin saw John Charles McQuaid alive.

†

4

The Official of the Roman Curia

1

In the Papal Hospice of Saint Martha, where the Consilium had its headquarters, Augustine Hogan and Michael Cremin shared an office which looked out over a narrow Vatican alley and the unassuming front door of a division of the Apostolic Chancery. When the New Mass came, and the Consilium merged with the restructured and renamed Congregation of Rites, they remained there with their shelves of files, their palm trees and their unresolved dilemmas.

It was the nature of the time, of course, but in Gus's view, there had been far too much conflict between them. Conservatives and progressives were at each other's throats, in Rome, as elsewhere, but things need not have been as bad as they were, not in their office, at least. Gus had always trusted Michael. In some ways, that had been the easy option, because Gus was in bad health. Tuberculosis. He had had a short bout of it in his youth, and the doctors were confident that he would beat it this time, too. It meant, though, that his duties tired him more than could have been expected, and he had needed to rely on Michael for many things. Not that there should have been cause for concern. Michael was clever and efficient. Lercaro und Bugnini, the powers in the Consilium, were impressed by him. They had even made him a Monsignor. Michael had been too young for such an honour, in Gus's view, but they had not consulted him on the matter, which rankled a little. Still, Michael was one of their own, a Dublin priest, like himself. That meant a lot to Gus in the cold labyrinths of the Roman bureaucracy. Even so, looking back over their time together, he found himself wondering if his trust in Michael had not been misplaced.

Late in 1969, when the work on the New Mass was almost done, an elderly woman from Ireland who was on a pilgrimage to Rome had come to Gus's attention. Alma Courtney was her name. In Saint Peter's Square one morning, she had been shocked to find that the water in the Bernini fountain had been stained with a blood-red dye. It was an act of vandalism, perpetrated in one of the holiest places on earth. Then, someone had pressed a pamphlet into her hand:

Romans! Today the Holy Mass has been put to death. The waters of Rome are turning red, just as the waters of Egypt turned to blood.

On that same day, Pope Paul's New Mass, the *Novus Ordo Missae*, the codification of the Rite of the Mass in the Vernacular, had come into force. Troubled by that blood-red water, Mrs. Courtney had written to the Vatican, demanding an audience with Monsignor Bugnini, who was known as the principal architect of the New Mass. Her letter had been passed to Gus Hogan. Gus had asked Michael Cremin to deal with it, resolving to meet the woman very briefly himself before her return to Ireland. Mrs. Courtney came early for the appointment. With growing indignation, she repeated what young Monsignor Cremin had told her. Gus tried to calm her, but failed. Respectful of the burden she was carrying, Gus sat back and gave her room to speak.

"We're not ruining the Mass," was the first thing Michael had said to her. They had met at the Bernini fountain, which was its normal colour again, and Michael had ushered them across Saint Peter's Square towards Saint Martha's, talking all the time. "You see, Mrs. Courtney, the New Mass is experiential. We're all at the table of the Lord together doing our thing. We've brought the Mass up to date."

"You might as well try to bring the sun, moon and stars up to date as the Mass," she told him. "It's plain nonsense."

"We've gone back to our original inspiration. Back to the early Church. To when they were trying to make the mysteries of the Faith intelligible for the first time. That's where renewal comes from. The source."

A short distance away, between Saint Peter's Basilica, the Camposanto Teutonico and the Palace of the Holy Office, heavy construction work was taking place. Work was also being done to the Basilica itself, and had been for some years, with unwanted annexes, and irregular protuberances being taken down. The noise of machinery was oppressive, and the air was full of the dust of collapsing masonry.

"And is this where you got the inspiration?" she asked. "In this unholy din? Would you not have wanted more peace?"

Michael ignored the remark and tried to explain something of the structure and tasks of the Consilium.

"Who worked for this Consilium, Father?" she broke in, wrinkling her nose. "Was there anybody who knows what things are like in a normal Catholic parish?"

"The bishops. The voting members were bishops. They had the pastoral experience."

Mrs. Courtney laughed out loud. "Young man, the bishops I know are far too busy for pastoral work. And they wouldn't be much good at it, either. But was there anyone there in that Consilium whose main work as a priest was dealing directly with ordinary Catholics? You're saying there was? Well, can I have their names?"

Inside the building, Michael procured a list of the personnel structure of the Consilium. He intoned the sonorous names as his finger found them: Cardinal Agagianian, Cardinal Bea, Cardinal Confalonieri, and so on, and then down through the archbishops, bishops, monsignori, and priests. They were famous names, many of them, but they were experts in different things, not simple pastors. At the name of Romano Guardini, Michael paused for a moment. Guardini had been renowned as a pastor. But his finest hour had been with the radical German youth movement fifty years previously, which wasn't the kind of experience Mrs. Courtney had in mind. Clearly, despite the repeated claims to the contrary, wide pastoral experience had not been a strength of the Consilium.

"Anyway," Michael continued, trying to rescue the matter, "there's no such a thing as ordinary pastoral experience. People are different. Places are different. You have to be creative. And no-one has experience of the new ways, because they're new."

"And that's what you call going back to the source, is it? Is that what the Apostles were like? Experimenting around the place as the fancy took them?"

Michael threw up his hands at such obduracy. "Madam, please, we're finding out new things about the early Church almost every day! History, archaeology, new methods of textual criticism. It's opening our eyes."

"Monsignor," she began again, with sharpness. "Who's saying to you that the original inspiration is lost, when every day for centuries everywhere in the world the bread and wine were consecrated in the exact same way at Holy Mass with the exact same words in the same Latin language? The inspiration couldn't ever be lost."

To his credit, Michael Cremin had tried to be patient. "We weren't true to the inspiration, Mrs. Courtney. We're only seeing this now. Through the advances in secular knowledge. The world has moved on faster than we have. It knows more than we do about some things. We have to be open to it."

"Catch up with the world, is that it? Have you ever stopped to have a good look at what you're catching up with? And what you're opening us all up to? The world belongs to the Devil; surely they taught you that in the seminary?"

"That is language. Symbolism. We need to look carefully at what it means for us today."

"I'll tell you what it means. Two world wars in the last fifty years alone. Millions and millions killed and maimed. The Holocaust. The famines in Africa. The Atomic Bomb. That's the world. And when you've finished catching up with it, there'll be no Church left."

"Madam, we can't turn our back on the march of history. We've been doing that for centuries and it hasn't worked."

"And what exactly didn't work, may I ask?"

"Our way of teaching, for one thing. The Mass is a good example. The faithful didn't understand the Mass in Latin. And the old Rite of the Mass prevented them from proper active participation."

"Father, I made my First Communion close on seventy years ago. Almost every day since then I have assisted at Holy Mass. Do you think that I am some kind of an idiot? Do you want to suggest to me that I spent 70 years on my knees having no interest at all in the meaning of what was happening in front of me? No possibility of knowing what it means? I can read, Monsignor Cremin. And

I had a Missal. With the Latin on one side and English on the other. How many times do you have to read a line of Latin in the Missal before you cop on what the English for it is? How often do you have to read the English before you understand it? And when something was too hard for me, I asked questions of the priests in the parish and I got straight answers."

"But Madam, there were many, many people who did not understand the Mass!"

"They were the ones who didn't care. And they'll never understand, no matter what language you give them."

Augustine Hogan looked across the coffee table at Mrs. Courtney. They were in the visitors' parlour on the ground floor. She was shaking her head so violently that the rest of her shook with it. It was as though she were shaking off a piece of clothing that was being tried out on her against her will. No, Michael had not dealt with her questions in the right way. Like so many other things he had been entrusted with. But what was the right way?

"Monsignor Hogan." She leaned over to emphasise her words. "The only answers that young man has are for the wrong questions."

Now Gus sensed what the matter was. He sensed it, but he could not put it into words. Not yet.

"I'm sorry that we've disappointed you, Mrs. Courtney."

She relaxed a little. "What's going on in the Church, Monsignor? What's wrong with us all?"

"You can put your mind at rest, Mrs. Courtney. The Lord said to Saint Peter: you are the rock. On you I am building my Church, and the gates of Hell will never prevail against it. We can take comfort from that."

She had brought her grandson with her, a little boy of ten or eleven, who was called Isaiah. The boy was sitting solemnly in his little grey waistcoat, dark tie and short trousers. Gus found himself growing sorrowful as he looked at the child. He had been with his grandmother that day with Michael. What example of the priesthood had Michael shown him? Gus wanted very much to spend time with Alma Courtney and her grandson, but there was no more time to be found.

2

Early in 1971, Augustine Hogan left Rome for a Swiss sanatorium, hoping to find solace there for his ravaged lungs. The Congregation for Divine Worship, as their division of the Curia was now called, would get on just as well without him, he was sure. They had Michael Cremin to run their little section of the Congregation, which oversaw part of the approval process for the translations of the texts for the Mass. They insisted on keeping Gus as the nominal head of the section, but it was not out of any sense of decency.

Gus had always loved Rome. He had loved the Church and had loved sacrificing himself for the Church, but now he was glad to get away. The past five years had sucked all the breath from his body. Perhaps this was God's way of telling him that his life was coming to an end.

It had all begun well enough. But in a way the signs had been there all along. Gus wanted so hard to understand. He began making the effort to understand, puzzling things out from his memories, jotting down tentative conclusions, trying to see things with the eyes of Jesus Christ, his dearest friend. He tried again and again, facing down the bouts of despair that choked him as much as the breathlessness, and he found that it gave him strength. Gus became able to leave his bed in the sanatorium for short periods. Soon he was able for short walks in the beautiful mountain air.

Tres Abbinc Annos was the lodestone that pulled things into line. This was the Second Instruction on the Proper Implementation of the Constitution on the Sacred Liturgy, which he and Michael Cremin had helped to prepare in 1967. All over the world, the wildest liturgical excesses had befallen the Church. Masses in Holland which included sexual activity. Masses in the Far East which worshipped the powers of nature. Masses in America where pizza and cola were consecrated instead of bread and wine. Masses where the congregation sat down for a meal in a restaurant. Masses where the congregation took drugs.

Tres Abbinc Annos had been intended to deal firmly with such abuses. To remove the permissive ambiguities in the legislation. To restore veneration to the Eucharist. But the Instruction had gone further. It had provided for the Vernacular throughout the Mass. This seemed a minor thing, seeing as the Vernacular was everywhere, anyway. It seemed harmless, compared with some of the things priests had been doing on the altar. But it was not a minor thing, if one considered the official assurances that had been given that the Canon of the Mass would remain in Latin, unchanged. It was not a minor thing to play fast and loose with such assurances. Under the old rubrics, the priest was to genuflect at the words of transubstantiation *hoc est enim corpus meum*. Under the new rubrics of *Tres Abhinc Annos,* the priest was not to genuflect at that sacred moment. He was to display the host to the congregation before genuflecting. Again, this seemed a small thing. But it meant that the symbolism of the Rite was changing. Beforehand, the person at Mass was together with others, but basically he was alone with God. Now, he seemed to be first and foremost part of some collective being. A community. The People of God, some of the Council documents called it. It was puzzling. God hadn't been pushed into second place. Not exactly. But He wasn't in the first place any more, either.

Now, Gus believed he could discern what had happened. The central reality of Roman Catholic practice, the presence of God on the altar, had been reconceived, re-fashioned. The new priority given to the Epiclesis was proof of this. It clouded the doctrine of Transubstantiation in a truly ominous way. This sacred event was no longer effected by the sole actions of the priest over the Offering. This event, if it still was an event with reality, had been re-ordered as a function of the narrative of the Sacrifice of Calvary, which began with the invocation to the Holy Spirit. Gus had lingering doubts that such a consecration could ever be valid. He suspected that without serious discussion, without the barest acknowledgment, even, the doctrine of the Real Presence had subtly changed. A great sadness then rose in him, because he feared that this would lead the Real Presence to depart from the Church.

The warning signs had been unmistakeable. So why had he kept on working? It was all Gus had ever known, to keep on working at whatever God had given him to do. No, he corrected himself. At whatever the Church had given him to do. It wrenched his heart to have to make such a difference, but it was the only way.

There had been a moment somewhere when words had ceased to mean what they were supposed to mean. When Yes had come to mean No and No Yes. And there had been a related moment, when everyone decided that it did not matter. If he could find that moment, Gus believed, then he would be able to breathe like a young man again.

The search for that moment took him back into his childhood. Dimly he understood that now it was only his moment that mattered, his lie, his sin. He still had not found it when the time came to go back to Rome. But Gus had strength again. Strength to face the inevitable.

Michael Cremin was part of that inevitable. Unlike Gus, Michael got on well with Annibale Bugnini. The powerful Vincentian had remained their superior, having become Secretary of the Congregation with the rank of Archbishop. Ineffectual cardinals came and went as Prefect over him, but they were totally dependent on Bugnini. Gus felt no animosity towards any of them. It was a vast parade of human weakness, in which he, too, had his part. He felt no animosity towards Michael even, although he saw now that Michael had betrayed him time and time again.

When the chaos of the Vernacular had threatened to overwhelm their little section of the Congregation, Michael had dealt with it. And Michael had disobeyed him. When the bishops of mainland Spain and the bishops of Spanish South America had quarrelled over wordings for the Mass in Spanish, Michael pointed out to Archbishop Bugnini that it was not due to theological differences but to their shared colonial history, one side the oppressor, the other the oppressed. Similar problems were arising between many language groups around the world, and the usual theology could not survive it. The solution the Congregation had adopted was to permit variant translations in cases of local necessity, leading to the co-existence of different Mass texts in the same language, each of them able to claim validity. Precisely this Gus had been working hard to prevent.

"You're the straw that breaks the camel's back," Gus had said to Michael, bitterly. "You've destroyed all that was left of the unity of the Church."

"Exaggerating as usual, Gus," Michael had answered. "Just because you can't see the unity being demonstrated to your face doesn't mean that it isn't there. There's unity in the diversity."

After that experience, Gus had tried to find a way of bringing Michael back to Obedience. It had little to do with the ecclesiastical controversies around them; it had a lot to do with Michael's priesthood. Obedience was everything for a priest. He, Gus, had been Michael's teacher in the seminary. This disregard for Obedience must be in some way his fault. And Michael wasn't the only one.

There was a new breed of priest everywhere: opinionated and disrespectful, intolerant of the old ways and of the older men who adhered to them. Deans of Formation like Gus had been responsible for them. Gus tried to talk with Michael and to get him to listen, but that did not work. And he spoke to senior officials, including Annibale Bugnini, but that did not help either. Gus had even approached Cardinal Knox, the then Prefect, after a high-level meeting, but he need not have bothered. It was Cardinal Villot, the Secretary of State, who answered.

"Unity in diversity? Most prescient. Most astute. Be thankful to God, Hogan, that He has given you such a talented assistant."

Gus stammered out something about Michael's difficulties with Obedience. The tall Frenchman bore down on him like a cold wind.

"You are the head of section, are you not? And you are unable to cope. Perhaps you should offer the Holy Father your resignation?"

That was the kind of place the Church was becoming. A place of lies and confusion. Worse even. A place of delight in confusion. A place where the lie was admired. Gus, to his great sorrow, saw that he had a part in it.

3

In April 1972, John Charles McQuaid died in retirement in Dublin. After the funeral, which many Rome-based Irish priests had attended, Michael returned to his duties at the Congregation to find that Gus Hogan was back at work, too.

"Good to see you, Gus!"

Gus Hogan was supposed to be dying of tuberculosis in Switzerland, but there he was, turning up unannounced to get on his nerves.

"We've just buried His Grace, Gus."

"The end of an era." Gus was smiling strangely. He had a visitor with him, a police officer.

"A break in, or something, Gus?"

"No, Michael. A body in the Tiber."

The police officer handed Michael a photograph. River rats had dealt with part of her face, but there was no mistaking who it was: Laura Moro, his girlfriend of some years before.

"Accident, suicide or murder, we do not know, Monsignor! This young woman did not live wisely. But you can confirm that you were not acquainted with her?"

The lie came easily. "I can't remember ever seeing this poor woman, Inspector. But you know how it is with us priests. We have to deal with all sorts of people. All the time."

The Inspector's smile vanished. "How strange, Monsignor Cremin. The young lady kept a diary in which you figure prominently for a time. She must have had prodigious gifts of the imagination!"

Michael ignored him and went over to his desk. Luckily, the policeman was on his way out. He had no jurisdiction in the Vatican, of course.

Gus Hogan came and stood over him, his arms folded, sombre. "What have you turned into, young Michael?"

Michael ignored him.

Laura was by now only a memory, and Michael felt little more than mild regret over her death. Later, when he was alone, the sadness came. He and Laura had made each other their own. They had been one flesh. One spirit, even, insofar as those chaotic waters of passion were spirit. To lose her had been like losing a limb, only worse. Laura had been beautiful, but it was not her beauty that he remembered most, it was his loss, and the pain of that loss.

Laura was dead, but Gus Hogan had a new lease of life. And he was full of energy. Gus was asserting his authority in all kinds of ways. He was putting in odd hours at the office when Michael was not there, and he refused to tell Michael what he was doing. Gus was an Apostolic Protonotary. A man in such a position could wreak havoc. And if Gus had a relapse and went back to hospital, the whole thing, whatever it was, would become Michael's responsibility. And now there was the suspicion that Gus knew all about Laura. A fear took root in him that made him fall asleep too late at night and wake up too early in the morning. The fear of being found out.

Michael could perhaps have talked with Archbishop Bugnini, to whom he was close. But being ambitious, Michael could not afford to admit that there might be a crisis looming, and that he was incapable of handling it. Instead, he paid a visit to a friend at the Secretariat of State, Felix Kostuva SJ. Father Kostuva had alarming news to give. Gus Hogan had indeed come to the attention of the Secretariat. There were people making enquiries in bishops' chanceries around Europe on Hogan's behalf. Irregular enquiries. The purpose behind it was still unclear, because Hogan dissembled when challenged. Most disquieting. The menace of Lefebvre, no doubt. These intégristes! Berating everyone about Obedience, when they themselves refused it every hour of the day. A great shame on the Church. Before long, His Eminence, Cardinal Villot, would move to crush Hogan and his like. Michael would do well to choose his friends carefully.

The information had cost Michael a Havana cigar, which he could ill afford, but at least he knew now how thin the ice was. He had to get to the bottom of Gus's scheming before it was too late. The best bet, Michael felt, was to sound out his old acquaintance, Liam the Librarian. If anybody could tell him what Gus was up to, it was Liam.

For reasons of his own, Liam the Librarian was lying low. Eventually, Michael came across him in the yard behind the kitchens of the Irish College enjoying a smoke. He had cupped the cigarette in the palm of his hand like a naughty schoolboy trying to keep the glow from being seen. Liam's face had shrunk around his cheekbones. He looked like a sack of corn with holes in it and all the grain leaking out.

"Gus Hogan, you say?" The librarian's eyes disappeared behind his eyelids and became unreadable. "Gus thinks the New Mass is the work of the Devil."

Michael felt better. "So Gus is, eh, no longer fully sane, then?"

"Do I detect a note of satisfaction, Michael Cremin, in your scummy little Vatican voice?" Liam took a last violent drag of tobacco smoke and crushed the butt under his heel. "Listen here, Monsignor Michael. Gus Hogan is a good man. Not like me. And not like you. And nothing's going to happen to Gus because of you. Because if it does, you'll wish you'd never been born. So you just keep on licking arse around the Vatican, and leave Gus alone."

Michael paled at Liam's ferocity. But he gave his acknowledgement, smiling a little.

Liam the Librarian was dying of cancer. Of late, he had come to prefer the company of people he used to sneer at: those quieter men in the Irish College who had been leading humdrum lives of prayer and faithful observance. Liam even prayed with them sometimes. The Rosary. The Stations of the Cross. And he went to them for Confession. Michael felt a certain disgust for these stirrings of Liam's conscience; he knew him too well to regard them as genuine. Liam just wanted some insurance in case the things he had stopped believing in turned out to be true.

But try as he might, Michael could not rid himself of the fear that he was about to be disgraced. This nightmare prospect seemed confirmed by every turn of events. Cancelled appointments. Late replies to letters. Unavailable senior officials.

While Michael was thus agonizing over his situation, and using increasingly implausible excuses to stay away from the office, Gus sent a note over to him at the Irish College. The note specified the place and time for a meeting. It was an unusual note, more like an ultimatum than an invitation. But Michael complied.

The place was a fish restaurant near the Spanish Steps. Gus had brought a woman with him, a washed-out individual with lifeless hair and too much make-up. She was sitting rigidly at the table when Michael arrived, clutching her handbag, the fingers trembling lightly on the straps.

Michael offered his hand politely, but she pushed it away. "I am the mother of Laura Moro. And you are the man who killed my daughter."

Her voice carried, and the restaurant was full. Michael was sure there were heads turning in his direction.

"I didn't kill your daughter," he whispered, appalled.

"Who can believe you, Father? The kind of priest you are. And you lied to the police about her."

"Signora, I knew your daughter. But it was a long time ago."

"You took her virginity. You, a priest!"

No, no, he wanted to say, but the shock of her words had made him speechless.

"And the child in her womb, the child she killed, that was your child! And you feel no remorse?"

Michael managed to get out the semblance of an answer. "These are very private matters, Signora!"

Laura's mother turned to Gus Hogan. One small tear was etching its way down her cheek. The caked facade was about to crack. "Don Agustino," she whispered. "It is true what I told you. How can I believe in God, now?" She rose from the table and pushed a way through the crowded tables towards the door.

Gus was quietly drumming the table with his fingers. When he looked up, his face was inscrutable. "Michael, could you not have told her you were sorry?"

For what seemed a long time, Michael could find nothing to say. When the waiter came, he sent him away, unable for the thought of food. Gus, too, ordered nothing.

"I'm sorry, Gus," Michael croaked.

"No, Michael, you're not."

Was that all Gus was going to say? This castrated celibate who knew nothing of what he was feeling? This canon lawyer dry as dust who couldn't do anything unless there was a regulation somewhere telling him to do it? At that moment, Michael hated Gus Hogan. Gus was the pair of eyes that see nothing. The ridiculous side of the Church. Michael wished fervently that Gus would crawl off somewhere and cough himself into his grave. Like Laura. The thought of her lifeless body was more than he could bear. He walked home alone, imagining that he was carrying her home in his arms, intending to bring her to his bed and warm her back to life with his embrace. But he put it from him. She was gone.

4

In the night after that meeting with Laura's mother, Augustine Hogan had a near-fatal relapse and was rushed to hospital. When the danger lessened, he was transferred to the Swiss sanatorium where he had been treated before. In all probability, Gus was close to death. If he survived, he would be incapacitated for a long time, if not permanently. Michael took in the news with considerable glee. After a while, he began to hate himself for it, and to ease his conscience, he went out into the city to buy a card to send to Gus on his sick bed. While he was there, he came across a few Irish Franciscans of his acquaintance who were staying at the College of Saint Isidore and were studying at the Pontifical universities. There was a coffee bar close by, and they went in together for a quick refreshment.

"So it's yourself then, Mick?" Michael looked for the man who had addressed him. It was an older friar, who had been late in joining the group. There was an odd quality to his voice, and the younger friars seemed to melt away, leaving Michael alone with him.

Michael was a little angry. No-one ever called him "Mick." It took a moment, then he guessed who it must be. Benignus Breen.

"We never got around to meeting in Louvain, did we?" Michael replied, innocently.

The smile froze on Father Breen's face. "Ah, Louvain?"

Michael studied the slightly unsavoury Franciscan before him. The only real hair he had left was in his nose, thick tufts poking out through his nostrils, waggling as he spoke. His eyes were those of a man owned by others.

"1960, Billy. You wrote a report about me back to Dublin every month."

"Did I?"

A brass neck, this Franciscan. "Yes, Billy. I read them."

Billy Breen forced a laugh. "You know how it is sometimes!" He spread his hands, sloshing his coffee around, and leaned over for a sly whisper.

"They wouldn't have wanted reports on just anyone, would they? Listen, Mick, I'll level with you. They're getting round to appointing a few new bishops. There's a new man needed back home. For Limerick. And I'm checking out a couple of things. For the Vatican. There's a name that crops up. A Monsignor of the Curia. So, eh, what do you think of Gus Hogan?"

Michael was beginning to feel uncomfortable. "Gus is very sick."

"I didn't know that. Let's just assume he'll be back on his feet fairly soon. So, eh, what's he like?"

"Gus is a distinguished man of the Church."

"Of course, he is, Mick! But what's all this about Gus dragging his feet on the Vernacular?"

"That's nonsense!"

The Franciscan smiled approvingly. "Of course it is, Mick! So, what's he like personally?"

Michael felt the relish spread inside him. Gus Hogan, he found himself saying, was a keen musician. He liked to relax by playing slow mournful tunes on the violin which he had composed in honour of the Blessed Virgin Mary. With a dark thrill, Michael realised that such a detail laid Gus's psyche wide open. It was no secret that Gus was finding it difficult to work with Archbishop Bugnini, and there was a nun from the kitchens who sometimes accompanied him on the piano. And then there were Gus's disparaging views on the new Directory for Masses with Children, which he thought would deprive children of any chance of acquiring the Catholic Faith. Michael was amazed at a picture which suddenly seemed inevitable, even though it had not been there before. Personal difficulties with superiors. Friendships with nuns. Emotional outbursts over children. It took less than a minute, and Monsignor Augustine Hogan, Protonotarius Apostolicus and Professor of Canon Law, was revealed as an unstable character with a troubled vocation. There were, of course, other difficulties. Gus's sympathy for traditionalist causes, for example. And his chronic ill-health.

"So, Billy, it won't be His Excellency Bishop Hogan for Limerick, will it?"

The Franciscan glanced at his watch. "Who said Gus was ever in the running? Isn't there a younger man in the Curia with all the expertise that's needed? An up-and-coming young fellow who Gus has been keeping down for years?"

"Are you suggesting ......"

Benignus Breen raised his finger to his lips. "I won't wait around for the penny to drop. But you won't forget your own. I know that!"

It took some weeks of anxious waiting, but then it was confirmed. They were not going to disgrace Michael. They were going to promote him, once more.

5

Early in 1974, when the giant wheels of the Church seemed at last to be turning at an even speed, Michael Cremin was charged with a diplomatic mission to Switzerland. Together with Felix Kostuva SJ from the Secretariat of State, Michael was to form part of a delegation to the rebel Archbishop, Marcel Lefebvre, who had set up his headquarters in a disused Abbey in Ecône in the Canton of Valois. Unlike his compatriot, John Charles McQuaid, Archbishop Lefebvre had taken a clear public stand against the Council reforms, and had become an outcast. Now he was threatening to ordain priests for the Old Mass on foot of an obscure legitimation from the local bishop. There was a warning letter from Pope Paul to be delivered in person to Archbishop Lefebvre, and there was to be an admonitory letter read out during Mass.

To everyone's surprise, Augustine Hogan was appointed to lead the delegation. Michael was troubled by this news. Gus Hogan was a known traditionalist sympathizer, so his presence might be interpreted at first sight as a peace gesture. But Gus was very sick and he knew nothing about diplomacy. He was likely to mess it up, if he survived the journey at all. Michael detected in this scenario the cold, manipulative hand of the Secretary of State, Cardinal Villot. Villot must have decided to set an example: a task Gus could not succeed in, but could not refuse; a public disaster which would enable a salutary punishment to be roundly meted out.

Michael decided to do what he could to save Gus Hogan from this fate. He got as far as one of the secretaries to Cardinal Villot, who brushed him aside like a bothersome fly. What was the Monsignor worrying about? Was there not a trained diplomat with them, the excellent Monsignor Kostuva, who would see to the diplomatic aspects? And did it not concern the validity of Vernacular versions of the Mass, which was Monsignor Hogan's remit? And was Hogan not in Switzerland, already? Round the corner, so to speak? And how long was a convalescence supposed to take, anyway? Michael sat in discomfort as the cold-eyed prelate took off the mask of courtesy. Only recently, Monsignor Cremin had been betraying that old fool Hogan to them, now he wanted to protect him. Surely an intelligent man like Monsignor Cremin would realise the risks he was running? One did not go far in the Church with sentimentality.

All through the night-long train journey from Rome, Felix Kostuva got on

Michael's nerves, fidgeting and biting his nails, and making conversation about Louvain, where he had apparently spent a few months during the Council while working on his doctorate. When the train crossed the border into Switzerland, the guard handed Kostuva a note which he read quickly and crumpled up in his hand. A telex, he whispered. An urgent summons back to Rome. When they got out at Sion, the regional capital, the Croatian Jesuit changed platforms and took the next train home. Michael did not believe in that opportune telex, but he did not care. He had smelled the fear in Kostuva. Let Kostuva scurry away like a drenched rat, if he needed to. Michael was determined to take good care of Gus Hogan. Kostuva's absence would make it easier.

Gus was waiting by the taxi rank as arranged. Michael made a lame excuse for Felix Kostuva, and handed Gus the despatch case which contained the stiff-backed envelope with the papal seal. They settled into their taxi, saying little. Gus had to save his breath, of course, but Michael knew there was another reason: so deep an estrangement that they were in different worlds, fenced off by mutual disapproval. With a surge of regret, Michael saw that it was largely his fault. He resolved once more to do whatever he could to help Gus Hogan.

A few miles down the motorway, in the midst of an icy silence that nothing could melt, the taxi clattered to a halt in a lay-by, with smoke coming from the bonnet. They could not understand the Swiss dialect of the driver, and with an ill-humoured gesture, he left them and trudged back towards the town. They looked at each other, neither of them knowing what to say or do. Behind them, a side road fell away towards the River Rhône. An ambulance appeared there, crawling up the steep incline in high gear. Seeing their predicament, the driver wound down a window and cordially offered them a lift. He had borrowed the ambulance for a few hours, he explained, brushing his slightly wild hair out of his eyes. And he would gladly drive them to their inn at Saxon, which was not out of his way at all. He even had some kind of a screwdriver with him which easily opened the boot of the taxi and enabled them to get at their luggage.

Philip Mahler, such was the ambulance man's name, was an artist by calling, but there was no money in it, in his experience, hence the ambulance driving. For many years he had been searching for beauty, comparing his flashes from other worlds with the persons and things before his physical eyes, and trying to give form and colour to the result.

"I take people's picture," the artist confided. "Then I look for the settings where they divest themselves. And that's what I paint. People divesting themselves."

"Divesting themselves of what?" Gus Hogan asked, seemingly interested.

"Of everything."

"There can't be much in the painting then, for people to look at."

"The truth is there."

"Where?"

"It's left behind."

"Would you paint me, Mr. Mahler?"

"Oh, I would, Father, but I'm only learning. There's a better artist than me who's teaching me. And she might have put you in already."

Michael had no patience for this half-witted conversation. He had not slept on the train from Rome and was thinking with longing of a hot bath and of fresh clean sheets to lie between in comfort. But they were expected in Ecône at two-o'clock. There would be no time to rest.

In Saxon, they took possession of two simple rooms furnished with a heavy frugality that Michael thought must be peculiarly Swiss. Gus then prevailed on the innkeeper to drive them the few miles to the seminary.

The young priest at the gate lodge, a courteous Spaniard, was happy to engage in conversation while awaiting instructions from his superiors.

"This gate before you, Venerable Sirs. It does not open for the New Mass. That would be a vain hope, I assure you."

"So it is said, Father."

"You know the famous Father Jungmann, I presume?" the Spanish priest continued. "Of the theological faculty at Innsbruck? I heard him say recently that the Holy Spirit always finds an answer for the Church. But that it is not necessarily the best answer. I am certain that he was referring to the New Mass. Can it be that Father Jungmann, of all people, has at last recognised the errors of the Second Vatican Council?"

"An Ecumenical Council does not err, Father," Gus wheezed in reply.

"Ordinarily not, I'll grant you," the young priest answered. "But because there are such obvious errors in the Teaching of Vatican II, we are forced to conclude that it was not in its totality a valid Ecumenical Council. It is logical."

"Logical to you, Father," said Michael.

"Look at the intention in which it was convoked. A defective intention, you must agree. To open the Church to modern times. To modern times, My Lords! It was the 1960s! Complete disrespect for all forms of authority! Pope John opened the doors and windows on a hurricane!"

"God works as He chooses to!"

"Precisely, My Lords. And look at how God is working in the fruits of this Council. Not 10 years have passed, and look at the attendance figures for Sunday Mass. In Holland down by 55%. In France down 65%. And this despite many relaxations of discipline! Obviously, the faithful do not like this New Mass they were given."

Michael spoke up with asperity. "It's a Mass the faithful can understand. And it's separating the wheat from the chaff. If they don't like it, they can leave!"

"They are leaving, Monsignor. In their millions. And it is not only the faithful who are leaving, it is also the priests. Look at vocations. In the U.S.A. down by over 60%. In France down by 80%. Can it be, Your Reverences, that God is no longer calling young men to the priesthood in the post-conciliar Church?"

They were interrupted by the telephone. The young priest in the old-fashioned soutane stood to attention, hanging on every word in the earpiece. He put down the receiver and turned solemnly to the visitors.

"His Grace, My Lord Archbishop Marcel Lefebvre, will not receive you. Paul VI and his circle must realize that they now have the very Church that they deserve. That is the only basis for discussions. And, please, with many most filial and fraternal felicitations to the throne of Saint Peter, you will be on your way."

Gus Hogan gave Michael a sign forbidding all protest. With the heavy gates still closed against them, they walked back down the mountain road towards Saxon, weary, perhaps, but with time enough to take in the surroundings. Archbishop Lefebvre had chosen a place of great natural beauty for his last stand: vineyards, a rushing waterfall, snow-capped mountain peaks as far as the eye could see. And wonderfully clean air. Gus was thrilled to find that he could breathe easily, and could walk the distance without too much trouble.

Michael's mind was on other things.

"That letter, Gus," he began, a little hesitantly. "We can't bring it back to Rome."

"And why can't we, Michael?"

"Cardinal Villot won't like it."

"Does that matter, Michael?"

"He'll have the skin off our backs."

"And what are you proposing?"

"That you trust my political instinct."

"I am inclined to do so."

It may have been the touch of the mountain sun easing his mind as well as his lungs, but to Michael's surprise, Gus accepted his harsh analysis. They had been sent out to deliver a papal despatch that was secretly known to be undeliverable. So let it be said that it had been delivered. And let Lefebvre deny it, if he chose to. Those who were pulling the strings did not care. They were pursuing other purposes. So the letter had to disappear. To muddy the waters sufficiently until things could move on for the better.

Back at the hotel, Gus and Michael bought a bottle of cognac, and while they sipped a little from the fine liquor, with its colour of sun-lifted autumn, they burned the unopened letter in the ashtray in Gus's room. The red wax of the papal seal entered into some odd chemical union with the glass, leaving it badly stained, but they were able to clean it by filling the ashtray with cognac and setting it alight. The flames reared out of the sculpted form like angry horses, and Gus began to cough and wheeze. It sounded like his lungs were full of stones. Concerned, Michael gave him a handkerchief. He was shocked to see it stain with so much blood.

"You know, Michael," Gus whispered, "it's been a long, long, time since I felt I was doing anything for God."

It was a tone of utter exhaustion, and Michael's heart sank.

"Obedience, Michael. The resolve to obey God's Will. That was always the guarantee that we'd get it right. No-one wants to obey anyone or anything now except themselves. But you obey me now as your superior. Go to your room, and have a look at these papers for me, if you've time. But leave me here now in peace."

Was that all? No searching questions about intrigues at the office? No reproaches over dead girls pulled out of the Tiber? Michael shrugged his shoulders. Gus was tired, of course. And he wasn't well, at all.

6

Michael lay for a long time on the bed in his hotel room, staring at the ceiling. The pages Gus had given him lay strewn over the carpet where he had thrown them. It gave him a headache to do so, but he went over the main points one more time.

Josef Jungmann had been right. The Old Mass of Pope Pius V was indeed an untidy sprawl of a building, its different parts built at different times for different purposes, with whatever materials had been available, and by the builders of the day, with all their imperfections. This he had proved in *Missarum Sollemnia,* that landmark of liturgical history from 1948. It put an end to the mistaken view that the Mass Rite was beyond change. The Mass had been changing since its inception. It was also true that the old Roman Canon especially could be considered a disorderly thing that flouted the good liturgical principles established at the Second Vatican Council, as Cipriano Vagaggini had claimed in his book of 1966. But in a deeper sense, Gus was saying, these experts were wrong. Only an architect of a strange new school, an anti-architect, in fact, could regard this building as uninhabitable, or aesthetically displeasing, particularly the central part of it, the Canon, which was in daily use, and had been for centuries.

But that was not the real issue, according to Gus. The real issue was the appalling hubris of a small handful of theologians. In 1966, Johannes Wagner, the Relator of Coetus X of the Consilium, had ignored the assurances given regarding the preservation of the Roman Canon, and had obtained Pope Paul's permission to create alternative settings for the Eucharist. In this way, a circle of ambitious men, self-empowered to sit in judgement over past and present, became able to impose on the Church their own desires for the future. They had no conception of what they were doing. They had no love, no devotion, for that very Rite they had celebrated for decades, and which should have been the cherished centre of their priestly lives. Why had they done it? Because of the resentment they bore against the Mass. The Old Mass, in Gus's view, had required the priest and people to put their everyday lives behind them in order to be free for the Real Presence. The rubrics made one empty of self, at least in aspiration. But there were some who could not bear it. They turned against the Mass, using the instruments of theology for the purpose. And there was always a secret centre, a black satanic few, who understood what was being achieved, and revelled in it.

Michael shook his head. It was so predictable. Any change to the Mass had to be evil, because the Mass was not supposed to change. The Old Mass had been a New Mass once, the New Mass of the Council of Trent. Surely this proved that New Masses were legitimate? And that Black Mass nonsense. Such charges had been levelled at Martin Luther, and any other reformer you'd care to name. Why couldn't Gus see how ridiculous it was? Anyway, there wasn't anything in the New Mass that was actually new. Devising it had been more of a streamlining operation, with elements being restructured rather than replaced. It retained most of the old ritual elements and a lot of the old language. It just wasn't in Latin, and it wasn't fixed on the past.

Before him, underlined by Gus in thick black ink, was a quotation from Pope Saint Pius V, himself:

Let all everywhere adopt and observe what has been handed down by the Holy Roman Church, the Mother and Teacher of the other churches, and let Masses not be sung or read according to any other formula than that of this Missal published by Us. This ordinance applies henceforth, now, and forever, throughout all the provinces of the Christian world [...]

We likewise declare and ordain that no one whosoever is forced or coerced to alter this Missal, and that this present document cannot be revoked or modified, but remain always valid and retain its full force.

Let all everywhere. Henceforth, now, and forever. Always valid. Cannot be revoked or modified. Such language. It was like forcing people to travel by horse and cart when they had motor cars. It was like forbidding them to travel anywhere at all. It was ludicrous.

What this pope was responding to, according to Gus, was the near destruction of the Church during the Protestant Reformation. As Renaissance Humanism gave way to Deism and the Enlightenment, and with the corruption of the Church still a vivid warning, man was setting himself up behind the borders of what was deemed natural. Soon it would become possible for the generality of men and women to shape their lives without any reference to God, at all. This hell on earth, hidden in the opium-smoke of a thousand distractions, was the future of mankind. The Mass of Pius V had come at a time when the Catholic Church had risen to meet the challenge. It was a deliberate closing of the ranks against the onslaught of error, based on the efficacy of a normative Rite assembled on the evidence of trusted usage. It was the work of men in adversity, their traditions broken, who were purifying themselves in the struggle for the essentials. God had guided them and had blessed them.

With sadness, Michael saw what Gus wanted him to believe: the Old Mass had never been an expression of arrogant Catholic triumphalism, as was often suggested. Quite the opposite. The Old Mass had been something to shore up the hull after the seas turned angry, after half the crew had deserted, and the Barque of Peter had taken damage and was listing dangerously. Who could have imagined that those ship's officers who remained would begin ripping open the timber to let in the sea? Either they were mad, or they were paid for the task, and had been traitors from the beginning.

Michael knew that Gus's quiet lament was intended for his eyes only. There was a second sheaf of papers that Gus had given him, a tissue of half-truths, question-begging and glossing-over in defence of the New Mass, which would be read out the next day under obedience to Cardinal Villot. Why didn't Gus simply thumb his nose at Villot and throw in his lot with Lefebvre? He'd be much happier. And why did he go to the trouble of preparing two sets of papers? Despite everything, Gus Hogan was still trying to educate him.

7

The next morning, Michael Cremin and Gus Hogan, still in the role of papal legates, set out for the parish church of Riddes, a village close to Ecône. They were formally greeted by the Vicar-General of the diocese, who, like the bishop, was a supporter of Archbishop Lefebvre. The rebel Archbishop had refused to attend, and the Vicar-General had gone home again, leaving the unwelcome legates in the care of a nervous parish priest. First he introduced Michael Cremin to the near-empty church. The memory of Gus's judgements from the night before was still fresh in Michael's mind, and he intended to take some of the unpleasant wind out of Gus's sails before giving him the pulpit.

"Most of us can remember the Council, and what a great event it was. I recall Archbishop Roberts saying one day, our mother the Church is getting on in years, and like all venerable old ladies, she has bulges in all the wrong places. With the New Mass we have less flab and we can now see the beauty of Mater Ecclesia a little bit better!"

There was silence. The token presence of Lefebvrists saw nothing amusing in his words, and sat stony-faced in their grim, black soutanes. The sprinkling of chance observers seemed a little cowed.

In the flat air of the Church, a piercing voice resounded, high-pitched and commanding. Michael knew it of old.

"How well he speaks, our fine young Monsignor!"

Reddening to the roots of his hair, Michael looked towards the speaker, who had stood up to attract attention. "Jean Nordheider, ladies and gentlemen. Of the Catholic University of Louvain. Not, however, a Catholic, I hasten to add!"

There was a rush of disapproval from the scattered audience, but Nordheider quelled it with a smoothing gesture and a winning smile. "I assure you I am, as always, here only as myself. I would never have thought that a walking holiday in this lovely place would catapult me into the very centre of one of the formative issues of our time! What I say is, we will not hear the truth in a sermon from a Monsignor of the Curia."

In the confusion that followed, Gus Hogan signalled to Michael to stand down. With slow dignity he took Michael's place at the pulpit, leaning his arms on the marble rampart and gazing over at Jean Nordheider with equanimity. He turned to the Parish Priest who was sitting below him in the front row. "Has the Blessed Sacrament been removed, Father? Please take Our Lord to the protection of the sacristy."

The priest hurried away as bidden, and Jean Nordheider stepped out into the aisle. "So. Monsignor. Are you willing to speak the truth?"

Poor Gus was on public display, and there was nothing Michael could do to help him. Yet there was more. A whiff of adventure, inebriating in the uncertainty of the outcome.

"Monsignor!" Nordheider began, savouring the syllables, "Would you agree that the old Canon of the Mass, declared inerrant by popes and their minions over many centuries has now been abolished?"

"No, sir," Gus wheezed in answer, his voice growing clearer with the effort, "in Missale Romanum, Pope Paul expressly included the Roman Canon as part of the Rite."

"Ha! Then where is it in the New Mass? Pray, tell us!"

"It is Eucharistic Prayer Number One."

"And is this Eucharistic Prayer an obligatory Eucharistic Prayer?"

"No."

"So there are Masses said where this Eucharistic Prayer is not said?"

"Yes."

"Yet, you wish us to believe that it is an integral part of the Rite?"

"Yes. I am pointing out that the Roman Canon was expressly and intentionally not removed from the Mass. By order of the pope. The Canon is therefore still an integral part of the Rite."

"But it is an integral part of the Rite that may never be used?"

"If you wish, sir."

"I do not wish, Monsignor. We take note that the Monsignor will have us believe that the Roman Canon is an integral part of the Mass through the vehicle of Eucharistic Prayer Number One, even though it is conceivable that Eucharistic Prayer Number One will never be used. A strange form of integrality or integrity, you will agree. In fact, to claim that it is an integral part of the Rite smacks of the abuse of language. But let us look at the substance of the matter. Are you saying, Monsignor, that Eucharistic Prayer Number One was promulgated by Pope Pius V in 1570?"

"No. But it is largely the text from that time."

"Did Pius V not give us a text in Latin? Is it then the case, Monsignor, that Eucharistic Prayer Number One, by some crafty sleight-of-hand, is in reality not a vernacular prayer, but only another prayer in Latin?"

"There is a Latin text for those who need to use it."

"And is that Latin text the text promulgated by Pius V in 1570?"

"Not exactly. There have been minor changes. Peripheral changes. For example, a re-ordering of sections for greater clarity. And the invocation of some of the saints has been removed, because their names are unknown to most of the faithful today."

"And good riddance, too, I dare say. But would you term the Consecration periphery, Monsignor?"

"No, of course not."

"Is it not the case that the Consecration in all the Eucharistic Prayers is the same?"

"Yes."

"But is it not the case that the wording of the Consecration in the Vernacular differs from the Latin wording of the Roman Canon?"

"Well, yes."

"My dear Monsignor, surely it is obvious to any intelligent six-year-old that an alteration to the Consecration in the Eucharistic Prayers means that the Consecration has been altered?"

"I do not see your point."

"Monsignor, the words of Consecration of the Wine as they flowed mellifluously from the pen of Pius V were as follows. *Hic est enim calix sanguinis mei, novi et aeterni testamenti: myterium fidei: qui pro vobis et pro multis effendetur in remissionem peccatorum.* Is this so?"

"Yes."

"Monsignor, the wording of the Consecration of the Wine in Eucharistic Prayer Number Two in English is: *This is the cup of my blood which will be shed for you and for all men so that sins may be forgiven*. Is this so?"

"Yes."

"Ladies and gentlemen, I rest my case!"

At this, there was a ripple of laughter. Nordheider had not rested any case whatever. He was simply putting Gus Hogan at a disadvantage. If that was all he intended, Michael thought, it would be a lucky escape. But there was more to come. When Jean Nordheider got to his feet again, there was no mistaking the lithe satisfaction. He was a cat settling in for the kill.

"I would never have imagined that I, an unbeliever, would have to instruct a distinguished man of the Curia in the basic elements of theology! Well, the Church is not what she used to be. Monsignor, does the Consecration of the Wine in the old Roman Canon read *pro multis* or *pro omnibus*?"

"It reads *pro multis*."

"You will agree, Monsignor, that if it reads *pro multis*, it does not read *pro omnibus*?"

"Yes."

"And you will agree that the English of Eucharistic Prayer Number Two, *for all men,* would best correspond in Latin to *pro omnibus*?

"Yes."

"Then surely you must also agree that the Canon has been altered?"

"There is no alteration. That is forbidden."

"Forbidden! I am glad to hear that there are things that are still forbidden by the Roman Catholic Church! If she were unable to forbid things, where would she be! Are you saying Monsignor, that in essence, *pro multis* and *for all men* mean exactly the same thing?"

"That is, in general, the position of the Church at this time."

"That is, in general, the position. Monsignor, was it also the position of Pope Pius V in 1570, in general, or in particular?"

"Sir, these are phrases that you are bringing together. Why assume that Pope Pius V, 400 years ago, would have brought them together?"

"It is the Church that brings them together, Monsignor! And bends the meanings of words to do so!"

"The words mean what they've always meant."

"Then the equation of *pro multis* and *for all men* is not a matter of the meanings of words?"

"Not entirely. It is also a matter of ecclesiastical practices, in this case the practice of understanding our tradition, so that we in the Church today can be properly loyal to the truths of Revelation."

"So the meanings of the words have not changed?"

"They have not, sir. It is we who have changed."

Jean Nordheider let Gus's words ring for a moment in the silent church, then shook himself free of whatever they had conveyed to him.

"Monsignor. For whom, in your view, was the Blood of Christ given? For many, or for all?"

"Eucharistic Prayer Number Two states that the Blood of Christ is given for all."

"And was that the view of Pope Pius V in 1570?"

"No, I don't believe so."

"Was Pope Pius V then wrong in his view?"

"He was right. For his times."

"How persuasively he speaks, the very reverend Monsignor! You are saying that at the time of Pope Pius V, the Blood of Christ was shed only for a certain group of individuals within mankind, those who believed in Him, no doubt. Today, it seems, the Blood of Christ is shed for all mankind, regardless of whether they believe or not. An exquisite thought. But Monsignor, what exactly took place that suddenly permitted the salvific power of the Sacrifice to be extended to all? Was it perhaps the massive outpouring of Grace at the Second Vatican Council? Were we all so uplifted by that great event that we are all saved already? Has the renewal of the Catholic Church between 1962 and 1965 produced such a wondrous leaven that there is now no need for an individual to have faith at all?

Perhaps President Nixon and Chairman Mao will automatically go to Heaven together with all the millions they have killed? Who knows, perhaps even I will go to Heaven and there join Voltaire and Nietzsche in poking fun at Saint Peter!"

"No, no, there must be faith. And repentance from Sin."

"Then, Monsignor, there can be only one conclusion. The New Mass includes a new Consecration. Whoever attends this Mass and receives Communion, does not receive the same body and blood of Christ as he who received Communion at the Old Mass. So, Monsignor, what has happened to Jesus of Nazareth? Has He been fired? Replaced by a less demanding Messiah?"

"He remains."

"Then, Monsignor, He is now outside the Church."

It was turning into a disaster for Gus Hogan, but he did not seem to mind. He leaned forward and spoke into the microphone with as much clarity as his ravaged breathing allowed.

"Here today, I have been defending what I believe to be indefensible. And I'm sorry I have to do it. As regards the Mass, I still say the Old Mass, and I always will."

Michael sat rapt in wonder as those quiet words worked out their meaning in him. Before that sparse congregation, most of whom had understood nothing of the exchange, Gus had put an end to his career. It was a strange way to do it, so publicly, but also so quietly. Concerned, Michael followed Gus Hogan as he left the pulpit and went to the sacristy. Gus was on his knees before the Real Presence. With the same unusual quiet of before. With growing discomfort, Michael fell to his knees behind him. Gus was divested, he thought, using the word the ambulance driver had used the day before. Divested of everything that normally mattered. A denuded man. An empty space formed by his shoes and his cassock. A nothing, except for the attempt at prayer. And there was a silent plenitude about it stressing the air so much that Michael could not breathe.

"When's the last time you were on your knees, young Michael?" Gus asked, as he helped Michael to his feet. But he did not wait for an answer. "I won't listen to you now. Our Lord might choose to let me breathe again for a while, and I have promises to keep."

The parish priest held the side door of the sacristy open for Gus to leave. There was a deference in the gesture, Michael thought. It was unusual to see deference being shown to Gus Hogan.

When Michael turned round, he found a short, fat and rather surly gentleman contemplating him from the inside door. He proffered a note. "Compliments of Dr. Nordheider." It was an invitation to lunch. Curtly, Michael refused. He could think of nothing he would like less at that moment than to spend time with Jean Nordheider.

That night, in the country inn not far from Ecône, Augustine Hogan died in his sleep. The room-maid found him in the morning, and the innkeeper went over to Michael, who was breakfasting, and whispered the news. Michael took a deep draught of coffee, swirled it around to clear his mouth of the remains of the breakfast roll, and tried hard to swallow. It didn't all go down at once, and he almost choked.

How serene Gus looked, Michael thought, when he saw him, his heart beating fast. He hurried away, and was back in less than a minute, with the purple stole of penance around his neck and the Breviary in his hand. He knelt by the bed, bent his head close to Gus's cold cheek and murmured the ritual pleas for forgiveness, hoping they might warm his departed soul.

Michael was close to tears. He had to repeat some of the prayers, because he stuttered and made a mess of them. Poor cold Gus, he thought. The least he could do for him was to pray the age-old prayers properly. It struck him that it was Gus's own Breviary he had been using, the Breviary his parents had given him on his Ordination. And he had been praying in the Latin the Church had abolished. Praying for Gus, as he passed away into the endless cold. No, Michael later decided, there was no denying what he had seen in that sacristy in Riddes. Gus did not belong to the cold. Loving-kindness was a word one of the Bible translations used. Gus had been enfolded by loving-kindness. It was something he could not explain, and he filed it away for future reference.

With great sorrow, Michael accompanied the remains of Gus Hogan back to Rome. One of the saddest things was finding out how little he had known him. Gus turned out to have had another life parallel to his professorial and Curial one. The life of a pastor of souls, a life well hidden. Years afterwards, the Irish College was still dealing with a motley assortment of visitors asking for the grave of "Don Agustino" so that they could go to pay their respects.

†

5

A Guest of the Benedictines

1

The snowdrifts of mourning melted slowly, and Michael Cremin needed the rest of the year to get over Gus Hogan's passing. When Christmas Eve came, Michael was invited to assist in St. Peter's Basilica as the Holy Door, which had been walled-up for 25 years, was opened by the pope for the Holy Year of 1975. It was an honour, of course, but it seemed connected with his receding chances of a bishopric. Michael was still on the list for Limerick, but a minor favour was often used to prepare one for an official disappointment.

A Holy Year was a jubilee, a special time of forgiveness and reconciliation. But for Michael, there was no shaking off the sadness. The life of Gus Hogan, the loneliness of that life, still pressed upon him, revealing how much he had added to Gus's burden. There was nothing he could do about it now.

The events that marked the Holy Year gave a special place to Cardinal Suenens and his new pentecostalist movement known as Charismatic Renewal. Places of pilgrimage were awash with people suffused with the emotional religiosity peculiar to pentecostalism, praying loudly and incessantly 'in tongues' or lying in odd places in near-trance states which they termed 'slain in the spirit,' while being lovingly tended by admiring friends.

The high point was a special Charismatic Mass in Saint Peter's Basilica on Pentecost Sunday. Cardinal Suenens was the principal celebrant, and the pope was present at a side altar. Saint Peter's was full of people standing and waving their hands, or sitting on the floor, indulging in their personal modes of prayer.

At Communion, there was a great throng of people clamouring to receive the Host, and the priests found that hands were reaching into the ciborium to help themselves to the Body of Christ. Under the impression, no doubt, that this was a new kind of valid practice, the priests began to encourage it. Some priests threw Hosts up in the air, or emptied their ciborium over the people on the floor, before struggling back to the Altar to pick up a fresh supply. From the side altar, amplified by the microphone, came the aged and cracked voice of Pope Paul: "Jesus is Lord! Halleluiah! Halleluiah!" Then Paul appeared on the steps to the nave, a ciborium in his hand, and joined in with feeble gusto, pressing Hosts into waiting mouths and hands, and flinging them into the air to land where they might. Some were trampled into the floor and became part of the grime between the tiles, others stuck to shoes and were dragged outside to be trampled underfoot in Saint Peter's Square. Some Hosts vanished into pockets and handbags for later consumption, or to be kept as souvenirs.

There was a time in the priesthood when rules would not have been broken, not in such a place, not in such a way, because the sense of wrong-doing would have been too great. Even after the Council, such disregard for the Eucharist had been thought to be confined to the Dutch Church and to fringe characters in America and the mission territories. And to have been stopped. The prospect of the pope treating the Host in such a blasphemous way was so terrible that many refused to believe it. Some said that the man in white at the side altar of Saint Peter's had not been the pope at all, but an impostor. The real Pope Paul was being kept under lock and key by Cardinal Villot. The real Pope Paul was so sick of the post-conciliar Church that he wanted to change it back again, and they would not let him.

To Michael Cremin, the impostor theory explained one strange contradiction, at least. Only a few months previously, Pope Paul had strongly condemned the emerging pentecostalism in the Church and had seemingly put a stop to Cardinal Suenens and Charismatic Renewal. It was odd in the extreme for him not only to hand Saint Peter's over to Suenens, but to actually appear there himself in the role of an enthusiastic Charismatic, as wild with the spirit as anyone.

Ultimately, it was all easily resolvable, Michael thought. It was simply the tenor of Paul's pontificate. Instead of man being brought to God, God was being brought to man, and things always got a little out of hand in times of innovation, even the Body and Blood of Jesus Christ.

Once, during a period of inner emptiness, and prompted by something, he did not know what, Michael dreamed of Pope Paul. He saw him as the rumours depicted him: locked away in some far wing of the Vatican, his mind clouded by wrong advice and wrong medication, only dimly aware of the horrors which beset him. The dream had been so typical of Paul VI that Michael laughed at the memory of it. It was not like Paul to be able to turn the ship around. Paul would not even know where to find the wheel, let alone the strength to make it turn. He might find a way back all by himself, perhaps; an old man on his knees in a darkened room, longing for God, fighting for a moment of lucidity to repent of his sins, a pope without a Church, a pope so careless of his patrimony that he had lost it by the wayside.

To deal with his sadness, Michael had begun having sex again, using prostitutes recommended by Vatican friends. But not even the hit of orgasm could lift that leaden cloud for long. This sadness weighed even on the sunlight that came in through the high Roman windows of his office. Even the oranges and grapes in the fruit bowl seemed to droop. Even the water he poured over his hands from the stone jug on the metal stand seemed tired and dusty. It was in his mind only, but day after day, when he walked home through the narrow, crooked streets where the poor people lived, the long lines of washing strung from house to house were a chorus of ghosts wailing and flapping their hands at him in distress; but he could not help them.

One lonely evening, not far from the Tiber, in the long shadows when he was out late, and they were salvaging a dead body from the river, he thought he saw Gus Hogan standing on the river bank below him, waiting to give the Last Rites. Gus was dead, of course, and it was some other priest. But the nameless girls he had slept with were reflected for a moment in the blaze of a car headlight, and they looked just like the Hosts thrown up in the air in Saint Peter's to land without protection among the uncaring.

When the chance came to go to America, Michael was glad to take it. Rome was starting to drag him down.

2

The Congregation for Divine Worship hoped to put relations with the American-based ICEL, the International Committee on English in the Liturgy, on a more congenial footing. To all outward appearances, relations had always been excellent with the ICEL. Its Chairman, Frederick R. McManus, had been a member of Archbishop Bugnini's secret pre-Consilium working group of 1964. As long as Augustine Hogan was alive, however, they had been playing a double game. In 1969, the Consilium had issued a cautiously progressive Instruction on the principles of the translation of liturgical texts, *Comme le Prevail*. The ICEL had made themselves a rather bold English translation of this policy document, and had then wanted to cover their backs by procuring Vatican approval. Vatican approval in this matter ordinarily meant the approval of Gus Hogan. The ICEL version of the Instruction had but one purpose: that the ICEL might thereby be empowered to downplay the literal meanings of the Latin words in favour of a recovery of the supposed original intention behind the Latin text as it would communicate itself to their specific historical time. There was no way that Gus Hogan would ever approve this rendition, so Michael approved it in his name, and obtained Archbishop Bugnini's initials on the document. When Gus found out what had happened, Michael was able to point to Bugnini's initials, and Gus was silenced on the matter. And so it continued. The ICEL addressed its requests for approval not to the Relator, Monsignor Hogan, but to his assistant, Monsignor Cremin, who saw to it that Gus never set eyes on them until the matter to be approved was already established practice. There was nothing wrong with this, of course. They were battling a traditionalist onslaught, and Gus just happened to be on the wrong side. Now Gus was dead, and Michael and his American friends could work together openly, at last. In addition to Professor McManus and his group, there was Father Robert Hovda, who had an unprecedented understanding of semiotics. Michael hoped to learn at first hand about the new dramaturgical techniques which Bob Hovda was beginning to explore in rejuvenating the Mass.

Despite their hard work, the New Mass was not quite what Archbishop Bugnini, and Michael with him, would have liked. The Novus Ordo and the Instructions which followed it were compromise solutions, and the true progressives in the Church were restricted in scope. There was nothing that could be done but work to strengthen the new National Episcopal Conferences and the Diocesan

Conferences on Liturgy, and to encourage local Ordinaries to give as great a role to lay people as possible. This was a sure promise of permanent innovation. In time, the new would arise by itself and would sweep aside the old with the unimpeachable logic of natural necessity.

3

After a succession of ICEL workshops at New York's Fordham University, the chain-smoking Father Hovda took Michael around a parish he helped out with, Saint Joseph's in Greenwich Village. It made him feel like Jesus, he confided, when he spent time among the low-lifers and deadbeats of the Village, where it was always inspirational and relaxing. The Village was an exotic place. Long-haired people sat around in the street playing sitars and didgeridoos. Clothing from far-away India and Nepal seemed all the rage, at least among those who wore clothes, and wherever one looked, a clash of aquamarines, crimsons, and saffrons leaped at the eye, while the sense of smell revelled in the waft of oriental spices, sharpened in places by the heady flush of roasting coffee.

"We need to get the artists back into the Church, Michael," Father Hovda explained. "Get the poets working on the texts for the Mass." He pointed to a grimy bar window just in front of them. "That's where Ginsberg and the boys hang out." He peered through, and waved Michael over. "See that guy there sleeping it off in the corner? That's Benjamin Dukamski. The poet of the colour green. He's doing a new Gloria for the Mass."

Hovda was a well-known figure. He slapped his hand against outstretched open palms, embraced individuals of either sex here and there, and returned loud hails of welcome from open windows.

"You know how it all began, don't you?" They had stopped at a street cafe for a rest.

"How what began?"

"Liturgy."

"The Last Supper, wasn't it?"

Hovda seemed amused. "I mean our liturgy. Ours for today. It was good old Virgil Michel. You remember what Nietzsche said? You gotta have chaos inside you to give birth to a dancing star. That was Virgil, sure enough. He'd been in Europe with Lambert Beauduin and when he got back to Saint John's, the place was a living hell. It was the 1920s. And Virgil cracked up. So they sent him out to the Chippewa reservation to get well again. Best thing they ever did. You gotta imagine what it was like out there, the wide open plains and all the communal living close to nature. Just magic."

Michael knew the story. After a mystical experience among the American Indians, Dom Virgil had returned to his monastery with a burning conviction of what liturgical celebration should be: artistic and social, an expression of a whole community's love of beauty and its striving for justice. Virgil Michel died long before the Second Vatican Council, but Saint John's Abbey kept his torch blazing. Some of those inspired by him were called to Rome for the Council, as periti, and more. Two of them, Archbishop Rembert Weakland and Father Frederick McManus, now headed the Bishop's Conference on the Liturgy in America. With Hovda as their right-hand man, they were teaching priests to celebrate the Mass as an event of positive experience, which would speak as much to the senses as to the intellect, and could integrate elements from the cultures and subcultures of the congregation without fear.

"You see, Michael, Virgil realised before anyone that the Church was wrong about the Mass. The Mass had gotten to be too abstract. A poor, lonely guy fiddling around on an altar, afraid he's making a mistake in the ceremonial, and everyone just passively watching him. Virgil saw this had to stop."

Bob Hovda was refreshing. He had no time at all for the hierarchical thinking that everyone in Rome took so seriously. He had been a socialist once, and a Lutheran, and a Methodist, before converting to Catholicism. He paid no attention at all to the Holy See and its activities, and titles like Cardinal and Archbishop brought out the sardonic humour in him. He was a thorn in the side of his own bishop in Fargo, North Dakota, whom he regarded as a failure.

"Michael, where do they drain the humanity out of potential hierarchs? Is there a special processing plant over there somewhere? And what kind of acid do they mix with the shit that takes its place?"

They chuckled together over their umpteenth pot of coffee. Bob's apartment in the Lower East Side was an odd place, but it suited its occupant: scruffy, smelly, run-down, with draughty windows and bad plumbing, but with a rich and idiosyncratic collection of artwork. It was hard to say what predominated: the cigarette ends, the booze, the haphazard piles of books, or the inspired glass work and pieces of pottery.

Michael was happy to tell Bob about the famous European liturgists he was acquainted with: men like Johannes Wagner of Trier, Josef A. Jungmann of Innsbruck, and of course, his own superior, Archbishop Bugnini. Bob Hovda held each and all of them in low esteem. "We need guys like you in charge, Michael," came his raspy whisper. "Not some pen-pusher who gets all scared by inclusive language. And not these autistic professors who can't even hug anybody."

Michael was greatly impressed by Bob Hovda. At that time, Bob was putting together a book from his notes for his liturgical retreats for priests, and he showed Michael the work-in-progress. *Strong, Loving and Wise*, was to be the title. Strong. Loving. Wise. It was a wonderful ideal for the priesthood. And the priest described there was a virtuoso of his art, presiding over the assembled community with word, gesture, voice quality, eye contact and clothing. On the altar, that model priest was a master of psychodynamics, while off the altar, he was a warm and suffering human being, who had already been there wherever the people were, and who had already been wherever they were going. There was compassion, sensuality, a feeling of wide open spaces, a coming to rest, a freedom. By comparison, the Europeans were lukewarm intellectuals caught up in paralysing trivia.

"You see, Michael, the Mass should involve everyone the way they feel like being involved. That's what brings God to the people. Not some Latin crap from the Middle Ages. And not this Novus Ordo crap they stole from the German Protestants and are trying to sell to us like it was something new. A guy who plants grain and brings it in when it's ripe, and whose brothers and sisters all grind it down and bake bread with it, he knows about transubstantiation. It's the song they all sing around the campfire when the bread's passed around fresh and warm; that's Liturgy, Michael. And the joy that fills them, and makes them dance around in each other's arms, that's what reverence is."

How right he is, Michael thought, as they opened another bottle of bourbon.

There was so much still to be done on the unresolved issues of the English-speaking liturgy that Michael had to prolong his stay. He was able to broker a reconciliation of sorts between Robert Hovda and the ICEL, who had fallen out over the texts of some of Hovda's poet friends. He was also able to help with some difficult organizational matters. Father McManus wanted only the best and brightest on his team. But the best and brightest tended to spend only a short time with him, then to abandon the ICEL in frustration. Some of them even abandoned the priesthood. The nub of the problem was that McManus was too tolerant of the conservatives around him, who were basically hostile to the ICEL programme, and he was far too democratic when it came to the flow of information. Michael recommended the Bugnini organisational model from the Consilium. The ICEL structures were quietly toughened up, with information circulating only on a need-to-know basis. Michael and Bob Hovda celebrated this turning point by getting madly drunk in Greenwich Village.

Subsequently, Father Hovda suggested that he and Michael take off westwards, to Collegeville, Minnesota and stay for a while in the famous Abbey of Saint John. There would be no overriding purpose to it, no hectic schedules, no pressures. Just letting time pass, and taking in some of the natural beauty there. Michael was happy to accept. St. John's had been Bob's home as a seminarian in the 1940s, and it still had the reputation of spearheading American liturgical reform. It was easy for Michael to obtain permission by telex from Rome. Archbishop Bugnini had once again seen off a Cardinal Prefect, this time the dithering Cardinal Tabera, who had been moved to the Congregation of the Affairs of Religious, leaving Bugnini in sole charge of Divine Worship. The Archbishop was delighted with the progress in America so far. Despatches of urgent business could reach him as easily in Minnesota as in New York. He trusted Michael and he gave him a free hand.

In the end, Robert Hovda was called away on official business, and Michael travelled to Minnesota alone.

4

St. John's Abbey combined the peace of the enclosure with a bracing openness to the outside world, and Michael was delighted to be there. There was a constant coming and going of visitors, sightseers, teachers and students from the most disparate religious and cultural backgrounds. St. John's was also a place of slow-moving time cycles and vast expanses of space; of wide, restful lakes and endless forests. The Benedictine Community included some of the most gifted people Michael had ever come across. Launcelot Deeler OSB was a trailblazer in youth and community education. He often took groups of young people on weekend retreats in log cabins on the shores of Swenson Lake, where there were intense interactions and refreshingly few taboos. Godfrey Diekmann OSB, who had been an influential peritus at the Council, was head of the liturgical centre at the Abbey and famous throughout the world. There was fine scholarship there, and art and music of the highest quality. An occasional visitor was the former Abbot Primate, Rembert Weakland, who had started off as a monk of Saint John's, and was now the Archbishop of Milwaukee, and one of the most talked-about people in America.

These charismatic men were true heirs of Virgil Michel. They had weathered every ecclesiastical and social crisis, even the American traumas of the 1960s. An extreme faction, politicised by the assassinations of the Kennedys and Martin Luther King, demanded that Liturgy engage directly with the terrible global evils that were threatening all life on the planet earth, especially the war in Vietnam. For them, there was no better place to celebrate Mass than chained to the railings of the Pentagon with the gun barrels of the military trained on the hosts and chalices in their hands. Some of these activist priests ended up in jail for long periods. Others died in the jungles of South America side by side with Marxist revolutionaries. Their teachers, the old-style radicals, were very much in sympathy, of course, but they preferred a more gradual approach. Let people be free in their faith, they argued; let them find personal joy through the unfettered exploration of the love of God in their lives, and justice would emerge naturally, all by itself.

It was at Saint John's Abbey, as the restful autumn came and went, that Michael Cremin was introduced to Zen Buddhism. A pupil of Roshi Philip Kapleau had entered Saint John's Abbey as a novice, and the Abbot had given him permission to continue with his practice of Zen. Brother Pius, as he was known, thrived as a monk, and inspired others to follow his example. The Roshi and the Abbot believed that only good could come of the encounter between Benedictine spirituality and the wisdom of Zen, and a regular meditation group was set up at Saint John's. However, the distance from Kapleau's headquarters in Rochester, New York, was considerable, and there were hardly any pupils who were advanced enough to be sent out as teachers. After Brother

Pius moved to a Canadian dependency of the Abbey, the Zen group was left to itself. Despite this lack of competent direction, or perhaps because of it, the meditation sessions were well-attended both by the monks and by laymen and laywomen.

The Zen at Saint John's was by now a lot less stringent than Philip Kapleau's own style, and it was no comparison at all to the style of the Roshi's Japanese masters. But it was still splendidly different. Instead of knees aching from hours of immobility on hard wooden boards in draughty oratories, there were now aches and pains from sitting immobile in approximations to the lotus position. Instead of fighting off boredom and sleep during the recitation of the Psalms or the consideration of Gospel verses, the meditators struggled to stay alert while reciting Buddhist Sutras and trying to keep their awareness empty.

Zazen, as the periods of meditative sitting were called, was not by definition prayer in the Christian sense, because the non-dual reality towards which it tried to point the meditator's experience was not thought of in personal terms. Nevertheless, a Catholic priest could detect many affinities with the prayer traditions of his Church.

As the weeks went by, Michael took pleasure in a sense of growing stamina. At first, he was able to bear the pain in his legs and shoulders for only 5 minutes or less, then for 20, then for close on thirty, and at times he reached levels of awareness where there was no pain at all. He would always have to let two rounds of walking pass him by while he massaged the blood back into his legs and became able to stand. When he was able to sit on the hard black cushion with relative ease, using the half-lotus position, he began attending the Sesshin. These were intensive meditation periods lasting a week or ten days. There were eight hours and more every day of sitting in silent immobility, broken every thirty minutes or so by a few rounds of ritualised walking. Every morning there was a short formal lecture by the person presiding, who was usually someone recommended to the Abbey by Zen insiders.

It was one of these who gave Michael his first koan, the koan Mu:

A monk approached the Master Joshu and asked, does a dog have true reality? Joshu answered, MU!

The word Mu meant something like 'nothing', or 'have not'. By answering the question in this nonsensical way, the master provoked the pupil into escaping the fog of language which was blinding him to reality. Towards the end of the Sesshin, Michael's turn came to go for the ritual private consultation with the teacher. "What is Mu?" Michael was asked. A huge sneeze erupted from him, and he burst out laughing. The teacher, who was a stockbroker from Eugene, Oregon, bowed low before him, told him he had solved the koan, and gave him a new one.

Michael assumed that this was progress and was very pleased. But he was also struck by a certain absurdity. What Roshi Philip Kapleau's former pupil had brought to St John's was an extreme form of mortification which not even the Trappists or the Carthusians would have deemed safe. Despite this asceticism, or perhaps because of it, it was ultimately superficial. The same progressive Catholics who sneered at the primitivity of their own dogmas would become wildly enthusiastic over the nonsense statements of the Zen koans. Priests and nuns who knew the Bible thoroughly were using Sutras they could barely understand to practise contemplation. They had so rich a spiritual tradition of their own, but there they were, those worldly Benedictines and their friends, Michael included, mixing together everything that appeared before them with a spiritual tag and lapping it up like cats at the cream.

Michael came to see that few of those Zen students were as good as they seemed. Many did nothing much apart from engaging very publicly in zazen from time to time. During the demanding sesshin, there was all kinds of cheating to make things easier. Some of them would miss out an afternoon zazen period to go to bed for a while. Others had supplies of tobacco and alcohol in their rooms to help things along. Among the more serious students, there were personal crises and mental breakdowns. There was supposedly an enlightenment experience once, who was sent to the Roshi for verification, but never arrived there, and never returned.

What Zen could do, however, Michael concluded, was point to something which the post-conciliar Church was beginning to discover: there was a natural way to God, open to all with enough will and perseverance. Few would ever walk it, perhaps, but it was there. Thinkers such as Aldous Huxley were right to speak of a perennial philosophy, an underground font of wisdom, constantly flowing since the dawn of mankind, but owned by no single tradition, and accessible to all who were prepared to shoulder the burden of searching. God and mankind were partners in the creation of reality. God was always the other side of the coin, immanent in everything said and done by men and women.

One lazy Sunday, Michael put these thoughts into a letter to his old friend, Gerry Hegarty. Gerry was still in Dublin, having put aside his dislike of the new Archbishop, Dermot Ryan, to accept a role in the financial administration of the Archdiocese. Gerry had been reading the Anglican apologist, C.S. Lewis, and this prompted his response. One could be like God and very far from Him, he wrote back, and one could be unlike God, and very close to Him. That was the difference between Lucifer and Jesus. And if Michael thought about it, Gerry wrote, he would have to agree that there was only one phenomenon that was immanent in everything men and women said and did, and that was Sin. Partnership with God was for the saints who no longer sinned, or at least, did not sin very much, and who immediately repented when they did. And no saint would ever use words about God the way Michael did. Michael should think about it. A lot.

Michael did not think about it. By the time he had figured out what Gerry was trying to say, he had become involved in something else at St. John's, and he had no more interest in his friend's ramblings.

5

One Sunday evening, after the usual 90 minutes of zazen, Michael had been approached by Launcelot Deeler. Dom Launcelot, a thin, bearded man with bad skin, had told him that some of the younger men had taken a liking to him. They wanted to invite Michael to one of their little circles.

"We smoke some weed there," he added. "And we listen to the spirit."

Launcey, as he was known, led Michael to a room at the top of a long flight of stairs in a disused part of the Abbey building. It was round in shape, with a conical half-ceiling of stained wood, and it was laid out with rugs which had been thrown away by their owners, judging by their threadbare appearance. There were no furnishings, apart from a selection of pipes and incense burners, and a supply of old cushions.

"Does the Abbot know about this place?" Michael asked.

"He likes to think that he doesn't."

There were nine or ten people reclining on the cushions. A hashish pipe was being passed round. When Michael and Launcelot Deeler took their places, they formed a complete circle, lying with their cushions against the wall, their feet pointing inwards. Above them, suspended from the conical ceiling on piano wire, but close to the apex, invisible from anywhere except where they were lying, was a framed picture of two men kissing.

"What's that?" Michael asked as the pipe was passed to him.

"Just one blow," whispered his neighbour. "Hold it in as long as you can."

"I mean up there. Under the roof."

"It's an icon."

"Of what?"

"It's Launcey's icon of the Kiss. Judas and Jesus."

Michael coughed out the acrid smoke as it bit into his throat and lungs, and then fell back as the drug took effect, a gentle drowsiness, soon followed by a quickening of the mental associations, as concepts, tastes and smells swam in and out of each other with slow pleasure.

"You guys into Judas, then?" Michael asked. A great ease was spreading inside him.

"Yeah. We're the Judas Society."

Launcelot Deeler was reclining opposite Michael, one knee pulled towards his chest, the other long leg stretched out lazily.

"Judas is the real hero of the Gospels. What would Jesus have been, if Judas hadn't done what he did? Judas was a great, solitary man; he took all the shadow there ever was and gave it a name, so we could see it, all by himself. He's the one."

They dreamed in silence for a while.

"The spirit's saying to me there's a Karmic connection between Judas and Friedrich Nietzsche."

"Yeah. Human, all too human."

"Beyond Good and Evil. That's the place to be."

"Thus spake Zarathustra!"

In this round of drugged assent, Michael drifted off to sleep. When he awoke, he was in his bed in his usual room in the main monastery building. A slight headache and a dryness of the mouth remained from the night before. He could not remember how it had ended.

The Judas Society was the half-serious name those youngish monks had chosen for their club. What brought them together was an interest in extending their spiritual experience, particularly in ways taught in non-Catholic and non-Christian traditions. By choice, they were process theologians, and believed in the Death of God. By this, they meant going beyond God as He was falsely described in the Jewish and Christian scriptures, whom they sometimes termed the Old God. They were preparing the way for the New God, or God as he would then be, when liberated from the falsifications of ignorant and fearful men. This New God would emerge out of the free affirmation of their experience. They preferred spiritual highs of the classical type, which included the use of mind-expanding substances, but at a pinch, they were prepared to admit that all experiences were spiritual, once you had achieved the right perspective. The more intense the experiences, the better. They were avid readers of Lao Tse and the Beat Poets, of Alan Watts and Carlos Castaneda, of Hermann Hesse and Friedrich Nietzsche. For the men of the Judas Society – they had not got as far as including women – there was no difference between being a teacher and being a pupil, being a priest and being an unbeliever, being right and being wrong. St. John's Abbey and their Catholic lives ought to be big enough and generous enough to have room for it all.

6

When the time came for Michael to return to his duties in Rome, he had spent almost nine months in Collegeville. There seemed no urgency about getting back, so he decided to travel first to Dublin, to spend a few days with his parents. The flight schedules meant a wait of some hours at New York's John F. Kennedy Airport. In one of the concourses there was an art exhibition, and Michael, hoping to pass the time, went over to take a look. The artists, who appeared to be associates of the famous Andy Warhol, were best known for their depictions of pop icons, such as Marilyn Monroe, and of drinks cans and other objects of consumption. In this exhibition, they had turned to sacred themes. There was a painting of a metal tube crucifix from which scruffy bartenders were filling glasses of beer in a run-down diner. There was a church done out like a hot-dog stand. There was even a painting of a priest saying Mass. The more Michael considered this last picture, the more it impressed him. It depicted the Consecration. But what the priest was elevating was not a Chalice; it was a bottle of beer, and the acolyte kneeling beside him was not an altar boy but a naked young man. The vestments of the priest had been torn open, revealing part of his back, which was bleeding from a wound. Michael was much taken by this picture. It was something like an epiphany. But an epiphany of what? Then, rightly or wrongly, something hit him: the tragedy of the Mass, as Gus Hogan had seen it. The shoddiest human products dumped on the altar in the place of the sacred species. A priest incapable of reverence, and slowly dying as a result, turning to perverted pleasures to distract him from the grim reality. A congregation looking the other way. And in that painting, the priest had his back to the congregation. He was celebrating the Old Mass, not the New. The Old Mass, it seemed, was still needed for a worthwhile blasphemy.

For all its vividness, the epiphany was quickly over, like the sound of one hand clapping, or the look of the face that had been his before he was born, as the Zen koans put it.

7

The Cremin home in Dublin seemed at first to be the same comfortable place it had always been. But as Michael walked through the familiar rooms of his childhood, a subtle difference became perceptible, one that he could not place. Things were much the same as during his last visit, much the same as always. Busts of composers and virtuosos of the piano and the violin still filled the empty spaces on ledges and shelves. There were still books of music and books about music wherever one looked.

After breakfast on his second day, Michael saw the reason. It was the absence of Ludwig van Beethoven. The wild-haired portrait of the composer glowering furiously over a manuscript, which had always hung in the hallway, was no longer there. A much gentler portrait, one of Franz Schubert, hung shyly in its place. A walk through the house confirmed his impression. Beethoven, one of the heroes of Michael's youth, had been expelled from the family home completely. Not even the recording of the Ninth Symphony with Karajan and the Berlin Philharmonic, not even the Emperor Concerto with Wilhelm Backhaus, and the Vienna Philharmonic under Carl Schüricht, which Michael loved above all, had survived this strange new regime.

"I was tired of him." His father's voice had a new ring to it.

"Tired of Beethoven?"

"Tired of that clenched fist being shaken in my face."

That did not explain much, and Patrick Cremin refused to be drawn on the matter. Michael's stepmother seemed more disposed than usual to speak to him. She had given Patrick a book about Beethoven as a birthday present. For some reason she could not understand, Patrick had been deeply shocked at the book's revelation of the composer's personal life. Apparently, Patrick had always believed that the composer of such lovely music must have been a very nice man, and a pleasure to know and deal with. But Beethoven's character, if one was not too blinded by his genius to see it, had been ugly in the extreme: petty, vindictive, exploitative, selfish, jealous, arrogant, graceless and hard. Having considered this, Patrick had decided that he would have nothing more to do with Beethoven. Michael's stepmother did not care how badly long-dead composers had behaved when they were alive. It was the music that counted, she thought. But her husband could not be prevented from purging their home of Beethoven and his music. At the same time, he made many other changes in his life. He gave up watching boxing matches on television. And he was showing an enthusiasm for prayer which his family had never seen in him before. His father was getting old, Michael thought, wryly.

"Beethoven was a monstrous egotist," his father explained one day, during a lazy afternoon in the garden.

"What's that got to do with his music?"

"Everything. That's what the music is all about. Self. Big, bloated, grasping self."

As a comment on music, that remark seemed nonsensical. But his father would not budge.

"There's a saint I've been reading about," Michael's father continued, "Saint Thérèse, the Little Flower. It's when I began to wonder if the Little Flower would have liked listening to Beethoven that I saw the reality. Would you recommend the Little Way, as she calls it?"

"No. I would not recommend the Little Way." Michael matched his father's firmness of voice. "I don't think it's a good way at all. Not in our times. And I wouldn't say she knew much about music, either. But I won't argue with you."

"And you can listen to Beethoven here anytime you want," his father answered. "Just let me know when you're bringing him in. I can go somewhere else while he's here."

While Michael was considering this remark, and enjoying the bright colours of the sun-rich garden, a courier arrived bringing an envelope with the coat of arms of the Holy See. Michael opened it with the silver letter opener his father fetched for him. It was an invitation to call on the Papal Nuncio. His father read the significance from his eyes.

"You know, Michael," Patrick Cremin ventured, after a long pause. "We've had a good enough relationship, over the years. But you never ever told me anything of what you were thinking."

"I don't recall you asking."

"No, I didn't ask, I suppose. It would have been hard to ask. But do you know what I'm thinking? I'm thinking you'll have to be more careful in the priesthood. Especially over there in Rome. I never thought I'd ever have to say something like that, but there you are."

Michael wondered whether he should thank his father for that odd statement. He decided that he did not want to.

At the appointed hour, a nervous Michael Cremin was received with measured cordiality at the Nunciature in Dublin's Phoenix Park. Artfully, the Nuncio poured tea from an antique silver teapot and engaged Michael in small talk about people and places they both knew in Rome. Almost imperceptibly, the Nuncio brought up the matter at hand. Monsignor Cremin's work in the Curia was very highly valued. But the Holy Father now wished to elevate him to the Episcopate. He was to be the next bishop of Limerick. There was a pause for surprise and reflection, as courtesy required. Then, Michael, with great satisfaction, declared himself the Holy Father's unworthy servant.

In Rome, Michael Cremin's leave-taking was to be a short one. He had little time for the toadies who were queuing up to wish him well. And his friends were few. The only important call to make was to Annibale Bugnini.

Bugnini, the Titular Archbishop of Diocletian, had remained the central figure at the Congregation for Divine Worship. Recently, Michael had heard him speak of a "phase three" of some grand plan of liturgical reform which was not public knowledge. This plan was to bring about a new incarnation of the Mass in each area of cultural identity. It had sounded like a permanently evolving set of expressive behaviours, with the features of a "discourse" and a "radical practice," as they were being described by some Marxist-oriented social theorists. It was a far cry from what the Mass had been for most of its existence.

Michael found the Archbishop at his desk. He was not alone. Beside him, whispering, was Felix Kostuva from the Secretariat of State. Bugnini was nodding with a wan smile. The metal-rimmed spectacles below the white, receding hair gleamed weakly in the faint light from the window.

"Your Excellency, what a pleasure!" Kostuva called out. Michael could see that it was not a pleasure at all. And what was Kostuva doing, greeting a visitor who was there to see Archbishop Bugnini?

Felix Kostuva seemed to sense Michael's query. "His Grace is leaving us!" he exclaimed, with a wave of his hand which might have signified deference.

Archbishop Bugnini came out from behind the desk, the usual bland half-smile on his face. "The Lord be with you."

"His Grace has been appointed to Teheran! As Apostolic Pro-Nuncio!"

Michael responded as he had to. "How fortunate for that land and its people, Your Grace!" He extended both his hands in a formal greeting, and bowed slightly. "Our prayers will accompany Your Grace on this most significant mission."

Again it was Kostuva who answered. "The good news has spread of the Holy

Father's paternal regard for the Diocese of Limerick. Most consoling! The people of Ireland are most dear to the heart of the Holy Father!"

"Most dear, of course," echoed Archbishop Bugnini, signalling to Michael that he should leave.

Michael backed towards the door with studied formality. Something was afoot. Something serious. Iran was a place where there was hardly a Catholic to be found, and where a man like Bugnini would have almost nothing to do. Its capital, Teheran, already in the beginnings of an Islamic revolution, was one of the trouble spots of the world. The poor man was not likely ever to return.

Rumours abounded in the slipstream of Archbishop Bugnini's departure. Bugnini the Freemason, worming his way into the confidence of unsuspecting popes and cardinals. Bugnini the secret heretic, serving strange gods for 30 years and more at the heart of the Roman Catholic Church. Bugnini the subversive in charge of the liturgical reforms, dismantling all that was holy, bit by bit. The traditionalists, delighted at such grist to their mill, crowed jubilantly in the world press, while the Vatican kept to its customary enigmatic silence.

The rumours peaked when an Italian newspaper published the names of some two hundred high-ranking prelates who were alleged to be Freemasons, including many cardinals and Curial officials, Bugnini among them. Old documents which referred to a grand Masonic plot against the Church were also made public, with considerable shock effect.

An acquaintance of Michael's, a man known to have his ear to the ground, saw these confused events as evidence of a split in the secret societies. Power now lay with a younger faction, in whom the post-conciliar Church did not inspire the same deep hatred that their elders had cherished for the old Church. Believing their historic mission regarding the Catholic Faith to be accomplished, these men now sought to commit the resources of the Lodges to the project of European Integration.

The Congregation for Divine Worship was quickly restructured. The new strong man was Ferdinando Antonelli OFM, who represented a new breed of pragmatic conservative. Unlike the traditionalists, these priests were prepared to accept the post-conciliar reforms and to try to make them work, no matter how much they might deplore some of the detail. A liturgical scholar of note,

Antonelli had been a wayfarer, then a rival of Bugnini. Soon, he would become a cardinal.

While the Bugnini affair was at its height, Michael could not help noticing the smug smirk on the face of Liam the Librarian. In a quiet moment at the Irish College, Liam confirmed his suspicions. He, Liam O'Casey, had passed on the absolutely certain proof of gross betrayal that had forced the unwilling pope to take action. He and Gus Hogan had worked together on the matter. Much of the evidence had mysteriously disappeared after Gus's death. But there had been enough to seal the fate of one of the main men, Bugnini. It was not easy to separate truth from lie with Liam the Librarian. Nonetheless, as his death drew unmistakeably closer, Liam had been unburdening his conscience in many surprising ways. There was no predicting the result when a worm like that began to turn.

8

It had been 5 years and more since Michael had last seen John Gregory. With the help of a friend in the police force, Michael tracked him down to a fishing village north of Ostia on the Tyrrhenian Sea, an hour or so from Rome. It was early afternoon when he arrived, and he came upon John Gregory in the driveway of his home, where he was at work loading a small van. He greeted Michael warmly, but with some reserve.

"We've been evicted," he explained gesturing towards the stacked furniture. "By order of the Vatican."

They took a short walk together and spoke of what had become of them. John had sold his taxi business and had gone to work for Father Thomas Clavis, with whom he was now living, together with a housekeeper, Patrizia, and her family. Michael related how he had helped to see the New Mass through. When he told him that he was now a bishop, John did not seem to want to reply.

"And how is Father Clavis, then?" Michael finally brought out, breaking a stiff silence.

"Come, he's expecting you."

Michael shook with annoyance. How could this man be expecting him when he had not told anyone he was coming?

It was Magdalena, the daughter of Clavis' housekeeper, a girl of some beauty and of unusual depth and quiet, who led the way. The old priest was sitting in an armchair on the downstairs patio, his hands folded over each other on a walking stick, waiting.

"My Lord Bishop! But you will forgive me if I do not kiss your ring?"

Michael grimaced with irritation, but the old priest seemed not to notice.

"An insignificant old priest like me, My Lord, too stupid even for the Spirit of the Council! The New Mass is simply beyond me! The Church has given up on me!"

Michael was disarmed, and he could not help laughing.

"Father, my late colleague, Augustine Hogan, retained the Old Mass to the end. And this despite his position with the Congregation for Divine Worship. He had great love for the Old Mass."

"Love, My Lord? What is that? I am too stupid to know. Please, enlighten me."

"God is Love, Father. That is our Faith."

"Can God love such a worm as me, My Lord? Why, I can do nothing for God!"

"It is out of His great Mercy, Father, that He loves what is unworthy of Him. That is our Faith."

"Thank you, My Lord. But permit me to put some thoughts before you, poor though my thoughts must surely be in Your Lordship's eyes. Let us imagine a priest. Shall we say, a priest who is deliberately unfaithful to his calling. A priest who invents his own morals. A priest after the manner of Friedrich Nietzsche, in fact, a revaluer of values, an admirer of the Will to Power, an affirmer of his life in this world without concern for an Afterlife in the next world, a priest, My Lord, who no longer believes in God at all, to go by his conduct of life. Now, does God love that man?"

Michael swallowed hard. This was a strange turn for the conversation to take, and young Magdalena had joined them again, a witness, uncanny in her silent beauty.

"Yes, Father. God loves that man."

"What does God love in that man? Surely it cannot be the fornications, the intrigues, the betrayals?"

"It is what that man was meant to be in the eyes of God, and still can be; that is what God loves."

"So it is a necessity then? God MUST love me?"

"Father, our lives are dependent from beginning to end on the love of God. That Love can no more be withdrawn than the rivers can flow backwards or the sun refuse to shine."

"Such love, My Lord. Such great love. But if you choose to live by night and so erect buildings in which you see only by artificial light, the sun does not refuse to shine, but surely you are refusing to permit the sun to shine on you?"

"What is your point, Father?"

The old man's head sank down against his breast. He seemed to have fallen asleep. Magdalena moved over to him and adjusted the rug which covered his knees. Exasperated, Michael turned to go.

"My Lord!" The old man called after him. "This is my point: we the creatures of God are free to choose. God is everything and everywhere. If you turn away from God, you must turn towards nothing and nowhere. Our Nietzschean priest is a man of Hell. A lover of death."

Michael stood framed in the doorway to which Magdalena had led him, and answered calmly.

"There cannot be such a priest, Father."

"Of course, not, My Lord, of course not. Thank you for correcting me."

Michael was glad to be heading back to Rome. John Gregory's hand had been cold and clammy in his grasp, like the hand of a corpse. The whole house, in fact, was a cold and lifeless place. And the garden, too, behind the gate, despite the healthy grass and the well-tended shrubs and flowers, that garden was a chill place, a place where nothing much would ever grow. It was death pretending to be life. That old man, Clavis, was a creepy fellow.

The further the car took him from the village and the closer to Rome, the better Michael began to feel. The old man was probably insane, not unexpected a fate for an entrenched traditionalist.

Still, it was sad to lose one's friends, Michael mused. It was the lot of a priest, of course, not to have friends. A priest was not a human being. A priest was a last resort for help, available to anyone at all hours of the day and night, without any needs of his own. But for many years, instead of ministering to the needy and the suffering, as he had done, briefly, in the Wicklow mountains, Michael had been a Monsignor of the Curia. Now he was a bishop. He was a management professional, helping an institution to function. Apart from that, he did pretty much as he liked. Perhaps that was why he felt so lonely, as he took his leave of Rome. He was lonely for the priest he might have been.

†

6

The Bishop of Limerick

1

At the time of Michael Cremin's installation as Bishop of Limerick, the triumphalist words of the late Archbishop McQuaid were still ringing in Irish ears: nothing had changed in the Roman Catholic Faith, or would ever change, because the Church did not change. The Mass in English and Irish may have come, and the altars in the churches may have been turned to face the people, but it was of no more significance than painting the walls a new colour or fitting new doors to the church buildings.

It was a climate of complacency, and the new bishop had little respect for it. He intended to build up a diocese in the spirit of the Second Vatican Council; one where there would be no fearful clinging to the past. His Episcopal motto was appropriately post-conciliar: Joy and Hope. The people of his diocese were to wake up to their true dignity; they were to set loose their spiritual energies and revitalise the way they lived. Belief in God and in His Son Jesus Christ meant belief-in-action, by which both the believer and his or her world were constantly being transformed. This transformational faith was nothing less than the core energy of mankind. It constituted humility, in the sense of a celebratory earthiness, which was the true meaning of that paramount Christian virtue. Of all the powerful forces of history, the Church offered the most sophisticated means for the cultivation of human potential which had yet emerged.

Such language meant little in the sleepy backwater of Limerick, but Michael Cremin was not overly concerned. Influential figures in Rome had led him to believe that after a few years in Limerick, a senior Curial position would be within his grasp. He would sow in Limerick in order to reap elsewhere. The bishops of the Irish Episcopal Conference remained suspicious of their new colleague. He was too liberal for them, and too young, and he had too much liking for publicity. But they were aware of his Vatican connections. They were courteous to Michael, but they steered clear of him. For his part, he would be jetting back to real life in Rome, soon enough. He would deal with their inertia from there, if he had to.

2

According to *Christus Dominus*, the Decree on the Pastoral Office of Bishops approved by the Second Vatican Council, bishops were appointed by the Holy Spirit as teachers and pastors, and the Holy Spirit was given to them. A bishop's diocese was not merely a subordinate branch of the Church; it was the whole of the Church locally present. A bishop was nothing less than the Vicar of Christ in his jurisdiction. In practice, a diocese demanded of a bishop the less exalted skills of organisational leadership. Financial control, resources management, personnel decisions and strategic planning of every kind were likely to take up his time. As a member of a regional Episcopal Conference, supra-diocesan functions would add to his formidable workload.

Michael Cremin, as Bishop of Limerick, was co-opted onto the governing body of All-Hallows' College in Dublin, a non-diocesan institute for educating young men for the priesthood. Michael saw the hidden potential in this role, and he surprised his fellow governors by bringing more commitment to it than anyone else. They were happy to leave the work to him, not noticing, or not caring, that it gave him more leverage than many would have welcomed. Traditionally, Limerick's new priests were educated at the national seminary in Maynooth, but Michael found he preferred the tougher, more self-reliant young men who emerged from All-Hallows. One of his long-term aims was to gather together an elite group of priests who would share his mind, and on whose loyalty he could depend. All-Hallows was a promising source. Also, the College was visited regularly by bishops from around the world who needed new priests. It was the perfect way to stay on the inside regarding ecclesiastical developments. Welcoming these bishops and helping them out meant that Michael Cremin was included in their gossip and was consulted by them on major issues.

Among the students at All-Hallows was a young man called Isaiah Courtney. As a boy he had visited Rome and had met Michael Cremin. He had never forgotten the young Monsignor who had troubled his grandmother so much. Isaiah had grown into a critically-minded young man, and he was regularly in trouble with the college authorities. The last straw, almost, was the issue of the spiritual gifts of women. On reading the autobiography of Saint Thérèse of Lisieux, Isaiah had been struck by a passage where she writes of having in her heart the vocation to the priesthood. If a woman could feel like this and still attain sanctity, it seemed that the Church's prohibition of women priests might not be justified. There was also Thérèse's ardent desire to do good on earth after her death. If Saint Thérèse was now serving God in this way, which, as a good Catholic, he was willing to believe, it seemed that she must be doing so as a woman. There must therefore be a feminine dimension to holiness, and perhaps even to God Himself, that the Church had ignored. A voracious reader, Isaiah had then stumbled on rumours of women priests in the persecuted Church in Communist countries. Hoping to ascertain the truth, Isaiah had ignored his summer pastoral assignment and made his way to Europe. In Vienna, he gained access to a private archive maintained by an Austrian civil servant, where he found the evidence he needed. On his return to Dublin, the authorities at All-Hallows ordered his expulsion. At this point, he appealed to Bishop Cremin.

Isaiah Courtney had recently seen the Bishop preside over Holy Mass. The encounter in Rome at his grandmother's side was still fresh in his mind, and he was intrigued to see how little Michael Cremin had changed. He was still young. He still had the looks of a film-star, though a rather dour one. He still bristled with ambition. There was something dark about him, the way he sat there at the altar yawning from time to time. The Mass did not seem to concern him much. He was a living question mark over the sacred mysteries he was serving. He had been a new kind of priest, now he was a new kind of bishop. Isaiah discovered that he was quite afraid of this man. But when he asked for help, he obtained it.

Bishop Cremin promptly called a review meeting. Nervously, Isaiah Courtney sat in the conference room with the President of the College, while the Bishop himself chaired the proceedings from the head of the polished oval table.

"Bishop Cremin, how can there be a clandestine Church?" The Father President frowned at the thought. "Even at the time of the catacombs there was only the one Church. Persecuted, but not clandestine. We know this!"

"Mr. Courtney?"

"The Church behind the Iron Curtain is split, Your Excellency. There is the officially-tolerated Church which is nominally loyal to Rome, but it's full of Communist toadies. And there is a clandestine Church which goes its own way and keeps the Faith alive. It tries to keep its priests and bishops a secret. My essay is about one of them, Felix Davidek."

"Bishop, it is simply ridiculous. This Davidek is a known quantity, I can say. A lunatic. And in his lucid moments almost certainly in the pay of the secret police."

"Mr. Courtney?"

"A heroic Catholic, Your Excellency, a saintly man."

"Well then. Let's hear the facts, shall we?"

Isaiah told what he knew. In 1948, after the Communist putsch in Czechoslovakia, a few courageous priests had refused to co-operate with the atheistic new regime. Small groups of committed Catholics formed around these priests, who began to work outside of the surviving diocesan structures, which were believed to be infiltrated by the Communists. They claimed legitimation from special faculties supposedly granted in 1948 by Pope Pius XII. They were known as the Church of Silence. After the Soviet invasion of 1968, the Church of Silence was targeted for destruction. It is said that one night, the late Padre Pio appeared in a dream to Jan Blaha, a wayfarer of Father Davidek, who had built up an underground community in the area around Brno in Moravia. In this vision, Davidek's community was empowered to create an Episcopal structure in order to provide apostolic legitimation in the unforeseeable circumstances that were coming. The Jesuit Order was active in support of the persecuted Churches of Eastern Europe and had clandestine bishops of its own. Blaha and Davidek sought out one of these, Peter Dubovsky SJ, who was operating from Augsburg in Germany. They were judged acceptable by him and were consecrated as bishops. On his return, Bishop Davidek implemented a number of emergency initiatives; one of them was the ordination of women. The women he ordained were charged not to engage in a public ministry, but to administer the Sacraments only in the event of their being imprisoned.

"Who does young Courtney think he is, Bishop? Running off to the continent questioning everything."

"Really, Father President. The young man has not finished speaking. What do you conclude, Mr. Courtney? That the Church is wrong to exclude women from Ordination?"

"No, Your Excellency. I only ask a few questions. For example, the Real Presence. If the Church believes that the Real Presence is given only by her Sacrament of the Eucharist, how can she tolerate the thought of a women's prison without the Eucharist? If she is not empowered to permit women to consecrate the Bread and Wine in a place where men are not permitted, she is declaring that there are places in the world where God can't be present. I think that is a blasphemy."

"Really, Bishop, the whole matter is completely over this fellow's head. And that's being generous to him. We don't want to say he rejects the law of the Church, now, do we?"

Isaiah spoke up. "The Real Presence is real. It's not a legal thing. So it is independent of the laws of the Church."

"Look at how he speaks up, Bishop!"

Bishop Cremin raised his hand for silence.

"Father President! Why are we afraid of an enquiring mind? Let the young man ask his questions. Let him go to an Institute of his choice for further study. I will pay for it. Finish your work on the Davidek group, Mr. Courtney. And when you're finished, have a look at the persecuted Church in 17th Century Japan. There'll be plenty for you to think about."

The President's face changed colour a number of times. No matter how much he wanted to be rid of Isaiah Courtney, he could not afford to alienate Bishop Cremin, who was not just a governor, but also a benefactor of the College. There was the pressing matter of the leaking roof in the priests' library, which the Bishop was being asked to pay for.

The Diocese of Limerick under Michael Cremin had indeed grown into a powerful financial force. When he had first taken over, Michael had appointed a millionaire lapsed Catholic named Leo Murphy to run his financial affairs. Leo

Murphy proved to have the Midas touch where Limerick was concerned, and it was badly needed. Within a few years, he had made the virtually bankrupt diocese into one of the richest in Europe. The aggressive fiscal style raised many an eyebrow, but most people were convinced by its success. Even the Vatican approved. Bishop Cremin had become a regular supplier of funds to the special projects of the new Pope, John Paul II.

The Father President was a realist. "Good. We'll hang on to Mr. Courtney and make something of him, if Your Lordship so wishes."

"Young man, are you determined to be a priest?"

"I am, my Lord Bishop."

"Then you shall be one of my priests, God willing!"

This was the moment Isaiah Courtney had been waiting for. It was the sign of the Church's acceptance of his vocation. Not the final sign, but a clear confirmation, nonetheless. Isaiah felt good about himself, for the first time in a long time, and he was too young, or too ambivalent, to question it.

Bishop Cremin, of course, had other things in mind than the self-doubt spirituality of old. One of the books he encouraged the young man to read was *Infallible? An Inquiry* by the radical Swiss theologian, Hans Küng. It was the first of many shocks the young man was to receive. Küng's demolition of the dogma of Papal Infallibility brought Isaiah face to face with some unpalatable truths: his faith, like the faith of many around him, was not the child-like trust the Gospels spoke of, but senseless obedience, infantile in the refusal of responsibility. If Küng was right, the truth was not preserved by God protecting Church leaders or sacred texts from error, the truth was preserved in the midst of many dreadful errors, and despite those errors. It was almost like saying that God did not preserve the truth at all, at least not in the way everyone had come to expect, and certainly not in an institution such as the Church.

In sorrow and anger, Isaiah Courtney wrote to Bishop Cremin to denounce Hans Küng. Küng was a total rationalist. Küng had more time for the likes of Hegel and Marx than for the Saints and the Blessed Virgin. Küng might well have fallen away from the Catholic Faith. Hadn't the Vatican ordered his dismissal as a teacher of Catholic theology?

The Bishop wrote back thanking the young man for his questions. He suggested that the real issue might not be that of how good a Catholic Hans Küng was, but whether his arguments were correct. If not, surely they could be refuted?

It was a reasonable point, and Isaiah began to look into the matter more thoroughly. He became aware that for all the Vatican-inspired scrutiny of Küng, no theologian was attempting a refutation of his central arguments. Instead, they were working overtime to discredit Küng's person. This was not the love of the truth that was supposedly at the heart of the Catholic Church. It made Isaiah uneasy. He wrote again to Bishop Cremin. Perhaps a theologian had to love the truth before he could recognise the truth. Perhaps the willingness to make the sacrifice of the intellect was part of that love. Where was this in Hans Küng? Küng was the most famous theologian in the world. It had gone to his head.

This time the Bishop's reply contained no praise. Isaiah was told bluntly to decide what he wanted to be: a coward afraid of the truth, or an upright man willing to look the truth in the face.

By return of post, Isaiah Courtney told the Bishop that he had no time for cowardice. He wanted to be strong. He wanted to be free. Strong and free to serve God.

3

With Bishop Cremin's financial support, Isaiah Courtney completed a Master's thesis on the lore surrounding Saint Mary Magdalene. Since the popularisation of the Dead Sea Scrolls and the Nag Hammadi findings, mass-appeal titles had been revealing the supposed hidden history of this saint. Isaiah's work supported some of these accounts in places, but his professor insisted on imposing a more orthodox interpretation. The young man wrote to inform the Bishop of this obstacle.

"We have power, we in the Church," the Bishop wrote back. "Power over how millions of men and women understand themselves. Power over the past and the future. If the truth makes us less effective in our work, perhaps that is a reason for saying that it is not the truth. My advice is this: change the university. Find a professor you can work with, and submit your thesis there."

Isaiah did so, and a year later, he was awarded his degree with high honours.

"That's how it's done," Bishop Cremin said, when they met shortly afterwards.

"Finding the self-confidence to manage the discourses yourself. Playing to win. That's the game the Church plays."

"Are we serving God?" the young man asked.

"Of course we are," was the answer.

Bishop Cremin had considerable interest in all new advances in biblical scholarship. He actively encouraged the young man's interest in the Jerusalem Community, which had been headed by James the Just, the brother of Jesus, after the Crucifixion. Some scholars of Judaism who had studied the New Testament from a Jewish perspective, were arguing that the man referred to as Saint Paul had actually been expelled by these Judaeo-Christians for propagating a teaching of his own invention. A teaching which those who had known Jesus well found utterly ludicrous. If these scholars were right, the origins of the Church needed to be completely rethought. The founder of Christianity was not Jesus of Nazareth, nor anyone who had known him personally; not Saint Peter, not any of the Apostles who had travelled with him in Galilee and Judea. The founder of Christianity was Saul of Tarsus, and it was the psychological power of his religious experience that had animated him, not the humble discernment of the spirit behind it. With financial help from Bishop Cremin, Isaiah Courtney studied with one of these scholars and came to share some of his views.

Again, his misgivings forced the young man to write to the Bishop: "if you accept what Professor Maccoby says, then you must accept that the Church has not in the least been faithful to the teachings of Jesus of Nazareth. How can you spend your life serving a structure built on so many lies and betrayals?"

The Bishop replied promptly: "I am happy to try to serve God to the best of my poor abilities. And if I may advise you, the extremes of historical critical studies are as pernicious as blind faith in the texts. Truth is not abstract, it is only true in the application. Use the extremes to see clearly where you want to go. Use what works. Forget the rest."

Again, Michael Cremin seemed to be right.

4

Pope John Paul II, who had begun to reign in 1978, had emerged as a colossus on the world stage. The strange death of his predecessor and the succession of scandals surrounding the Vatican finances had dealt the Church some serious blows. But by sheer personal force, the Polish pope was bringing about a resurgence of the global power of Catholicism. Many young men who were studying for the priesthood were taking heart from his example. But to Isaiah Courtney, Pope John Paul was a man of theatrical gestures rather than moral credibility, a man of externals. Ernesto Cardenal, the priest-poet, who had become Minister for Culture in Nicaragua, was a case in point. After his ordination as a priest, Father Cardenal had formed a Christian community with the illiterate poor on an island on Lake Nicaragua. It thrived there to international acclaim until 1977, when the experiment was destroyed by the armies of the dictator, Somoza. Claiming to have become a Marxist revolutionary through reading the Bible, Cardenal was a hero of liberation theology and an inspiring personage. In 1981, Pope John Paul II visited Nicaragua. At Managua airport, with the TV cameras running, the charismatic pope in his flowing white robes chastised Ernesto Cardenal, and told him to regularise his status as a priest. He never did, and was eventually suspended from the priesthood. Yet, despite their materialist persuasion, Cardenal and other Marxist priests were not in danger of excommunication. They could dilute their priesthood with atheist philosophies to their heart's content, as long as they did not make too open a challenge to the status quo as regulated by Rome. In stark contrast, excommunication, perhaps the ultimate punishment, was to strike that beacon of Catholic Traditionalism, Marcel Lefebvre.

Though under suspension since the mid 1970s, Archbishop Lefebvre had always maintained that he and his Society of Saint Pius X were completely loyal to the Holy See. With advancing age and declining health, Lefebvre grew worried about the future of the Society, and through it, the Old Mass of the pre-conciliar Church. To ensure its survival, he ordained four auxiliary bishops as his successors. Previously, the pope's emissary, Cardinal Ratzinger, had promised the full rehabilitation of Lefebvre and his Society, including the right to consecrate one successor-bishop of his choice, if Lefebvre would make the required gestures of submission. The old traditionalist could not overcome his mistrust, and went ahead on his own. The complex juridical issues were to divide experts for decades, but in effect, Archbishop Lefebvre was deemed to have excommunicated himself.

The fact of Excommunication was proclaimed by a Decree of the Holy See with the title: *Dominus Marcellus Lefebvre*. Isaiah Courtney read it in the porch of

Westminster Cathedral in London in the summer of 1988. There and then, he decided that he could no longer go forward for the priesthood. Felix Davidek had been a heroic and saintly bishop, and the Church was destroying his example by denying its existence. As for Archbishop Lefebvre, there was hardly a diocese in French-speaking Africa which did not owe its survival to him. If priests of this calibre could end as outlaws, what hope was there for him? He could not serve this Church. As soon as he was able to, he informed Bishop Cremin of his decision to leave.

At this time, the Bishop was emerging from a bruising battle over the renewal of the Sacrament of Penance in Limerick. This core Catholic practice had been renamed the Sacrament of Reconciliation with the optional form of a free and open conversation between penitent and priest. Bishop Cremin wanted to go further. He wanted to harness the full potential for transforming lives. The concepts of Sin and Remorse were out, he declared. Instead, priests were to speak of Moral Challenges, which would be addressed not by negative prescriptions of acts of penance, but by a positive focus on life-targets for personal growth. Some older priests, unwilling to play the psychotherapist, had denounced the Bishop's innovations to the Vatican. These priests got nowhere, of course, and Bishop Cremin, in anger, had cleared them from his diocese. For this, he had been pilloried in the newspapers as 'Michael the Cruel.' Shortly afterwards, with excellent timing, an article had appeared in a prestigious theological journal entitled *Bishop Cremin's Abolition of Sin.* Concerned friends in Rome had then intervened, and so, not long after their humanist metamorphosis, 'moral challenges' became 'sins' again in the Diocese of Limerick. The crisis was over, but the name 'Michael the Cruel' now stuck to him like iron filings to a magnet.

Belying this new reputation for cruelty, the Bishop wrote to Isaiah Courtney full of concern for his vocation. The young man was to come and see him as soon as possible. He still hoped that he would some day work for him.

"Isaiah," he began, giving the young man his full attention. They were walking briskly in the grounds of his residence. "You are wondering why good people who sincerely seek the Holy Spirit can end up on opposite sides of a dispute. Well, misinterpretation is the norm. To misunderstand is the first step on the path to truth."

"There has never been anything worse for a Catholic than excommunication. Why would the Holy Spirit put up with misunderstandings that have such terrible results?"

"Perhaps because all that we men and women ever give to the Holy Spirit is misunderstanding. We see everything in the light of our own concerns. It cannot be otherwise."

"Your Excellency, tell me who is right: Archbishop Lefebvre, or the Church which says he is excommunicated?"

"Both, I'd imagine. In their own way. And neither. It's not about our Catholic Faith, really. It's about power. It's about how the lives of the multitudes are to be regulated. The players of the game use the Will of God like they would use any other token of their strength."

"Bishop Michael, your opinion has the advantage of being generous to both sides, but it just confirms what I've suspected. The Church today is a case of the blind leading the blind. Either it went badly wrong somewhere, or it was always wrong. Is Jesus Christ the Head of this dreadful institution? Could He not have given us something better?"

"We know very little about Jesus. Very little about what He really taught. As distinct from what people said about Him. We look back over our tradition and find the way forward. That is the Church. It is an axiom by which we live that it is the Holy Spirit that guides us."

"It sounds to me like you don't really believe."

"Isaiah." The Bishop spoke with kindness. "Of course, I believe. I believe because I have to. But in one thing, at least, the Church is no different from any other religion that we know of. She entertains all kinds of fantasies about the glory of her origin. The real work is in the day-to-day activities. Shaping the future. For mankind."

It was the person more than the argument that persuaded him, but Isaiah decided to persevere. Michael Cremin had shown sustained generosity to him. And he had impressive stature. Whatever he said was widely listened to. In fact, Cremin had long had the aura of a leader-in-waiting. Added to that was the charisma of someone unfairly passed over. It had been the uninspired and uninspiring Dermot Ryan, the Archbishop of Dublin, who was appointed Pro-Prefect of the newly-constituted Congregation for the Evangelization of the Peoples, a position reckoned to be the third-highest in the Vatican. When Ryan died shortly afterwards, the pope filled the position with a minor Curial official who happened to be a fellow Slav. Cremin was almost certainly too young to head a major Vatican congregation, but a promising position could easily have been his in the Curial reshuffle which followed. Cremin was passed over again for the See of Dublin, which went to a pragmatic conservative, as the See of Armagh had done some years previously. In Rome, a tide had turned. Vigorous progressives were out of favour. It was a time for cautious men who could be relied on to toe the official line.

Despite the adverse intellectual climate, Michael Cremin took the opportunities his minor diocese provided. When Archbishop McNamara of Dublin locked horns with civil society over the fractious issue of contraception, his media-savvy colleague, Bishop Cremin, kept a deafening silence. But it was clear enough where the future lay: not with blustering old men who liked to lay down the law, but in free and dignified moral choices, personally verified. It was Bishop Cremin they turned to when this truth needed to be articulated. Michael Cremin may not have been a major leader, but it was obvious that he should have been. He did not stand for the Church as it was, but for the Church as it should be and could be. It was inspiring, while remaining strangely ill-defined.

5

Isaiah Courtney's odyssey towards the priesthood gradually slowed to a halt. Unable to cross the final bridge, the young man spent weeks in remote monasteries agonizing over the state of the Church, and beseeching God for a sign of His Will. He did not receive one. To him, that meant that he should continue, giving the institution of the Church the benefit of his many doubts. Nevertheless, the more he reflected on his faith, the more convinced he became that something disastrous had befallen the Roman Catholic Church. Only a few decades previously, this structure that was now moving towards the end of the Second Millennium with the name of Catholic would not have been recognizable as the Church. Still, there was a veneer of normality. The institution was doing most, if not all, of what the Church had always done. But somehow, it seemed drained of life and colour. The substance that remained was burning itself out in a thousand sideshows. The central drama it had once preserved was being staged somewhere else, if it was not lost forever.

When Isaiah saw this clearly, one rainy afternoon in Mount Mellary Abbey, his own fire was burning out. Close to a breakdown, he returned home. Days turned into weeks, but he just sat around the family home, able for little more than staring into space. An insight had asserted itself, an insight he could not easily deal with. All this time, he had been following a star pointed out to him by another, by Bishop Michael Cremin. He could not see that star himself. For Cremin, that which was viable was true. The Catholic Faith was there to make a human life viable from birth to death. Insofar as it did this, it was true. Isaiah could find nothing in that message to inspire him. No longing for justice. No appreciation of the beauty of God's creation. No attempt to grasp the mystery of suffering. No compassion. No love. If the Catholic Faith was only true in this sense, then it was not true at all.

There was no way around it. He would have to repudiate Michael Cremin and all he stood for, once and for all. A horrible thought.

One Sunday, a concerned friend took Isaiah with him to Mass at the Carmelite Convent in Limerick. The nuns were visible behind the high railing that protected their enclosure in the public chapel. One nun stood out from the rest. Isaiah found himself watching the little things that she did, such as the way she turned the pages in her prayer book. There was an uncommon grace about her, almost like a halo. Her name, he discovered, was Sister Marie of the Holy Trinity.

Unexpectedly, Isaiah received a letter from Bishop Cremin. It was an official kind of letter, and made no reference to Isaiah's nervous exhaustion, which the Bishop might not have known about. The Bishop wanted to stress a particular aspect of priestly formation. He was urging Isaiah, like other future priests, to seek the friendship of women who were following the religious life. Young men and women with a religious calling could benefit from wise friendships with the opposite sex through which they could share the difficulties of their path and offer each other mutual support.

Immediately, Isaiah thought of Sister Marie. The beauty and the grace he had seen around her, he wanted to see it again, and to become part of it. He hardly believed it possible, but when he asked permission to seek her out, it was granted.

The Carmelites were technically a closed order. After the Second Vatican Council, this had ceased to mean that the nuns were completely shut off from the outside world. Even so, the Prioress did not permit Sister Marie and Isaiah Courtney to meet privately. If Marie was to help him, it would be through prayer. The Prioress encouraged them to exchange letters, and these letters became a lifeline. The anomalies of history and theology ceased to trouble the young man. Instead, he learned to ask where his fears and resentments came from. He began to see how much of his life had been lost, because it had been defined falsely by desires and ambitions. Like a fresh sea breeze, Isaiah began to taste what it meant to be free. Paradoxically, that freedom entailed continuing with his vocation to the priesthood. In a thank-you letter, he told Bishop Cremin that he was spiritually alive like never before. His doctoral studies now seemed a worthless vanity; he asked permission to abandon them. He longed for nothing more than a life of hidden service, a life of struggle to do simple things perfectly in the presence of God.

Bishop Cremin replied tartly that he had no time for the aspiration to hidden service. He wanted the opposite. He wanted brilliant men who would hone their brilliance into effective weapons and rejoice in doing so. Men with whom he could build the Church of the future.

When the Prioress eventually permitted a short meeting, which she chaperoned in person, Isaiah showed the Bishop's letter to Marie, who read it carefully.

"The poor man," she said, after reading it. At that moment, had Marie advised him to, Isaiah Courtney would have broken off all contact with Michael Cremin. Instead, she showed him how little the Bishop actually mattered to him.

Again, Bishop Cremin was locked in a dispute with the Irish Episcopal Conference, this time over the new civil legislation for Divorce. He had been sponsoring fundamental research into the theology of marriage with the aim of modernising the Church's concept of this elective state. Arguing from the more generous practices of the Eastern Rite Catholic Churches, he was proposing that partners in a broken marriage be free to marry again under certain circumstances. The Episcopal Conference strongly disagreed, as ordered to by Rome. During this difficult period, Isaiah Courtney called to see the Bishop, who had forgotten that he had granted him an appointment.

"What brings you here, Isaiah?"

"Bishop Michael, I am over my difficulties. I am ready to go forward for Ordination."

"Are you?"

"I want to follow the Holy Spirit of God, whatever it might mean for me. Open-ended. If it means ignoring all the theology and history that there is, it's fine by me."

The Bishop turned round, his face a mask "Well, sir. You will first go back to the seminary. I will not have a priest of mine doing things he knows nothing about. Do the final year again. Or I will not ordain you. *Laudetur Jesus Christus!*"

"In aeternum, Amen," Isaiah answered, trying to hide the joy rushing through him.

At All-Hallows College it was unprecedented for a student to repeat a period of formation he had already completed satisfactorily.

"Got on the wrong side of Michael the Cruel, have we?" the registrar grimaced. "At least you're getting a second chance. No-one else ever did."

It was a second chance of an unusual kind. Bishop Cremin lost interest in Isaiah Courtney. There were other young men whom he was trying to educate. Where Isaiah Courtney had failed, one of these might succeed. It proved a blessing for Isaiah. He cleared a space inside himself which he could retire to in prayer, and which he kept scrupulously clean and quiet. In that space, he was able to listen and learn. There was a womanly touch to it. He was sure that God's touch would be like this, if God were a woman. No barrack-room commands to do this, or do that. No expeditionary sorties into the mind to plant slogans like flags to be defended against all comers. Above all, a closeness of presence, not always fully there, but never far away, like that of a mother. Gentleness and patience, and the chance to respond because you chose to, having recognized it to be right and good, and to do so out of a movement of love.

6

Michael Cremin already knew the Carmelite nun, Sister Marie, quite well. They had first met some years previously, shortly after Michael's installation as Bishop. Caught by a shower of rain, Michael had been rushing to his car in a hotel car park in Limerick. When he thought he had almost made it, someone stepped out in front of him, blocking his way. A young girl, her hair bedraggled from the rain. She had no coat, no umbrella. And she was so nervous she could not get the words out that she had planned to say.

"Your Excellency," she stammered, "Will you help me?"

With a flick of his finger, Bishop Cremin could have left the girl to the assistant who was beside him holding an umbrella. But there was something about this girl. She just stood there looking at him, a drowned waif, the rain running down her bare arms from her hair, and something stirred in him. Helplessly, he gave her an appointment for the following day.

The girl from the car park arrived on schedule, accompanied by her mother. Marie-Louise Costelloe was her name, and she was fifteen years old. She wanted to be a Carmelite nun. She hoped that Dr. Cremin, who was her bishop, would persuade the Carmelites to accept her before the usual age of entry.

They had to wait, of course, for the Bishop himself. The waiting room was cold, dark and draughty. To make it less forbidding, Marie began drawing with a pencil on a sketch pad she had brought. When the Bishop strode in, the floorboards creaking under his brisk step, it was these bright sketches that caught his eye. The girl had talent.

"Tell me your reasons for wanting to enter the convent."

"Your Excellency, I know only one reason. God calls me, and I come. He suffered so much as to die of love for me. I want to suffer for love of Him."

Love? What do you know about love? he wanted to say, but checked himself. On a hunch, he tried another tack. "Do you take singing lessons?"

"Your Lordship!" her mother broke in. "Marie-Louise won a scholarship to the Conservatory in Paris!"

Michael was perplexed. With her round face and her large, brown eyes, she was pretty, but no beauty. For a moment he saw Laura's eyes looking down at him from a Roman window far away in the distant past. He shook the illusion away. This girl had nothing of Laura's hard selfishness. She was more like Corinna Fielding had been, before rejection had marked her.

"I can't change the rules for you," Michael said, quietly. "I didn't make them and I can't change them. You're just too young. And you'll say goodbye to art and music in the convent. Do you know that?"

"All is in God's hands." She smiled at him with disturbing innocence.

Is it really, Michael thought. Why wasn't it in her own hands? He could not think of a worse waste than a talent for art and music entering a closed order of nuns. Anyway, there was no reason why she could not wait until she had finished school and then go through the established procedure like everyone else. He told her to be patient and to apply to the convent in the usual way, carefully hinting that she might be turned down.

"They have already turned me down. And Your Excellency will not support me. But may I petition the Holy Father?"

Michael was tired. "I'll get back to you on that," he said, already moving on with his thoughts. He had a government minister coming. "Leave your name and address on the way out, and I'll get back to you."

In the end, Michael agreed to refer the case of Marie-Louise Costelloe to Rome. He did this only to find a kind-hearted way of getting rid of her. To his consternation, Rome granted the petition. There seemed no sense to it, but some months later, still aged fifteen, Marie-Louise Costelloe entered the Limerick Carmel as a postulant.

Most Church leaders would have approved wholeheartedly of a new vocation to the religious life. Bishop Cremin did not. He believed that this growing young woman was making a mistake. It seemed tragic to him that she could have so much love inside her, but was choosing never to share it, unless it would be through the abstract means of contemplative prayer.

Unable to intervene as he might have liked, and unable to voice his mind too openly, Bishop Cremin resolved to keep a discreet eye on this girl. He was troubled by what came to his attention. The convent authorities saw no reason to tailor the Carmelite Rule to Marie's needs. She wore unsuitable clothing, ate unsuitable food, slept in unsuitable conditions; and she was assigned tasks of work which were out of harmony with her nature, even though there was plenty of congenial work that could have been assigned. It was the pre-conciliar way in all its casual brutality: senseless mortifications, programmatic humiliations, the routine devaluing of individuality. It was not what he wanted in his diocese. But he could not stop it. Not very easily. The religious orders were independent of him in many ways. Anger burned in him. He had felt strongly about Contraception and Divorce, and the other issues he had fought over, but not as strongly as he did about this girl. And he was powerless. A new and unpleasant feeling. He calmed himself. He had been in Limerick longer than he had intended. A little too long, perhaps. With a sigh, he accepted what he could not change. But he could not put this woman from his mind.

Years later, when Michael Cremin encouraged Isaiah Courtney to visit Marie, it was for mutual spiritual encouragement, certainly, but there were other reasons, too. For one, he felt that the entrenched male chauvinism in the Church had to come to an end. This was impossible unless young men and women learned to treat each other as equals in the search for God. For another, he hoped that their growing spiritual relationship would not lack an earthy groundedness. He longed for a generous, life-affirming interpretation of religious vows, in which Marie and Isaiah would be young together and would be generous with physical tenderness. Perhaps they would fall in love and become sexually fulfilled with each other, becoming adult and self-effective as they did so. He wanted it for them because he had a soft spot for them and because he believed it was right. But they would have placed no value on it. Led by Marie, Isaiah was trying to live a life of trust in God. Not the unthinking, childish trust of before, but a child-like trust, serene in abandonment to the Divine Will. There was only the present moment, and it contained everything. Whatever one met in the present moment, it was all a potential enclosure in which God had arranged everything to lead one towards holiness. The present moment became such an enclosure by the deep power of trust. Isaiah Courtney was indeed in love with Marie. In time, it went the way of her love for him, which was subsumed in her love for God.

One by one they failed, all the young men Michael Cremin had selected for his special kind of training. In turn, they were abandoned by him or left him of their own accord. He was hurt by their failure, and it surprised him to be hurt.

He had taken a personal interest in each of them, had suffered for them and suffered with them, only to see them fail and turn away from him. Still, he had thought he was proof against such emotional wounds. It drove home to him what he only dimly perceived: the loneliness of the life he had chosen.

7

When Ireland, which up to then had been a small and struggling island republic, signed up to the great process of European Integration, a growing diversity of lifestyle and religous choice became evident among the people. The Irish Episcopal Conference took a dim view of these signs of progress, but Michael Cremin did not. It was the proof of what he had been saying for years. A new Ireland was coming. It would be an Ireland of open borders and open minds, hard-wired to the nodal points of change in a single globalised society. He believed the Roman Catholic Church to be indispensable to this process. The Church was the oldest surviving example of a globalised society of shared intent. In her post-conciliar manifestation, the Church had discerned where humanity was heading. She had the wisdom and the power to guide and to lead.

At the diocesan level, Bishop Cremin's response to cultural diversity was a diversity of spirituality. One of his first initiatives was called Art of the Spirit. He let it be known that the churches of Limerick were too dark, and he invited all interested people to come and brighten them up. Limerick, however, lacked artists with a sustained interest in decorating churches, and the plan never got off the ground. He then launched a bolder initiative called Divine Experience, which had its focus in workshops in which people could try out different kinds of spiritual exercises. For this, he opened his diocese to a broad range of providers, from the Catholic Orders with their venerable charisms, to new lay movements and ecumenical communities, to Sufi, Hindu and Buddhist groupings, and to exotic builders of bridges across the religions. He provided long-term accommodation and finance for their projects, and he defended them ably when Ireland's sleepy conservatives were stirred up against them. It was an expensive initiative, but the Bishop had money, and to all outward appearances, it was a long-lasting success.

Strangely, while Church circles in different countries were celebrating his successes, the Bishop found himself growing more and more dissatisfied. His diocese was alive like few dioceses known to him, but it was also strangely dead. He had re-invented his diocese for the sake of the fulfilled human being, but there were no examples of such fulfilled people actually coming his way. When he dreamed of such a person, it was of someone with the face of Marie-Louise Costelloe that he dreamed; a young girl lying in wait for him in the rain, astonishing him with words that were laden with spirit.

After her solemn profession in her convent, Bishop Cremin had written to Sister Marie to invite her to sample the spiritual diversity his diocese was now offering, and to perhaps consider making a contribution herself, at some point, from the Carmelite tradition. The answer had come by return of post, and it was a refusal.

It made the Bishop think. When he had set up the spiritual initiatives, it was for all those like Marie, sure enough, but they had their unique focus only because of Marie. It felt wrong to him that she was refusing him her co-operation. And her apparent ingratitude wormed into him like a poison.

Michael found himself thinking more and more of Laura, his Roman girlfriend of times gone by. He found himself longing for Laura and for the love she had never given him, for the love she had been unable to give him. He longed so much for the impossible that he felt his heart was breaking. And Marie's answer, ten years and more since he had heard it spoken: He suffered so much as to die of love for me. I want to suffer for love of Him. What cooling, soothing words they were, even now.

Marie was exceptional, and Michael Cremin knew it. It made him defenceless. Michael had never been defenceless before. To protect himself, he rationalised what he knew. Spiritual people were quite ordinary, really. Wisely, the Church made certain of saints only after their death. What power the saints had was in the stories told about them and in the inextinguishable need of men and women for inspiration.

Francis of Assisi, for example: a man in love with God, even though he had never seen Him, rushing to abandon everything on account of a few words of the Gospel that had lighted up in his heart.

The greatest saints were like that. They were consumed by a thirst they did not try to slake, because long ago in a far distant place they had come upon a running stream of great purity, had tasted a few drops from it, and now nothing could satisfy them apart from that hidden water, which they would never be able to find again and call their own, but which might well up again for them at any moment without warning. It was a life of poverty on many levels, chosen freely, because all the possible satisfactions were worthless in comparison with this, their soul's joy.

But it was all imagination. Fiction, ultimately. Saints were like great heroes or great lovers. They belonged in a book. They were literary motifs, the motifs of an age long gone. And yet in Marie, such motifs were present before him, seemingly real. And Marie was keeping out of his way. Like Isaiah. Like all the others. There were no spiritual people around him at all. There were no loving people around him, at all. He presided over the dead crowds who filled the dark of his churches. He was a purveyor of illusions to people he had come to despise.

8

Since the Second Vatican Council, theological scholarship, like almost everything in the Church, had been contested by two main factions. The pragmatic conservatives, the successors to the hapless traditionalists, maintained an international journal, *Communio*, with which to air their views and further their cause. The editors, among them Joseph Ratzinger and Hans Urs von Balthasar, steered a course pleasing to the Vatican and were elevated to cardinal for their efforts. Their rivals, the progressives, also maintained an international journal, *Concilium*. Its editors, which included Hans Küng, Karl Rahner and Yves Congar, were blasted remorselessly by Vatican disapproval. In the person of Küng, they were compensated by the adulation of the secular press, which gave their opinions wide currency, even among those with little respect for theology. To both journals, Michael Cremin submitted academic papers from time to time, and both journals rejected them. Though a bitter pill to swallow, it was something he understood. Michael's thinking was no longer at the cutting edge. A bishop simply did not have the time to keep up to date. Although his papers were usually good enough for the second rank journals, publishing in them gave him little satisfaction. He believed he should be up there with the best.

When the problem of Intercommunion between the different Christian Churches arose, Michael sensed that a new chance had come. For Pope John

Paul II, the prospect of non-Catholics partaking of the Catholic Eucharist was intolerable and this constituted the official line. In a new book, *This Is My Peace*, Michael argued that when Jesus had invited moral outcasts to seek Salvation from Him, he had included followers of other religions, and had extended also to them the invitation to the greatest possible degree of intimacy with Him. The Church must do likewise. Within the framework of a Liturgy of Hospitality, the communion wafer could be shared with non-Catholics without prejudice to the reserved nature of the Eucharist. It seemed to make the impossible possible, but it was not to be.

"*Laudetur Jesus Christus!*" intoned the Papal Nuncio.

"*In aeternum, Amen*," Michael answered. Beside him Felix Kostuva, a senior official of the Curia, made the Sign of the Cross. They were facing the Nuncio, who had shown them to an antique sofa behind a marble coffee table. When they were seated, the Nuncio poured tea from a silver teapot. Behind him, through the bay windows they could see Dublin's Phoenix Park bathed in sunshine. In silence, they sipped their tea.

"His Excellency is most concerned for our separated brethren, of course," ventured Kostuva.

"His Excellency's many pastoral merits are cherished most dearly by the Holy Father."

Even Felix Kostuva wilted at that. There had been a special shade of emphasis on the word 'many'. No matter how numerous these merits, they were not enough.

"Your Grace," Michael began, but got no further. The Nuncio's raised finger was ample warning.

"Shall we contain the damage, Excellency?"

Michael almost choked on his tea. Damage? What damage! But at a sign from Felix Kostuva, he acquiesced. The alternative was his destruction. This had been made terribly clear. The dossier in Rome was full of the kind of detail that could be turned one way or another. A Visitation would be unavoidable. And it would be led by the Metropolitan of the area, Archbishop Claffey of Cashel and Emly, who would jump at the chance to settle old scores. A co-adjutor would be a certainty. Within two years, Michael Cremin would be one more broken stick among the driftwood of history. But it was preventable. Kostuva had been sent over to prevent it. Michael still had friends in high places. He looked the Papal Nuncio in the eye and smiled. Power was power.

A few months later, admirers of *This Is My Peace* were discomfited to find a sequel in the same style from the same author repudiating much of what he had said before. *The Rock of Peace* was its title. Puzzled journalists who inquired at Michael's chancery were fobbed off by under-secretaries reading platitudes from prepared scripts. Quietly, *This Is My Peace* vanished from the bookshops, and was replaced by *The Rock of Peace.* The shameful sequel had been ghost-written, and Michael did not care about it. But it was the end of whatever status he still had as an academic theologian. And he cared about that. He cared more than was good for him.

Now there was a new feeling about everything. Michael's enemies were arrayed against him, and he was alone. For the first time ever, Michael wondered where he would find the strength to keep going. He had already written to Gerry Hegarty, his old friend from the seminary, to persuade him to join him in Limerick. Now he tried harder. He spoke urgently and frankly about his needs. He wrote to Gerry's Archbishop, David Carroll, reminding him of significant favours owed. Finally, he offered Gerry the position of Vicar General and Chancellor, the most senior position he had to give.

In fact, Michael already had a vicar general, Father Fergus Honan, whom he cordially despised. After the repudiation of *This Is My Peace*, the Papal Nuncio had wanted to ensure that Michael's wings would remain clipped, and Fergus Honan, a crony of Archbishop Claffey, had been imposed on him. By creating a second post of Vicar General, which he was within his rights to do, Michael intended to beat Claffey and the Nuncio at their own game. The office of Chancellor had control over all legal, financial, personnel and administrative matters in a diocese. A Chancellor who was also Vicar General was a power second only to the Bishop.

One morning, shortly after his arrival, and bleary from lack of sleep, Gerry pointed towards Leo Murphy, who was lounging in a doorway chatting with some of his aides. "Bishop Michael. That man, there. It's either him or me."

The corridor went quiet.

"What's the problem, Hegarty?" sneered Leo Murphy. "The realities upsetting you, are they? Try the investment portfolio of the Holy See!"

Gerry walked over and closed the door on Leo Murphy's aides.

"The portfolio we're talking about is the one here in Limerick. Armaments. Unregulated pharmaceuticals. Contraceptives. Night clubs in Bangkok and Las Vegas. It's crying out to heaven, Mr. Murphy. There's nothing Christian about any of these investments, even when they're legal. And a lot of them aren't. Either that changes right now, or I'm leaving."

Michael looked into the innocent blue eyes of Gerry Hegarty. They were the dancing light blue he remembered as a child from the May altars to the Blessed Virgin in the schoolroom, all decorated with fresh flowers. He needed Leo Murphy, but he needed Gerry Hegarty even more.

Together, Michael and Leo Murphy walked over to the high window which looked out onto the lawn. Leo was a vain man. It would be unhelpful for him to lose face.

"Leo. You know how much I've been relying on you."

"This'll cost you, you know."

"Name it. It's yours."

"I want the annulment."

Michael groaned inwardly. Leo's sex escapades had been filling the local newspapers. And his wife was very devout. Fellow bishops had commented more than once about the credibility of the diocese, if it was relying on such a man.

"It'll take time, Leo."

"You'll look after it?"

"I will."

Leo clapped Michael on the shoulder, and with a wide grin and a confident stride, he pushed past Gerry Hegarty and left the building.

"Is he gone so easily, then?" Gerry asked, suspiciously.

"You're in charge, now."

"We'll have to watch your back for his shadows. A man like that always casts a few shadows."

Leo was gone, but Gerry Hegarty's energy and sheer success transformed the diocese. When transparency, sustainability and the ethics of investment became the watchwords, the Diocese of Limerick was one of the few in the Church to have satisfactory policies in place. It enhanced Bishop Cremin's standing considerably. When Michael next drank tea at the Nunciature in the Phoenix Park, the beaming Nuncio conveyed the pope's invitation to become a special advisor to the Vatican on sustainable investment. *This Is My Peace* was well and truly forgotten.

9

The creation of two posts of vicar general had one unanticipated effect: the bishop himself now had much less to do. For many years, Michael Cremin had been accustomed to working fourteen hours and more a day, seven days a week. Leisure time had long been a harried cluster of minutes snatched from the blind onrush of his duties. With Gerry and Fergus doing most of the work, Michael's days felt different. He regularly had a few hours in the evening, and even an afternoon or two in the week, for leisure interests. He took up golf, but dismayed at his clumsiness, he gave it up again. He took piano lessons, trying to fulfil a long-cherished dream, but he had to concede that his fingers were too old to acquire dexterity, and so he gave up. He tried many things like this only to abandon them, giving himself an odd sense of failure.

Work had protected him all this time. It was inhuman, but that workload had been like a belt tightened around his life, keeping it together. Now that the belt had loosened, his life began to reveal aspects that were strange to him. Long-buried emotions came out, clamouring for a place he did not have to give them. He would seek relief by striding around the City of Limerick in all weathers, wearing civilian clothes, going nowhere in particular, but going there with controlled exertion, like the people working out in the fitness studios he sometimes passed.

If it had not been for these walks, which took him further and further from his residence, and indeed from all that was familiar to him, he might not have seen the other side of Limerick: the ugliness that goes unchallenged, particularly by someone of his social standing. Teenagers selling themselves on the streets to be able to feed their drug addiction. Terrorist organisations and crime syndicates setting up their brutal fiefdoms in housing estates. Schoolchildren threatening each other with loaded shotguns. Knife fights which were intended to end in death. There were so many places stained with blood and despair. The Bishop came back to them again and again, standing for long periods by burnt-out cars on neglected thoroughfares, observing the marks of lives given over to violence and destruction.

There were bishops, of course, for whom violence was a constant companion. Cahal Daly, for example, who had recently become a cardinal. Daly was not close to Michael, but he had once confided to him what his life had come to in the sectarian strife of Northern Ireland: an endless round of terrorist crimes and the failures of government, of tragic deaths and tense funerals; condemning violence to people who refused to listen, staying up all night with devastated families, trying to find the right words to help them in their suffering. Daly had kept up his philosophical work, despite the pressures; it was a respite for him, an oasis of peace inside the mind. But what respite was there for a young woman whose husband had been killed, whose children were now fatherless, facing into a lonely crushing future? Prayer, perhaps? Daly liked to think so, but when he made his way to the bereaved homes, he often found that his heart was ripped open, and all he could do was sit with the family and cry.

When Michael Cremin walked the aftermath of gang rapes and ritual beatings, he was far from shedding tears. He was not personally involved, at all. In those lawless places, life in the raw was baring itself unashamedly. Strong convictions and strong emotions were demanding expression. Seething energies smashed all given forms, because no form could contain them. Michael began to like what Limerick was showing him: cruel men and cruel women doing what they did because they had little choice, the titanic clash of necessity, as unforgettable as an exploding star. He began to wonder whether the time might not have come for a theology of violence, a theology of excess, a dionysian theology.

Seeking inspiration, he turned again to Friedrich Nietzsche, whom he had not read in many years. When he opened *On the Genealogy of Morals*, it was all there for him as he knew it would be: the origin of good and evil; not in God, but in man's attempt to affirm himself. Good was a judgement of themselves and their kind by aristocratic masters: a self-judgement by fearless persons who were free to act as they willed. Evil was the judgement by slaves and cripples of those others whose vital expression they could not share, so that in turn they might be able to apply a good judgement to themselves; it was a derivative judgement, and fuelled by resentment. This was the slave-morality which had emerged from Christianity. If objective evil existed at all, it did so because of the enervating judgements enforced by him, Michael Cremin, and by priests like him, deforming humanity with life-denying teachings, leaving the healthy will with no object for its striving except nothingness. And indeed, why not let life be life? For a moment, Michael was brought back to his student days in Louvain, to the excitement that had lifted him on first reading this German genius, back to the cauldron of energies that had seemed ready to burst from the pages of those books. But there was no excitement now. There was only a weary recognition. He, too, had chosen to believe in the right of energies to their expression. The absolute right to be. But there was far too much noise about it all. Nietzsche was noisy. It pained him, this incessant clamour. He put the book from him and read no more of Nietzsche.

Instead, he picked up a book his new secretary, Miss Wynne, had recently found for him: a collection of Gospel verses made by the French mystic, Charles de Foucauld. In the modern way, a lot of the book was taken up by fatuous commentators who felt it necessary to explain Brother Charles to the reader. Charles himself had simply made a list of the sayings of Jesus he thought especially beautiful. Just a list, nothing else, over a few short pages. No concern for systematic location or for historical verification. No concern for anything except the spiritual power of those words, words which had filled his Saharan sanctuary with unimpeachable light each time he read them. Michael acknowledged the poetic force in those lines. They had a massed warmth, like logs crackling on a fire. They had beauty. But on closer inspection, it was a broken and distant beauty, like an ancient and priceless cup no-one could drink from any more. He put the book from him. He was not able to learn from Charles de Foucauld.

From there, Michael was led to other mystics, to Catholic saints whose writings he had read years previously, and remembered, having been stirred by the starkly violent images they used to speak of the ecstasy of union with God. Was this the dionysian theology? No, the mystics meant a different kind of violence.

The God of Love had no place for cruelty.

Michael tore up the notes he had made for his new theology and threw the pieces of paper from a little stone bridge. He watched the tiny scraps flutter down into the dirty waters of the River Shannon, and thought about himself with regret. How much more difficult it was to discard the parts of what he was that he had no use for, the parts that gave him no joy.

In a way, Michael Cremin was looking for redemption, but redemption was only a concept. Thinking about it did not help him to feel good about himself. What he needed had become distilled into a pair of eyes he had seen in a dream, once, he thought, a long time ago, without noticing it, the eyes of a beautiful woman. They were a sort of hazel in colour but the pupils were darker, enfolding wells of the deepest and purest spring water and there was a rich and solemn silence in them like in the churches of old during the Old Mass when he was a child. He had no clue whatsoever as to those eyes or to their owner. As a child, he had believed that they were the eyes of his real mother, the beautiful and loving presence who had been driven away by the person his father had married. If he could find her, if he could find the bearer of those eyes, he would take off all his clothes and stand naked before her, but he would not ask her to look at him, although he hoped that she would. The months had become years, and times and places had flowed into each other without ever a trace of her, except in some memory of a dream. But he thought there might be some small solace in trying to remember her, the Lady of the Eyes.

Michael began collecting prints of paintings of women, books of nude photographs and the like, which he studied carefully. Once, he came across a Tarot card, the High Priestess, and he was sure that he had found the Lady of the Eyes. But the more he contemplated the image, the more his certainty faded. On another occasion, he thought that he had found her in the Lady Mistress who was the subject of certain Pre-Raphaelite paintings. Prompted by a book review, he turned to the Grail Romances, and he thought for a while that Wolfram von Eschenbach's Grail Queen, Repanse de Schoye, might be modelled upon his Lady. But always, rational convictions reasserted themselves, and he locked away the Grail legends, and the books of Godwin, Waterhouse and Millais, and went back to another long involvement with the personal problems he barely understood, while the machinery of his self-maintenance continued to turn over effectively.

It was on a spring morning, one that did not seem at all fresh and bright to him, that Michael received an unexpected letter from Marie-Louise Costelloe. He read through it, during a late breakfast. Sister Marie wanted to follow an example set long ago by Saint Thérèse of Lisieux. She wanted to consecrate her life to something referred to as the Holy Face. She asked his, her bishop's, permission to do so.

Michael shook the toast crumbs from the page, and sighed to himself. Poor Marie. She had become part of the herd in that convent. She seemed to believe that spirituality was all about getting permission from higher-ups and copying something some canonised saint had done. A pity she had not taken up his invitation of a few years previously, and taken courses in Zen, or Wicca, or the Goddess. And this little Thérèse. Pope John Paul II intended to make her a Doctor of the Church. Another sign of how he had been declining, recently. He would have to discourage this bizarre consecration, obviously. Still, care was needed. He would first have to see what basis for action there was in canon law. He picked up the phone and called Gerry Hegarty.

"Gerry, what can you tell me about the Holy Face?"

"Nothing, at all, Bishop Michael."

"Find out about it for me, will you, please?"

Oddly, the tabernacle in St. John's Cathedral flashed into his mind. The Sanctuary lamp had run out of oil and nobody seemed to be doing anything about it. He'd have to sort it out himself, obviously.

Michael got up and went in search of someone who knew where the oil was kept.

"There's no oil, Bishop," mumbled the sacristan.

"Go and order some, can't you?"

"Can't be ordered, Bishop. You see, the way we do it here is, the first Mass the Bishop says when he's new, we shove a few barrels of oil onto the steps there, and that blesses the oil, see, and that's the oil for the lamp. Then when a new bishop comes we do it again. That's how it's done."

Michael had never heard anything like this before, and he had been the Bishop for almost twenty years. It wouldn't be the first time that one of the half-wits of the city had ended up on his payroll.

"Get out another barrel, will you, please?"

"There's no barrels, Bishop. You see, when you said your first Mass here, they forgot to put the barrels out. So there's no oil from Your Lordship. We've been running on the leftovers of the last fellow's oil. And now it's all gone."

"Use some other oil, then!"

"Won't work with other oil, Bishop."

"Well then, we'll have to change the lamp, won't we?"

The sacristan shook his head at the impossibility of the suggestion, and went to put away some vestments that were just back from the laundry. Michael decided that he would retire this man at the first decent opportunity.

10

Later that week, while he was walking from the Cathedral to his residence, Michael remembered Marie-Louise Costelloe and the Holy Face. Back at his desk, he rummaged among his papers for her letter. Then, he studied the expert opinion Gerry Hegarty had procured for him. There was more to this than met the eye. He would have to bide his time.

Michael called in his secretary and dictated a note to the Carmelite convent. An application by Sister Marie was under consideration. The devotion in question belonged to a bygone age of piety. Any value it may have for the Church of their own day needed careful elucidation. Mother Prioress would be so kind as to write to him stating her grounds for granting approval in the first instance.

Afterwards, Michael paced up and down, pondering the matter. It was not just the Carmelites. The Poor Clares were at it, too. As for the Cistercians, that new Abbot was so conservative he had removed all the TV sets from the monastery. The Orders couldn't be trusted. Nor could the new lay movements, Focolare, and the like. Outdated principles of formation and ruinous devotional practices. The whole gamut of fear-choked refusal from the dark ages before the Council. And whenever he had reason to enter their Houses they fawned over him in a truly disgusting manner. Hypocrites. All smiles to his face while they opposed him behind his back.

Above all, something would have to be done about Saint Thérèse of Lisieux. Ideally, she'd be put where she belonged: among the embarrassments of the preconciliar era. But the date had been set when she would be declared a Doctor of the Church. Thérèse Martin had made of herself an example to be imitated. With the status of Doctor, there was likely to be more imitation of her than before. His own educational programme had no place for mindless imitation. Risk-taking, experimentation, self-expression, that was the way. If her example took hold, he could say goodbye to his vision of a better Church.

The Holy Face was a case in point. By this was meant the Hidden Face of Jesus, the face that Saint Veronica saw as He walked the way to Calvary. It was a tortured face full of cuts and bruises and dripping with blood, a face that men and women hide their own faces from: a beauty hidden by a horrible wound, the great beauty of Jesus, unrecognisable to anyone who did not love Him. Devotion to this Holy Face entailed not only continual meditation on the suffering of Jesus but also the imitation of this hiddenness in one's everyday routines: hiding away any excellence or achievement, finding there the Dark Night, and in that crucifying aridity the patient wait for God.

There had been a certain justification to it, of course, in Thérèse's time. Life was tougher back then. Life chances were almost non-existent, especially for women. In self-sacrifice, the values of compassion had been demonstrated. Values of self, ultimately. Today, with people better placed to realise themselves, Thérèse was the wrong example. Granted, a Doctor of the Church was an unimpeachable authority. But there were other unimpeachable authorities. Other Doctors. Saints with voluminous writings of great obscurity who could be used to dilute the message, make it safe, healthy. In his own diocese, he was not completely powerless. Official disapproval was still an effective weapon in the Catholic Church.

Then he remembered the sanctuary lamp in the cathedral. He would have to do something about the oil for that lamp.

A knock on the door shook Michael free of his reverie. It was James Lawless, who ordinarily worked for Cardinal Bernardin of Chicago. Michael knew him well, having used him for secret money-runs to Poland in the 1980s. A request had come from the Secretariat of State in Rome. Unofficially, in accordance with the strangeness of the matter. In a televised speech, Pope John Paul II had made an apology to womankind for many centuries of discrimination on the part of the Church. This surprising passage had been smuggled past the official speech writers and inserted without proper approval. It was an audacity, to say the least, and angry officials wanted to get to the bottom of it. The trail led back from the pope's Polish entourage in Rome to a man who went by the name of Jimmy the Steeple, a devotee of Our Lady of Garabandal. Apparently, this Jimmy the Steeple, who lived as a hermit in the pine forests near Garabandal, had given the controversial lines to a Polish priest who was on a pilgrimage to the area. This priest had later given them to a Polish bishop who had personal access to the pope. It was all highly irregular, and Michael could understand the concern of the Secretariat of State. It was not about women, as such. If a Jimmy the Steeple was able to write things into the pope's speeches, then the Church was out of control. The audacious piece of text seemed to have originated with Jimmy the Steeple's Irish connections, hence the request of the Secretariat of State to Michael.

Michael listened intently as Dr. Lawless gave his report. Jimmy the Steeple had refused to talk to him, but he had picked up the trail easily enough, all the same. Things came together with an old priest living in retirement in Dublin. The spirit-presence whom this priest claimed to be serving had wanted the pope to apologize for the Church's treatment of women, and the instruction had been conveyed to the pope in the way described.

Michael was dismayed. Nonsense about spirit-presences did not belong in a report to Rome. Was there a concrete agenda, perhaps?

Dr. Lawless was reassuring. "Bishop, this priest told me something. He has effaced his priesthood. Those were his words. As far as I can see, it means he's not a priest any more. That's good for us. If he opens his mouth again, we can slap him down any time we like. It's the sick visionary mindset. Trying to hear the voice of God. A private line to the Almighty. A special mandate to break with the organisation whenever it suits. My advice is, just ignore it."

A shiver of foreboding crept down Michael's spine.

"This priest who has effaced his priesthood. His name?"

"Didimus Thomas Clavis, Bishop."

"That will be all."

"Yes, Bishop."

11

The Vatican's Prefecture of Economic Affairs required Bishop Cremin in Rome for a time. He was a highly-regarded member of the Catholic Episcopate, and different Curial congregations, including the Secretariat of State, invited him round and sought his opinion on matters of interest. The question of Didimus Thomas Clavis was dealt with over an informal glass of wine with the official concerned. Pope John Paul sometimes listened to self-styled mystics from the lunatic fringe. A great hindrance to the Church when he did. Thankfully, his successor would be a much more rational person.

When Bishop Cremin returned to Limerick, he announced a Canonical Visitation to the Carmelite Convent. Ostensibly, this was a routine affair, as a bishop's jurisdiction extended in certain matters to the religious orders in his diocese.

The Visitation, however, was unnervingly thorough. While accountants checked the account books and engineers checked the buildings, furniture and equipment, Bishop Cremin himself, with crosier and mitre, sat in the Bishop's throne in the chapel and required each member of the Community to give account of her commitment to her chosen way of life. As expected, there were concerns to be noted; psychological issues, laxities of observance, failures of convent management, none of them particularly serious. But they gave him what he wanted: grounds to move against the Convent, should he choose to, and therefore the required element of control over the Prioress.

The last of the nuns was the one he wanted to see the most. The Prioress had to take her by the hand and lead her to him. This nun was wearing an unusually heavy veil, the kind of veil that might have been common a hundred years previously. It covered almost all of her face and made her unrecognizable.

"Your Excellency," the Prioress whispered. "This is Sister Marie of the Trinity and of the Holy Face."

Michael smiled to himself. She was already using that title, even before he had approved it. It would be all the easier now to forbid it. Making the Sign of the Cross, he began the opening prayer. But it was the Prioress who gave the response.

"Mother Felix. Is Sister deprived of the power of speech? And is this, this garb, prescribed by the Rule?"

The Prioress flushed with embarrassment. Rome had warned her that the Bishop was on the warpath. They were on the Bishop's territory. Little more than guests at his pleasure. They didn't even own the premises that housed their Community.

"My Lord Bishop. Sister Marie has just returned from medical treatment. If I may speak with Your Lordship on the matter?"

Mother Felix broke the news in her private parlour, and her words spread their own kind of veil over the small, sparse room. Marie had contracted lupus, a form of leprosy.

"The doctors here can't know much about something like that," Michael muttered. The sense of superiority had left him now. "Surely a second opinion ....."

"We've had a second opinion. Poor Marie is very ill. And her nose and face are an open wound. That's why she's wearing that veil that upsets you so much, My Lord. She is quite disfigured already. And there is an unpleasant smell, like the smell of a decomposing corpse. She finds the thick linen cooling, and it holds a piece of gauze in place which is impregnated with something for the inflammations. The only good thing to say is that there is hardly any risk of contagion. Her voice, too, is affected, which is why I answered for her in the chapel."

"You've had a second opinion, have you? Well, get a third one!" Michael was struggling to remain calm.

"Your Excellency! It is a waste of time and money to consult another doctor."

It was the fault of the Holy Face, Michael was thinking. Marie had brought this on herself. Wanting to consecrate herself to the Holy Face. Now her own face was peeling away. It had to be psychosomatic. She should see a psychiatrist. He would get her to see a psychiatrist. But the Prioress would not be moved. The illness was attacking the internal organs, and there was very little that the doctors could do. Marie was slowly dying.

"I won't have it, do you hear? Nothing's incurable. You've just got to try hard enough. I'll get to work on it."

The Visitation was over. Together with the Prioress, Michael returned to the chapel for Solemn Benediction. Despite the turmoil in his heart, he conducted the ceremony as he always did, with consummate dignity, leaving a lasting impression on all who were present.

While he was getting ready to leave, Sister Marie made a request to see him. The Prioress led him to the visitor's parlour, where he found Marie waiting on her knees.

Her eyes were unchanged. They were as beautiful as they had been when he had first seen them in a rain swept car park so many years before.

"I've heard," he said. "I'll look after you."

Her mouth was veiled, and her words were whispered from far away. "I ask only for your blessing, My Lord. And to be permitted to thank you for your gracious approval of my Act of Consecration."

Approval? He hadn't given approval. But he couldn't withhold it now, could he. She could have approval for anything, anytime. Michael raised his hands to bless her, and the blessing came from a depth he did not know he possessed.

Michael Cremin was true to his word. After the Visitation, the convent was deemed to be in good order. Money and facilities were provided so that Sister Marie had access to the best medical care available. Through the Roman superiors, he tried to persuade the convent to dispense her from some of the restrictions of the Rule.

Michael was beginning to believe that he was doing some good, when a letter arrived from Marie. She asked him to refrain from any further attempts to lighten the burden for her. She wished to offer herself in loving submission to the Will of God. She asked him to do the same.

Michael read and re-read this letter. He had loved Marie-Louise Costelloe from the moment he first saw her. And the more he had tried to get her on his side, the more she had eluded him. Now she was gone from him completely. Was this the way of love? This emptiness? This death?

12

Those who were close to Bishop Michael Cremin began to notice a change in him. Towards Beatrice Wynne, his secretary, he became cruel and sardonic, taking pleasure in belittling her and her work. Luckily, he was often abroad.

During one of these absences, Beatrice, on the advice of Gerry Hegarty, arranged for a supply of sacred oil from Mother Felix at the Carmelite Convent, and the sanctuary lamp in the cathedral was now lighting again.

When Michael returned and discovered the source of the oil, it made him angry, but also curious. Beatrice had disobeyed him, in a way. It evoked an element of respect. Then, for the sheer sport of it, he fired her. Beatrice went without complaining. Next, he turned to Gerry Hegarty. It was only a small matter of a few litres of oil, and Michael had no real reason to discipline Gerry. But there was still the issue of the Holy Face.

"This is your doing?" Michael placed the copy of a letter on the desk in front of his Chancellor and Vicar General. Gerry picked it up and ran his hand over the image of the bishop's seal of office, with which he had stamped the original.

"You were out of the country, Bishop Michael. And the thing had to be decided."

"Gerry. Have you seen her? She's got a leprosy condition. Her face is peeling away, for God's sake!"

Gerry Hegarty spread his hands in exasperation. "I didn't know that. But I don't see why it matters. Will you tell me, please, what the problem is?"

Michael didn't know how to answer him. Leprosy wasn't just an illness. It was a biblical affliction, a scourge of God. As such, it wasn't real, it was a literary motif, though a powerful one. It was archetypal, to use a hackneyed Jungian term. What was he to say? That the literary motifs should stay inside their books and not turn up in his diocese? That the Church had moved away from the old-style victim theology, when there was a classic victim rotting away on his doorstep, so to speak?

"This place is a shambles, Gerry."

"It is. You know, Michael, you don't recognize yourself any more."

"So it's my fault?"

"You're the Bishop."

"So I did that Sister in, just like I'd thrown acid at her, is that it?"

"How would I know? How would I know why good people get terrible illnesses? How would I know why innocent children die terrible deaths? Maybe we need their sacrifices. The Bible is full of that. Whole communities are rescued by someone who atones for them, by patiently bearing afflictions. Jesus Christ, for example. Remember Him?"

"I won't put up with this, Gerry."

"I know, Michael. I know you won't. So my time here is done. I'm offering you my resignation."

The Bishop waved his hand in a tired manner. There was a flash-fire hatred for Gerry Hegarty leaping at the walls of his stomach, but he wanted to keep it down. He couldn't afford to lose Gerry. Not just now.

"No, Father, resignation not accepted."

The Bishop and his Chancellor looked at each other across the charged silence. Gerry Hegarty had never let him down. If Michael had a real friend in the world, that friend was Gerry. All the worse, now, if Gerry chose to defy him. The worse for Gerry. A young priest from the diocesan staff appeared at the door, and the tension eased slightly. He was sorry to interrupt, but there was bad news from Dublin. Mr. Cremin, the Bishop's father, had just died. The silence came over the room again, this time more heavily. The young priest felt his nerve breaking and he slunk out the door. Slowly, Gerry Hegarty stood up, crossed the space that separated them and put his arms around Michael. Michael tried to push Gerry away, but far, far in the distance he heard a humming-bird lift its voice in song, and the grief rose up and hit him, blow after blow. Then it began sucking at him like an open drain.

Patrick Cremin had died happy. Dorothy, Michael's stepmother, was sure of it. Not that it was much consolation. To Michael, his stepmother was the cold shadow which choked his childhood memories, the alien thing he had fled from into the musical worlds to which his father's record collection had opened a way. Some years before, Dorothy had more or less admitted to him that she had married his father for his money. As long as he had known her, she had been not only cold and heartless, but totally superficial. Old now, and good-looking no longer, she wanted him to believe she had made Patrick happy.

Music might have brought happiness. Michael remembered the rush of delight on Patrick's face whenever the lush strings of the Cavatina from *Cavelliera Rusticana* filled the living room. But Dorothy had never liked it, and he had stopped playing it. As they lowered the coffin into the grave, Michael thought back over how long it had been since he last saw his father. It seemed like years, and into the silence inside him, he murmured an apology. As was expected, he led the graveside prayers, which he knew off by heart, but the words meant hardly anything. His mind travelled away from him and was lowered into the grave with his father's coffin, dispassionate as it took in the dull clods of earth and the little shower of stones on the shiny wood. A death rattle for the man he had once been closer to than anyone, but whom he had never really got to know. Had Michael loved his father? Michael didn't know, but he certainly wished that he had loved him. Being a father was like being a priest. It was lonely.

He happened to glance around the faces of the mourners. Among them was Beatrice Wynne. She came towards him and touched his shoulder, shyly. When he looked into her pain-filled eyes and saw that she was crying for him, who did not deserve it, he could not help himself. He bowed his head and rested it on her breast. She put her arms around him and held him, and he shuddered for a moment with the weight of his pain. Then he was himself again, shaking hands, breezily accepting condolences, and Beatrice was gone. After that day, Michael was determined that Beatrice would come back to him. Beatrice, however, had met a young man in North Wales and wanted to make her life there with him. With great difficulty, Michael freed his schedule to be able to attend the wedding. Inexplicably, a mechanical defect brought his car to a halt on the Dublin road, and he missed all the flights that would have got him to Bedgellert in time. While he was waiting for transport home, Michael had time to reflect. Why had he treated her so badly? There was no explanation. But he regretted it. Deeply.

One day, not long afterwards, Gerry Hegarty walked into his office unexpectedly.

"Fintan Kelly's in hospital dying with a brain tumour. Did you know that?"

"Who's Fintan Kelly?"

"One of your priests, Michael."

"I can't be expected to know everyone's name at the drop of a hat, can I?"

"And Barry O'Connell's mother died yesterday. Cancer. You never talked to him."

"I was busy. Why didn't Fergus Honan do it?"

"Fergus did, but it would have meant something if you'd done it. You're the Bishop."

"I was busy."

"You had two years, Michael. She'd been dying for two years."

"I said I was busy."

"Busy doing what? Wheeling and dealing in the Vatican Congregations. Going everywhere in the world except Limerick. Doing anything and everything except your job here in Limerick."

"Change, Gerry. Transformation. Changing things for the better. That's the job. And it's not just here, I can tell you."

"Ah, Michael. You've achieved a lot, I suppose, as people normally count achievements. But..."

"Be clear, will you, for once?"

"If you ask me, your achievements are dangerous drugs. You gave in to the temptation to fill your life with them, and now they're destroying you."

"Gerry, I've had enough of this. Have you no work to do?"

"It's the simple things, Michael. You've lost hold of the simple things. You don't want to just get a bit of fresh air out on a walk in the hills like anyone else. You want to climb Mount Everest. You think that your life is all about climbing Mount Everest."

"And what's wrong with climbing Mount Everest?"

"Bishop Michael, why would God want anybody to climb Mount Everest?"

Because it's there, Michael wanted to shout at him. But Gerry was hitting him with something else.

"Michael, I'll say this to you only once. Because it hurts me to talk to you like this. You're turning into your own shadow."

Michael began to shake. He was a caught fish, dangling on a hook, his mouth gashed open. He had nothing at all to say. Who was Gerry Hegarty to torment him like this? The ground was cracking open in front of him. There was a hole opening up, a hole full of darkness like his father's grave.

But his mind was working too fast for him. He was in that grave already. He knew it, and did not know it.

Then he was a bird in the air. He was caught in the slipstream of a giant aircraft that was plummeting to destruction.

You rode the air currents again and again, to feel a quick surge of force, trying to make the force yours for a time, but when you succeeded, it fizzled away to nothing. The man of power was able to hold out a little longer, that was all.

Was he truly able to hold out? To endure to the end? Of course he was. He was Michael Cremin, priest of himself.

Shortly afterwards, Michael found himself on the wrong side of his doctors. The stress levels, Your Excellency. Was there heart disease in the family?

Michael refused all further tests for the moment. He had to go to Rome the next day. There wouldn't be a free space in the calendar for a while. The tests could wait.

When Michael got back from Rome, he had long periods of nightmares, in which Marie-Louise Costelloe figured regularly. He turned to a mixture of whiskey and sleeping pills to drive the nightmares away. When the nightmares passed, and when an exertion of the will separated him from the whiskey and sleeping pills, a lassitude would take hold of him which could last for many days, days in which he was barely able for his many tasks. The only remedy was hurtling around the country roads in the fastest car he could find, pushing the engine harder and harder, until he was certain that the slightest mistake would mean his death.

One night, he was caught by the police, but they were kind enough to keep it out of the newspapers.

"Your Lordship might want to consider taking a holiday from time to time," remarked Mr. Justice McCurtin during a special sitting of the Court at Michael's residence.

Michael told the Court that he would indeed consider a holiday. In the end, he did not go anywhere on holiday, because there was nowhere he wanted to go. When he got his driver's licence back, Gerry Hegarty insisted on keeping charge of the car keys so that there would be no more wild driving around the roads of Limerick.

There was no remedy now for how Michael felt. He could not fall asleep properly, even with sleeping pills, and he was walking with a heavy stoop, as if he was carrying a ton weight of scrap metal on his shoulders. Even his food did not taste like it ought to. And there seemed to be no fresh water anywhere. Whenever he poured himself water for his thirst, the water was invariably stale and dead. It was horrible, like drinking the dust from the roads.

In the end, there was nothing for it but to take time off. Under an assumed name, Michael travelled to Hamburg in Germany. The sexual services of the Reeperbahn seemed to purge him with excess, and Marie and his father were driven from his mind.

While he was in Hamburg, his birthday came around. Treating himself to a last erotic workout as a celebration, he achieved a sense of vitality he did not want to lose. Deciding to extend his holiday, he chose America. The connections from Hamburg were good, and the formalities were easily dealt with. Limerick could wait.

†

7

Semi-Retirement

1

The wrought iron rails of the balcony were cool to the touch. The night was clear. The lights going on and off were bright snakes sliding to the traffic that ribboned the streets far below. Ahead, the high-rise buildings parted, and there was a clear view over the public parks to the shimmering water of Lake Michigan. The Archdiocese had been generous to Michael Cremin. The apartment was in the Loop area of downtown Chicago, right at the centre of everything. He looked at his watch. He had a woman coming.

His recent birthday had unsettled him. There was an unwelcome finality to everything. He had never been loved. He had never loved. But he knew what love was. Love was the painful longing that the word evoked.

The Loop was affluent, anonymous and full of distraction. You could forget yourself there, but Michael had not been able to do very much. Most of the time, he had just lain in bed, shivering. Now, there was no time left. The flight home was early the next morning. Why had he asked this woman to come? The only reason he could think of was that she was paid for by the Archdiocese.

Michael walked back inside the apartment. So far, he had been too tired to read, but a book in the antique bookcase caught his eye. He took out the book and turned it over in his hands. The author was his old friend, Robert Hovda. The cover photograph was a good likeness, from the days when Bob wore a thick beard. Bob was celebrating Mass, standing behind an altar, his arms extended, one of the sacred vessels in each hand, his eyes lifted slightly and suggestive of heaven. It was one of Bob's favourite poses: looking towards heaven, but standing firmly on his own two feet while he did so, and never losing eye contact with the community. Bob was dead, now. Six or seven years ago. Michael had a faint memory of hearing the news.

Had Bob Hovda ever been happy? Calm down, a bishop had said to him once. Calm down, you're getting a Messiah complex. Isn't that what we're supposed to have? Bob had answered. Bob was too big a man to kiss the behind of a bishop.

The past came alive, and the familiar rasping voice filled Michael's apartment as neatly as the Chicago traffic jangling through the window. Where the hell do they drain the humanity out of people to make them into Church hierarchs? What kind of acid do they mix with the shit that takes its place?

No, Bob Hovda had been angry rather than happy. And there were long periods when he had found more solace in booze than in Jesus Christ. Michael returned the book to its place. Bob had been human and flawed, and he wouldn't have minded anyone saying so.

Idly, Michael took out another book, a big Bible in shiny leather. The pages were still uncut. Behind it on the shelf, and hidden by it, were books of a different order: treatises on occult practices and tantric sex. Unlike the Bible, these had been read. They were well-thumbed and greasy, and they smelled of the herbs and essences whose use they recommended.

On the potency of that fragrance, Michael was spirited back to Rome, to the time when he was young and was struggling for the conciliar renewal of the Church, battling for the New Mass and its survival. There had been a shadowy German on the fringe of things, a monk whose name in religion could hide him well, and who was reputedly close to Johannes Wagner, the head of Coetus X of the Consilium. Emboldened by the new freedoms, this monk liked to pepper his Masses with elements borrowed from occult traditions. Satanism, his detractors had whispered, but never too openly. Michael put the books back. He wondered who the previous guests had been.

The doorbell rang. The woman was punctual. As he went to the door, Michael realised that he was too tired for her. Even so, he did not send her away.

When the woman had made herself comfortable in the bedroom, he asked her to pose naked for him. That was what he thought he wanted. Just to look at her naked body. In silence.

The woman did as she was asked, and Michael began to study her, not knowing what he was looking for. The woman picked up a long scarf of red silk and began to dance for him, back and forth over the bedroom carpet.

The dance meant nothing to him. The energy of it was put there by an actor; by a woman simulating what she imagined beauty would have to be, on the stage of his observation, and it disgusted him.

Magically, the slow circles of scented red silk turned dark and violent. He became aware of a powerful engine throbbing somewhere in the building. The new dance seized hold of the woman and drove her faster and faster. She reached a pain threshold, and, with a scream, she pushed herself into a world beyond.

The strong rhythms of the engine reached for him, but all he had was the uncertain shifting of his manhood. He did not want this sex.

Troubled, he asked the woman to lie with him with her arms around him, and to be tender with him, like a lover might be, when passion had come to rest, and the couple were close to sleep.

She refused, and Michael drifted into a half-sleep. Sexuality was life-force and was inexhaustible, so he had thought. But not his sexuality. His was a climbing iron abandoned long ago on an arctic glacier, and he felt corroded and lonely.

The Lady of the Eyes, how he longed for her, as for a mothering sea that would wash warm over him all night long.

But it was the hired woman who roused him. She had tallied the charges and was ready to leave.

Afterwards, Michael sat down in an armchair and put his head in his hands. The parched and cracked ground inside him longed for rain. But where was that rain?

One solitary tear crept from his eye, lost itself down his hard cheek, and died on his lips, leaving behind a shy taste of salt.

Michael missed the taxi he had ordered. Then he missed his flight.

Yes, he was unhappy. Deeply so. And he was completely unable to do anything about it. He, Michael Cremin, was a priest. Empowered to administer the

Sacraments of Jesus Christ. He was a bishop, upon whom Apostolic authority had been conferred. But the Grace and comfort of the Holy Spirit meant nothing to him. And the Resurrection? The great miracle it was his job to preach to others? No, the Resurrection had changed its meaning long ago. The New Testament, once one had got beyond the mystification, told only of how the Apostles had remembered their dead teacher, that was all. And the Lady of the Eyes? She was like Jesus Christ. Some illusions took a long time to fade, that was all.

Michael looked up and saw only the blotchy grey of a snaking night mist. He well remembered his own dead teachers. Incompetent, most of them. Augustine Hogan, for example. As Dean in Clonliffe, all those years ago, Gus seemed never to have heard of toothpaste, and his bad breath alone had made talking with him a serious mortification. And seeing Gus privately for anything had been pointless. It was as if a statue, a talking one, draped in black, had been put behind a desk for the seminarians to gape at. The belittling of individuality was normal back then. But even that had been beyond Gus. He had been too squeamish to crush people with humiliation.

As he rounded a corner in his memories, Michael walked into his office one morning in 1970, shortly after the New Mass had come. Gus was in conversation with Josef Andreas Jungmann SJ, the historian of liturgy, who was a consultant to their Congregation. Standing to one side, watching sardonically, was another formidable scholar, Johannes Wagner.

"Cardinal Ottaviani, I say," Jungmann was insisting, "never understood the meaning of Active Participation. I am not sure whether you do either, Monsignor Hogan. So I will tell you. When I was a curate long ago in the Tyrol, our parish priest thought it would be a good idea to have the statue of Christ hanging from a rope thrown over the beams of the rafters. It was the Feast of the Ascension, you see, and at the right point during his sermon, he gave me a sign, and I pulled on the rope, and lo and behold, up rose the statue into the rafters of the church. I suppose he thought this a clever way of teaching about the Ascension. But all he taught us was that Christ was somewhere up there, far from our daily lives, and unreachable, because that's where we had put Him. It could not be clearer how wrong our liturgy was."

"We are bringing Christ back to the people," Wagner added.

Gus Hogan was badly flustered. "Allow me one comment, Fathers. Permit me to tell you of the late Padre Pio, a simple Capuchin Friar, as you know, and a stigmatist. I attended one of his Masses, of the Rite of Pius V, of course. Father Jungmann, the place was bursting at the seams with people young and old, and they were on fire with faith! It was a very active participation! Just of a different kind!"

"Monsignor! They were not active at all! The priest was at the altar saying and doing everything and they were doing nothing!"

"They were reverent, Father. Reverent! They were participating in a mystery. And the way of participation was through silent reverence! And I can tell you, the place was on fire with the quality of that reverence!"

"Really, Monsignor! A man of your intelligence! These devotions to purported cases of the stigmata, these projections of subjectivity, surely you can see, they simply block Christ from our view. We must teach the Resurrection, as a human thing, and a communal thing. As that event that makes us human in this world together. That, Monsignor, is Liturgy."

"Words, Father, empty words. If you do that the way you say, you're trying to bring Christ to people who don't want Him. And that's a waste of time, if there ever was one. As for those who do want Him, you're making it more difficult for them. Who can be quiet and reverent at Mass now?"

"Really, Hogan!" Johannes Wagner had had a contemptuous twist on his lips. "Do you expect us to have the stigmata before we can celebrate Mass?"

It was an insult, and Gus had wilted before it. Poor Gus. Whenever he talked with real theologians they folded him up like bored students making a paper plane to send flying towards the dustbin.

Poor Gus. He had never felt at home in the post-conciliar Church, even though he was one of those with the task of getting it to work. A bit of a joke, really. Not that he would have been better off with the Lefebvre people he used to try to protect. The Lefebvre people did little but set up faschistoid priories in which to feed their siege mentality on conspiracy theories. That wouldn't have suited Gus: he believed in God too much. Poor, poor Gus. Always out of place. Except for that time in Switzerland, using the last of his breath to do what he believed was right. He had not been right. Still, it had been impressive to see him try.

In Chicago, the morning had come. Through a gap in the curtain, a strong finger of sunlight was moving in the room. Pointing brighter and brighter as it illuminated first this object and then that one, before gathering them into its trailing wake.

There was a mirror on the wall, directly in the path of the sun. When the light reached it, he saw a human face, but a face so unlike himself that he cried out in pain. His fine head of hair was decimated like an old man's, and there was a haggard expression that combined suffering with a faint ludicrousness. He closed his eyes and looked at what remained to his darkened sight. That stricken face was not his, but the face of Gus Hogan. That was how Gus had looked the last time Michael had seen him alive, in Switzerland, all those years ago. Michael opened his eyes again. That face was feverish and emaciated. The face of a tortured man. But an unearthly peace rippled through him like a quiet wind. Poor Gus had all the breath he needed now, Michael thought.

"You're telling me to beware, Gus? The moment of death is a long one? It takes up all of life. Is that it? That there is a point of no return? I have reached it? Ah, Gus!"

Gus's voice was audible now. "Young Michael, you can still turn back and live."

"Do you have to torment me like this? Have you not forgiven me, wherever you are?"

"It is I who seek forgiveness," came the answer. "I allowed you to prevail in your dying. I had no voice just now because I was afraid to use it as I should have done when I was with you. Forgive me, young Michael. But above all, see yourself as you are!"

"Gus, oh Gus. If you only knew what I was doing to you!"

The sun, by now a great shaft of blinding light, exploded into an eternity of arrows, hailing down on him from every direction and from none. Michael Cremin saw and heard no more.

2

They found him shrunk into the armchair, his head on his chest, unconscious. A quick phone call, and Michael's world was reduced to the wail of sirens, the rattle of stretchers in ambulances and the thick mist of narcotics. But there was time enough to save him.

The heart of a poet was the centre of the world, and that was why a poet's heart was always broken. Thus Heinrich Heine. But what about the heart of a bishop? Full of dis-ease and unable to break?

Recovery from the heart attack was long and complicated. It kept him in Chicago for some weeks. Later, it confined him for some months to a rehabilitation institute in Dublin.

From his sick-bed, Bishop Cremin provided faculties for the ordination to the priesthood of Isaiah Courtney. Photographs of the occasion were sent him. In one of them, Marie-Louise Costello was clearly recognizable.

"Still alive, then, is she?" the Bishop mumbled, saliva dripping from his mouth. His face had gone slack from the medication, and he could not control his mouth properly. He wished Isaiah well in his priesthood.

When Michael Cremin returned to full-time work, it was to hand over his diocese to an Apostolic Administrator, Dr. Jeremiah Newman, a minor, but respected post-conciliar theologian. Michael had written to Pope John Paul asking for leave of absence. He had written of the need to seek God's Will anew in the face of the closeness of death. In a way, he meant it.

They lined the hallway of the chancery to see him off, all his personal staff. He needed a stick to get down the steps, and he saw their concern for him even as they were cheering him and calling out their good wishes. Michael creased his face into a smile and slowly lowered himself into the limousine.

That was what the cameras preserved for the admiring public: a great man made old and infirm, but unbowed and undefeated. They were reminded of the heroic pope, John Paul II.

3

In the Liturgy of the Hours, time rose and fell with the plain lines of melody, and the ageless praise of the Psalms lifted to the beauty of God with the sureness of a returning tide. The Christian life, with its movements from darkness to light and from suffering to joy, was incarnated in the singing like a light in a bowl, and the offer of Salvation filled the open spaces as gently as the perfume of flowers.

The effect of the liturgy was profound, as Michael Cremin was discovering once more. The old concepts of Sin and Forgiveness, those tokens of the Christian narrative, had begun to work for him again, but in a new way. Sin did not matter, as such, but it was a useful reframing concept. One could reconsider everything and revision it oneself. God did not matter. What mattered was the idea of God. The thought of a forgiving and saving God was an efficacious and deeply satisfying thought. It was the clear thought that sanctified, not the doubtful reality behind the thought. A bracing insight.

On leaving Limerick, Michael had flown again to Chicago. He had stood once more in the luxury apartment on the twenty-third floor where he had come so close to dying, wondering what he would find there. But there was no trace of what he had lost. Perhaps it had been dispersed by the ammonia vapours that drifted from the carpet; from the places where the cleaning fluids had bleached it clear of stains, but not quite of their smells. They identified themselves to him as he stood there leaning on his stick: the pungency of burning herbs, the sexual juices of men and women, heavy like old fruit, and underlying everything, the concealed pus of unacknowledged pain. Whatever he was looking for, he would not find it there.

Death is now a welcome guest. That sad line from a sad opera had settled around Michael Cremin like a thread drawing tight. The car radio had sparked into life with it: the lament Purcell had given to Dido as she dies by her own hand for her love of Aeneas. Pure heart-break, unmistakeably feminine.

Michael had been pondering an offer of hospitality from an old friend, Jerome Theisen OSB of Saint John's Abbey, who was now the Abbot Primate in Rome. As Dido sang out her heart to him, he decided to accept the invitation. Before nightfall the next day, he had taken up residence in Minnesota as a guest of the monks.

It proved to be the right decision. Michael was nourished by the prevailing calm of the monastery, and soon after his arrival, he felt strong enough to put away the walking stick.

It was the clear human thought that sanctified. Holiness was a human excellence, the paramount human excellence: a synonym for self-realisation. What Catholic teachers had presumed to be the Grace of God, and had fought for gamely in mad battles with their human inclinations, was, in fact, a natural occurrence, if it was to occur at all.

Michael compared it to prospecting for water in the desert. If one went about it the right way, it was inevitable that water would be found.

So how come he could not find the water?

Certainly, there were many voices praising a variety of waters at Saint John's. The clumsy radicalism of the first post-conciliar years had come of age in a thousand many-splendoured manifestations, and the calm of the monastery, always rather deceptive, had openly ceded ground to a busy actionism. Saint John's had declared itself a place consecrated to struggle and mystery. A world in many colours was what the monks and their friends believed themselves called to create, and to celebrate, jubilantly and rather loudly.

Michael ignored most of it. The Abbey church was full of ritual theatre drawn from all religions and none, but he did not go there. When he said Mass, it was quietly, in the chapel of the enclosure, and reverently, for him. On special nights, on the grassy areas outside, women empowered each other and themselves in Wiccan rituals, but he paid them little attention. By day, the Abbot was affirming the goodness of sexuality, gay and straight, while trying to deal with cases of sexual abuse among the monks. Not even these protracted acrobatics could hold Michael's interest. He was pondering the deeper things of the desert, a desert private to himself, cheerless and empty, where there was nothing for his thirst.

4

Michael Cremin was still famous, and the Benedictine authorities prevailed on him to offer a course of lectures at the University which was attached to the Abbey. He chose a subject on which he felt he could still make a contribution: the history of the Liturgical Movement, which had given the Church the New Mass.

It was easy enough to paint the usual picture. But Michael felt the need for a more critical exploration. He owed it to the students, he felt. They had a right to look behind the received accounts and to try to make something out of whatever reality they might find.

The students believed that the Liturgical Movement had begun in earnest at the National Congress of Catholic Works held at Mechelen in 1909. And so it had, with Lambert Beauduin's revolutionary paper *La vraie priére de l'Église*. People needed to be grounded in their prayer, as a student told the class in a short presentation. Therefore, liturgy was not essentially directed towards God but towards God and the congregation, who were built up in the Faith through actively participating together. Active participation was impossible if the liturgy took place in a dead language unknown outside the liturgical setting. Michael was pleased with the student's conclusion. A truth of human life, she stated, a stark human necessity, had taken its rightful place in the liturgical equation: the fact that humans are expressive beings, who must shape themselves and their world through symbols and experience. In his response, Michael commented that it was worth taking a closer look at one of the forerunners, Dom Prosper Guéranger, of the Abbey of Solesmes in France. In the 1830s, Abbot Guéranger had also established a principle of active participation in the liturgy. However, the liturgy he had in mind was not a new, democratic one, but the Old Mass of Pius V, and the participation was individual and interior, using the quiet mind and the quiet heart rather than communicative and social skills. Through his books, lay Catholics were enabled to give their lives an intelligent pious structure by using the Breviary and the Roman Missal. And so, Michael offered, Active Participation was every bit as traditional as it was modern. And it was fully compatible with the Missal of Pius V, if you wanted it to be. Many of the post-conciliar reformers had been more interested in persuasion than in the actual truth.

"So the New Mass is wrong?" someone called out.

Michael did not answer. It was not a good question. Too simple to reveal anything useful. Instead, he told them about the reforming theologians he had known who had worked hard to create Paul VI's New Mass. Surprisingly few of these trailblazers had maintained belief in the rightness of their achievement. Josef Jungmann SJ and Ferdinando Antonelli OFM had recorded their unhappiness in diaries they left for posterity. And Father Stephen Sommerville, for many years one of the principal figures in the ICEL, was now claiming that the replacement of the Old Mass was nothing less than the triumph of Evil in their day. Even Pope Paul VI was on record as holding similar depressing views. For many of them, the post-conciliar Church with its liturgies had revealed itself as Frankenstein's monster, and they looked back with regret on the assistance they had given at its making.

It was a most remarkable disquiet of conscience for men who claimed to be following the Will of God, and a most remarkable disunity. It weighed heavily. It required explanation. Granted, the most influential theologians of all, Hans Küng, for example, or Karl Rahner, seemed to keep the progressive flag flying to the end. But Rahner, for one, was a puzzle. The German writer, Luise Rinser, had recently made public her long-running and supposedly platonic love affair with Rahner. To the fury of the Jesuit Order, which was unable to win against her in the courts, Ms. Rinser was amusing the world with luscious extracts from her letters to the great theologian. If Rinser was telling the truth, as she probably was, it was arguable whether Rahner had believed in God at all.

Perhaps these theologians had not questioned themselves and their motivation enough. Perhaps they had not cleared the rotting corpses from the well-springs of their thoughts and their feelings. Take another venerable personage, the German educator and member of the Consilium, Romano Guardini. Father Guardini had always felt himself a lonely outsider, lamed by shyness and depressions, never able to fit in. Perhaps it was a psychological need that led him to work so hard to realise the supposed community value of the Mass. Perhaps his emotional life was such that he could not make a difference between his own psychological needs and the spiritual needs of others.

But why was the Reverend Professor dishing up a load of speculation? This class was about theology and Church history. What were they supposed to learn from all this gossip?

Michael knew the answer he wanted to give. But he was unable to give it. He was a bishop of the Church, after all. He belonged to the Church. He belonged to the Church like a ghost to a ruined castle. Even though it might set him free, he could not begin tearing down what was left of the walls.

Michael acknowledged the students' questions. He was sick of theology, he told them. And sick of history. Theology and history had no answers to anything.

It was up to them, really. Up to each of them and his conscience, if he had one. They should take a look at where they were. This very Abbey had been one of the spearheads of the liturgical reforms they had been discussing. And look at it now. A worthy façade, and behind it anger, confusion, despair. Sexually active monks had been preying on vulnerable people here for years, and they were only trying to deal with it now.

"Professor! What have these scandals got to do with the liturgical reforms?"

Helpless now, Michael told them about his old superior, Gus Hogan. If Gus was lecturing to them, and not the tired old Bishop of Limerick, they would be asking themselves about the meaning of reverence, which Gus felt the New Mass was lacking in. Gus had believed that if someone lacked reverence for the Real Presence he would be unable to respect or cherish anything that was good. Including the children in his care, if he was a priest.

"Tell us what you really believe!" somebody called, but Michael decided that he had said enough. He often felt like Karl Rahner or Romano Guardini, he told them. But he had no desire to make a theology out of his predicament and teach it to them. Anyway, he did only what he liked. There was a lesson for them, if they cared to look for it. To underline that fact, he was now ending the course. There would be no further classes. If they wanted to hand in a term paper, they were welcome to do so, and he would grade it for them, but they shouldn't expect him to set the theme. Let them do whatever they liked, and be graded on that.

Michael walked out, leaving a totally silent room behind him. It reminded him of Jean Nordheider in Louvain, all those years ago. Discomfiture and stony silence had been the marks of Nordheider's presence. Now they were his marks, too. Michael wondered if Jean Nordheider had also felt the cold of the desert, and the unspeakable horror of the cold. He doubted it, somehow. Jean had never seemed to care.

5

In reality, Michael Cremin's decision to leave Ireland had not been such a happy one. Uppermost in his mind had been a personal matter of the greatest urgency: a strange and powerful experience during his heart attack which so far he had kept secret. This experience now lay behind everything he thought, did and said. It was a cold that burned in him constantly, like the opposite of a fire. It consumed him like a shrinking enigma, in which he was reduced to a single dense point of despair. With his lecturing over, he felt the inclination to engage with this dreadful event, in the hope of banishing it forever.

First, he had been drawn down a tunnel of light, such as he had read of in published accounts of Near-Death-Experiences. Then a mirror had come upon him from nowhere, a mirror that was also a living being, and he had seen the Knowledge that the living mirror reflected, the Knowledge of an utterly failed existence; and that existence was his. All his life had run before him in that instant, like a film that was fulfilled in one single present moment. He saw the moments of joy and pain, all the acts and the omissions, and underlying them dark, dirty motivations, horrific lusts and hates, and terrible calamities, all of which grew increasingly foreign to him. In that quiet mirror, a face had slowly formed itself, the face of a monster. It was a filthy dangerous thing, a thing of stinging arrogance, slobbering with lust. It was a thing he had never imagined could ever exist. From a world that could not possibly exist. Silvery music was playing, and the mirror was asking whether this creature was he, the self that he had made in the course of living. Michael could not believe that it was he in that mirror glass. That horrible visage was a trick of Hell, and he turned towards the vast and many-splendoured expanses to where great companies of spirits were beckoning him, laughing and celebrating.

He expected that they would lead him to Paradise, but they did not. He found himself in an underground City, and then in a cell in a prison hospital. The place stank horribly of fear and pain and despair. There, a doctor came to see him. This doctor had time on his hands. He took pleasure in explaining to Michael what was going to happen to him. He was to be castrated. His testicles would be squeezed to a pulp in a little metal press. The pain of it was absolutely unique. Then his scrotum would be slit and the juice from his testicles would be collected in a glass and brought to the Commandant of the prison camp, who was a very powerful individual, and who used this juice as an energy drink. If there was any meat mash left over from his squashed testicles it would go to the Commandant's dogs, who were very dangerous animals, and always ravenously hungry. They would devour any living thing in their vicinity, if they were permitted to, except their master, of course. Then, like all new inmates, he would go to the surface and be chained to a thousand other castrated prisoners who worked together as a unit. He would spend all of eternity as part of this slave gang, which was chained to the giant wheel that they were pushing round and round. The wheel worked a filter pump which created a certain kind of water that the Commandant liked to use for his little vegetable garden. There were other slave gangs, of course, thousands of them, working other wheels with other functions, or doing other useful things. The Commandant was not an unreasonable individual. He kept the prisoners alive as long as they were able to work. If a prisoner did not like this destiny he could try to escape. He might manage to get out of the prison compound, and into the reaches of the City, but he would be spotted immediately. The first citizen who saw him would crush him like a man killing a fly, except that it would be done by a simple glance of the eyes. Theoretically, he might escape into the open and try to survive there all by himself. But no-one had ever succeeded in doing so. The air and the earth and all organisms that dwelt or grew in the open were deadly poisonous. There was nothing to eat. Nor was there much light. It was also terribly cold. Fatally cold, actually. And the dogs? It was their special treat to be let loose on those who tried to escape. Sometimes the Commandant deliberately let a prisoner think he had escaped into the open in order to have some sport with his dogs. Pointless complaining about it. As for now, well, he would now take off his clothes and bend over, please, because he, the doctor, was going to have sex with him. Before the castration, of course. No fun in it afterwards. And if he wanted to resist he was welcome to, because he, the doctor, preferred rape to consensual sex any time. He was just a little tired right now, or he would have raped him the minute he came in.

Michael was taken by the doctor from behind. His insides were rent open and seared and shrivelled. But he had woken up in a different kind of hospital, with very different doctors, and he was alive.

"All the accounts I've read of such experiences are positive. Lights. Friends. Loved ones. All these good things."

Michael sat easily in the plush armchair, but his mood was sombre. The therapist, Celsus McCutcheon OSB, shifted uncomfortably. The Benedictine psychiatrist, an authority on Near-Death-Experiences, did not yet know what direction the therapy should take.

"Michael, the good ones are the ones that get reported. The ones that seem to point to the afterlife. These other ones, these bad trips, they're actually more numerous, but we class them as hallucinations, you know, connected with this life, and with where you are right here."

"So it's not just me?"

"Almost everyone who comes back from the point of death relates something similar, but it often stops just after things turn negative. The mind starts to bring itself to an even keel again. You just went a bit further than most."

"What if it's real? If the beyond is really like that?"

"It's not real."

"How do you know?"

"I know that God is good. And there's no way your concentration camp situation can be squared with what I know to be the goodness of God."

"It's Hell, Celsus. It's supposed to exist, isn't it?"

"That's imagery. It tells us something. Like your dream. It doesn't mean that your ultimate destination is in the force of the image. It's an extreme. Hypothetical. It's a what-if situation. What if there is no loving God who saves you. You experienced a counterfactual."

"But why would God want to save me?"

"Because that's what God does. Would you condemn someone to hell-fire for all eternity? Of course you wouldn't. Surely God is at least as merciful as you are? Michael, you're way out in the wilderness. You gotta let yourself be loved! Get that feeling back inside you that you are a great lovable man."

Celsus McCutcheon was surprised at how easy it was proving to find the way. These words, he would not normally use them, they just popped into his head, and they were perfect. The therapy would take a new line he had wanted to try out for some time.

"You know, I think this needs a non-discursive kind of handle on it. I think you did some Zen when you were here before? Well, that's where I'd like us to go on this. No need to focus on all this detail. So why don't you just do things that make you feel good for a while? Eros is medicinal, you know that. You could get fixed up there. And you could join the guys in the Dojo? Give Zazen another shot? Clears the channels real fast."

6

Do things that make you feel good, Celsus McCutcheon had said, and Michael tried. The Zen Dojo made him welcome, but the people there disappointed him. They were practicing Zen for the sake of personal effectivity, and he left them to it. He went looking in the fresher worlds of the forests, listening to the morning sounds of the animals and birds and to the breathing of the wind in the maple trees.

One day, back at the Abbey, a package was waiting for him: a thick brown envelope delivered by hand to his pigeon hole. It was a paper by one of his students, the only submission so far from his course on the Liturgical Movement, and he retired with it to the monastery library. The paper proved to be a comparison between the Old Mass and a supposed Rite of the Holy Grail; far-fetched, but not without charm. The Old Mass and the Rite of the Grail Castle, each in a different but complementary way, were described as dramatic events of a special kind. They were both authored by God, at least in the essentials, and they both re-enacted the same archetypal occurrence: the overcoming of death by divine intervention. The main difference was that the Mass was open to all, whereas the Rite of the Grail Castle was secret. The Rite of the Grail and the Rite of the Mass were connected through the Chalice, which was a symbol of the feminine, and which drew down the reality of the Grail into the Church and the mundane world, and renewed that world. The words of Consecration in the Old Mass contained a hidden reference to this: the words :Mysterium Fidei: enclosed in their odd colons. What seemed to rationalist minds to be a clumsy interpolation was, in fact, a window to another world, the world of the Grail, which was a world of Salvation, but one which lay short of Heaven even though it touched on it. In the New Mass, the words and signs of Consecration had been broken up and the pieces shifted around or removed completely. The New Mass no longer possessed this opening to the world of the Grail. Strangely, the reformulations had cost the Old Mass this opening too. The capacity of people to respond to the presence of God had changed for the worse, and with this, the Mass Itself had changed. Traditionalist groupings had preserved the outer form of the Old Mass, but they had not been able to rescue its wider meaning. This could not be rescued by the acts of men, because it did not belong to men. Nor could it be restored by the act of a future pope. That window to another world had been put into the Mass by God. It was God. But God had allowed men and women to remove it. The liturgical reforms after the Council had deprived the Church of the vessel of spiritual power that had been inherent in the Mass. That spiritual power was now gone.

As an example of academic work, the paper was not of good quality: the writing was impressionistic; there were no sources to speak of. The Church had never possessed a Rite of the Grail, Michael was sure. The world of the Grail was pure fantasy. But there was an original thread of gold there that was worth exploring. Michael penned a short note to the student offering an appointment.

It was an attractive, but troubled, young woman who came through his door. The marks of self harm were unmistakable.

“At least you believe in something,” he said, pointing to her paper.

“Actually, I don’t.”

Michael looked narrowly at her, but decided to let the remark pass. “Where did you get these ideas?”

The paper was her own, she told him, but she had taken inspiration from old sources. Her family had a long history, one dating back to France and before that to Ephesus at the time of Saint John. Her sources came from the lore that they had handed down through the generations.

“If you don’t believe in anything, at least you believe in learning something.”

“Depends on the teacher, maybe.”

Michael appraised her. “I hope it’s not me you mean. I’m not able to teach. I find the truth far too difficult.”

“In your last class you tried to tell the truth.”

“So you believe in the truth? There might be a way forward in that.”

“So you’re not sending me away?”

“No, I’ll help you.”

She put her hand on his, and it seemed to him that the bond had been there already. Isadora Nightbird was her name.

7

Celsus McCutcheon had listened with studied sensitivity as Michael told him of Isadora.

"You seeing this girl? How long?"

"A few weeks."

"Slept with her?"

"No."

"That's not like you, Michael."

"She's a kind of wise fool. You see, that crazy paper, it said more about the Liturgical Movement than any amount of books or lectures."

"Why don't you just admit that you want her sexually? You don't need any excuses to want her sexually."

"She's not the kind you can touch, Celsus. She has this wild imagination that's throwing things at me, things she can't know much about."

The psychiatrist leaned forward in his chair. "It's not about this girl, Michael. It looks like the eternal feminine is reaching out for you. We know where we're coming from on this, don't we? An intimate encounter with the feminine. We celibates need that from time to time. The alchemy of physicality."

"I promised I'd help her."

Guilt, thought Celsus McCutcheon. Guilt was the problem here.

"Michael, I think right now we feel a kind of freedom in this regard, don't we?"

"Do we?"

"You know, this is the first therapy session we've had where you aren't obsessed with that bad trip that was messing your life up. You are a great lovable guy, and when something happens to remind you of that, you freeze all over with guilt."

"I don't want to go around feeling lovable."

"The Church has changed, Michael. You know that. You were right there making the changes happen. We're not big into guilt any more. No-one is. Why should you be?

"Fine, Celsus. Guilt isn't the word. It's about responsibility. I feel responsible. And I don't just feel it. I am responsible."

The psychiatrist looked at his watch. The session was over. He was not certain that they had made any progress. "You just keep me posted, OK?"

Yes, Michael was responsible. He had always been responsible, and he had always known it. So why were things as bad as they were? Something had dawned on him. Isadora Nightbird was Laura Moro. Collegeville, Minnesota was Rome in 1964. His life was bringing the same kind of experiences to him again. It was like Nietzsche's Eternal Recurrence of the Same. Things came back, but they came back worse, unnecessarily so. Yes, he was guilty, with all the paralysis it entailed. He was guilty of what he had become.

During a walk in the forest, Isadora told Michael a little about her childhood. She had grown up on a farm only ten miles or so from the Abbey. When she was fourteen, she had lost her maidenhead to the fingers of a priest. Isadora did not blame the priest much, because she had liked him touching her. She never had intercourse with this priest, but two of her friends had. These girls had been missing for years. Isadora believed that the priest had killed them, probably because they had become pregnant by him.

"Have you talked to the police?"

"I can't trust the police."

"Can you trust me?"

She stopped on the forest path, and looked at him. Then she leaned over and kissed him.

"Don't do that, Isadora."

He was unprepared for her anger. Her eyes flashed, and her grip on his arm grew so tight that it felt like an iron claw.

"I'm not going to let you go," she said.

They were at a place where a number of paths crossed. He stopped, and removed his arm from her grip. She continued walking. He waited there in the stillness watching her disappear, trying not to want her to turn round and come back to him. But she did not come back.

Then, out of the blue, Michael found a note from Isadora in his pigeon hole, *I went to the police about the priest who touched me*, it read.

The same day, the police arrived at Saint John's. They arrested Launcelot Deeler, Michael's old friend from the Judas Society. Launcy had not aged well, and was often ill. Michael had not seen much of him since coming to the Abbey. He joined the throng that watched silently from the steps as the police bundled Launcy into the patrol car. An indictment for sexual abuse, rape and murder. It was barely imaginable. Then, Michael's eyes were caught by the sleeve of Launcy's jacket as it slid open, revealing a long and skinny arm. There were tracks of puncture marks along what was left of the veins. Heroin, whispered someone who knew him.

When Michael walked back up the steps and into the red-tiled hallway, the Abbot was waiting for him, sombre. A message from the Papal Pro-Nuncio. A crisis in Limerick. Bishop Cremin was to return to his diocese without delay.

8

It was a rainy September morning. Michael Cremin turned a bleak eye on the three men who were arraigned before him. He was in charge again in the Diocese of Limerick, and he intended people to know it. Things were worse than he had expected: financial chaos and a paedophilia scandal.

These disgraced priests were the first item on his agenda. Michael looked them up and down. An unsavoury lot. Bishop Newman had incardinated them. He alone knew why. Jules Murrigan, a scrawny fellow from Co. Galway. The pot-bellied Bosco O'Loughlin, who in better days had been a champion swimmer. And this fellow with the blotchy skin, whom Michael's eyes came back to. Yes, it was he, Benignus "Billy" Breen, whom he knew from Louvain and Rome.

"Howyeh, Mick!" Breen's associates giggled at his bravado. "I said to the lads here, Mick Cremin looks after his own. That's what I said."

"Did you?" Michael's eyes bored into those of the priest.

"We go back a long way, Mick, you and me."

"Did the Friars throw you out, Billy?"

"Just having a break. The Order's gone down an awful lot, know what I mean?"

Again a snigger, more confident this time.

"I'm going to drum you out of the priesthood, Billy. You and these two. Then I'm going to put you in jail."

"We're innocent until proven guilty. And it's all lies, anyway, Mick."

Michael tapped the folders of evidence he had been given. "As far as I'm concerned, you're guilty until proven innocent. And that won't happen." He turned to Fergus Honan, who was still the vicar general. "Get them out of here. They're suspended. No privileges."

Father Honan began to usher the men towards the door. Billy Breen swung round in anger. "Ever hear the saying about the monkey? The higher he climbs up the ladder, the more you see his arse. Think about that, Bishop Mick Cremin."

Michael addressed Father Honan. "They're in diocesan housing, I believe. I want them out by the end of the month. Eviction orders."

Fergus Honan pushed the disgraced priests out the door, and then stepped back. "I'll tell Gerry Hegarty to get other accommodation for them."

"No, Father. No other accommodation. As far as I'm concerned, they're homeless. And not Hegarty. You."

The vicar general began to splutter, but held himself in check. The bleak eye of Michael the Cruel told him all he needed to know. If he wasn't careful, he was finished, too.

There was no doubt about the guilt of these men. Michael set up a victim compensation fund, selling a prime piece of real estate to do so. He spent time with the victims, their families and their friends. He briefed the media personally and with total frankness. He went on television and apologized, granite-faced and convincing.

He was a sharp contrast to his fellow bishops. Those with similar cases were dithering between denial and inept containment, causing untold damage to the reputation of the Church. Understandably, their first concern was pastoral: to help the victims, certainly; but also to minister to the sinning priest, to try to protect him from the final spiritual consequences of his acts so that he could repent of what he had done and become able to make amends. After all, that was the task of the Church: to minister to sinners. But all too often, they were perceived to close ranks for the sake of the criminal, forsaking justice and compassion to protect their friends and colleagues.

Michael Cremin's primary concern was public relations. He saw what many bishops could not see: that the Church had declined massively in stature, and was now but one player among many in pluralist civil society. A discredited player, at that. The likes of Jules Murrigan and Billy Breen were only the tip of the iceberg. The Church was destined for a niche existence in a reduced milieu, assuming she survived at all.

At the end of the month, when the bailiffs arrived to evict the priests from their homes, they found Bosco O'Loughlin dead in the armchair in his living room. Empty packets of sleeping pills and pain killers, and an empty bottle of whiskey littered the rug beside him. The film Jesus of Nazareth had been playing all night with the repeat button on. Jules Murrigan had fled the country the day before. Billy Breen, who lacked financial resources and could not afford to escape, was already on remand in Limerick prison. Michael heard the news of Father O'Loughlin's death the same day. "Newman will do the funeral," he commented, and returned to his papers.

Michael Cremin's next concern was the organisational chaos Bishop Newman had unleashed on his diocese. Discreetly, Michael brought back Leo Murphy to run his financial affairs. There was no help for it, he told Gerry Hegarty, who called to protest. Bishop Newman's financial management had been disastrous, and he needed his diocese back where he had left it, on a solid footing, with money of its own.

After just over a year had passed, Michael Cremin was able to report to the Vatican that the situation in Limerick had been remedied. This was a considerable achievement, and the Secretary of State, Cardinal Sodano, invited Michael to Rome for a private dinner. The Cardinal went to great lengths to treat him as a guest of honour: the food and wine were of the finest, and Michael's opinions were asked on a variety of current issues. His Excellency's firm handling of the Limerick affair had been admirable in every respect. Rome was full of his praises. But more of the kind was coming. Most unfortunate. Would he care to act as an advisor on this issue for the Vatican? Excellent. But there was another matter. Most delicate. The failing health of the present Holy Father. As a bishop of their trust, His Excellency would surely see the urgent need to plan for the transition? The Holy Father's pilgrimages and his acts of personal piety were a great blessing, no doubt, but surely, the government of the church could be left in the capable hands of his cardinals? Many bishops thought so.

Michael returned to Limerick uplifted. Pope John Paul's active life was as good as finished. Others were ruling in his name, whether he liked it or not. And when he thought of the backward-looking and divisive line this pontificate had been taking, he found it very much for the better.

Michael was a bishop of their trust. That meant a lot. Whatever new regime Cardinal Sodano would heave into power, Michael's years in the wilderness were drawing to a close.

9

On his return from Rome, Bishop Cremin found a letter waiting for him on the subject of Billy Breen. A number of Limerick priests had signed a petition calling on him to make a gesture of mercy towards Breen. The priests condemned Billy Breen's crimes unreservedly; even so, they feared that the Bishop's treatment of Breen bordered on the unacceptable. Breen had acknowledged his guilt in full and wished to make his peace with God. Father Benignus OFM, as they called him, was a priest of their diocese. He needed his bishop to minister to his spiritual needs before it was too late. It would be unjust and unchristian to refuse.

Michael wondered sourly what had made this degenerate so popular with his priests, but he saw no way to refuse the request. He had indeed been harsh with Billy Breen. Not only had he deprived him of his priestly faculties, but he had refused to provide bail for him, which meant that Billy would languish in prison until his trial. Billy Breen had been locked up for over a year already and he had to be kept apart from other prisoners for his protection. His health had broken down. The medical reports indicated that he was dying. This was no great loss, as far as Michael was concerned, but a gesture would be a good thing. A Christian gesture. Yes, he would hear Billy's confession and administer the Last Rites, if need be. He would carry out those symbolic actions which they had both been pretending to live by all these years. He would do that for him, if that was what he wanted. And he would see to it that word spread in all the right places that he had done so.

Benignus Breen OFM was housed in a particularly depressing wing of Limerick Prison. A deferential prison officer led Michael through the echoing corridors and into the cell. The officer, a small, balding man with a wispy moustache, was a long-serving member of a Catholic lay organisation, Communion and Liberation, which he was clearly delighted to mention. He had specifically asked for the honour of assisting His Excellency this day. Communion and Liberation was one of the New Religious Movements so favoured by Pope John Paul II. These conservative lay people were serious pests, in Michael's view; but he smiled at the man with as much warmth as he could muster. He might yet prove useful.

In the cell, posters of forests and meadows graced the walls. The plenitude of greens, blues, yellows, and reds, caught the attention, providing relief from the gun-metal grey that dominated the place. They were being good to Billy Breen, allowing him to have such things on the walls.

Billy was the first to speak. "You know, Mick, I wouldn't be here at all if it wasn't for you."

"Go ahead, Billy."

"If a fellow like you could get ordained and keep getting promoted and end up a bishop, it's a sign to us all that anything goes, Mick."

"At least you're being frank, Billy."

"You're an honest man, I suppose, Mick, in your own way. You practice what you preach, most of the time. I remember one of your sermons way back when you took over as bishop. All about the Church today wanting you to live a fulfilled life. Not a shred of morality in it. After I heard that I began fiddling around with the young lads. It's not that long ago, really. One thing led to another, you see, and the first time, Mick, he led me on. It wasn't the first time for him. He was a right little whore. If he's up there on that witness stand all self-righteous, there's no justice at all."

"And the rest?"

"The other times, I was guilty in every way and I'm sorry and I don't mind paying the price. But I'll say this to you, Mick. You're lucky it's not the little boys that turn you on, or you'd be in here with me yourself."

"Billy. There's ways and means. I know priests who take off the collar every now and again and go to Denmark or the Philippines. They get it out of their system. They don't destroy young lives."

"They're destroyed anyway. What kind of a world are we giving them? Men like Haughey and Mitterand running countries, and men like you running the Church. I saw it all years ago in Louvain. That Italian chap who killed himself. There was a Jesuit sent over from Rome to hush it up. To protect your career. I had to swear an oath to keep my mouth shut. And I did, Mick. I protected you. All these years. They made it worth my while, I'll say that. But I might have talked, all the same. You know, I exchanged a word with one of them last year when all this began to break. I have a cousin, Mick, who was always very good to me, and her child is very ill. Without any warning the hospital cancelled the operation. The child might have died. And when I said I wouldn't break the agreement, the operation was back on schedule again. That's what they're like, Mick. People are saying I am the most evil man in the world, but they're a lot more evil than me. And they're running the Church."

"I'm sorry you think that, Billy."

"I'm sorry for the young lads. Did you ever stick it in like that, Mick, did you? I'd say you did in your time."

"No."

"You don't know what it's like, so. To be against God and against nature and nothing you can do about it. To say Mass and have Him there with you knowing He knows everything. It's a terrible, terrible thing. Will He forgive me, Mick?"

Michael looked blankly at Billy Breen. He knew what platitudes to bring to his lips, the phrases both he and Billy had known off by heart for years. But he could not speak them. His voice felt like a cracked old flower pot someone had rammed down a disused toilet. And Billy's burnt out eyes were boring into his, seeing through him.

"You're not answering me, Bishop Mick Cremin." he whispered, a light brightening deep inside him. "God doesn't want the likes of you answering for Him! Oh, Merciful God!"

Something broke inside those tired, bloodshot eyes, so stranged with light, and Father Breen collapsed onto his iron bed, sobbing. It was a pitiful sight, but there was something more to it, something that warned Michael away.

The prison officer was speaking into his portable radio, calling for assistance. He took Michael's arm. "We'd better take you out, My Lord. The medics'll handle him."

To get rid of the prison officer, who was still dancing attendance, Michael raised his right hand and gave the age-old sign of blessing. When he managed to get away, and the last of the security gates had closed after him, he put Father Benignus Breen from his mind.

When Billy Breen died, Michael Cremin was in Castelgandolfo breakfasting with Pope John Paul II. The pope, who was in considerable physical pain, had always been able to rely on Bishop Cremin, he told the guests in his Polish-accented Italian. Some years ago, Cardinal Casaroli had wanted him to resign. But it was Casaroli who resigned. Peter remained. In the Garden of Gethsemane, Peter had abandoned Jesus in his hour of need. This successor of Peter would never give in to infirmity. Jesus Christ would determine when his time was up. Jesus Christ and no other. Was it not so, Bishop Cremin? Michael nodded obediently, and looked into the eyes of Pope John Paul. They were clear, despite the medication. And angry. The old man was still a force to be reckoned with.

†

8

The Celebration

1

Leo Murphy's marriage to Melissa Norton-Murphy had finally been annulled, much in the same way as the marriages of various European royalty: by prevailing on the pope to overrule his own tribunals. Leo was living with his new companion, Janice Carmody, in Farrelstown Castle, which he was renting from the Diocese of Limerick. The annulment came through shortly after an important day for Bishop Cremin: the fortieth anniversary of his ordination to the priesthood. In Leo's view, nothing could be more fitting than a great celebration. The annulment and the victory it represented may have been uppermost in his mind, but he felt it was Bishop Cremin who should be celebrated. The Bishop was a great man, and it was high time that this was told to the world.

The day of the feast dawned, but Michael Cremin did not want to attend. The congratulations had been coming in for weeks already, and he had hoped to leave it at that, without a celebration, and to end the occasion with a few notes of thanks sent out by his secretariat. In some respects, his recovery from the heart-attack was only apparent. There were nights when he dreamed again of his visit to Hell, and he awoke from those nights well before dawn, in the grip of a despair that was thick and choking. Was this the true morning, he would ask himself: this grey shroud emerging from behind the disguise of the night? He had begun to leave a fire burning in the grate, and when such a morning came, he would lie there looking into the little shapes cast by the remains of the fire, saddened by the fact that he could see so little. He cursed knowledge and the urge to understand. He cursed God and Man. He cursed friendship and love. He cursed the past, the present and the future. Then he would loll in the bedclothes overcome by a fit of laughter at the absurdity of it all.

No, this place with the dying fire, this was not home. Home was still a transfigured fireside in Foxrock, with his mother cuddling him, which he could not remember her doing, because she had died when he was small, abandoning him to a world of strangers, and with his father defending him against the terrors of the dark, which he had often done, but never sustainably. Home had never been the succession of functional clerical dwellings he had come to know, slippery underfoot from floor polish, where the heating in the bedrooms never worked, where the food was miserable, and the faces that crossed your path on the way down to a meagre breakfast veered between the scowling and the servile. Home was not this lonely bedroom of a bishop, where there was no-one to share his bed but the sneering fingers of flame in the dying fire. He knew of dioceses in the Church where the bishop would cruise the local seminary for sexual partners, having made sure in advance that enough willing young men had entered there to study for the priesthood. He knew bishops who had secretly married and were raising families. He knew many others who longed for a woman's touch and who drowned that longing with alcohol. There was a peculiarly Catholic irony about it all. Bishops like himself, who could separate sex from relationships and morality, got away with it easily. But those who cared, and who tried to offer their love to their companions, found themselves in furtive relationships they were unable to stand up for, heaping misery on themselves and their partners. Eamonn Casey, for example, the former Bishop of Galway, who had fled the country in disgrace some years previously. When news of Casey's love-affair and his illegitimate son got out, Michael had felt sympathy for him. If Casey had been a bishop in the mission territories, no-one would have batted an eyelid, and his considerable talents would not have been lost to the Episcopate. Michael's own domestic arrangements had always been frugal; ascetic, even. Most of his girlfriends had been business transactions with escort services. Now he was over sixty, with his vital forces at an ebb. Even if the Church abolished celibacy, which he hoped it would, there would still be nothing to drive away the cold for him.

No, he did not want this celebration. Once, the year before, when walking in the grounds of his residence, he had come across a hole in the perimeter wall. This section of the wall adjoined a school playground, and he had looked through the hole at the children, who were out playing during their morning break. There was a good teacher in that school, and the children loved her. It was in their faces when she gave them her attention, it was in the way their faces lit up at such a moment as if they were beings of sunlight. It was beautiful, and Michael turned away, discomfited. Nobody smiled at him like that. Not ever. The next morning, Michael walked back to that section of the perimeter wall, longing to see again those smiles of joy, but somebody had gone to work there. The hole was gone, and with it that opening to a better world. But he could not forget.

In the end, Leo Murphy sent a limousine to collect him. Strangely, the driver looked like John Gregory, the taxi-driver he had been friends with in Rome. It was unmistakeably John Gregory. The same red hair and red beard. Michael began to wonder if it really was John, but it could not be. What would bring John Gregory to Limerick? And what could halt the decay of things so that a man could be permanently a certain age like John Gregory seemed to be?

"How is our mutual friend, Father Clavis?"

"No doubt he is looking forward to seeing you again, Your Excellency!"

Yes. It was he. John Gregory. The answer proved it.

No. It was not he. The answer did not prove anything. It was an empty courtesy. Nothing more.

When they arrived at the Castle, the driver held the door open for him, but there was no time for Michael to study his face more closely. He was immediately thrown into a flurry of outstretched hands and flashing cameras. Even the television people were there, with one of the better-known reporters. Delivering the old confident smile and the expected platitudes, Michael felt animated again, but he would make as early a night of it as possible.

2

There was a guest book on a table in the hallway in which the party guests were asked to inscribe themselves. Michael turned over a few pages. All the pages were laid out like gravestones. People were chuckling over their host's sense of humour, as they put their names on their own gravestones, but Michael saw nothing amusing in it. The guest who had arrived before him had signed himself as Augustine Hogan. The one before that was Laura Moro. The page before that, an opulent gravestone, was Jean Nordheider's. Quickly, Michael thumbed back and forth through the pages, till he found what he was looking for. Someone had signed himself in as Angelo Poggi. They were all there, all the ghostly figures who had populated his life. It was sick, sick, sick.

"Michael, are you unwell?"

Leo's concern seemed genuine. It couldn't be Leo's doing anyway. He did not know about these people from the past.

"How well he looks, our esteemed Bishop Cremin!"

It was the nasal whine of Louvain, forty odd years before. Michael turned to face him.

"John Northrider, Most Reverend Sir!"

Michael, always perfect in public, shook the outstretched hand warmly, while his mind raced elsewhere. He had misread the name, that was all. When he was free again, he glanced once more at the gravestones of the guest book. He had misread all those names. Laura Moro was Laura Moran. Angelo Poggi was Angelo Prunty, the Galway businessman. Augustine Hogan was in reality Austin G. O'Hagan.

Already, though, they were being shepherded towards the dining hall. There were dignitaries to be greeted, which could not be done without a ritual sip of champagne and some small talk. Their wives placed no small importance on having Michael's ear, even if it blocked the way for others. He was a bishop, after all, a handsome and famous one, to boot, and they were in the main loyal daughters of the Church, who liked to deplore the general decline of faith and morals.

His own morals would be a shock to them. They would think him an atheist, a traitor. But he wasn't an atheist. He was an enlightened Catholic. The Roman Catholic Church, and indeed, most of the varieties of Christianity there had ever been, were examples of a creative appropriation which had more to do with the exercise of power than with any final truth, which was, of course, inaccessible. To a certain kind of mind, it was the Will of God that things should evolve in this way, and that the empty truth be kept secret. Perhaps it was necessarily so. Only the rare and solitary scintillae among men had the stamina for the truth. If Michael were to answer the question with honesty, he would say that in his understanding, God did not yet exist. God had yet to emerge into existence out of the fragments of meaning that were scattered throughout the primordial darkness with uncertain viability. The difference between this and atheism would be too much for most people.

The banqueting hall of Farrelstown Castle still retained the nave of the old church it had once been, in times gone by. The stone flagging had been laid with fine carpets and some dozens of tables were set for the guests. What had once been the Sanctuary was now a raised area, and there Leo had placed a long table, reminiscent of the King's table at a feudal banquet. There were thirteen places there, all facing into the banqueting area. Twelve plus one, Leo whispered to him, as they took their seats, with Michael to his left. The place to his right remained empty.

Leo had created seven levels out of the enclosed space of the former church. Seven, that is, if one included a roof platform, which was accessible by means of a staircase in the small spire. This had been achieved by constructing a series of low wooden ceilings, staggered step-like, one above the other, and each a different colour as it led to the next level. The whole formed a wide ascending spiral which made ready different futuristic spaces for work or leisure. The roof platform was of black stone, and was exposed to the sea wind.

"Where did you get the staff, Leo?" Michael was observing how the dinner was being managed. There was a woman in charge, a woman who seemed vaguely familiar to him, clearly a woman of formidable strength, with what seemed her daughters, one dark, one fair. These three were not only directing guests to their places with deft courtesy, but were co-ordinating a small army of doormen, attendants, waiters and waitresses.

"Do you not know? I thought Hegarty would have told you. Or are you no longer on speaking terms with Hegarty?"

"Oh, Gerry does his own thing."

"They're looking after an old priest who moved over here from Wales. Some kind of mystic, apparently. They're in the old cottage by the sea."

"Where?"

"The old cottage by the sea. The one Hegarty kept for the diocese."

"I don't know about this cottage by the sea."

"I've often told you. You give Hegarty too much of a free hand."

The many courses of fine food were not to Michael's taste that night, but he got through the meal and the speeches easily enough. After the dessert course, Leo whispered to Michael to come away with him. By a secret flight of stairs, Michael was led up to the third of the seven levels Leo had made. This was where the organ loft had once been. It had been turned into a meeting room with opaque, sound-proof glass. It was furnished with tables of anthracite and armchairs of dull yellow flaked with black. A cleric was waiting. He was dressed in unassuming black, but Michael recognised him. It was Felix Kostuva SJ, his old acquaintance from Rome, now an Archbishop of the Curia, and a key figure at the Secretariat of State. Kostuva extended both hands in greeting.

"The warmest wishes of His Eminence on this happy occasion. And of His Holiness, of course."

"His Eminence is more than kind. As is His Holiness. We in Limerick add our voices to the great multitude who are beseeching Our Lord for the speedy recovery of the Holy Father."

Archbishop Kostuva nodded briefly. Only now did they sit down. The visitor folded his hands together and looked blandly at Michael.

"His Eminence will continue to have particular interest in the affairs of the Diocese of Limerick."

Michael understood. The meeting was over. And it had gone well for him. Enquiries had been made. The information was favourable. Michael withdrew, his heart beating faster. Kostuva had not come all this way to exchange a few well-chosen words. It was the prelude to something greater.

The party had livened up during his short absence. The banqueting hall, now a ballroom, was full of dancing couples elegantly accompanied by Viennese waltzes from the smiling musicians on the stage. Space cleared immediately for the great Bishop of Limerick, and good manners required Michael to dance a round or two with some of the more important guests. Then, a gesture from the doorway caught his attention. It was Leo signalling discreetly to him. Michael crossed the floor to reach him. Without a word, Leo made way for Archbishop Kostuva.

"His Eminence will see you now."

Michael jumped with surprise. Was the Secretary of State here in person? Felix Kostuva motioned for silence and led him upstairs.

It was not Cardinal Sodano who received him in the glass enclosure, nor any cardinal he knew. This cardinal's garb was not of the usual kind; he was dressed like a cardinal of a different century. And his face was hidden. A black linen cloth covered his features, except for slits for the eyes, nose and mouth. Over the forehead and eyes, a mask of hammered gold had been fitted. He might have stepped from a scene of a film.

"Do not inquire who I am." The masked cardinal was French, judging by his accent.

Michael detected a peculiar smell on the air, a smell which he remembered from a train journey across the Alps many years ago. It was Felix Kostuva sweating. Sweating with fear. At a sign from the gloved hand, Kostuva withdrew.

"Your Eminence?" Michael emphasised the question.

The cardinal ignored the move. "Your Excellency. Our host has a sense of style, has he not?" He gestured around the space Leo had created, and the gesture drew power. The space seemed quelled by the masked presence. In a corner, a table fountain built of slate was throwing an oddly dark water into the air.

"Why would our host have dark water, Excellency? Kostuva assumes it is a temporary condition of the pipes. But it is not a temporary condition of the pipes. I do not believe in meaningless co-incidences. Do you, my dear Bishop Cremin?"

Michael did not answer.

"You are an open book to us, Excellency. We know everything you have ever done. There is not a word you have spoken anywhere that is not known to us."

"You say "Us"?"

"We are the Church within the Church. Chosen for secret leadership."

"A Lodge?"

"We are a Lodge, if you like. We are few in number. Some of us are cardinals. Our leader is not. He is not even a priest. The Church as you know it is a vehicle of our making. The pope does our bidding."

"What do you stand for?"

"Our beliefs are yours, Bishop Cremin. Jesus is a myth. We have been using the power of this myth. To pacify the masses. As for the reality, William Blake put it so well: energy is eternal delight. We follow the energy of the Spirit. Through the forming impact of the Will. We are men of power. We choose men of calibre to join us. From an early age, their lives are steered by us. You are such a man. Since 1960, and before, your life has been engineered by us. You are our artefact. Soon, you will be a cardinal. And soon, the Holy Father, Pope John Paul II, will pass from this life. We are making of him a saint for the masses. A long, slow, public decline into almost total incapacity. A heroic struggle against infirmity. We will reduce the whole of Christianity to a feeble old man kneeling on television repeating simple slogans with his last few breaths. It will have incalculable psychological force. There will be spontaneous outbreaks of prayer. There will be a surge of new vocations to the priesthood. In short, miracles. We have promised him this. That he will die a saint. And then? Then the conclave will elect you. You are to be the next pope. And you will serve the greater good as we direct."

"And if I refuse?"

"You will not refuse."

"And what if you're making a mistake?"

"Mistakes have been made on occasion. Yes. Errors of judgement. Betrayal. Cowardice. Inefficiency. We have alternative scenarios. We have put many centuries into shaping the papacy to our requirements. But we are doing the same with the Dalai Lama. The United States was decreed. But we are also forming the European Union. If you fail, there will be another. But you will not fail."

"If this is true, what happens now?"

"You will build conservative credentials. You must embody the charism of unity. We have a number of scenarios. One of them is like this: after you become a cardinal, you will have a vision of the Blessed Virgin Mary. You will enter a monastery to spend the rest of your life in humble prayer and penance. But the Holy Father will summon you to Rome. He will clasp you to his bosom in Saint Peter's and entrust you with a Rosary Crusade for world peace. You will become known personally in every diocese in the Catholic world. In every home on this planet. You will travel the world, and your Rosary Crusade will become a long prayer marathon for the dying Holy Father, Pope John Paul II. And your first act as pope will be to expedite his canonization. This is how it might be."

"And then?"

"Who can say? You will be told in the right way at the right time. But some things are more likely than others. You will rehabilitate the traditionalists. You will restore the Old Mass. You will lead a resurgence of fundamentalist values. We will require a unified front in the cultural wars that are coming."

"The choice is mine to make, is it not?"

"You made your choice before you were born. But let it be as you wish. At the appropriate time, we will come for you. That will be all."

"Your Eminence."

3

Michael Cremin felt the need to think things through. The masked cardinal could well be part of some elaborate joke. But Kostuva's presence meant that it was serious. Archbishop Kostuva did not travel to a backwater like Limerick simply to amuse a minor bishop at a party. Ordinarily, Michael would have no time for secret societies. He had always gone his own way. But there was no denying that the Church was full of cabals, and had always been. In every age, there had been secretive associations, formal and informal, pious and not so pious, that had claimed leadership. Most of them had vanished quickly enough, but the ugly inspiration always seemed to re-assert itself. Even so, he was his own person. Independent. That was how he intended to stay.

He remembered the seventh level, the roof platform, and he began climbing the stone steps. The next pope. The next pope. It echoed in his head as if a crowd of bats had broken loose and were screeching it from the hollow places around him.

Archbishop McQuaid, all those years ago, had been the first to single him out. A year in Louvain. Postgraduate studies in Rome. Confidential tasks. It had meant a lot, to be special. It meant nothing to him, now.

Michael misread his position and found himself in a room which had emerged unexpectedly into his path, a room suffused with red light. There was a chair there in the red glow, an ornate high-backed chair, like the bishop's throne in a cathedral, and the chair was occupied. Michael shook himself hard, but there was no mistake. The throne was occupied by none other than John Charles McQuaid. The Archbishop was dressed simply. His hand did not sport the fat Borgia amethyst of old, and the skull cap he wore was not of archiepiscopal purple, but of unadorned black, and was frayed at the edges. Indeed, his appearance as a whole was oddly scruffy and unkempt. The voice was humble.

"A stranger priest in the diocese of Your Lordship. Entreating permission to speak. If Your Excellency be so kind."

"But Your Grace!"

"There's no Grace that is mine. Nor yours. Mister."

The Archbishop had taken off the skull cap and was scratching at his head. The bald skull was a hideous sight. The stretched skin was cracking. Little explosions were loosening a thick ooze of red-specked pus, and this was food for legions of tiny crawling things which seemed to be living inside the Archbishop's brain. They were the strangest maggots imaginable, with the appearance of strings of letters and words.

"The vermin of confusion, Mister. Not a pretty sight, I know."

Michael fell to his knees.

"Up, Mister. None should ever have knelt before me."

"Your Grace," Michael whispered, rising. "Are you alive?"

"Where you are, Mister, is part of where I am now. You were my eyes once. And you tried to tell me the truth. Once. I would not have it. Now I am told to tell you the truth. Once. If you will have it. What you see before you is what I might now be, but for the Mercy of God. Except that it's what I am, I think. You see, a mirror appeared before me, and showed me this wretch that you now see, and I was asked if I saw myself or another, and I answered, God help me, that poor wretch with his head addled with the vermin, that is not me, that is another. And so I wait from one end of time to the next and scratch at this confusion wondering who that wretch was. I am completely unable to say that that wretch is me."

"Your Grace's many years of faithful service surely deserve better than this!"

"No, Mister."

"Your Grace, I have just been told that I will be pope."

"I grieve for the Church that deserves you in the papacy. I should never have ordained you. Turn back, Mister, and begin again. Resign your Episcopal office. Implore your laicisation. Ask forgiveness of those you have wronged. Make amends. Beg permission to go to Calcutta and dig latrines for the poor. And now, I must show you this."

The Archbishop vanished, making way for a sight that was indescribable. A strong force was there, unspeakable in its brutality, a force that reached everywhere, and Michael was slowly being devoured by it. It was toying with him, waiting for the moment of maximum gratification to complete the kill.

Michael staggered back and tripped, falling heavily. When he came to himself again, he was in a room which the builders had not yet finished. The red tapestries were only plastic sheeting, with a strange reflection of colours from lamps somewhere below. And the bishop's throne from which Archbishop McQuaid had spoken was a tall mirror, which someone had pushed in there out of the way.

Michael found a short flight of steps, which led up to the roof platform. He stood on the platform for a long time, leaning against a railing, slowly growing calm again as he was swept by the strong sea winds and the rain.

Somewhere in the distance, a cock crew. But where he was, there was no sign of morning.

†

9

The Cardinal

1

Farrelstown Castle, which Leo Murphy had returned to the Diocese of Limerick, was situated on the Shannon Estuary. After Cardinal Cremin had returned from Rome and the official greetings at Shannon Airport had been concluded, this was where the limousine had taken him. The building work was finished at last. Farrelstown was indeed a residence fit for a prince of the Church. It was also close enough to his diocesan headquarters, and he could keep abreast of the business of the Church while he was there. Above all, apart from the staff, who would come and go as he commanded, it was completely empty. The new cardinal preferred to be alone. A letter had been waiting for him. He took it up and read it once more.

My dear Michael,

Forty years, and you have been on the increase, I on the decrease. Now, as you approach your zenith, I approach my nadir, but gladly. I am retiring from the University on May 15th, next. It is time philosophy was released from my unworthy clutches. There will be a small get together at the Department to see me off, and I would be pleased to welcome as my guest of honour my most eminent student, perhaps my only student. Will you come?

May your Eminence be more than a mere title.

Yours ever,

Jean Nordheider

Would he come?

Yes, he would come.

2

The new cardinal had prepared his speech with care. The Fifth Century Roman Emperor, Julian the Apostate, was the theme. Jean Nordheider had always liked this enigmatic and challenging figure, who had renounced Christianity and tried to impose the religion of the Sun God on his fading Empire. Poor Julian. He had not seen the futility of what he was doing. He had not seen that it did not matter who or what the people worshipped. It had never mattered. In essence, the worship of Sol Invictus and the worship of Jesus Christ were the same worship, because it was the habitus of worship, that human excellence, that counted, and not the supposed object of the worship. Some Gods were better than others at bringing out this excellence in people, but that was the extent of it.

After the get together, the cardinal and his mentor travelled to Arenberg Castle and took a stroll by the river as they had often done so many years before. So much had changed, in the world, and in themselves, and yet so much had remained the same. Jean's distinctive nasal voice had flattened and turned slightly hoarse. And there was no mistaking the chronic shake of his fingers. But he had not changed to suit his advancing years. His playful, ironic manner now seemed empty and insolent. Seeing Jean like this evoked harsh images: an aging prostitute in Hamburg's St. Pauli, plastered with make-up to appear younger, unable to look clean and fresh. But the cardinal knew that he, too, had little enough to show for his early brilliance.

"I can still remember our discussions of Plato's *Republic* right here, all those years ago."

"So can I, Michael."

"Plato thought you could educate for the Philosopher King, and at the same time educate for the general population. Nowadays, they all think the opposite. Adjust education down to the masses, and leave it there. The lowest common denominator. It was always the other way around. Educate for the best, and the rest will follow. The Gospels have this insight, too. The parables of Jesus. All the layers of meaning. The right teaching for the best and the worst, all at once. It's what I wanted."

"And now you have no Philosopher King, only the disgruntled masses?"

"Precisely."

"Michael, that is only what one would expect. I have always refused to debase myself in such a way. I have had the sum total of one pupil in all my career."

"And all the thousands of students in your courses over the years?"

"I took no notice of them. In my lectures, I spoke only to myself. Rhetorical poses have their own especial charm, as you know. Except when you came to me for instruction. Then I exerted myself, of course."

"For a few short months!"

"But you kept coming back for more!"

"When did I do that?"

"Each time we met. In Rome. In Ecône. Do you think I lowered my scintillating intellect to the dreary subject of the Mass for the benefit of Monsignor Hogan? No, Michael. I did it for you. Silently, you called out to me. And I answered, as a teacher must. I took it upon myself to point the way. I saw many years ago what could become of you, and like Socrates, I became a midwife to what I saw, so that it could become incarnate and enter this time and place. Why, I am almost the Virgin Mary!"

"So, I am that lone pupil?"

"You are the sorcerer's apprentice. In person! Except that I did not teach you to conjure up the demons. I taught you to exorcise them. By refusing them your assent. I taught you to refuse your assent to everything that was not worthy of assent. To all the superstitions of religion, to all the myths of meaning that have chained men up since the dawn of rational thought. So, Michael, answer me, has anything proved worthy of your assent? Has any one of the old truths stood the test of your scepticism over all this time?"

"No."

"The existence of God?"

"No."

"A social utopia, perhaps?"

"No."

"Sex, other pleasures?"

"No."

"So. What remains worthy of assent is the power of assent itself, no? That alone. The Will to Power. Your life is the proof of it. As I knew it would be. Be like me, Michael. Assent to permanent assenting. In the dramas of your desires. That is the very principle of a self."

The cardinal thought again of the aging prostitute on the Hamburg street. A sour waft of urine reached his nostrils. Jean's body was starting to fail him. That permanent assenting was nearing its end. A useless principle, like all the others.

"Some say I might be pope one day, Jean."

"Pope! That would be perfect for you, Michael."

That would be perfect for you, Michael. He had heard those words before, or words like them. They had not been true. Nothing had ever been true. And Nordheider's mask was slipping. Old age was at him. Inexorably revealing what was underneath. A no-face. Nothing.

3

Without telling anyone, the cardinal delayed his departure from Louvain by a day. The limousine took him across the town from the Arenberg Campus to Cardinal Mercier Square, where he got out and walked slowly through the old town with its shops, street cafés and student bars. Louvain was more colourful than he remembered, more international in flair, but still bourgeois and very quiet.

Close to the Town Hall, he came upon an old beggar woman singing for alms. She had chosen a place where the stone pillars of a colonnade would give her resonance and she sang surprisingly well. When she saw the cardinal, or saw perhaps his clerical dress, with the scarlet braid of high office, she began to sing the Ave Maria, to the music of Schubert. For a moment, everything was fresh with beauty, and the cardinal was lifted to a lighter place, where, through the gentle hold of the melody, Corinna Fielding, his first girlfriend, came before him. The cardinal saw her as the teenager he had loved, or had thought he had loved, all of forty years ago, with her curling hair long and golden and her smile full of trust. A trust he had broken. You don't love me, she had told him, you just love the idea of yourself loving me. She had been right, of course. As if that mattered now. He had given his life to God. To whatever God was.

The cardinal checked his pockets but found only a two-euro piece to give to the woman. He dropped the coin and had to get down on his knees to go after it. He happened to glance between the pillars, and spotted someone he knew, sitting at a street table not far away. Felix Kostuva of all people. Since Leo Murphy's party he had not seen Kostuva. But he had not been free of him. Or of his mysterious friends. At the consistory, a Brazilian cardinal, another of the new elevations, had taken him aside. "Your Eminence," the Brazilian had whispered, "A fraternal greeting. You and I, we were both chosen before we were born."

The coin forgotten now, the cardinal stayed behind the pillar and watched. Jean Nordheider was at that table too, sharing a bottle of wine with Kostuva with all the ease of long friendship. The cardinal felt the beginnings of emotion. What could have brought these two together, with such familiarity? A suspicion pressed down upon him with sly urgency. A suspicion that knew no bounds.

A little way behind him, the old woman finished her song. *Sancta Maria. Mater Dei. Ora pro nobis peccatoribus.* This is what his priesthood had come to. Two old men in a street café, and a song that knitted the past together with luminous thread.

Jean Nordheider had opened his mind and set him free. And the knowledge he had acquired had fooled him and his freedom had enslaved him. The Church had made him great. And he was nothing. Again, he remembered Corinna and his betrayal of her. It was such a small thing, really. But when he followed the thread, he saw a land dried out. He had changed the course of a river.

With the ticking of the wristwatch close to his ear, as he leaned against the fat, grey, pillar, observing them, his friends, his enemies, his emotions were erased by brush stroke after brush stroke of helplessness, leaving him flat and numb. There was no way forward. And no way back. Here he was. At what he thought was his source. Where there was no renewal. No hope.

Help me, he whispered into the crevices of the crumbling stone, and the cobwebs shivered in the ghostly stream of his breath.

4

When he got back to Farrelstown Castle, Michael Cremin decided that the best course of action would be to confide in Leo Murphy. Leo was a friend. With money and power. And no scruples. Where there is no way forward, make a way, blowing everything to smithereens, if need be. There was a certainty as rock solid as anything had ever been. That certainty was his refusal.

While he was staring out of the high bay window overlooking the deserted lawns, the telephone rang. Leo was extremely busy, but he would make time for him. Could he come to Dublin? The National Gallery of Art?

The place for their meeting proved to be beside one of the jewels of the Gallery's collections, *The Taking of Christ*, a representation of the betrayal of Jesus by Judas. Not long before, experts had concluded that this large, brooding canvas was by the fourteenth-century Italian, Caravaggio, and was, in fact, one of his masterpieces. For years, the painting had hung unrecognized over the mantelpiece in a Jesuit House in Dublin, until someone had thought it worthwhile to give it the proper attention.

They were lucky with the timing of the discovery, Michael thought, looking at his watch. If Dermot Ryan had been Archbishop at the time, that painting would never have got as far as the National Gallery. It would have ended up in Dermot's living room, for him to show off to his visitors. Not before they had found out that it was a priceless Caravaggio, of course.

Leo was late, and to while the time away, Michael studied the picture. It was remarkable for its controlled violence. Judas was an ugly character with thick ears, blunt, graceless hands and eyes that looked into nowhere. One of the men standing behind him, the one enfolding the whole scene in his dark red cloak, was Caravaggio himself. He had a sneer on his face, as if he was made for better things, as if this fateful scene did not concern him at all. Michael chuckled at the audacity of it. Putting yourself into such a picture in such a way. Making your own ironic little comment on one of the generative figures of Western culture, on the greatest of those generative figures.

"Isn't it strange how a kiss could do such a thing?" Came a voice close by. It was a visitor, a woman with garlic on her breath.

Perplexed, Michael looked again at the picture. The kiss that Judas gave to Jesus was like the tip of a battering ram. Then, like a stab wound to his heart, he became aware of the face of Jesus. Jesus was fully conscious of what was happening to him. The betrayal was complete. There was nothing to ease the pain of it. Jesus offered no resistance. He had no protection against it. The kiss of Judas drained all the life and colour from him, and he sank away, destroyed.

Michael turned towards her. "Madam, modern research suggests that Judas had a political motive. And theologically, we can say that God made use of him. Judas opened the way for the sacrifice of Jesus on the Cross."

"He was too beautiful."

Michael looked at the agonized face of Jesus, and the tortured eyes looked out at him, still shocked at the mark Judas had made on him with a kiss. What was the point of denial.

"Yes, Madam, he was."

How armoured he was, too, against seeing the truth, his great self as much a lost and shapeless cage as the hulking Judas on the canvas before him.

Time passed, and still there was no sign of Leo Murphy. Disappointed, Michael drove back to Limerick. Later, he found out that Leo had been detained by the police. But by that time, Michael could do nothing to help him. Pope John Paul II had died. Michael was urgently required in Rome.

5

After the obsequies for the dead pope, Michael Cremin stayed on in Rome. Cardinal Ratzinger had summoned the Conclave for nine days hence, and despite the unavoidable get-togethers with other cardinals, Michael found that there was time for relaxation. One morning, he put away his cardinal's robes, dressed in jeans and an anorak and treated himself to a visit to the Vatican museums. He had last been inside them some forty years before when the Mass was still in Latin and the congregation was kept away from the altar by ornate barriers and by the forbidding back of the priest. Discreetly, Michael moved from room to room, stopping briefly whenever something caught his attention. He found that he was moving through time, from the frescoes of Raphael with their celebrations of light, order and colour to darker, more modern images. Finally, in the Borgia apartment, he was brought to a standstill by a bronze sculpture of Pope Paul VI. In this image, Paul had shrunk to about a third of his normal size, and the cape and mitre dwarfed him even more. He looked like a rotten old tooth on which the crown had been shaken loose. To the right was a painting of the Crucifixion by Gerardo Dottori, which Paul had donated from his private collection. The Christ figure seemed to be formed of triangles inside a blue pyramid. The head seemed caught in the apex of a different, unrelated triangle. At the feet of the Christ figure, bathed in blue light, were two nude women, waiting. The Crucifixion seemed to take place in a landscape ravaged by nuclear war. From Raphael's heavenly scenes, they had come to this absurdity. Where could they go next? Nowhere, basically. It stopped there. There was nowhere left to go.

Michael returned to Limerick and Farrelstown Castle to rest for a day or two. But the eyes of the wizened Paul VI and the burning clouds and skimpy triangles of the Dottori Crucifixion came with him and disturbed his peace of mind. He was beginning to dislike Farrelstown Castle. The seven levels of the old chapel seemed tawdry to him, and all the careful workmanship on view seemed to lack a soul.

Unable to rest, Michael began to wonder about the old cottage by the sea. He had meant to have a look at that cottage, ever since Leo Murphy had mentioned it to him at the party, but he had never got round to it. He called for a map of the Farrelstown estates and had it rolled out before him on the big polished desk. To his surprise, the estates stretched almost as far as Foynes, and included a good stretch of the estuary coastline. The cottage was marked on the map by a cross. Cillbrian was the local name for the place. The approach was by means of the public road and then by a right of way over a difficult expanse of rock which was impassable at high tide.

Michael put on a tracksuit and running shoes and summoned his driver. An hour later, he was making his way across the stony formations, climbing towards a recess surrounded on three sides by the rocks. There, a cottage of bleached stone nestled in a small, cheerful garden. The doors and windows were wide open to the sun. In the garden, sitting in a wheelchair, was the old man Michael had known in Rome as Clavis. He was dictating what seemed to be answers to letters to a companion. Michael recognized her, too: the woman from the fishing village near Ostia, Patrizia. Her daughters were also there. He could see them clearly through the open windows. It may have been some unusual play of the light, of course, but they did not seem to have aged much in the intervening years. The daughters could have been grandmothers by now, but they were still young girls on the threshold of their lives. They had been at that party Leo had organised for him. Doing the catering. Michael remembered the vacant place to Leo's right at the table of honour. Had they been the reason why the masked cardinal had stayed away?

Some distance from the strand and the house was a boat, held fast by a shining chain fixed to a wooden stave in the mouth of a small cave. They had arrived there by sea.

"The Reverend Didimus Thomas Clavis, I presume."

Clavis himself was much the same as he had been in Rome. "Have you come to repent, Your Eminence?"

Michael looked at the old man in the wheelchair, whose eyes were surprisingly young and cheerful. Repentance, what is that? he wanted to shout at him, but he checked himself. It pained him to turn away, but he did so, and made his way back to his car and driver.

That old priest was a hopeless simpleton. Able only for black and white. Utterly incapable of tolerating the grey. The grey that made up almost all of existence. The grey of the liveable compromise. Evidently, there was a strong attraction in such a black and white view of things. It was the attraction of the Book of the Apocalypse, with its blatant reduction of everything to Evil and Good, with nothing in-between. You were damned or you were saved, and God imposed His firm justice without qualification. It was the justice of a rock hurled from a mountain, hopelessly crushing whoever stood in the way, no matter who he was. Saint John wallowed in this language of warfare, portraying a God who pits everything against everything else, unleashing a mad orgy of destruction throughout the universe, while He keeps a protective hand over a faithful remnant and guides them to safety. The remnant were Good. The rest were Evil. There was nothing in-between. One had the utterly ludicrous scenario of God declaring nine tenths and more of His Creation to be irredeemable and allowing it to perish. If that was true, what was the point of anything, at all.

Wearily, Michael acknowledged that he should have given Clavis an answer. He should have said that he didn't need anyone to tell him that he had failed. He knew it already. His life was almost over, but he could not look back on even one single moment out of all the countless millions of moments granted to him that he would want returned to him again. It was not that he had tried and failed. He had failed even to try.

With an ache in his heart, an ache that might have been left there a long time ago by a long-departed lover, Michael pined for Mercy. Yes, the Book of the Apocalypse was probably true. At any rate, it was a certainty that of all those that he, Michael Cremin, had come to know, either personally, or through their public deeds or their writings, hardly any at all had been remotely close to goodness. And he himself? He was there with the worst of them. Unimaginably far from goodness. Yet, aware of it, and of what it meant.

Michael Cremin returned to the old cottage by the sea. When he climbed down from the rocks into the sheltered recess, he found that Clavis and his entourage had departed. Disappointed, Michael was about to head home, when he heard something stirring. The sounds came from the tiny kitchen of the cottage, where he came upon a nun bending over an artist's table, where she was stitching together the pages of a book. She straightened up from her work and turned to face him. A white veil covered her features, and behind it, Michael could make out the awkward bulge of heavy bandaging. The veil was there to hide the open sore that had once been her face.

"Marie," he said.

"Your Eminence."

"Where is he, Marie? Clavis, I mean."

"He has been called away."

"I seem to be in the habit of arriving too late." Silence spread like the aroma of a funeral wreath. It was all so sad. "What will become of you, Marie?"

"God is looking after me. Go, please. Do you see that cave over there? The place where the stave is at the mouth of the cave? Try to look there." She was pointing through the window to the rock cave where Clavis' boat had been moored.

The place where the stave is. Michael crossed the short distance to where the garden ended and the rocks began. The stave was at an angle. The shining chain which had held the boat fast was hanging loosely to the ground. On a flat rock at the mouth of the cave, bread, water and wine had been laid out. The rock was like an altar in Penal Times to which a priest had come in secret to say Mass.

"That priest is you, Father."

It was a nun who had spoken. Not Marie. Younger. Hardly more than a girl. She was dressed in an antiquated habit, of the kind one might see in old photographs. She had an exceptional presence. Michael felt he must know this nun from somewhere, but he could not place her. He wanted to ignore her, but he could not. And there was a truth on his tongue like a dull blemish he could not avoid exposing.

"I can't say Mass for you, Sister."

"You are an ordained priest. In good standing. What can stop you from celebrating Mass?"

What was he to say? That the Mass was a sham? His priesthood, too? What was the point in mincing his words. The young nun had a simple, direct manner. He would be simple and direct, too.

"I have lost the capacity."

"You speak truly, Father. Your Masses are blasphemous. One small step away from a Black Mass."

Michael laughed at her. "That's the best use for the Mass. Turn it on its head. A backdrop for blasphemy. The sacred is sacrilegious. It always was. Need I go on?"

"Please don't. But think of Jesus. He offered Himself. You might choose to imitate Him."

"And what would you know, whoever you are?"

"I tell you this out of the love of God and out of God's love for you. A week from now you will become pope. Those who organize your election will demand many things. Among them will be a return to the certainties of the pre-conciliar Church. The restoration of the Old Latin Mass. But God will ask more of you. God will show you the true horror of the last forty years. You must realise that it is too late. God will ask you for the sacrifice of the entire Church. You will declare to all who are prepared to listen that the Church has failed and has come to an end. You will tell them that God will not refuse anyone who is willing to repent, but that there will be no Church to help them. God will teach directly, if there is a willingness to listen. To learn how to listen."

"Let me tell you about God, Sister. I am qualified on the subject. God does not teach. God does not love. God is a force. A superior kind of electricity. God is blind to us and our feelings. Indifferent. Amoral. We harness this force. We bend it to our will. That is our role, we of the Church: to harness this force in the Church's way. The other players in the march of history do the same. They harness the force in their way."

"And this is what you choose to believe?"

"It is what I know."

"You speak of what you have made of God. You and all men and women like you. You speak as a drug addict might speak of the drug. And you speak of what will finally bring all life to an end in this world. Soon mankind will be no more. These are the end times. They have come because of you."

"Why do you tell me this?"

"My heaven is to serve God in this world."

Michael looked at her with weary recognition. "You are Thérèse of Lisieux."

"I am."

"You are Thérèse of Lisieux, Saint of the Church, who has been dead for over a century. All my life I have rejected you. Hated you. And here you are, escaped from your grave to torment me."

"Do you still choose to hate?"

"I am too tired to hate."

"Celebrate the Mass once more, Father. Offer yourself as Jesus did. Celebrate the Mass that is lost. Lost by your doing. What of those whom God cannot reach, because they have turned away? What of the sick, the helpless, the enslaved? And what of the animals, the trees and flowers, the mountains, the rivers, the earth herself? All that those who turned away have touched with their darkness? The Mass was their protection, too. It was a hermit's stillness in a place of noise. It was a pool of fresh water where there was only dryness. It was cool, mountain air where poisonous gases had spread. It was the secret word of truth out of which our hearts were beating."

"If I listen to you, I listen to my death. You are my death."

"You have never lived. Come with me into the cave of sacrifice. There, I will help you with the Mass. I will help you to see. You will see what makes you what you are. And how you can still change for the better."

"I can never change."

"Is it to end like this? In this despair?"

"You always said No to life."

"I said Yes. To God. Who is life and the all of life. I turned away from all that was not God. And God took me for Herself and gave Herself to me."

"Herself. I may as well give up."

"You may begin again."

Touched by her strange constancy, Michael Cremin felt something stirring. It was hope, fluttering inside him like wings that sense a breeze.

"Where is this new beginning?"

"The new beginning is everywhere. It is now."

On the thorn of his assent, Michael felt the arms of Thérèse holding him upright. They were arms of warm breath, without mass, without material force, but there was a power in them unlike any he had ever known. It was the power of the still centre of the turning wheel, when everything is inside the wheel, and turns with the wheel, and one cannot easily see the centre, or that the centre is everywhere.

"Love is everywhere. It is all that is."

And so it was. The radiant power of the still centre of the turning, a power that was not a force, but a burning flame of light came to him, on the gentle reach of mercy. It burned him, this mercy, but he did not turn away.

A light began to shine on the horizon. He longed to step out towards it, but he could not.

A silence came over them like a scarf of silk in a fresh morning wind, and then the light was gone.

"You must become able for the light," Thérèse said to him.

Michael stood still, considering. It had been seven years and more since he had first caught a glimpse of his true self in the mirror. In a way, he had always known. It was inexpressibly merciful to ask for his assent.

A hope lifted, a flower opening to the morning, and Michael reached for her hand. She led him into the cave of sacrifice. She showed him the Liturgy that was written on its walls.

With her help, he was able to begin again.

The following contains a list of writings, works of art and religious terms which occur prominently in the story. A short explanation is given in case one is needed.

Writings and Works of Art

Also Sprach Zarathustra	Thus spoke Zarathustra. Philosophical work written by F. Nietzsche in 1884. Proclaims the Death of God, the Superman as His successor, and the Eternal Recurrence of the Same
De Ecclesia	Working title of the Schema on the Church discussed at the Second Vatican Council
De Sacra Liturgia	Working title of the Schema on the Liturgy discussed at the Second Vatican Council
Dead Sea Scrolls	Ancient Jewish writings discovered around 1950 in caves near the Dead Sea
Directory for Masses with Children	A document issued by the Congregation of Rites in 1973 to guide the introduction of children to the Mass according to their capacities
Dominus Marcellus Lefebvre	Vatican document issued in 1988 establishing the excommunication of Archbishop Marcel Lefebvre
Gaudium et Spes	Apostolic Constitution on the Church in the modern world promulgated in 1965 by Pope Paul VI in accordance with the Second Vatican Council
Unfehlbar? Eine Anfrage	Infallible? An Inquiry. Book published by Hans Küng in 1971 questioning the dogma of Papal Infallibility
L'Histoire d'une Âme	The story of a soul. The spiritual autobiography of Saint Thérèse of Lisieux. Edited and published posthumously in 1898
Lumen Gentium	Apostolic Constitution on the mystery of the Church promulgated in 1964 by Pope Paul VI in accordance with the Second Vatican Council
Missale Romanum	Apostolic Constitution of Pope Paul VI in 1969 promulgating the new Mass Rite devised by the *Consilium*
Missarum Sollemnia	Standard work on the history of the Mass of the Roman Rite written by Josef A. Jungmann SJ in 1948. Notable for its genealogical method which elucidates different points of origin for different parts of the Rite

Mit Brennender Sorge	Encyclical issued in German by Pope Pius XI in 1937 concerning the situation of Roman Catholics in Hitler's Germany
Nag Hammadi Findings	Ancient Gnostic writings in Coptic discovered in Egypt in 1945
Pacem in Terris	Encyclical issued by Pope John XXIII in 1962 concerning the establishment of peace, justice, charity and liberty through conformity with the divine order
Quo Primum Tempore	Bull of Pope Saint Pius V in 1570 promulgating the new norm of the Rite of the Mass as decreed by the Council of Trent
Sacrosanctum Concilium	Apostolic Constitution on the Sacred Liturgy. Promulgated in 1963 in accordance with the Second Vatican Council by Pope Paul VI
Schema XIII	Draft document concerning the relations between the Church and the world discussed at the Second Vatican Council. Forerunner of *Gaudium et Spes*
Summa Theologiae	Also known as *Summa Theologica*. Last work of Saint Thomas Aquinas. Written 1269-1274. Built on a carefully ordered sequence of questions, it seeks to relate human life, the cosmos and God systematically
Syntactic Structures	Seminal work of theoretical linguistics written by N. Chomsky in 1957. Attempted a comprehensive theory of the human language faculty from mentalist assumptions
The Apocalypse	A book of the New Testament attributed to Saint John the Beloved. Contains a visionary account of the battle between Good and Evil, the end of the world and the final victory of Good
The Bible	The authoritative collection of Christian sacred writings. Consists of the Old Testament, containing Jewish scripture, and the New Testament, containing specifically Christian writings
The Crucifixion	Futurist painting by Gerardo Dottori (1928)
The Republic	Philosophical work written by Plato ca. 380 BC dealing with the nature of a just city. Contains the *Parable of the Cave*
The Taking of Christ	Painting by Caravaggio (ca. 1602) depicting the betrayal of Jesus by Judas

Tres Abhinc Annos Second Instruction on the Proper Implementation of the Constitution of the Sacred Liturgy, issued by the Congregation of Rites in 1967. It simplified the ritual gestures required during Mass and permitted Latin to be replaced by the Vernacular, throughout the Mass, including the Roman Canon

Zur Genealogie der Moral On the Genealogy of Morals. Philosophical work written by F. Nietzsche in 1887. Traces the origin of Christian moral judgments to power relations and the resentments they evoke

Terms from theology and Church history

Afterlife The next life. Life after death. In many religious traditions death is believed to involve some form of divine judgment which determines the nature of an individual's subsequent existence

Canon of the Mass see Roman Canon

Coetus X Section of the *Consilium* responsible for the creation of the *Novus Ordo Missae* after the Second Vatican Council, headed by Johannes Wagner

Congregation for Divine Worship Division of the Curia responsible for liturgical issues. Successor to the Congregation of Rites

Conservatives Term used for those bishops and theologians who tried to steer the Catholic Church away from radical changes at the Second Vatican Council. Their main concerns were the demarcation of the Church from the world, the primacy of the Pope, the preservation of Latin as the liturgical language and the maintenance of discipline among the clergy and laity

Consilium *Consilium ad exsequendam Constitutionem de Sacra Liturgia.* Curial body set up in 1964 by Pope Paul VI to implement the programme of liturgical reform decreed by the Second Vatican Council

Council of Trent — Ecumenical Council of the Catholic Church held in Trent, Italy, from 1545 to 1563. Defined the Catholic Faith anew to face the challenge of Protestantism

Curia — The central administration of the Roman Catholic Church. Based in the Vatican

Diocese — Principal administrative unit of the Roman Catholic Church. Headed by a bishop

Divine Office — Prayers offered every day at set times by Catholic priests and religious, consisting mainly of verses from the Old and New Testaments arranged thematically. In monasteries, these are usually sung by the whole community together

Epiclesis — A prayer to the Holy Spirit to accept the offering of bread and wine at the Eucharist. In contrast to Orthodox liturgies, the epiclesis is not prominent in the old Roman Canon. The epiclesis is a prominent feature in the Mass of Paul VI

Ecumenical Council — A formal gathering of the bishops of the Roman Catholic Church assembled together with the pope or his legate in solemn deliberation on matters determined by the pope. The first of these was held at Nicaea in 325 AD. The most recent was the Second Vatican Council

Eternal Recurrence of the Same — A concept in the philosophy of F. Nietzsche which serves to obtain an ethic of life affirmation

Eucharist — The re-enactment or commemoration of the Last Supper, i.e. the Passover meal celebrated by Jesus and his friends shortly before His crucifixion. This ritual is the centre of the different Christian liturgies. It is one of the Catholic sacraments

Faith — Belief and trust in God. Usually connotes informed assent to defined truths of religion

Fall — See Fall of Man

Fall of Man — The act of wilful separation from God in which, according to Christian theology, all men and women share as an aspect of their being

Fatima — see Marian Apparitions

Garabandal — see Marian Apparitions

Grace — Supernatural participation in the life of God by the gift of God

Holy Grail A store of spiritual power mentioned in Arthurian legend, medieval epics and mystical traditions. It is often believed to have the form of the cup used by Jesus at the Last Supper

ICEL International Commission on English in the Liturgy. A joint commission of the bishops' conferences from English-speaking countries based in Washington DC. It has the task of preparing English versions of liturgical texts

La Salette see Marian Apparitions

Last Rites Sacrament administered to a dying or recently deceased person

Liturgy Public prayer of the Church according to prescribed rituals

Liturgy of the Hours see Divine Office

Marian Apparitions Supposed appearances of the Blessed Virgin Mary, usually to ill-educated people in remote places bearing a message of apocalyptic content. Examples are the apparitions at La Salette (1846), Fatima (1917) and Garabandal (1961)

Mass of Paul VI see Novus Ordo Missae

Mass of Pius V The norm of the Mass of the Roman Rite codified and made binding in perpetuity by Pope Saint Pius V in 1570 on the instructions of the Council of Trent. In general use until ca. 1969

Mass of the Council of Trent see Mass of Pius V

New Mass see Novus Ordo Missae

Novus Ordo Missae Unofficial term used to refer to the Mass promulgated by Pope Paul VI in 1969. This was a Mass in the Vernacular in contrast to the Latin of the Old Mass. The changes include turning the altar to face the people and the more active role given to the congregation

Old Latin Mass see Mass of Pius V

Old Mass see Mass of Pius V

Ordinary A person vested with local authority in an ecclesiastical jurisdiction

Papal Infallibility A dogma of the Roman Catholic Church which states that under certain conditions, the Pope is preserved from error in matters of faith and morals

Pentecost — The coming of the Holy Spirit to the followers of Jesus of Nazareth after the Resurrection, as described in the Bible. In some interpretations, this event brought the Christian Church into being

Peritus — An expert in theology who provides advice to an Ecumenical Council. At the Second Vatican Council, periti accompanied individual bishops or were officially appointed to the Council as a whole

Post-Conciliar Church — Term used for the Roman Catholic Church after the implementation of the reforms of the Second Vatican Council

Pragmatic Conservatives — Term of convenience used for those bishops and theologians who wished to preserve a strong centralised institutional Church while accepting the post-conciliar reforms

Prayer — Sacred encounter between the loving person and God

Progressives — Term used for those bishops and theologians who tried to steer the Catholic Church in a more liberal direction during and after the Second Vatican Council. Their main concerns were the discarding of outdated concepts and practices, the introduction of a vernacular liturgy, ecumenism and religious liberty

Real Presence — The hidden but effective presence of God within creation, usually signified by ritual signs

Repentance — Contrition for one's sins and acceptance of God's forgiveness

Roman Canon — The central and oldest part of the Mass of the Roman Rite, which contains the consecration of bread and wine. It begins with the words *Te igitur* and concludes with or before the *Pater Noster.* In the reform of the Liturgy following the Second Vatican Council, the Roman Canon provided the model for Eucharistic Prayer Number I

Roman Catholic Church — An institutional structure centred on practices of worship which claims an unbroken line of descent from the Apostles. Probably the oldest and largest Christian denomination. Claiming to be the sole locus of salvation, it has wielded immense power in world affairs

Sacrament — A symbolic encounter between a believer and God by means of ritual acts and objects through which divine grace is imparted

Salvation — Liberation from Sin and death by the Grace of God

Second Vatican Council Ecumenical Council of the Roman Catholic Church held at the Vatican 1962-1965. Convoked by Pope John XXIII as a pastoral council with the purpose of entering on a dialogue with advances in secular knowledge, it led to changes of revolutionary import for Roman Catholics

Sin The state of alienation and brokenness which accompanies the estrangement from God arising from self-will

Society of Saint Pius X International priestly society based on traditionalist principles. Founded in Switzerland by Archbishop Lefebvre in 1970, it preserves the Mass of Pius V in defiance of many of the post-conciliar reforms

Spirit of the Council A rhetorical figure used after the Second Vatican Council to justify reforms which went beyond what the Council had explicitly decreed

Traditionalists A loose coalition of Roman Catholics who tried to refuse the reforms which followed the Second Vatican Council in order to adhere to a strict interpretation of Catholic tradition

Transubstantiation The change of bread and wine into the Body and Blood of Christ, which, according to Catholic teaching, takes place at Mass as a result of the consecration

Tridentine Mass See Mass of Pius V

Vatican City State in Rome which is the seat of the Pope and the Curia. Used more generally to refer to the centralised government of the Roman Catholic Church

Vernacular The language in everyday use in a locality, as opposed to a reserved language for liturgical purposes

About the Author

Born in Ireland and educated in Ireland, England and Germany, Eamon Kiernan read Linguistics and Education. Teaching is his main occupation. He considers writing to be a form of spiritual questioning.

Publications to date:
The Inness of With, Gehrden, Aontau, 2002 (poetry, English)
Im Horizont des Wortes, Gehrden, Aontau, 2003 (Phd thesis, German)
The Secret Teaching of the Knights Templar, Koblenz, Aontau 2006 (English, translated from the German of Hans Prutz)
The Vineyard of the Nietzschean Priest is his debut full length serious novel. Kiernan resides in Germany where he lectures in English.

Tuborg Havnevej 19
Hellerup
2900 Copenhagen
Denmark
http://www.whytetracks.eu.com

Lightning Source UK Ltd.
Milton Keynes UK
13 December 2010

164333UK00001B/38/P